HOLIDAY CHEER
ANDREW GREY AND

T0280043

by Andrew Grey

Stardust

With Georg's life in Germany and Duncan's in Boston, the chance for more than a holiday fling is as elusive as stardust.

Sweet Anticipation

When Greg offers to help with a bachelorette party, he comes face-to-face with the man who got away—baker Rhys. Working on the party food together might be a chance to reconnect.

Rudolph The Rescue Jack Russell

When Alex accidentally bonds with a rescue dog, it's the first step to overcoming one of his fears, but now he's anxious about taking care of little Rudolph. Fortunately he has sexy shelter volunteer Luther to help him understand the magic of unconditional love.

By Amy Lane

Regret Me Not

Pierce's life recently went to crap, and Hal is at his own crossroads. Pierce must find the knight in shining armor he used to be before Christmas becomes a doomsday deadline of heartbreak instead of a celebration of love.

Late for Christmas

When perfectionist Cassidy gets distracted and hit by a tree, he comes under the care of his neighbor, doctor Mark—the distraction. Mark sees Cassidy's loneliness, but also his surprising kindness and creativity. Can he convince Cassidy he doesn't have to be perfect to be loved?

ChrisMyths

Shelter worker Eli can't provide a big happy family, so he doesn't blame his boyfriend, Andy, for going home for Christmas. But Andy's heart is in Brooklyn with Eli, and he has an army ready to put in the elbow grease to save Christmas—if he can get Eli to believe in him too.

Holiday Cheer

from Andrew Grey
& Amy Lane

Published by
DREAMSPINNER PRESS

8219 Woodville Hwy #1245
Woodville, FL 32362 USA
www.dreamspinnerpress.com

This is a work of fiction. Names, characters, places, and incidents either are the product of author imagination or are used fictitiously, and any resemblance to actual persons, living or dead, business establishments, events, or locales is entirely coincidental.

Holiday Cheer
© 2024 Andrew Grey and Amy Lane

Stardust originally published by Dreamspinner Press, December 2014
Regret Me Not originally published by Dreamspinner Press, December 2017
Sweet Anticipation originally published by Dreamspinner Press, December 2019
Late for Christmas originally published by Dreamspinner Press, November 2021
ChrisMyths originally published by Dreamspinner Press, December 2022
Rudolph the Rescue Jack Russell originally published by Dreamspinner Press, December 2022

Cover Art
© 2024 L.C. Chase
http://www.lcchase.com
Cover content is for illustrative purposes only and any person depicted on the cover is a model.

Digital ISBN: 9781641087896
Trade Paperback ISBN: 9781641088084
Trade Paperback published November 2024
v. 1.0

TABLE OF CONTENTS

STARDUST

CHAPTER 1

THE MACHINE made large, slow circles, liquid sheening on top of the glass that was being shaped, slowly, atom by atom. At least that was how it seemed. The process was exacting and would take a very long time. Every curve had to be perfect. I knew it was loud in the room below where I watched through panes of glass. It had to be, with all the machinery that moved and gleamed in the bright lights. People in white cleansuits moved around the huge mirror. No contamination could be allowed in the room; nothing could be allowed to spoil the glass. It had taken weeks of work to get it this far and there would still be many more.

"Did you volunteer for this?" an unfamiliar voice asked from behind me. I turned and nodded automatically. "What were you thinking?" he asked in a pleasing German accent.

"I had nothing else to do, and by agreeing to come here, it allowed the other members of the team to spend Christmas with their families." I smiled, and he did the same. A nice smile, more sincere than the polite ones I was getting used to seeing. His smile went to his eyes and was genuinely warm. I'd seen him around the plant the past few weeks, but he'd never approached me, and I'd done as instructed and remained in the area set aside for me to do my work. "I'm Duncan Haversmith," I said, extending my hand.

"Georg von Mittelbach," he said. I'd seen his name plate on an office, and in my mind I'd pronounced it "George," but he said it like "Gay-org" and it fit him really well. He was tall with dark hair, precisely cut, and deep brown eyes. I assumed he was one of the managers, since he had an office. "I have been asked to act as your liaison to make sure you have everything you require."

I was confused. "What about Hans?" I'd been working with him for the past two weeks.

"He went on paternity leave. His wife had a baby."

"Oh," I said, resisting the urge to turn back to watch the grinding process. I probably should have, because it would have given me a chance to cover my surprise. Hans and I had been working together for two weeks and he'd never mentioned anything about it.

"Sometimes—" he began and then paused. "I traveled to the US on business a few years ago for a few months, and you are much more open about your personal lives in the office. We tend to be a little more… private."

I nodded. I had noticed that. "I guess I'm sad I never had a chance to offer my congratulations." I'd been working as the liaison for the consortium that had contracted the mirror while it was being ground for a new-generation space telescope. The project was led by NASA, but a number of universities were also taking part. As an astronautical engineer, I led the team back at MIT that had designed the mirror and its housing.

"Please." Georg smiled again. Dang, he was beautiful when he did that. No, beautiful was the wrong word—he was stunning, and his deep eyes shone in a way that reminded me of the shine of the water that both lubricated the mirror below as well as carried away the microscopic material ground away. "It's his fourth baby. He should have it down to a science by now." His smile brightened, showing off perfectly white teeth. My stomach did a little flip. It was brief, but a slight jittery feeling remained, one that told me Georg might be gay. Of course the way his gaze lingered a little longer than was necessary was also a clue. "How long will you be here?"

"I'm scheduled for another six weeks at this point, but I'm supposed to remain until the mirror is finished and packed for shipment." I motioned to one of the chairs around the small table that filled the tiny room I'd been given as a work area. Since it was only me, it was fine. I rarely had visitors—only Hans, and now Georg. Most everyone else went about their business with little concern for me.

"There isn't going to be a lot to see in the next few weeks." Georg began setting a file on the table. "We are on schedule, and barring some hidden flaw in the glass itself, which isn't likely, given our quality standards and the testing that was done before the process began, we should finish grinding and polishing on December 30. Then we can complete the packing process and we'll fly it to the US and make delivery. I will admit, it seems excessive to have you here the entire time. There will be very little to see."

"I understand," I said. I really did. "This seemed like overkill to me, but they wanted someone here to communicate back and relay any issues. You are aware that this is the second mirror. The first one got halfway through the process and had a flaw. That was a different company, of course."

"Of course," Georg said with another smile, this one with a hint of pride. "Is there anything else I can do for you?"

"Not that I can think of," I said. "Except maybe recommend a few places to visit this weekend. I've been here a few weeks and have explored a little of the tourist section of Munich, but I'd like to do something different." It was harder than I expected to be able to get around and see things since I didn't speak much German. As long as I stuck to the areas frequented by tourists I seemed to be fine, but I had been hoping to see other areas.

"Of course," Georg said, growing quiet. "If you like, I can show you around a little."

The offer took me slightly by surprise, given how standoffish most people had been. "That would be very nice."

"What would you like to see?"

"Whatever you'd like to show me," I answered. It seemed like the right thing to say. "I haven't been here before, so everything is new."

"Is your wife along with you?"

"I'm not married and I'm here alone." I sighed, and I knew I should have done a better job of suppressing it. Georg shifted his gaze slightly. "The plan was for my boyfriend to join me for a few weeks—at least that was the original plan. He decided his interests lay elsewhere a few months ago." That was putting it mildly, but going into the gory details wasn't appropriate. Hell, I wasn't sure if what I'd already said was appropriate and wished that I'd kept my mouth shut. What if Georg was a huge 'phobe and I'd just talked myself out of someone to spend a little time with?

I had found that the weekends could be surprisingly long. There was a lot to do right nearby, but not having anyone to do things with made the hours crawl by and made most things a lot less fun. I was already beginning to tire of my own company.

"So you are gay," Georg said matter-of-factly. "I am the same." Maybe that explained why Georg was being so friendly. Not that I thought Georg was hitting on me or anything. But everyone else had been rather standoffish and Georg was so relatively forward.

"Do you have a boyfriend?" I asked, hoping it was okay to ask.

"Not at the moment," Georg answered, his smile brightening. "I have a meeting shortly, but I wanted to make sure you were up-to-date. I'll come in each morning and brief you on the current status and any issues we encounter." He checked his watch. "Tomorrow I'll have more time and we can firm up plans for Saturday." He gathered up his papers and left the room after a nod and a small smile.

Once I was alone again, I turned back to my view of the mirror. For the first time in a while, I smiled and really felt it. Maybe I'd made a friend and would have someone to do things with occasionally. I was going to be here for another six weeks or so, and I needed to make the best of it.

A few minutes later, I turned back to my computer and decided to get back to work. I had other projects I could work on and figured I should make progress on those. After all, I hadn't been sent here on an extended vacation.

After working the rest of the morning and afternoon refining my design for the cradle that would hold the mirror in place on the telescope, I went to my hotel. I had the choice of watching television— mostly shows I couldn't understand—reading, or surfing the internet. Thankfully, the rate negotiated for my stay had included Wi-Fi access. Unfortunately the service wasn't robust enough for me to stream video, so I ended up reading some before turning out the light.

"HOW IS it going?" I asked when Georg entered my work area the following morning. I had been looking forward to seeing him and firming up plans for the weekend. I needed to get out and spend some time with other people—the solitary life was starting to get to me.

"Very well. The mirror is still on schedule with no issues. Right now we are using coarse material to shape the glass and that is going just perfectly. There was a power issue during the night, just before the men came in this morning."

I sat up a little straighter. Any sort of interruption to the process could be catastrophic. The glass had to be so precise that if the machinery stopped and rested for too long in one spot it could create issues in the surface of the glass.

"It was not an issue. We have backup systems and the process was largely uninterrupted. It moved more slowly for a few minutes, but there was nothing that would impact the lens."

"Very good," I said with a smile. Exakt Optik apparently had contingency plans for most every situation. I had recommended that we use Allianz up front, but the powers that be had chosen another vendor. That choice had costs months of delays when they encountered issues, and I had been able to convince management that the second attempt should be undertaken by Exakt. It looked like I might just be proven right. "I knew Exakt was right for this job."

"Why were we not chosen the first time?" Georg asked as he took a seat.

"Politics," I answered. The real answer was that a US firm had professed to have the capability to complete the job and there had been pressure to choose them. Unfortunately, their claims weren't up to their abilities. Georg nodded. "But it will work out in the end."

"Yes," Georg said. "What did you do last night?"

I colored slightly. "I got something fast to eat and spent the evening in my hotel." I was not going to admit that I was so tired by the end of the day that I ate American fast food. It sounded terrible even to my ears, and I vowed not to do it again. I knew there were many much better things to eat nearby. The problem was I didn't necessarily know where they were. This was an adventure and I needed to treat it as such rather than being so timid all the time.

"Where are you staying?"

"At the Hotel Jungen." It was just a few minutes away and made my commute very easy.

Georg smiled. "Good. I will meet you there tomorrow morning at nine o'clock, if that is okay?"

"Of course," I answered excitedly. I gave him my phone number, just in case. "That would be great."

"Some of my colleagues and I are also going for lunch today. If you would like to join us, you would be welcome. It's just to a small restaurant in town here, but it will allow you to see the place, and you can eat there if you like after work sometimes. It will be better than 'something fast.'" I got the idea Georg knew what I'd meant. "Food should be savored and enjoyed. This is a nice place serving good German food. It will keep you warm when it gets colder."

"Thank you."

"I'll come here and get you at twelve o'clock."

I expected him to stand and leave, but he sat back in his chair, watching me for a few minutes. Then he reached back and closed the workroom door. "May I ask a question? If you do not want to answer, it is okay."

"Sure." What was I going to do? If he wanted to talk, I could spare a few minutes. Otherwise it would be back to designs or watching the progress on the mirror, which was quickly losing its fascination.

"What is it like to be gay where you come from? I have heard stories of people being hurt. Can you get married where you live? It's very confusing to us here."

"Well, I live outside Boston now, and I can get married there. Massachusetts was the first state to fully legalize gay marriage. And I suppose there are places where it isn't safe to be openly gay. Where I live is perfectly nice. People are supportive and understanding there. 'Live and let live' and all that. What's it like here? Do you have any issues?"

"Most younger people do not care. They accept it," he said with a shrug. "Older people, like my grandfather, have a more difficult time. They cling to the older ways and beliefs."

"Does your family know about you?"

"Yes. It took a while for my grandfather to... agree to disagree about it?" I nodded because he'd used the term correctly. Georg's English was very good, and I wished my German was a quarter as proficient. I could understand more than I could speak. I knew I was relying mostly on gestures and body language as well as picking up other clues. But I tried as best I could, and most people were helpful.

"Is he still alive?"

Georg shook his head. "He died last year." It was obviously a painful subject, and I wished I hadn't asked. "I like to think he began to understand. He was very... or it was very important to him to have someone carry on the family name." Georg shifted in his chair, which seemed a little strange. He impressed me as a confident man in control of things whenever possible. He was also incredible to look at: dark hair, strong jaw, full lips. If you changed his clothes and put him in another setting, he could be a model, or put him in jeans and a heavy shirt, on a horse, with a day's beard growth, and he'd fit in as a cowboy. Georg had obviously been active much of his life.

"I'm sorry. It's hard to lose people we love." I knew that feeling all too freaking well. "You still have your parents, right?"

"My mother." This discussion seemed to be making Georg uncomfortable, and though it had seemed like a natural progression, I wasn't sure how we had gotten onto this topic. "My father died when I was very young."

"Are you an engineer?" I asked, trying to change the subject.

"I'm a senior project manager. Usually I would be involved in the initial bid and then manage everything down through delivery. Hans did part of that with your team. This project is a little unusual for us. We like the same people to see things through to the end. But in this case it couldn't be helped. I take it from the file that you helped design what we're making."

"Yes. I got my doctorate a few years ago, so while I'm a full-fledged member of the team, as opposed to one of the graduate assistants, I'm not one of the most senior members."

"You said you volunteered to come here," Georg said.

"I did. They wanted another member of the team, but his wife is expecting her first baby in a few weeks, just in time for Christmas. I volunteered so he could stay with her." There was no way I would have let Hildebrandt sit over here, worrying for weeks about his wife. The guy was nervous enough as it was and that would probably have sent him over the edge.

"That was kind of you."

"Thanks." I wasn't so sure how kind it was. He had someone important to enjoy the holidays with, and if he'd have come, it was likely the project would have ended up flying him back and forth multiple times. I could simply stay here for the duration and save expenses. My neighbor would watch my place for me, and other than that there wasn't much to keep me in Boston now other than my work.

"I need to get back to my desk, but I'll come get you for lunch." Georg stood and opened the door. He said a brief goodbye and then left, once again leaving me alone. I should have been getting used to it by now, but after having Georg stay and talk for a while, the feeling of being alone had intensified. I wasn't normally a very outgoing person, so I didn't know why I was so forward with Georg, but it had seemed to pay off, so maybe I would try to be forward more often rather than trying to blend in with the woodwork.

My phone beeped, and I picked it up, glancing at the message from Dr. Harper, the project director. The man rarely seemed to sleep. I texted him a brief update that everything was going well so far, and I got a smiley face in return.

GEORG RETURNED precisely at noon, and I followed him out of the plant and to his blue BMW coupe. I got in the passenger side and buckled up as Georg went around to the other side. "The restaurant isn't far," he explained and started the car, then pulled out and headed off through town.

"I love the way this area looks. People have lived here for thousands of years, and it feels like it." Everything felt solid and unchanging, a lot like Boston. "I was raised outside Dallas, and everything there seems like it just sprang from the ground yesterday."

"Are you an adventurous eater?" Georg asked.

"Yes. I like good food and I'll try just about anything." That had been one of the appeals to coming here. I'd sort of forgotten that and ended up eating at fast food way too often, for convenience. I smiled excitedly and saw Georg look across at me and smile back. "How old is the town? Was it destroyed during the war?"

"Bobingen is more than a thousand years old, and unfortunately it was damaged. Some of the important buildings were spared, while others were bombed. They've done quite a bit of restoration work over the years, and it is hard to tell what's been rebuilt. I doubt there are many tourists out this far, and I understand there was a lot of talk about just rebuilding in the modern style."

I watched as we drove down the straight old center of town. It looked like a fairy-tale place, with brightly painted half-timbered buildings, windows with overflowing flower boxes in holiday colors, and a city hall with a clock tower at one end of town and a stone church at the other. I wanted to lower the window and stick my head out so I could get a better view.

"You haven't been here before?"

"No." I sure as heck would have if I'd have known what awaited me.

Georg chuckled softly. "If you like this, then I can't wait until I show you around tomorrow."

"Sorry."

"What for?" Georg slipped his car into a parking space and turned off the engine.

"I have this tendency to bounce a little when I get excited." I had to remember not to do that. It had been okay when I was a kid, but now it came across as childish. I knew that. But there were times I still forgot and my natural energy took over.

"Bounce away," Georg said, still chuckling slightly. "It's nice that you're excited." We got out, and Georg watched me over the roof of the car, and I got this fluttery feeling in my stomach. For a few seconds Georg's gaze darkened. It might have been attraction, or I could just have been seeing what I wanted to see. Georg was attractive, to say the least. Of course his attraction to me was probably my imagination. It wouldn't be the first time I had misunderstood someone's attention. I turned and looked up and down the street, taking it all in even as still I felt Georg's gaze on me.

I turned back and saw Georg turn away. Suppressing a smile, I closed the car door and followed him toward a small restaurant. I suppose that during nicer weather tables would have been set up out in front, but now the space was empty. We entered and were shown to a table. "I thought others were coming."

"They had other plans," Georg said, coloring slightly. I wondered if that was true. If he had told a fib, it was flattering. "We usually have lunch on Friday afternoons, but things seemed to fall apart." Georg took a seat, and I sat across from him. He ordered a beer when the server approached the table, and I figured when in Rome… so I got one as well. Things were different here, I was learning.

"We would never have beer with lunch back home. Drinking on the job is frowned upon."

"I remember. Americans are very hung up on alcohol as I remember."

"To say the least," I agreed. When the beer came, the server left menus, and I sipped from the glass. "Man, that's good." I took another drink, the smooth, slight bitterness captivating my taste buds.

"Every town has their own brewery, and each kind of beer is served in a glass designed to enhance its flavor. Although there are some nationally produced beers, like in the US, beer is still very much a local and regional art."

I took another sip. "So in the next town...."

"You'll probably get a completely different beer made by a different brewmaster."

"That's cool," I said. I figured I could only have one beer, so I didn't want to drink it too quickly, no matter how good it tasted. Georg handed me a menu, and I looked it over. Of course I could read none of it. I knew a few of the dishes, but not well enough to be comfortable. Georg helped me a little, and I settled on the Schweinsbraten with potatoes and salad. He explained that pork was the main meat served in Bavaria, and their roast pork was simply the best.

Georg placed the orders, and I sat looking around the restaurant. It seemed to have been there for hundreds of years. The woodwork had darkened from thousands of hands touching it over many decades. "What's Christmas like around here?"

"Here in Bobingen, the town will put up their Christmas tree, and on market day it is transformed into their version of the Christkindlmarkt, the Christmas market where traditional Christmas crafts and foods are sold. They're very special. There are some more common items, like the wooden or wax ornaments, but the craftsmen in each town have their own traditions and they make unique things. You'll have to come in a few weeks. They'll set up down at the end of town around the church."

"I've heard of markets like those, and a few places in the US have them, but I suspect here it will be different." After all, this country was the birthplace of the Christmas tree, and I knew a lot of our Christmas traditions originated here.

"It will be," Georg assured me.

As quiet settled between us, I wondered what else we could talk about. We weren't out together on a date; this was a business lunch. But from the way Georg kept watching me, it was starting to feel like something else. I actually turned around to make sure he wasn't looking at someone else. His gaze was soft, kind, and yet it didn't waver from me for a second. What it meant, I wasn't quite sure, but I wasn't ashamed to admit that I liked the attention.

"Can I ask you how long you've been single?" Georg asked.

"Officially, three months, but emotionally longer than that. Jay was an interesting guy, but after dating him for a while I found out we didn't agree on some things. Like monogamy, for example. He didn't believe it was necessary." I sighed. "The last straw was when I came home from the university and found him in our bed with some stranger. I guess I knew he might be up to something, but seeing it…. I kicked his sorry butt to the curb." I didn't tell Georg that Jay had said his cheating was my fault for being so boring in bed. Jay had actually said that he had to force himself to stay awake when he was with me. I was dull and uninteresting, at least according to Jay, and it still stung. I knew I shouldn't let it get to me, but it had, especially the way Jay had said it in front of the guy I had just walking in on him screwing, both of them screaming and yelling at the top of their lungs.

No matter how many times I had tried to forget the whole incident, I couldn't get it out of my head.

"Your boyfriend wasn't worth your time." Georg didn't smile, but met my gaze steadily, his voice low and private. "Wipe him from your mind. He isn't worth thinking about or remembering."

"I agree." Our plates arrived, and my stomach rumbled as the scent of butter, fried potatoes, and roast pork reached my nose. Damn, it smelled like heaven. "I can't believe we're talking about this. I've known you two days and I've already spilled the beans about my useless ex." I couldn't remember feeling so open and easy with someone so quickly. Georg touched something in me, and I felt comfortable with him.

"It's all right. I like talking with you." Georg sipped from his glass and left his knife and fork where they were. "You're refreshingly open and honest. It's nice." Georg's smile was so warm it touched my heart.

"I'm just me," I told him.

"Well, then, this Jay couldn't see what he had," Georg said as he picked up his knife and fork and slowly began to eat. I watched him and mimicked his movements. Georg moved with practiced grace, so I felt like a country bumpkin at the table with him. We ate our lunch, and I tried to figure out how Georg could know anything about me. He was probably just being nice. I smiled and continued eating.

We grew quiet as we ate our lunch.

"Is it good?" Georg asked.

"Delicious," I answered between bites. "How is yours?"

"Very good," Georg said.

I cleaned the plate and finished my beer, then sat back, almost completely content. Georg continued glancing up at me as he ate, and I began to wonder what I could have done to capture his interest. I tried to think of the last time someone had been so attentive. I cringed when I remembered that Jay had acted much the same way, at least when we'd first met. A shiver ran though me as I wondered if events were repeating themselves.

Georg motioned, and the server brought the check. I pulled out my wallet, but Georg waved it off and handed the server some cash. He left and returned a few minutes later. Georg took his change, and we got up to leave the restaurant, putting on our coats before walking out to the car.

"Thank you," I said as we got in the car. "It wasn't necessary for you to buy me lunch."

"It was my pleasure," Georg said and then started the engine. We retraced our route and ended up back at the office parking lot. He shut off the engine and the heat inside the car dissipated as the cold from outside worked its way in. Georg didn't move. I wasn't sure what was going on and slowly opened my door.

"Thank you again for lunch." I got out and waited for Georg, and we walked inside together. I felt his gaze on me as we walked up the stairs and to my small work area. "It was very nice of you to keep me company." I wasn't sure what else to say.

Georg stood in the doorway. "I'm glad you enjoyed it." He said the words as though they had some deep meaning rather than simple pleasantries. "I'll see you tomorrow morning."

"I'm looking forward to it," I said and sat down to try to get some work done. Georg didn't leave right away, and after a few seconds I looked up as he turned and left the doorway.

I couldn't help wondering what this sudden attention was all about. Georg seemed like a nice guy, but what could I have possibly done to warrant this kind of interest? It was nice to think that he might be interested in me. Actually, it was really flattering. But I would be leaving in a few weeks, and after the mess and heartbreak with Jay, I didn't want to go running down any road that could lead to heartache. And getting involved with anyone over here was a recipe for disaster, even if he pushed every button I had in the attraction department. I suppose I was drawn to what I didn't have, and I'd always liked bigger, stronger, and darker men. Georg fit that bill perfectly.

I shook my head and pushed those thoughts out of my head. I was getting way ahead of myself. Georg was being nice, and I was jumping in, like I always did. I checked the clock and decided to get back to work. Maybe some rational thinking would help clear things up.

CHAPTER 2

"DID YOU forget what time it is here… again?" my friend Julie asked as she answered her phone.

I checked the clock and groaned. "Sorry. I'll let you go back to sleep."

"I just went to bed and wasn't asleep yet, so I'll let you keep your head… for now. What's up?" I heard her yawn and another apology was on the tip of my tongue, but I stopped it. It would only get her going again.

"I think I'm being dumb. I went to lunch with a sort of coworker yesterday, and I think he was flirting with me. We got through the whole gay thing, so I know he is. That isn't an issue, but what do I do if he is?"

"Flirt back?" she quipped. "Enjoy it. Hey, try finding out if he's interested and hump his bones. Hell, why are you asking me? It's been a year since I've gotten any action. That bastard took everything in the divorce, including my ability to stand the sight of men. You're an exception, of course, unless you keep calling me at this ungodly hour." I heard her huff. "Seriously, though, you may be misunderstanding him. It could be that he's just being nice."

"Okay. So what do I do?"

"Men are clueless." I heard her transcontinental sigh. "Ask him."

"Yeah, right. What do I say? 'Yesterday at lunch I thought you might be flirting with me. I was just wondering if you were?'"

"You could. Or if you're interested, you could just flirt back. If he continues, then reel him in. Why is it I have to give you advice on men? You are one, you date them—that should make you an expert. Lord knows there's been no hitch in my giddyap in a while."

"I take it you've been up watching old movies again."

"Yeah. I definitely need to get laid. But I can't figure out how to do that without actually spending time with men." Julie seemed to have gotten stuck in the men-are-pigs, post-breakup stage. I was smart enough not to mention she could find a woman. The last time I had, the screeching commenced and didn't cease for an hour. Apparently I'd hit a nerve, and she nearly worked my last one by the time we were done.

"Okay. Go out, find a man, take him home, fuck his brains out, and kick him to the curb in the morning. You'll feel better, he'll have gotten sex… win-win."

"Oh, you're no help," Julie said, and I walked into the bathroom to start cleaning up. I put the phone on speaker and quietly opened my kit.

"Sorry."

"Yeah… well. So what's this guy's name?"

"Georg von Mittelbach. He's one of the project managers. Tall, dark hair, gorgeous eyes. Oh, and dimples. When he smiles he has these Mario Lopez dimples that are hot as hell. He could step out of a magazine, if you know what I mean."

I could almost hear her smile through the phone. "When do you see him again? Is this some water cooler fascination?"

I rolled my eyes, forgetting for a second she couldn't see me. Next time we'd have to FaceTime. "In a few hours. He's showing me around today." I tried to sound cool, but failed miserably when my voice cracked a little. Damn, I hated when that happened. I wasn't a teenager, but fuck if it still didn't crack when I was nervous.

"Then have fun and see what happens. Above all, enjoy yourself. That's why you took that assignment. It was a chance to get away and get over the asshole. If you meet a handsome, dashing man, all the better."

"Thanks. You've been a big help."

"Next time call during normal business hours and I'll be more on my game." She paused. "Have fun, and I love you to pieces, you know that. Don't let that crap with Jay and the baggage from your family stop you from having fun. You have a chance to be the person you want to be, so go for it." She hung up, and I closed the app on my smartphone.

Julie was right. All the crap that had gone down in the past few years didn't mean anything. I was in a brand-new place and no one knew me. I could just be me without carrying all that junk along for the ride. I finished getting cleaned up and dressed and was waiting in the lobby of the small hotel when Georg strode in. He smiled when he saw me, and I stood and approached him.

"Are you ready to go?" Georg asked.

"Sure. What did you have in mind for today?" I was anxiously excited about spending time with Georg, hoping he'd like me and I didn't say something stupid.

"I thought we'd drive out to Füssen and visit the castles. It's not too far and there are great views of the Alps from there." Georg smiled. "It's touristy, as you could imagine, but it is fun, and some places are touristy for a reason. After that we can play it by ear if you like."

"I'm in your hands," I said without thinking.

Georg paused at the front door of the hotel. "I think I like that."

Did he mean what I thought he meant? I pushed the idea way. It didn't matter, because I like that he liked that. "I'm glad," I said catching Georg's gaze for a second as we walked to his car. We climbed in, and Georg pulled out of his parking space and wound through town until we reached the autobahn.

"How did you get into this line of work?" Georg asked as the car got up to nearly incredible speed.

"I loved Star Trek and science fiction as a kid, so when I decided to become an engineer, I wanted to design things that went into space. I got my PhD a few years ago and I was on the ground floor of this project, so I was asked to design components and sort of fell into designing the mirror. I have experience with optics, as well, so things fell into place."

"Is this the first big project you've worked on?"

"No. I worked on some satellites and things." I couldn't say any more about them, which was a real shame because they had been an incredible challenge. Those projects were where I had gotten my experience with optics.

"So you're a doctor?"

"Officially, though I never use it outside of an academic setting."

Georg chuckled. "Here it would be used all the time. Germans are really big on official titles, and if we go through all the work to get a doctorate, we seem to want everyone to know it."

"There's nothing wrong with that, I guess. I know people who use it all the time. The degree allows me to do what I really love. That's why I got it, not because I want to rub a title in anyone's face."

I looked out the window as the rather bleak landscape passed. I could imagine how gorgeous everything would be with the hills and valleys covered in green. "Will it snow soon?"

"Up in the mountains it already has. The scenery should be impressive at the castle." Georg looked over with another of his smiles.

"You seem excited. Have you been here before?"

"Yes." Georg chuckled. "I think it's your excitement I'm picking up on. I grew up here and I've seen this view more times that I can count. My father used to take me up in the mountains on our land to hunt when I was a child." Georg got off the highway and onto a smaller road, headed toward the mountains in the distance. "I know this entire area like the back of my hand, but with you I'm seeing it with fresh eyes."

"It's beautiful," I said and continued watching as the landscape changed.

"It's in my blood. This land, these mountains, they're a part of me." Georg sighed. "I've traveled and worked in other places, but this part of the world always calls me home." We turned a corner and the valley spread out beneath us. Georg pointed forward. "Look straight ahead. You can see the castle perched on the top of one of the peaks. That's where we're going—the white against the dark hills."

"Wow," I breathed and watched as the castle got closer and closer. It disappeared from view for a while as we wound around and eventually ended up in a small town. Georg parked, and we got out of the car.

I wasn't sure where to look first. In one direction was a golden castle on a hilltop, and in another was Neuschwanstein, towering above us.

"This is Füssen," Georg said. "The castle over there is Hohenschwangau, where Ludwig grew up and, of course, Neuschwanstein, the fairy-tale one he built. You'll need to bundle up and we can get our tickets. Then we climb up to the castle."

"We walk?"

"Yes," Georg said with a smile. "It's beautiful."

I had to agree with him. Since Georg had bought lunch the day before, and drove, I got our tickets, and we walked through town and then began the climb up the hill. The sun was bright and the air crisp, and the hill wasn't too steep. A few carriages came up behind us.

"We could have taken one of those," Georg said, but I shook my head. The view was spectacular everywhere I looked, and as we rounded a bend, the white stone castle loomed overhead. I wouldn't have traded that sight for anything.

"Jesus, it looks like something from Disney."

"They used this castle as the model," Georg said. I could see that, and we continued on our way, rounding the final bend and then entering the gates to the castle courtyard. We got in line for an English tour and waited ten minutes. We were shown inside and given a tour of palatial rooms with lavish decoration that looked more like theater sets than interior design. By the time the tour was over, my head was spinning. We stepped outside into a now cloudy day. The temperature had dropped as well.

"Do you want to get some pictures?" Georg asked.

I had taken a number of them inside with my phone.

"Sit on the wall and I'll take your picture."

I did, and Georg snapped a few.

"Would you like me to take one of both of you?" a lady asked as she walked past.

Georg handed her the phone, and we stood next to one another. After a few seconds, Georg put his arm lightly around my waist, and I moved closer to him. Smiling, we waited while she took our picture. After thanking her, we started the walk down the hill.

The wind picked up and flakes of snow began to fall. It was gorgeous and cold and wonderfully Christmassy all at once. Unfortunately as we got farther and farther down the hill, the cold began to win. I shoved my hands in my pockets and wished I'd worn another layer of clothing.

"Here." Georg pulled a light scarf out of his pocket and wrapped it around my neck. "It will keep you warm."

I pulled my hands out of my pockets to wrap the scarf, and Georg took one of them once I was done and threaded his fingers with mine.

"I guess I got my answer," I said.

"To what?" Georg asked, turned to look at me.

"I was wondering if you were flirting with me or if you were just acting extra nice." I moved closer, and Georg wrapped his arm around my shoulders.

"I was definitely flirting. Are you warmer now?"

I nodded, and we continued our downward trek. Thankfully the trip back to town took much less time than the trip up. We stopped in a couple of shops and I got a few ornaments. I didn't expect to use them this year, but I'd have them for next year. I looked at a few sweatshirts as a souvenir, but decided against them. "Is it time for lunch?" I asked after we'd left the shop and started walking through the town. I had lost all track of time and didn't care in the least.

"If you can wait, I thought we would go back to Munich and have lunch in the market." That sounded good to me, so we got in the car and Georg drove back to the city. I spent much of the time watching the scenery.

"Do you live in Munich?" I asked, turning back as the mountains receded in the distance.

"Yes. My family has a house there. It's been with us for generations." Georg seemed uncomfortable. "I inherited it from my grandfather."

"It must be very nice to have something like that. It means you have roots and a history." I had none of those things. My life often felt transient. I'd lived in multiple places: Dallas, where I grew up, Chicago for a while, and now Boston. "I like to think that wherever I hang my hat is home, but that sounds kind of dumb. I don't have a home. Not like that, anyway. I live in a small apartment near the university. It's one step up from student housing."

"Is that where you lived with… what's his name?" I loved how Georg refused to say Jay's name. It made me smile. Personally I didn't want to think about him. Not right now.

"No. I had to move. We had a place together, but neither of us could afford it alone." I sighed and wished I'd stop doing that. "It was for the best. I didn't want reminders of him around, anyway." Also since I was going to be gone for weeks, it didn't make sense to get a huge place if I wasn't going to be there a lot. "It's just a place."

Georg reached over and placed his hand on my leg. Warmth spread from his touch and radiated outward, warming my entire body. I tried not to shift too much, but I needed to make sure my cock wasn't poking straight out for Georg to see. My heart raced, and I turned to look at him as he drove. Could he feel the effect he was having on me? I hoped he could, and at the same time I hoped he couldn't. It was nice having someone interested in me, but getting involved with someone I worked with wasn't a good idea, even if we didn't have the same employer. I closed my eyes and willed my heart and dick to settle down. Neither listened.

"That's sad. Home should be where you feel safe and secure."

I looked to Georg and smiled. The sun was coming back out as we got away from the mountains and it shone brightly overhead. "If it's clear tonight, I'll show you what makes me feel safe and secure."

Georg turned toward me and then back to the road. He squeezed my leg slightly and suddenly I was afraid to move in case Georg remembered where his hand was and decided to pull it away. I wasn't sure what he wanted from me, and that was both exciting and terrifying. I liked the fact that he thought me attractive enough to be interested in me, because I sure as hell was interested in him. Who wouldn't be? I'd also had enough quickies and one-night stands to last me the rest of my life. I didn't need that any longer—a few hours of fun always left me with days of regret. Suppressing a sigh, I decided to enjoy what was happening for now. It was nice. Worrying would only take that away.

We approached the city and Georg removed his hand so he could shift gears. I felt the loss immediately. We wound our way through major city streets in the direction of twin church towers. "That's the Frauenkirche," Georg explained. "The Church of Our Lady." He continued through the old city and out a little ways to an older neighborhood with large homes. Some looked like they had been turned into small hotels. Georg parked in front of a stone building with an iron fence.

"Is this your home?" I asked, looking up at the three-story edifice. It was impressive. The gardens were well kept and the building looked like it had been lovingly maintained for a long time.

"This is my family's city home." He turned off the engine, and I shifted in my seat.

"I take it your family is wealthy." Not that it mattered to me.

Georg turned toward me. "My family goes back a long time in this region. There is an estate outside the city. It's open to tourists and does well enough to cover expenses and maintenance." He truly seemed uncomfortable.

"What aren't you telling me?"

"Within my family there is also a title: Count von Mittelbach. We also took the title as our name some time ago." Georg turned to me. "Since my father had already passed, that title came to me on my grandfather's death."

"So you're a count?" I smiled. The thought delighted me. "That's cool."

Georg shrugged. "The title has brought very little happiness to my family. My grandfather had one son and my father died when I was a child. It was my grandfather's wish that I get married and have children to carry on the family, but that isn't likely to happen." Georg opened his door and I followed suit.

"Why didn't you say something earlier?"

"I don't advertise the title." Georg looked toward the house. "If you're warm enough, let's walk toward the market and we can eat and look around. Afterwards I'll show you the house, if you like."

"I'm fine," I said as I stepped onto the sidewalk and waited for Georg. I let him lead the way, though I was beginning to wonder if this was a good idea. Georg had turned quiet and seemed to have withdrawn into himself. I shoved my hands into my pockets and walked alongside him, taking in all that was around me.

"I want people to like me for who I am," Georg said after we crossed a main street. "My grandfather always introduced himself as Count von Mittelbach. It was very much a part of who he was, his identity, and I guess I still think of it that way."

"I take it you've had people get close to you because of the title?"

"At university there was a parade of women interested in becoming Countess von Mittelbach." Georg chuckled. "They, of course, were disappointed. But my grandfather still pressured me to marry."

"Didn't you say he knew you were gay?"

"Yes, but he didn't care," Georg said, shocking me. "He wanted a great-grandson and that was all there was to it. He died last year, disappointed in me."

"You are who you are. And if that's your family's attitude, no wonder they were miserable. It's a title, not the end of the world. Aren't there distant relatives that everything will pass to?"

"No. And I'm thinking that's a good thing. The title will die with me, but the property can now be left to whomever I wish, unless I have a child." Georg shook his head slightly. "Let's change the subject to something more interesting than my family's ridiculousness."

"I think it's interesting, you being a count. It goes with your rather dashing appearance. But I liked you before you told me, so it's no big deal. Though I may gush once or twice, but it's only because we don't have counts back home, so it's a novelty. Well, the concept is a novelty, you're not a novelty." God, I was rambling like an idiot. "I'll just shut up now."

Georg laughed, full-on. It was a deep, rich tone that delighted my ears. I could listen to that sound all day. Georg stopped walking and continued laughing. I hadn't thought it was that funny and wondered if I'd said something stupid. "I've spent most of my life trying to deal with the ramifications of being Count von Mittelbach, and you sum it up in a few words. No big deal." I shrugged, and Georg's laughter died away.

"Maybe it's the American in me, but you are the person you are and should be judged by your own actions and behavior, not based upon how you were born." I wondered how to ask my next question, but I was dying to know. "Do you have to work, or do you do it because you like your job?"

"I love my job and I need to work. There is family money, but it pays for upkeep on the properties. Most of it was used up by previous generations who did nothing but live an unsustainable lifestyle. My grandfather never worked, and he was appalled when he had to sit me down to tell me that I would need to get a job after my education. He thought work was beneath us."

I didn't know what to say to that. The attitudes of one generation weren't the attitudes of another. "All that matters is what you think."

Georg nodded. "Sometimes I feel as though I'm working to preserve a ghost, a family legacy that no longer exists." He moved closer and lightly bumped my shoulder. "Okay, let's really change the subject now."

We were approaching the main square of the old section of Munich. I had visited once, but now the space had been transformed. Canopies lined the square, lit with lights. The air was permeated with the scent of onions, sausage, sauerkraut, and other scents I couldn't name, but damn they were amazing. I inhaled deeply and smiled. "This is heaven."

"Come on. Let's get some sausage for lunch. We can go to the Viktualienmarkt just up the way that makes some of the best." Georg took my hand. It was starting to feel sort of natural, and I liked it. Jay had never been a touch-centered person. He was more a sex-centered guy, and I liked that Georg touched. It was kind, gentle, and made me feel special, even if it was only for now. At the stand, Georg ordered.

I had expected something like a hot dog, but I was mistaken. The sausage was enormous, grilled and cut into pieces, served with pommes frites, or fries, and Georg added some of the ketchup to the edge. By the time he handed me the paper dish, I was ravenous. He and I moved off to a stand-up table, and I began to eat. The ketchup surprised me and I might never go back to the American version. It was tangy, a little spicy, and damn good.

"It's currywurst," Georg explained. "Think of it as the German hot dog, only better."

I nodded and continued eating. The wind blew through occasionally, and I really wished I'd stopped to buy that sweatshirt like I'd thought of earlier. Georg moved closer, shielding me from the wind and sharing his heat. It was thoughtful of him, and I stepped a little closer. "You always seem so cold," he whispered into my ear, his hot breath warming more than just the skin it touched.

"I should be used to weather like this after living in Boston. It was warmer up until a few days ago, and I guess I didn't dress well enough." I should have known, and I felt like an idiot. All I needed was another layer.

"There will be places to get something if you want it," Georg said as he finished. I could have eaten more, it was so delicious, but was satisfied for now. I used my napkin, and then Georg disposed of the trash and led me out into the market—and what a place it was, filled with booths of holiday crafts, baked goods, and decorations, most of them handmade and sold by the craftsman. I could not resist the painted beeswax and handcrafted wooden ornaments.

I lost all track of time as I examined each booth. I bought a carved incense smoker for Julie. She loved to cook, so I got her a baker, and the artist even signed it for me. He seemed thrilled when I asked him to. Once it was signed, a nice lady, probably his wife, packed it well, and I added it to my growing bag of purchases.

"I guess I didn't picture you for a shopper," Georg said.

"Then why did you bring me here? This is amazing. I can get most of my shopping done all in one place." Not that I had that much to get— some things for a few friends and that was about it. As night descended and the lights came on everywhere, I bought a final gift and added it to the stack. It was a simple ornament made of wood.

"Why that one?" Georg asked.

"It's a schoolteacher and it reminds me of my mother. I haven't spoken to my mom and dad since I came out." I turned away. Just saying the words was hard.

"Because of something that silly?" Georg asked. "My grandfather was old-fashioned and kept pressuring me to get married, but when I told him I was gay he simply shrugged and said I needed to get married, and then once I had a son, I could take whatever lover I wanted." Georg grinned. "That was his generation. Marriage was a contract between families to him. You used it to get what you wanted."

"That seems so… cold."

"The idea of marriage for love isn't that old. Marriage united families, kingdoms, and properties for centuries, usually at the cost of the woman. It didn't matter what she wanted, and I somehow doubt that in this modern age I could have found someone to go along with that arrangement."

I snickered softly. "Maybe one of those countess wannabes would have been a candidate. After all, she would get the title, and as long as you were up-front with her, then you could have what you wanted."

"As long as I kept the person I cared for in the closet and out of sight." Georg shook his head. "No, thank you. I'd rather have the title die out. It's probably time it did anyway. They are symbolic. Officially they don't exist. Though if I really wanted, I could probably will that along with the property. There is no aristocracy because there are no reigning monarchs in this country. What's left of the old aristocracy just kept using their titles. Some have money, most are broke, but almost all of them live somewhat in the past."

"You don't," I said. "And I think the title's cool. But you need a cape, like in the movies." I couldn't help laughing at the face he made. Then he shook his head and looked at me like I'd gone mildly crazy.

"We've seen everything and watched the glockenspiel at least three times," Georg said with an indulgent smile as we passed the last stall in the market.

"I like it." Every hour I'd felt my gaze drawn upward to watch the Bavarian knight battle his opponent. It was another of those things we didn't have at home.

"I know you do. But if you're ready we can walk back."

It was getting colder, and I quickly agreed. We walked briskly, the activity helping to keep me warm. Once we were in his neighborhood, on his quiet street, Georg put his arm around me and we slowed our pace.

"Thank you for everything. I had a real nice time today." I kind of figured that day was over. "You didn't have to do everything you did, but it was memorable."

"You're welcome. I had a good time as well."

We arrived at Georg's house, and he led me through the gate and up the walk. He unlocked the door, and we stepped inside. The house was dark, but he turned on the lights, and I gasped. The house was filled with antiques, paintings, and all the trappings you'd expect from very old, titled money. The house itself was stunning: carved woodwork and lush carpets that had probably been down for decades. They were worn, but added an air of solidity to the house. "Are those portraits of your ancestors?"

"Yes. That's my grandfather at the top of the stairs, and they get older as you go downward. My dad didn't have his portrait painted because he was never the count. Someday maybe I'll have mine done as a bookend to the end of the line."

I looked up the open stairs and my gaze traveled downward, going back in time. Georg had tried to make light of the fact that he was who he was, but I could tell it hurt him that all this would come to an end. I didn't have any answers and wasn't sure what to say. Georg had just shown me a part of himself that I was sure very few people ever got to see.

"The dining room is in here, and that's my office. The morning room is just off the kitchen near the back garden." He showed me through room after palatial room. "Everything is from my grandfather and great-grandfather. We never throw anything out, so things just get older and older." We went through and out the back door, stepping into the garden. I walked away from the house.

"I can turn on the lights."

"Please don't," I said softly and stopped in the center of a patch of grass, looking up.

Georg came and stood beside me. "The stars," he whispered.

"Yeah. They're what settle me. See, these are the same ones we see at home." I pointed upward. "They look the same no matter where I am, unless I go to Australia, of course."

"Is that all?" Georg asked.

"No. I look up at them and I see us, all of us."

"In the stars. Like astrologically?" Georg asked.

"No. Us. We came from there. All the elements in us. Everything about us was created and born in stars. The oxygen we breathe, the water in our skin, the iron in our blood, the stone in your house—all of it comes from the stars. When they explode, they blast their elements everywhere, and that gas, dust, and energy forms new stars, planets, and everything we are. So when I look up, I see the stars and I see them creating what will come next."

"So you're saying we're made of stardust," Georg said.

"Yeah, we are."

"I like that, because when you laugh I swear I can see the twinkle of stardust in your eyes."

I turned toward Georg, and he lightly worked his hand behind my head and slowly moved closer. At first I wasn't sure he was going to kiss me, or even if I wanted to be kissed. Jay's words rang in my head and they almost made me hesitate, but by the time I had thought about it, Georg's lips touched mine. At that point I let those concerns go and returned Georg's kiss. He tasted spicy and warm, and I turned slightly. Georg pulled me closer and deepened the kiss slightly, moving his lips against mine. Then, too quickly, he pulled away.

I breathed deeply to inhale the last of his scent before the cold night air carried it away.

"You hesitated. Did I do something wrong?"

"No," I whispered, not wanting to tell him that Jay had told me on numerous occasions that I kissed like a dead fish, and had even once proceeded to explain how I should be kissing. That, of course, only made me more self-conscious. I finally decided that was part of his plan. "Was I okay?"

Georg didn't answer with words and instead kissed me again. Then he backed away and gathered me close, pressing me to him. "Tell me more about stardust."

I wasn't sure how much I should say. "Well, all elements are made in the stars. Bigger ones make heavier elements, and when they die and explode, they seed the beginnings of new stars, planets, and even create the building blocks of life. You and I, nothing we see, would exist without them. They're like the mother and father of us all." I looked back up at the dark sky peppered with points of light. We could see more if we were outside the city, but there were enough to see standing in the dark backyard to make an impressive display. "That's why I do what I do. I hope someday we can see back to the beginning, to where we began."

"I don't understand," Georg whispered.

"That's why we're building the lens. The farther away we go, the farther back in time we travel—millions, billions of years. With the mirror we're building, we can see farther away than ever, maybe back to the very beginning. That's where we all began, and everything we see and touch had its start in those first stars." I swallowed and wondered just how incredibly geeky I sounded. If I wanted to say something romantic, I could at least have looked into his eyes or something, but instead I started talking about the origin of the universe. Yeah, I was the king of geeks. Crown me now and get it the hell over with.

I started to shiver, and Georg began moving us toward the house. "We should go inside. It's going to get very cold out here." I nodded, and Georg opened the kitchen door and we stepped inside. "The place can be rather drafty, but this room is almost always toasty warm." He took off his coat, and I did the same. I handed Georg back his scarf and sat at the large trestle table in the center of the room.

"I thought I would cook dinner if you're up for my cooking," Georg said.

"That sounds nice. I can help if you like," I offered, but Georg was already getting out what he needed, so I stayed where I was and he got to work.

"I don't cook very much because it's generally just me. So on my way home I either stop and have dinner or grab takeaway. I love kebab, so I get that once a week. It's Turkish food and very good. You should try it while you're here."

"I don't think I've had Turkish food before." Georg heated up a pan and began cutting up vegetables. "Where did you learn to cook?"

"I was interested in it, though no one ever taught me, so I took a class a few years ago. I got tired of heating things up, so I went to a culinary institute in the evenings to learn proper cooking." He pulled dough out of the refrigerator.

"What are you making?"

"My specialty. Vegetable strudel." Georg set the dough aside and dropped the vegetables into boiling water for a few minutes, then drained them and set them aside. He finished working with them and then stretched the dough out thin before rolling the vegetables into the dough. I watched, fascinated, as he shaped it, brushed it with lots of butter, and then placed it in the oven.

"I've heard of apple strudel, but not vegetable."

"It's really good. Now I just have to make the sauce to go with it and let it bake." Georg began working again and I watched. Before he got far, Georg opened a bottle of wine and poured two glasses, then handed me one. I raised it.

"To a wonderful dinner, and thank you for an amazing day."

We clinked our glasses and drank.

"I really hope you like it." Georg said.

After a few minutes the rich scent of baking dough filled the kitchen. Except for the modern appliances, the room looked like the rest of the house, like it had been trapped in the last century. It had a warmth, a permanency about it that was reassuring, like the table I sat at. How many people had sat at this table? Had Georg sat here when he was a kid, waiting for the cook to pull a batch of cookies out of the oven? I liked to think so. The wood had been worn smooth by decades of hands, and the occasional scratches told of use.

My stomach growled. The sausage I'd had for lunch was definitely wearing off. I was tempted to drink more wine, but knew that would be a terrible idea on an empty stomach, so I sipped from my glass. Georg finished the sauce and then set it aside. Once again I wasn't sure what we should talk about. Georg was busy, so I stood and wandered to the back door, looking out into the dark garden.

"My grandmother had a real talent," Georg said from behind me. "She designed the garden years ago, and my grandfather kept it just the way she had it. Now I do the same. She designed it so that no matter what season it is, there's something to see. The fountains she put in look wonderful whether they're running or covered with snow." I felt him move closer. "Is something wrong?"

"No." I chuckled and turned around. "I've never been good with the casual thing, if you know what I mean."

"I'm sorry, but I really don't."

"I did plenty of easy hookups when I was in college. It was simple and there were no attachments. Usually we were on different paths and our lives just intersected for a night or two."

"Is that a nice way of saying you had one-night stands?" Georg asked.

"Yes, I did. But I don't do those anymore." Why I was telling Georg this was beyond me. When I was around him, my mouth seemed to go before my brain engaged and I'd say the first thing that came into my mind.

"Neither do I," Georg whispered and lightly traced his fingers over my hair, sending a shiver down my spine. "I haven't done those things in quite a while."

"Have you had anyone special in your life?" God, I was rambling. I stopped myself as nerves jangled and my heart pounded once again, each touch increasing its speed.

"I have. But they never worked out. Guys thought being the boyfriend of a count was going to be glamorous and exciting. It seems I'm none of those things, and once they found that out, they decided they weren't as interested as they'd thought." Georg stopped running his fingers through my hair and then pulled away. I turned around.

"I don't care about the title or anything else that goes with it." I shrugged.

"I know." Georg smiled. "The one person I was reluctant to tell was the one who doesn't care. It figures."

"So is it?" I asked.

"What?"

"A casual thing for you? If it is, I can deal with that. I mean, I'm only here for a few weeks, and we can be friends and do things if you like."

"It isn't a casual thing." Georg slipped his hand in mine. "But yes, you're only here for a few weeks, and I can deal with that if you can." He stepped closer and I let him. Hell, I helped close the distance, and when our lips met, I clung to him as though I were a drowning man and he the only person able to save me. Georg wrapped me in his strong arms, and I went willingly. It didn't matter that I was only here for a short time. All that mattered was that I was here, right now, with him. I didn't do casual, but right now, I'd follow Georg anywhere.

His kiss tugged the air from my lungs, and as soon as it broke, I gasped for breath and returned for more. He tasted like cream, sweet and rich, and damn if I didn't want more. A timer went off in the kitchen, its ding reminding me of the bell that sounds at the end of a round in boxing. Georg moved away, and I hoped like hell I could keep my legs underneath me.

"I need to take dinner out of the oven," Georg whispered, and I nodded. He didn't move.

"Georg," I said softly, prodding him, though I had no idea why. The blood supply had left my brain and distinctly settled much lower. He turned back toward the kitchen, and I used the moment to adjust my throbbing cock. It had been a long time since I'd felt that kind of driving need for someone, and I wanted to scream that when I did, it had to be temporary, that the possibilities had a finish date.

I knew I should have dinner and ask Georg to drive me home. I could stay in one piece and keep it together if we went back to being colleagues with the distance of only a professional relationship. That would be the easy way, the prudent thing to do.

"Duncan," Georg called from the kitchen, and I followed the sound of his rich voice like he was the pied piper. My heart was already engaged and I couldn't walk away. A stronger man might have been able to do it, but I couldn't. I'd take whatever time I had and try to make this a happy holiday season. Live one day at a time—that was what I told myself. Enjoy what I had for as long as I had it. I walked into the kitchen and sat back down at the table, taking a drink of my wine as Georg fixed two plates.

"We can go in the dining room if you like." He set the plates on the table, and I placed my hand on top of his.

"Right here is just fine." I smiled slightly.

"You seem to have made up your mind," Georg said softly. I had hoped I wasn't being so obvious. "I hope it was in my favor."

I leaned across the table, and Georg did the same. Our lips met in the center of the narrow work table. "I made up my mind." Georg was worth taking the chance. We had weeks left together and we should enjoy them. If nothing else, I would have some wonderful memories to carry with me.

We sat back down and began to eat. The food was amazing—the pastry light, the sauce rich, the vegetables savory—as was the view across the table. I tried to keep a grin off my face and ended up looking away a few times so I didn't seem completely weird. At least doing something as normal as eating, even if the food was anything but normal, calmed me down and let me think and just be happy.

Once the meal was over, I was stuffed with the best dinner I could remember since I was sixteen years old, when my mom had made my favorite pot roast, just the way I liked it, with a touch of chili for heat, for my birthday. The memory of my mother stabbed at me for a second. It must have shown on my face, but I did my best to cover it. I took Georg's hand and let the memory fade. There was no use thinking about her or my father now. They had made their feelings very clear, and I had to live with it. I had done so for years, and it was no different now.

Georg cleared away the dishes and placed them in the sink. He took care of the leftover food as well, and then took me by the hand and led me back through the opulent rooms and up the main staircase, past all the portraits of his ancestors.

"Was the house damaged during the war?"

"No. This particular neighborhood escaped most of the bombing. My grandfather told me that most of the items were packed away and stored in the basement once it became apparent that everything was in danger. He said the only thing that happened was that part of the ceiling in the morning room came down from the shaking. We were very lucky, so the house here was spared, as was our estate in the country." We stopped at the top of the stairs, and I looked down at the main floor. Then Georg squeezed my hand and led me down the hallway to the room at the very end.

He opened the door and led me inside. The room was comfortable and relatively plain—not what I had been expecting. "The others are very fancy. But I can't stay in the room my grandfather used. It just didn't feel right, so I still use the one I've always had." The bed was large and solid, dark, with solid posts reaching almost to the ceiling. Georg closed the door and stood in front of me. Confidence went out the window right then and there; I could feel it sprouting wings and heading for the door. My knees shook and I tried my best to hide it. All those comments from Jay played in my head. I knew I shouldn't let them, but I couldn't help it.

"Duncan," Georg said softly. "You seem far away. We don't have to do this. I can take you back to your hotel if you want."

I shook my head and took a deep breath. I had to get that voice out of my head. Jay was an ass, and I couldn't let him define how I thought of myself in the bedroom. I locked my gaze on Georg's and moved closer. It was now or never, time to push away that part of my past.

Georg engulfed me in strong arms and pulled me close. He found my lips with his, the kiss confident and sure, drawing me out of myself. I clutched at Georg, holding him as I returned his kiss. Slowly light replaced the darkness and I let Georg in, and as soon as I did, the energy from earlier, Georg's energy that had left me breathless, did the same thing. I forgot about Jay and everything else as Georg consumed all my attention. All he'd done was kiss and hold me, and I was happy.

Georg unbuttoned my shirt and slipped it off my shoulders and arms. Then he tugged at my T-shirt, and I lifted my hands in the air. He pulled my shirt off and let it go. Warm hands, firm and gentle, caressed my chest and then stilled as Georg deepened the kiss, taking possession of my mouth with his lips and probing tongue. I moaned softly, and then louder and louder as excitement and passion built from deep inside. When Georg paused, it was to remove his own shirt, and I got to touch. My own skin was smooth, but Georg's chest was covered with dark hair, and I stroked it. It was rough on my hands, and I loved it.

He guided me toward the bed, and I went willingly, sitting on the edge and gently tugging Georg on top of me. He pressed his chest to mine, skin to skin, heat to heat. My pants were so tight now, it was painful. I sighed when I felt Georg's fingers on my belly, and when he undid my belt and opened the catch of my jeans, I sighed.

"You're very handsome," Georg told me, looking down as I lay beneath him. He traced my chest and belly lightly with his fingers, my muscles quivering beneath each touch. I wanted him badly and tugged him closer, sliding my hand down his back to his waistband. His pants were tight, so I was only able to slip my fingers underneath. Georg groaned softly as I slid my hands around his hips to undo his belt.

Georg backed away, withdrawing his contact. He opened his pants and slipped them off, then draped them across the back of the chair. Then he tugged at the cuffs of my pants, laughing when they slid off my legs. His joy and excitement filled the room. "You know, it's okay to laugh and have fun when making love."

I swallowed and wondered if Georg realized what he'd said or if he meant what he'd said. I assumed he was using the term generically. "It hasn't been like that for me." Jay was intense and controlling. Sex was not happy, but something else altogether. Georg stepped closer, parted my legs, and then leaned over me. He ran his fingers up my ribs, and I giggled and writhed to get away.

"See, you can laugh all you want. This is the height of what makes us human. In your terms, if we're all stardust, then this is the stars' greatest gift." Georg stopped talking and put his mouth to better use.

I arched my back when he sucked on my chest, driving forward for more, which he gave at the slightest indication. Georg seemed to read my body like a book. I didn't have to say what I wanted; he simply gave. If I hitched my breath, he stopped, licking that spot at the base of my neck once again until my eyes crossed, and when he tugged off the last of our clothes and we were together, body to body, lips to lips, heart to heart, it was perfect and felt so right. When he pulled away I ached for him, and when he was in my arms, I felt whole. How this could be after just a few days I didn't know, but I thanked the stars for it.

When we came together, Georg deep inside me, I gasped and held on, his movements slow, deep, and so meaningful that I knew it had to be my imagination. Hell, I had to be dreaming, except no dream felt like this. Even the best ones were one-sided, and this was anything but. Georg took me places I never dreamed possible, and when we reached the absolute heights of passion, my breath left me. I gasped for air, willing my brain to function, and dug my fingers into Georg's shoulders to ground me. I had to, to keep from flying apart into a million pieces. I could take no more, the pressure too great, and I tumbled over the edge… no… I rocketed into outer space, away from my body, until I floated free, weightless and wonderful, holding Georg to keep from flying away forever. I knew I had to be in space, because I saw stars.

CHAPTER 3

THE NEXT two weeks were magical. That was the only way I could describe it. At work, things were as they had always been—well, almost. Georg and I had lunch every day with his colleagues, and I got to know all of them. He stopped by my workspace each day and gave me an update, which was nearly always the same: everything was progressing on schedule. On Friday afternoon, a week or so before Christmas, I turned to watch the work on the mirror. The machine continued its work uninterrupted. Final polishing was in progress to get the specifications of the glass exactly right. With each movement, the mirror got closer and closer to completion, and it got closer and closer to the time when I'd have to go home. The mirror was expected to be completed just a few days after Christmas, and then it would be packed and readied for shipment. At that point, I'd be packing and getting ready to be shipped home as well. The thought unsettled me more and more each day.

I had sent my supervisor my daily update and tried my best to work on other things, but my mind wasn't cooperating. Giving up, I called Julie and talked to her for a few minutes. "Make the most of what you have," she said after I laid out how I was feeling.

"It isn't fair."

"No one said life was fair. You can't stay there, you know that isn't possible," Julie said gently.

"I know," I told her. "Things are the way they are. I don't have to like it, though." There was indeed nothing I could do except feel time slip by. "Before you go, I was wondering if you could do me a favor. In my living room, there is a small Tiffany blue box on the top of my bookshelf. Please pack it and ship it to me the fastest way you need to get it here."

"FedEx?" she asked. "I should be able to arrange that here from work."

"Perfect," I said and gave her the address here at the office. "Just let me know how much it costs and I'll pay you back." I recognized the sound that came through the phone. She'd smack me if I tried to pay her back. But still....

"I'll take care of it tomorrow and text you the info." She spoke more quietly. "I need to go before the spawn of Satan I work for hears me." She hung up, and I went back to work.

"Are you about done for the day?" Georg asked, standing in my doorway.

"I guess." I wasn't being productive and figured I might as well put what I was working on aside rather than screw it up and have to redo everything later. That would be just my luck.

"Good. I'm done for the day and I thought we might take a ride." Georg grinned, and I began packing up. It was nearing five o'clock anyway, so it wasn't like I was heading out early.

"Where are we going?" I asked as I followed Georg out of the building and down to his car. For the past few weeks I'd basically been staying with him. After a few days we figured out that both of us wanted to spend as much of our time together as possible, so I checked out of my hotel and Georg gave me one of the rooms in his house, though I'd never actually slept there yet.

"We have a tradition in my family, and I've kept it up because, well, it's something I did with my grandfather... sort of." We got in the car, but instead of going toward Munich, we headed away from the city. The landscape got more and more rural as we traveled.

"You really aren't going to tell me, are you?" I asked. Georg just looked over in the darkening car and smiled.

"It's a surprise." That was all he would say. We continued traveling and ended up passing through a minuscule town and then turning off the road and up a rather long drive. A house loomed in the distance with a few lights shining in the windows. "This is my family's estate. The main portion of the building is three hundred years old, and just like the house in town, we never threw anything out. The building is closed for the season. We move the antiques and art to controlled storage for the winter."

"Then why are we here?"

A man stepped out of a building next to the main house as Georg pulled to a stop. They spoke in German, and the man did a lot of nodding. "This is Werner. He's the caretaker. This is Duncan."

"Everything is ready," Werner said with a very heavy accent.

"Danke," Georg said and raised the window. He parked the car and we got out. "We're going to cut a Christmas tree. One section of the property is planted with pines, and every year we plant a few more so we will always be able to cut our own tree for the house. Once we cut it, Werner will deliver it for us tomorrow."

"Okay."

Georg popped the trunk and pulled out a handsaw. "Grandfather and I used to do this every year. It made the holidays special. Sometimes we had Christmas here, but it isn't practical any longer." Georg pulled out a long, heavy coat and handed it to me. I took off the lighter one I was wearing and put on the warmer one. Then I followed Georg across the land, which he seemed to know well, toward a stand of darkened trees. He handed me a flashlight and carried one himself.

"Isn't Werner coming?"

"No. This we always did ourselves. For the past few years I've done it alone." Georg waited for me to catch up and took my hand. "I tagged one a few months ago, so all we need to do is find it." He practically raced across the open land as the last of the light began to fade. We turned on the flashlights, and I wondered if it wouldn't have been more prudent to cut the tree in the morning when we could see, but Georg was determined, so we trudged on.

The stand of trees loomed over us, and Georg led us inside, weaving around the silent sentinels, shining his light here and there until he found the one he was looking for. "Are you kidding?" I asked as I looked up. The tree had to be twelve feet tall. Thankfully it wasn't particularly wide or we'd never get it in the house.

"No. This is perfect." He shone the light inside and shook the branches. "To get out any animals that might have made a home in it." Georg shook the tree again and then moved the lower branches to the side, and I heard sawing from under the tree.

I moved in near him, holding the tree and shining the flashlight inside to give Georg extra light. As he continued sawing, the vibration went up the tree and into my arm. It took a while, but the tree began to tilt. I let it move slightly and held it in place until the trunk gave way and the tree toppled onto its side. Georg stood up with a grin.

"What do we do now?"

"Haul it back up toward the caretaker's cottage, and Hans will handle it from there."

"I wasn't aware I would be used for manual labor. What if I pull a muscle or something?"

Georg moved closer. "I'll take good care of you." His tone sent a thrill up my spine. For that I'd haul the tree all the way back to Munich. Instead, we each grabbed a bottom branch close to the trunk, dragged the tree out into the open, and then steadily made our way across to the caretaker's cottage.

"Did your grandfather drag the tree?"

"He helped," Georg said. "He was funny about some things. He didn't believe we should have jobs like regular people, but he wasn't against work—he just felt it needed to be dignified somehow. Oh, and visible. If he worked, then others were going to see it so that his work would set an example. Grandpa could be a bit of an egotist." Georg chuckled.

We stopped halfway back to rest, and I couldn't help looking up. The clean winter air combined with the darkness of the country meant that sky was peppered with stars, millions of them, shining everywhere. "I used to hope that Star Trek would turn real so I'd be able to visit other worlds." I didn't look away but felt Georg get closer, and then he wrapped his arm around my waist. "They're out there, I know it. We've found rocky planets like our own that orbit in the Goldilocks zone, the band around a star that allows for liquid water. So I know there is someone else looking up at these same stars from a very different angle and wondering if they're alone or if someone else is out there."

"You're not alone, Duncan," Georg said from behind me.

"Yes, I am. Though I'm here with you and I've been with you for a few weeks, I only have a few weeks more and then the mirror is done. You'll ship it and me home, and I'll go back to the same life I had, boring and alone." Where this maudlin attitude came from I didn't know. What I said was true, but I didn't want to talk about that now. I still had two weeks or so and I was determined to make the most of them. "I'm sorry. I promised myself I wasn't going to bring that up. Things are what they are and neither of us can change them, only make the best of what we're given." I couldn't help chuckling. "I sound like a cheesy greeting card." I reached for a branch on the tree.

"I wish I could change things," Georg said, and I was grateful that I had made enough of an impression on him to be missed. He picked up his portion of the tree and we continued forward. "I learned long ago that there were things you have to accept." We continued walking a few more steps and then Georg dropped his branch. The tree fell from my hands as well. I turned to Georg, ready to ask him what happened. He cupped my cheeks in his warm hands and kissed me within an inch of my life. "I don't want you to go either. If things were different, I'd figure out a way to let you stay, but it isn't possible. You have skills that would be a huge benefit, but in the job climate here, it would take months for you to get a visa, and immigrating would be...."

I didn't get a chance to respond because Georg kissed me hard, taking possession of my mouth. His heat formed a bubble around us, a bastion against the impending cold pushing from all sides.

"I wanted you to know that I felt just the same as you," he said. "Sometimes it is hard opening up when you know the door is going to have to close again."

It was the same for me, and as Georg lifted his head, I rested my head on his shoulder, holding him as he held me. "We can only make the most of what we have." It seemed strange to feel this way after just a few short weeks, but the heart wants what it wants, and for the next little while at least, I was going to let mine free. I'd deal with the fallout when it came. "Let's get this tree where it needs to go so we can get somewhere warm and preferably horizontal before I start...." The urge to press Georg onto the ground was becoming a little overwhelming and frostbite on sensitive parts was not a welcome idea.

Georg nodded, and we picked up the tree and started walking faster and faster. By the time we reached the caretaker's residence, we were practically running and laughing our fool heads off. We set the tree where Werner indicated and said goodbye to him before getting back in Georg's car. Georg drove back toward the city, both of us still smiling.

"I've never cut a tree in the dark before," Georg said.

"Then why do it now? We could have come in the morning," I offered.

"Werner can bring the tree in for me then but he couldn't later in the day. Well, he probably would if I asked, but I know that he spends Saturday afternoons with his children. His wife has them most of the time, so I don't want to interfere."

I sat back and rode quietly, watching as the lights of the city increased and then surrounded the car. It was obvious that he wasn't going right back to his house, and we ended up at a small restaurant where we ate a quiet dinner and then drove home. I used the word "home" in my head. The drafty old place, as Georg referred to it, felt more like home than the apartment in Boston ever had. It would be strange returning to my solitary residence.

Inside the house, Georg led the way right upstairs, and he proceeded to give me a recap of the starry night sky we'd shared in the countryside, only this time I didn't even have to open my eyes.

I WOKE to a resounding knock reverberating through the house. Georg was out of bed in a flash, pulled on his pants, and bounded out of the room within seconds. I wondered what was going on, but the bed was warm and the floor was not, as I'd found out in the middle of the night when I got up to use the restroom. So I stayed where I was until Georg returned and joined me on the bed. "Hans brought the tree and we got it in the stand. It's in the hall and ready to be decorated."

"What time is it?" I groaned and pulled up the covers. It was cold out there.

"Just before eight."

I groaned again. "Don't the branches need time to warm up so they fall into place or something?"

"Yes, they do, but I'll have breakfast done in a few minutes, and then we can get the ornaments and decorate the tree." He paused and sat near me. "For the past few years I haven't had a real reason to do this. I put up the tree because it was what I'd always done, but this year I have you to share it with."

"Okay. I'll get up." I timidly stuck a foot outside the covers and then darted off the bed, pulling on a robe as fast as I could to keep the important parts from getting too shriveled. Georg laughed, and that sound alone was enough to warm me.

"Come on, go get dressed, and then we'll have something to eat."

I hurried to the bathroom and got cleaned up. Then I got dressed. I thought Georg must be downstairs, so I went to join him.

The entire house smelled of pine, the scent hitting me as soon as I opened the bedroom door. I walked down the hall and took the stairs. The tree had been placed in the main hall in front of the stairs so they wrapped partially around it. The tree came within a foot of the ceiling and filled much of the space. It was very impressive.

In the kitchen, I sat down at the table as Georg set out his usual breakfast of coffee, rolls, cheese, and some yogurt. I'd never been much of a breakfast person, so coffee and a buttered hard roll were enough for me. I cradled my warm mug in my hand, sipping my wake-up juice slowly. Georg was as excited as I'd ever seen him, and that was saying something. I had to admit, his energy was contagious. He ate fast and then hurried out of the room.

I swallowed the last of my roll and followed Georg, carrying my mug along with me. I found him in the hall, setting down a stack of plastic packing tubs. He hurried back up the stairs and returned a few minutes later with more. "Grandpa used to keep all this in boxes, but I switched to these a few years ago. It helps keep any dampness away."

"Do you need help?" I looked at the carefully labeled tubs and realized I would have no idea what was in each one.

"I just have one more trip." Georg hurried away, and I stepped back and let him have his fun. When he came back, he searched until he found the tub he wanted. "These are the lights. Grandfather used to use real candles, but I gave that up. It's too dangerous, and the last thing I want is for the entire house to go up in flames. The candles are traditional, but I think it's one practice we can afford to do without."

I pulled out carefully wound strings of clear lights, and after checking each one, I helped Georg string them on the tree. There were dozens of them, and he wound each string just below the tips of the branches so only the lights would show. He went up and down the stairs, using it as a ladder to reach the top of the tree. I fed him lights, and he placed them.

Once we had them strung, Georg opened the first container of ornaments and began unwrapping them from the tissue. I gasped when he handed me a blue glass ball painted to look like the night sky. "Like I said: no one ever throws anything out. These were hand-painted over a hundred years ago. My great-grandmother was very talented, and at that time, painting was an acceptable pastime for a lady of her standing. So she did a lot of these and gave them to family and friends for gifts. Thankfully she kept some of her favorites for herself."

"It's amazing," I whispered, cradling the irreplaceable object in my hands.

"Put it on the tree," Georg said, and I carefully looped the string around the branch. I unwrapped others and put them on the branches, spreading them around the tree while Georg added wooden ornaments with the patina of decades of hands and play. Beeswax ornaments and delicate straw items came next. I was scared to handle some of them, but Georg added them to the tree. The last items were delicate cut paper pieces, yellow with age.

The last item Georg pulled from the tubs was a star—brilliant, gold-plated, and stunning as hell. It wasn't one of those new things, plastic and lit, but antique and as beautiful as anything I had ever seen. I stood at the base of the tree and watched as Georg placed the star on the tree.

"It's the most beautiful tree I can remember in real life."

"We did it together." Georg came down the stairs and swooped me into his arms. He was like a kid, and his enthusiasm was infectious.

"What did you have planned for today besides constructing this masterpiece?"

Georg covered my lips with his, carding his fingers through my hair, and kissed my breath away. I clung to him and wasn't about to argue in any way, shape, or form. Somehow, he propelled us up the stairs and into his bedroom. We tumbled onto the bed, clothing hastily discarded and, skin to skin, we let our bodies do the talking while our lips were otherwise engaged. Small moans filled the room and grew louder and louder as our lovemaking grew in intensity. "Georg, please…," I begged into his ear, and he licked down my chest and belly. My muscles fluttered in excitement as he took me deep, encasing me in the wettest heat known to man. I grasped the bedding and let Georg take me where he wanted us to go.

"I have you for a few short weeks, so I intend to make the very most of that time." Georg's hot breath ghosted over my wet skin, and then he slowly took me between his lips. I threw my head back, moaned wantonly, and began the climb to heaven. I was nearly there when Georg stopped. "I want you."

"I need you." That was the only coherent thought I could muster. Supplies were by the bed, and when Georg entered me, stealing the breath I'd just been able to catch, I floated once again, flying higher than before until the wave of ecstasy broke and we were there, together, just the two of us, for what seemed like an eternity.

I knew I would give anything to have that bliss go on and on, but that wasn't possible, and when I came down to earth, I held Georg and wished for time to stop.

CHAPTER 4

TIME CONTINUED unabated, like always. Just before Christmas I stood looking out onto the production floor. The machines around the mirror sat still. The very last stages of the process were set to be completed. Tests would be performed after the holiday to make sure everything was perfect before the mirror was packed and prepared for shipment. My boss had said I could come home for Christmas and then fly back after the holiday, but I had politely declined. How could I explain to him that the last thing I wanted was to fly back to Boston—now or in the foreseeable future?

"What were you packing up so diligently last night?" Georg asked after he made his morning report. It was unusual because we tried to confine ourselves to work while in the office.

"When we were at the market I bought a gift for my mom, and I boxed it up and sent it to her. It doesn't matter if it gets there for the holiday or not. I'll be lucky if she even opens it, but I sent it anyway." I chuckled. "If she does open it, she's in for a surprise, because I put a copy of the picture of the two of us that we took at Neuschwanstein. She'll probably swallow her tongue, but if she does look, I want her to know I'm happy. The mailroom here was kind enough to help me ship it."

"The office is closing at noon today for the holiday, and I thought that tonight we could take a walk through the market one last time if you wanted. We can watch the glockenspiel."

"You know I love that thing," I said with a smile. Our time together was now measured in days rather than weeks, and soon it would be measured in hours. I had thought of trying to distance myself from him to save some of the heartache, but discounted the thought almost immediately. I'd only be punishing myself and Georg. Going home was going to hurt no matter what. So I kept pushing it all away to focus on the here and now. It was what we had.

"You do love it, and the town will be festive. There will be music tonight as well. Some of the various choirs will be in the square singing traditional German carols."

"Sounds great." I checked my watch. "I'll be ready to go in a few hours. Will we go right there?"

"I thought so. There's no reason to bring your computer—everything will be shut down, and you can lock this room if you want."

That sounded great. I could leave all that behind for a few days and enjoy things. "I'll be ready." I texted the project manager and let him know the upcoming schedule, and then once Georg left, I began wrapping things up.

By noon I was ready to go and I met Georg in the lobby. We left and drove into the city. He parked near the center. We walked through the market and then out along the old town streets.

"A lot of the city was bombed during the war. Most of the market square, which looks so old, is really a reconstruction of what had been there before. There wasn't much left, so it was recreated, as was a lot of the rest of the city. Our house was in one of the few areas that seemed to be spared." Georg looked over at me, and I wrapped my arm around his.

We continued walking aimlessly, and I didn't care where we went, seeing grand churches, restaurants, and quiet streets where I could almost hear the snow as it began to fall. Within an hour, it really started to look like Christmas, with a white coating covering almost everything. We must have walked a large circle, because as we got closer to the square, I heard voices floating on the air. It was one of the choral groups. We stood at the entrance to the main square, silently, and listened as song rang out across the square.

"Let's go home," I whispered in Georg's ear.

He nodded, and we walked back to the car and drove to the house. We were quiet in the car, saying very little. I descended into my own thoughts. It was getting more and more difficult to keep thoughts of our impending separation out of my mind. Once we got home, Georg made something for dinner and then spent the rest of the evening helping me forget what was coming.

"IT'S TIME to open presents," Georg called from the doorway to the bedroom. Georg had told me that, in his family, they opened presents on Christmas Eve. But other than to eat and do what nature required, we really hadn't left the bedroom, so Georg agreed that under the circumstances, following my tradition was best and I made it worth his while. I inhaled and realized that was probably not the best idea. I needed a shower, and we needed fresh sheets on the bed. Yeah, that was probably a stupid thing to be thinking as Georg stood in the doorway, wearing his blue robe, with an excited grin on his face.

"I know." I chuckled. "I need to shower, and so do you."

Georg hurried in. "There are presents to open." He had gotten more and more like a kid the closer we got to Christmas. I half expected him to grab me by the hand and drag me downstairs right that minute.

"They're not going anywhere… but…." I sniffed, and Georg took my hand and led me to the bathroom. We shaved before getting into the shower. After which I got my first present, which consisted of me pressed against the wall while I gasped for breath and tried to remember my name while he took me deep between his lips, the wall the only thing keeping me upright.

When we came back down the earth, I closed my eyes and held Georg as he used the handheld shower head to rinse away the remnants of our passion. I clung to him, needing his strength for what was to come. Each day brought us closer to the end, a parting neither of us seemed to want.

"Let's get dressed."

I nodded and pushed away from him. He shut off the water, and we stepped out of the tub. Georg handed me a towel, and when I turned my back to him, he gently patted me dry. The gesture was so simple, and gentle, while still intimate. I didn't move while I felt the fabric on my skin for fear the spell would break.

It did, of course, and we hung up our towels and dressed in comfortable clothes. Then we left the room and descended the stairs.

The tree was brilliant, and I stared at it as I took each step to the main floor. Additional gifts had been added to the ones I had bought for Georg and placed under the tree.

"When I was a child, the presents were brought by the Christkind, the Christ child," Georg said.

"Baby Jesus brought your presents, not Santa?"

"That's what I was told." Georg laughed. "It's actually an incarnation of the Christ child as sort of a sprite."

"Okay." I was hardly in a position to argue with anyone else's beliefs, and it didn't matter who brought the gifts. There were as many legends and stories about the beings who brought gifts on Christmas as there were cultures that celebrated the holiday. "For us it was Santa, except we didn't have a lot of money, so we got the poor Santa. The other kids in school got the rich Santa. At least that was what I deduced because that's how it seemed to turn out." I grew quiet and stared up at the tree. "I would have thought something like this had to be magical or something from the movies when I was young."

"I was lucky, I guess," Georg said, slipping an arm around me. "Merry Christmas."

"Fröhliche Weihnachten," I said, having asked one of the men at the plant how to properly say "Merry Christmas" in German. Georg smiled and then kissed me. "Let's open presents."

I should have known Georg wouldn't last much longer. "Do you want to open them in here?"

"How about the living room? I'll light the fire if you'll bring in the gifts. When I was young, my grandfather would have chairs brought in here, but we can be more comfortable in there, and the fire will help us keep warmer."

I agreed and carefully carried the presents from under the tree into the other room. I also brought a bag from the kitchen for the wrappings. By the time I was done, the fire was blazing, and Georg joined me on the sofa. He reached down and handed me a square box. "I thought you'd like this."

I carefully removed the paper and opened the white box, removing the tissue-wrapped contents. Slowly I pulled away the tissue and gasped. It was the star-painted glass ornament I'd first put on the tree.

"She always gave these as gifts to those people special to her, so I think she'd be pleased."

I nodded and couldn't say anything around the knot in my throat. "Thank you," I managed to croak after a few seconds and placed the treasure back in the box before hugging Georg. When I released him, he handed me a long, flat box that was very light. I tore away the paper and lifted the lid. Inside was a piece of paper. I opened it and began to read.

"This isn't a real Christmas present for you as much as for us. I convinced the company that I should be the one to accompany the mirror to the States and to oversee its initial installation. So if you're okay with it, my gift is that I'll be going back with you. Installation and preparation are expected to take four or five months." He turned to me and took my hands. "I can't give you forever, at least not now, but I bought us some more time to see if this is what we truly want."

I stared at the page as if it were a gift from God. "Why didn't you say anything?"

"I wasn't sure until a few days ago. I hope it is okay?" He seemed nervous, but that lasted until I pulled him into a hug.

"It's amazing." I was all smiles as I set the box and page aside. I moved all the presents out of the way before launching myself at Georg. For weeks I'd been worried about leaving, and now he was coming with me. We'd have months together, time to figure out what we were going to do. A weight of doubt and impending loss had been lifted, and I needed to celebrate. The sofa groaned slightly as I tugged at Georg's shirt, tossing it to the floor. I'd always wanted to make love in front of a fire, and it looked as though I was finally going to get my chance.

Georg swore in German when I licked at a nipple, arching his back and stretching out on the sofa.

"I think we need stuff," I whispered, my voice muffled by his skin. Georg got the idea because he jumped up, taking a few steps before stopping at the entrance to the room. "Be naked when I get back." He hurried away, and I pulled off my clothes as fast as I could. Footsteps pounded up the stairs and then repeated in reverse a minute later. Georg walked in, golden skin, dark hair, firelight playing off him as he walked naked to where I waited. The room heated as Georg came closer, until he stood next to the sofa. I shifted slightly, lifting my head. I parted my lips and slowly sucked him between them. He tasted incredible—spicy with a touch of salt and a pinch of musk, a perfect recipe.

A steady stream of German spilled from him. I didn't understand a word, but I knew exactly what he was saying. I sat up, taking him deep, and ran my hand up the back of his legs, then cupped his perfect ass. "Good God—" Georg cried, and I took him deeper as he thrust his hips slightly. "Is it too much?"

I didn't answer, just took him to the hilt and paused, relaxing my throat to take all of him. The cursing in both languages continued, and I backed off, letting him slip outward. Georg's cock throbbed on my tongue. I shifted my gaze upward, sliding it along his body, across his rippled stomach and strong chest to his half-lidded eyes looking back at me. The heat of his gaze sent warmth coursing through me. I wanted him badly and I had him. Squeezing his ass, stroking his smooth butt, I bobbed my head and listened as Georg babbled almost constantly.

"Wait," he whispered and pulled away, his cock slipping from my lips. "We need to come together."

I sat back on the sofa, swallowed hard as Georg lifted my legs and buried his face between my cheeks. In an instant I was in flight, soaring to the ceiling. When I could take no more of his lips and tongue—probing, tasting, driving me nearly mad—he replaced it with his condom-sheathed cock and pressed into me, adding stretch and fullness to the sensation. I wasn't sure if I dared tell him how I felt.

Georg captured my lips, kissing me hard. "Ich liebe dich," he whispered. I wondered how it was possible, but I clutched Georg to me.

"I love you too," I whispered and rode the wave of sensation, warmth, and newfound love until I gasped and cried out Georg's name as we came in a rush that left both of us unable to move. We stayed still for a long while. When he pulled away, I shivered and gasped, lowered my legs, closed my eyes, and let my mind float as long as it wanted. I was vaguely aware of Georg leaving the room and then returning. He wiped me up and then sat next to me, placing a blanket over both of us.

I curled into his warmth, resting my head against his shoulder. "I have something for you." I shifted and retrieved a small box from the small pile of unopened gifts.

"It's heavy." He tore away the paper and opened the Tiffany blue box. Then he pulled out the contents and looked at me, puzzled. "I'm afraid I don't understand." He held up an object about two inches long. "Is it a rock?"

I shifted closer. "Well, it's not just a rock. It's a hunk of iron. See the odd shapes and the way it looks sort of liquid?" Georg nodded. "That's from its trip through the atmosphere." I smiled as Georg's mouth dropped open slightly. "I wanted you to have something to remember me by. I wanted your gift to be special and to remind you of the time we spent together." I leaned closer and kissed Georg gently, watching the firelight dance in his eyes. "It's a meteorite—that was as close to stardust as I could get."

SWEET ANTICIPATION

CHAPTER 1

GREGORY HANSEN let himself into his sister's house, closed the door behind him, and headed right up the wide, imposing stairs. The brand-new house more closely resembled a hotel lobby than a home, but he kept that to himself because Annalise would take his head off if he said anything. Under normal circumstances, she could be trying when she wanted to be. But lately, as she wound toward the end of her third pregnancy… well, Gregory wanted to get out of the house with his balls intact, thank you very much.

"Is that you, Greggy?" she called from her room. No one else ever called him that, and he corrected the rest of the planet when they heard her use that nickname. He let her get away with it out of simple love and gratitude. After their parents had died in a plane crash when he was fifteen, she had raised him and seen to it that he had the best life she could give him. Annalise sent him to college, using the last of their parents' life insurance to pay the tuition, all four years of it. There was no grumbling that he was getting her share. She did it because, while she might be gruff, she had the biggest heart of anyone Gregory knew. It was just that few people outside the family ever got to see it.

"I'm here," Gregory said when he reached the top of the stairs, not wanting to yell. "I came over as soon as I got out of work." He reached the bedroom door and gasped. Annalise looked like hell. Her cheeks were drawn, her hair flopping down the sides of her head. No matter what, Annalise always looked her best, so this was a shock, even to him, who had seen his sister in rough times and some of her happiest. "What happened?"

"I'm tired, and the doctor says that this baby is… problematic. There are a few complications. So I'm apparently on near complete bed rest." She wiped a tissue over her forehead, which glistened with sweat. "Would you get me a glass of water?"

"Sure." He hurried away and returned with water and ice from the kitchen. He placed the large, covered travel mug next to the bed, then helped her sit up and grabbed one of her hairbrushes to run it slowly through her hair.

Annalise took a deep breath and began to cry. "Oh God, don't mind me. I'm just a mess." She cried harder, and just as quickly as it started, it ended.

Gregory continued brushing her hair, then got one of her hair clips and put it in place so her hair would stay. "What does Jonathan say?"

"He's going to take some time off when the baby comes, but until then, he needs to keep working because they'll only give him so long." She wiped her eyes and sighed.

"I can stay and help." Lord knows she had done enough for him.

"No. Jonathan's mother is going to come in a week or so, and she'll stay with me until the baby comes. She wants to spend time with James and Kevin, and she said she'll help make sure everything is ready for Christmas." Annalise reached for the nightstand and picked up a manila folder. "This is where I need your help." She handed it to him.

"What's this?"

"You remember…, Cynthia's getting married in two weeks. A big Christmas-themed extravaganza. She and her parents are going all out, and I'm supposed to be the matron of honor. More like giving birth to a turkey of honor at this rate." She rubbed her hand over her belly, and Gregory did the same, smiling when he felt the baby kick.

"This one is going to play soccer," he said with a smile, and thankfully Annalise flashed a quick one back.

"As long as it isn't with one of my kidneys, I really don't care what he does, just so he makes an appearance on time and is healthy." No test was necessary. Her husband Jonathan's family had only ever had boys going back at least six generations and probably longer, so it seemed Annalise was going to be awash in an even bigger sea of testosterone, no matter what.

"I asked the doctor, and he said that as long as I get plenty of rest, I should be able to go to at least some of the wedding." Cynthia was his sister's best friend, and she was like a sister to both of them. She had looked for love everywhere and found it in the man who moved into the house right behind hers. "Part of what I agreed to do was to plan the bachelorette party. I arranged the location and I already sent out all the invitations, but I can't do the rest." She took his hand. "Gregory, I need you to do this for me."

He opened his mouth to tell her no way in hell, but she seemed so hurt and worried and tired. "I don't know anything about these sorts of things."

"It's a party for a bunch of women. That's all. I made a list of the things that need to be done. Just please help me with this. This is a big deal. Friends of Cynthia and mine that we haven't seen in ten years are coming into Mechanicsburg just for this. I had planned something really special… but I agreed to do it before I got pregnant this time, and it means so much to Cynthia." She wiped her eyes again, and Gregory agreed to it without any more argument.

"As long as I don't have to be there or serve as the entertainment."

Annalise's expression shifted from tired to wicked in about ten seconds. "You might want to be there. I found a stripper. The guy is big, buff, and hunky as all hell. I hired him out of one of the gay clubs in Harrisburg, so it's likely he bats for your team. Though he said he dances at a ladies' club in York too, so maybe he's an equal opportunity butt-waver." She flashed him a grin, and Gregory rolled his eyes.

"I'll help you with the shower. Cynthia was always nice to me, even after you and Jonathan had two fits and a hemorrhage when I came out to you sophomore year in college." Gregory snickered, because, looking back, it was so funny. At the time it had been ghastly, with both of them staring at him like he had two heads. Things had improved for all of them over time.

"I feel like shit over that. Well, actually I feel like shit in general, but I do regret how we acted. We just didn't know." She squeezed his hand. "We know different now."

He nodded. "And Cynthia was there for me."

Annalise nodded. "She gave me hell and told me to put on my big-girl panties and get the f… over it. If anyone else would have said that, I'd have snatched them bald, but her I listened to, and I'm glad I did. I was closed-minded." She cleared her throat, reached for the bottle of antacids, and chewed on one. "Look, I made it pretty easy. Just follow the list. I already paid for the room, and the bartender is already hired, along with the entertainment. The rest of the stuff is listed."

"Okay. I'll take care of it. You just take care of yourself, and I won't ask for much in return. Maybe name the baby after me. Though 'Studmuffin Larson' doesn't sound too good." He jumped back as Annalise took a halfhearted swipe at him.

"Go take care of things and let me rest." She lay back down, and Gregory pulled the curtains closed before leaving the room. "And, Greggy, thanks."

"You're welcome." He went down the stairs, grabbed his coat from the rack, and pulled it on before heading out into the snow and yuck, driving back to his small apartment above the music supply store in town.

He made a call and put his phone on speaker. "Well, you'll never guess what I'm going to be doing for the next few weeks." He tried to make it sound really interesting.

"Entering the Mr. Tight Ass contest at Broncos?" Will retorted. "You know, we should go see that on Saturday. It should be something. Last year the guys mostly showed off their assets without the benefit of Lycra, and let me tell you, it was like a religious experience." He could practically see Will fanning himself.

"Nope. I was at Annalise's. She's on bed rest because of the pregnancy, and I have to plan her best friend's bachelorette party. Can you imagine how thrilling that's going to be?" Gregory tossed the file on the passenger seat to concentrate on his driving.

"Oh my God! Will there be strippers? Some of those guys are hot, and I heard they may swing it for the ladies, but when they go home, the butt swings all the way back to the gay side." Will cackled like the loon he was.

"Annalise already hired him. She gave me a list and asked me to finish planning the party. I have no idea what the heck I'm supposed to do. You remember the last party I had. Half the people got sick from some dodgy cheese dip, and I ended up hosing down my bathroom for the next week. I don't know anything at all about this stuff." There were some parts of gay life that everyone else seemed to get and for which Gregory seemed to have been passed over. Party throwing was one of them.

"You know I'd help you, but I'm leaving town for work in two days and I'll be gone almost until the holidays. It's business, but two weeks in sunny southern California and away from this crap? I'm so ready." Will sounded way too happy.

"Thanks a bunch." The one person Gregory was hoping would be able to help him navigate what for him was going to be a pain in the ass, and he was going to be heading to the sun. And to make it worse, Gregory couldn't be mad at him. "Some guys get all the luck."

"Dude, it's a party. Just look at what your sister gave you, get the stuff together, haul it over to the venue, and let the ladies put everything together. Just act helpless, and they'll come to your rescue." Will spoke as though what he said was obvious.

"You've seen how my sister does things." Annalise threw parties where everything was perfect, from the bows on the backs of the chairs to the centerpieces, and even the punch had the perfect amount of everything. Sometimes he wondered if his sister stayed up all night measuring tassels so they hung evenly and finding wine that made the perfect sangria. She was like a party goddess, and these ladies were expecting that when they arrived. Not whatever the hell Gregory was going to be able to pull together. "Thanks for nothing. I know you're going to be gone, but you were my last hope." He sighed. "I guess I'm on my own. I'll talk to you later."

"Where are you headed? I could come over if you want." That was a nice offer, but Gregory knew Will needed time to pack and get ready for his trip. Besides, he was going to need to figure this out.

"The weather is awful. Stay home. I'm going to have a few beers, eat some dinner, and then check out this list and see how godawful it really is." Gregory said goodbye and ended the call. He sighed and glanced at the folder of doom, finished driving the mile or so home, and parked in his spot behind the building. Gregory trudged through the now-half-gray, slushy mess to the back door and went inside and up the stairs. At least he had the apartment at the front of the building. He unlocked the door and went inside the partially lit apartment. Even though he had one with the front windows, it was already getting dark, and Gregory had to turn on the lights in order to see.

He heated some dinner in the microwave and sat on the secondhand sofa to eat it, turning on the HD television. He had basic cable, so the picture wasn't too bad, and he sat back with a beer, trying to relax. Gregory sent his sister a message to tell her that he had made it to his apartment in one piece, and then once he had finished, he pulled open the folder to see what his sister wanted.

Good God. There were party favors to get and assemble, decorations that he needed to buy the supplies for, and apparently twenty bows to tie, one for each favor. His sister had even supplied diagrams and websites for instruction. "How am I going to do this?"

Some of the things were doable. He could arrange to buy the bar supplies, since they were serving limited kinds of drinks, it seemed. But the food? The list was overwhelming, even with the recipes Annalise had provided. There was no way in the world he was going to be able to do this. Gregory was a danger in the kitchen. He could do simple things, but he had never baked. That was Annalise's specialty, and she had banned him from her kitchen when he nearly burned it down making french fries once.

"A cake…." Thank God he didn't have to make that. She had given him the name of the bakery she wanted it from, so he pulled out his phone to check their hours and get it ordered. Everything that it should say was there, so all he had to do—

"I'm sorry," the recording began. "Due to a death in the family, the Dutch Bakery will be closed for the next week and will reopen December first. However, due to this closure, we can take no additional orders for the holiday season. Thank you."

Great. Gregory messaged his sister as to what she wanted him to do and received a reply.

This is Jonathan. Please call me.

Gregory dialed his number, and Jonathan answered. "Gregory, Annalise is sleeping and I'm not sure how well she is right now." He was clearly scared. "I'm thinking of taking her to the hospital if she isn't any better soon."

Oh God. "What's wrong? She was tired but talking when I was there."

"That's good. I'm going to let her sleep, but I'm really worried." Jonathan was not a drama queen in any way. He was steady as a rock.

"Call me if you need to take her in, and let me know if you need anything. And take good care of her." He ended the call and set his phone to the side. He finished going down the list until the last item on the second page made him stop to make sure he was seeing it right.

Oh God, how in the heck was he going to get *those*?

CHAPTER 2

GREGORY WALKED down the sidewalk two days and a whole new weather pattern later. He checked the address to make sure he was in the right place. Will had said that a friend of his might be able to help with the cake and other baking. He found the house and knocked on the front door.

"Just a minute…," a mellow voice called from inside.

Gregory waited, soaking in the winter sunshine. The snow had melted, with only the piled areas remaining. He turned back to the door as it opened.

"Gregory?"

"Rhys?" Gregory asked. Damn, now he was even more off-balance, and his nerves shot through the roof. It wasn't every day that you stood face-to-face with the guy you'd dated for two weeks and fallen in love with even though you knew you shouldn't. "My God. I…. A friend of mine recommended you because I needed some special baking for a party." He shifted from foot to foot. "Maybe this is a bad idea."

"Nonsense," Rhys Denning said with a smile that seemed genuine. "Come on in." He stepped back, and Gregory went inside. The Christmas tree was already up in the living room, the lights on and twinkling. The house smelled like the holidays in every sense of the word—cinnamon, maybe cloves, a touch of chocolate. "What can I do for you?"

Gregory pulled his attention away from the decorations and the heavenly scent. "I'm sorry, I…."

"Is this because of what happened when we dated?" Rhys motioned to the sofa, and Gregory took a few steps and sat down. What the hell? What did he have to lose but his dignity?

"I guess. I mean, things were going well, and then…." He sighed and shrugged. "I guess things didn't work out." Even though Gregory had certainly wished they had.

"That was a long time ago, and I hate to say it, but I was an ass back then. You didn't do anything wrong. It was just one of those stupid timing things. I had broken up with a boyfriend I'd been with for two years, and he returned and said he wanted to try again. I was stupid enough to believe him and give him a chance. I should have told him to take a hike and seen where things went with you. It was always one of the things I regretted." Rhys sat back. "I really am sorry for what happened then. You deserved better than that."

Gregory wanted to put his fingers in his ears to clear them out to make sure he had heard right. "You did? You are?"

"Yes." Rhys smiled. "Now, does that help clear the air? I should have looked you up after that, but I was too embarrassed and I figured you would have found someone else. I didn't want to mess things up for you the way Hector had for me."

It surprised Gregory how open and forthright Rhys was. He wasn't really used to that. Gregory had been raised by parents and then a sister where he needed to peel the onion layer by layer in order to see what was on the inside. Just putting things out there wasn't in his family makeup. Gregory was actually wondering if Rhys was telling the truth or if he had some other motivation, when he stopped and smiled.

"It does, thank you," he said rather softly as he realized that Rhys didn't really owe him anything, and that his explanation was open and seemed freely given, judging by his expression and the shine in his blue eyes.

"Anyway." Rhys put his hands on his knees with a light slap that sent up a small cloud of flour from his dusty clothes. "What is it that I can do for you?"

"Well...." Gregory opened the folder and pulled out... the list. Over the last two days, it had taken on an ominous connotation in his mind. "My sister, Annalise, is pregnant and confined to bed rest. We were afraid she was going to need to be hospitalized, but she's doing better now." That was a relief. "Her best friend is getting married, and Annalise promised to be matron of honor and to plan the bachelorette party. And now she's asked me to step in because she can't." He sighed. "Plan the party, I mean, not be matron of honor." He snickered at the idea.

"Can I see the list?" Rhys asked, and Gregory handed it over. "Okay... we can do the cake, no problem... and the other desserts, no problem." He lifted his gaze. "What about the savory dishes?"

Gregory swallowed. "I burn water. I was going to see about a caterer, but everyone I called was already booked. She included recipes, so I thought that I would be very careful and try to make them. They don't seem too complicated, but I'm so terrible in the kitchen. Annalise tried to teach me, but she ended up kicking me out for safety reasons."

"I see...." Rhys continued smiling. "Let me check my calendar." He pulled out his phone, and Gregory wondered what he had in mind. "Yes. I'm free the day before and the day of the party. So I can make the rest of the dishes for you."

Gregory breathed a huge sigh of relief. "Thank you...," he said, and then remembered. "Umm, there's one more thing. She wrote a final item on a second sheet of paper." Gregory handed that over to Rhys, who took one look and burst out laughing.

"You have to be kidding?" Rhys snickered.

"It's a Christmas-themed bachelorette. Apparently the stripper is coming as Sexy Santa, and she wants trees on the cake, and the drinks are all holiday-themed." Gregory found himself smiling.

Rhys lightly bit his lower lip. "She wants forty-eight Santa-hatted, penis-shaped baguettes. What is she going to do with them?" His eyes sparkled.

"In her other notes, the plan is to use them as Christmas tree decorations and party favors." Gregory smiled. "I can just see the tree now." He covered his mouth to keep from laughing and failed when Rhys chuckled outright.

Gregory had missed that sound. Sometimes he still heard the clear, joyous laugh in his sleep. It was one of the things he had liked most about Rhys—his ability to laugh with others and at himself. Gregory was a self-conscious kind of guy, so he tended to be reserved. Rhys had been open, and he laughed easily, which only made those around him happy as well.

"I think I can help you with those as well. I have made baguettes before, and it's all about the flour. I have notes about the blend I used, so I could get a good consistency for the crunch."

"Oh thank God," Gregory breathed. "I want Annalise to be happy, but I also want Cynthia to have the best bachelorette party and wedding possible. She's a kind soul." And Gregory hadn't met many of those in his life. His sister was good and fiercely protective, but Annalise tended more toward the awful truth than kindness... if that made any sense.

"What about all the other decorations?" Rhys handed back the list, and Gregory placed it in the file for safekeeping. Maybe he'd take a picture of it when he got home so he'd have a record in case he lost it. "I remember you were always good at numbers, but not handicrafts."

"Hasn't changed. Annalise got all that talent."

Rhys leaned forward and patted his knee. "Don't worry, I can help you with all of it, if you'd like." He pulled his hand back, and Gregory swallowed, still feeling the warmth through his jeans. A timer rang in the kitchen, and Rhys jumped up. "I need to get some things out of the oven. Come on."

Gregory followed him into the kitchen and came to a stop in the doorway. It was like no home kitchen he had ever seen. Two large wall ovens, as well as a large, professional-looking stove, dominated one wall, with a large island prep area that included an inset butcher block, and lots of cabinets in black, with everything else in lighter colors. "I don't want to mess anything up," Gregory said as Rhys pulled a chocolate cake layer out of the oven, the scent making his stomach rumble with the numminess.

"You'll be fine," Rhys said as he set the first layer to cool and pulled out the second layer, before putting two more pans in the oven to bake. "It's a constant thing around here most days." Rhys checked the layers again with his finger, seemed pleased, and left them to cool. "I do any number of handmade cakes and bakery items a day. Each is made to order and special."

"I see." Gregory lifted his gaze from the cake layers.

"These are nothing like the grocery store cakes." Rhys handed Gregory a scrap piece of cake from his cutting board, and it was moist, light, chocolaty, and melted in his mouth.

"Oh my God...." Gregory moaned. And this was just the cake. It wasn't even iced. "What sort of frosting do you do?" He wanted another bite.

"All kinds—buttercream, fudge, mirror glazes as well. I can do fondant, but I don't like to. It looks pretty and is all the rage on cooking shows, but it tastes like nothing, and I don't like the mouthfeel."

Gregory tried not to snicker as he thought about something in particular with a really nice mouthfeel. "Do you do cupcakes and things like that?"

Rhys shrugged. "I have, but there are a lot of places that do them. If I get a special order, then I'll make them. I did wedding cupcakes last year for two hundred. It was a beautiful display. The cake for the party won't be anywhere that big. We could do a ten-inch round cake with three layers. Does Cynthia like lemon?"

"She adores it."

"Then lemon cake with a strawberry filling. I can ice and decorate the cake with a holiday theme like on your sister's list. The mini quiches shouldn't be a problem, and I can make savory cream puff shells that we can fill. That should take the place of the sandwich things your sister had on her list and elevate it just a little. I can help you pick out the things for the fruit and cheese, and I can make some of the dips and things."

"Thank you. You're saving my life."

Rhys nodded. "But I need a favor."

"Okay…," Gregory said cautiously, even though he would do whatever he had to in order to pull this off. He needed this to go well for Annalise and for Cynthia.

"I'm going to need some help. This is the busiest time of year for me. I have the layers for twelve cakes to bake today and twelve to put together, with people picking some of them up tonight. I can do that. It's not a problem because most of them are already done, and I can bake layers ahead. But with the additional work for the party, I'm going to be stretched thin."

Gregory understood. "Ummm, I don't know what I can do. You know I'm a danger in the kitchen, and there's no way I can do any of this." He motioned around the room and nearly knocked a pan onto the floor. "See."

"Really? I could use some help, and I can instruct you." Rhys got some layers out of the pantry and removed them from the plastic wrap. He started the mixer on the counter and left it running while he got a turntable out of a lower cupboard. "Making a cake is like putting up a building. You need to start with a good foundation." He put a round cardboard on the turntable and added the first layer. Rhys turned off the mixer, raised the beater paddle, and cleaned it with a spatula. "What I really need your help with will be the savory things. Also, if you want, I can help with the bows and decorations, but you definitely need to work with me on that."

"Okay," Gregory agreed. Annalise had asked him to make this happen, and he'd said he would. "What do you want me to do?"

Rhys seemed surprised, but Gregory had no place to be. "Open that door. There's a stack of aprons on the shelf just inside. Get one and put it on."

He did as Rhys asked, and when he turned back, the first layers had been filled and Rhys was adding the third. His movements were practiced, flowing, and almost erotic, especially the way he tilted his hips and body to make sure everything went on just right.

Gregory put on the apron and closed the door. "I'm ready, I guess." This was strange territory for him.

"Wash your hands well." Rhys continued working without looking up, using four layers and then lightly coating the outside of the cake with frosting before setting it in one of the large refrigerators next to half a dozen others. "That one is crumb-coated. Those are iced and ready to be decorated." He pulled open the door to a second refrigerator. "These are ready for pickup." There had to be six of them in there, all standing perfect and beautiful.

"I see." Gregory washed his hands and dried them on the towel Rhys told him to.

"Now. Take that sheet pan and put it over the top of those layers." Gregory got the empty pan off the table and did as Rhys asked.

"The bottom pan should be cool, so clamp everything together with your hands and flip it over. Take the top pan off and set it aside."

Gregory nodded, putting it where he'd gotten the other pan from.

"Now slowly lift the pans off the cakes."

"I did it," Gregory said when the cake stayed on the tray.

"Perfect. You can tap the pan lightly before you lift it off—that will usually free the layer… perfect. Finish the last one, then gently wrap the layers in plastic wrap so they don't dry out."

"This is sort of fun," Gregory said. He followed the instructions and soon had three trays of cake layers packed up. Rhys had finished another cake and put it in the refrigerator. He then helped Gregory pull out a rolling rack and showed him how to store the layers.

"Fill this one from the bottom up. That way I know the oldest ones are down there. Then if you want, you can do the next set of pans."

"All right." Gregory could hardly believe he was actually doing something useful in the kitchen.

"You're doing a good job." Rhys flashed him a smile that lingered longer than Gregory thought was necessary, and a little flash of heat and wonder shot through him. Was Rhys checking him out? Gregory hoped so, though he was a little leery from what had happened before, but....

Rhys's compliment must have jinxed him, because a cacophony of clangs broke the moment and Gregory sighed at the pans he'd managed to knock to the floor. "I did warn you." He was just a danger in the kitchen. This entire endeavor was going to be a disaster, and he was going to somehow mess up Rhys's kitchen. Maybe he should quit while he was ahead and before he injured someone.

CHAPTER 3

RHYS STIFLED a snicker. "It's okay. They were empty. Just pick them up and put them in the sink." Some of them had been clean, and he was going to have to wash them before he could use them.

"Maybe I can do the dishes," Gregory offered.

"Put the layers in the pantry first," Rhys said, and shook his head as soon as Gregory turned away. Knocking over the pans was no big deal. Sure, it was more dishwashing to do, but he had the last of the layers he needed to bake for today in the oven, so the pan drop hadn't affected anything. But Gregory's shoulders set a little lower, and his head hung. "It really isn't that big a deal. Don't sweat it, okay?"

"But I can't do anything." He came back out of the pantry and closed the door. "The last time I tried to help Annalise get ready for one of her parties, I nearly impaled her on a meat thermometer." Gregory was so earnest, and it took all Rhys's willpower to try not to laugh.

"Really?" he asked and snickered anyway, and Gregory nodded. "I don't even want to ask how you did that. But I remember seeing your sister once. She was pretty intense. So relax and try to have fun instead of worrying what you're going to mess up." He finished the crumb coat on the last cake and transferred it to the refrigerator.

The doorbell rang, and he hurried out front and ushered in Mrs. Halstead. "Are they done? I know I'm a little early," she said as she followed him through.

"I have them both. Let me get boxes for you." He pulled the cakes out of the refrigerator, and she exclaimed with delight, hands on her cheeks as she looked them over.

"I have parties Saturday and Sunday. The season is starting so early, and these are going to be perfect."

"I'm glad." Rhys got the boxes and put each cake in one, then handed her a box and followed her out to the car. After they were loaded in her trunk and level, she paid him and slowly drove away. Once back inside, he noted her payment on the receipt and put it in a drawer. Then Rhys returned to work.

"Those were beautiful," Gregory told him.

"I try to make each cake special and unique. You aren't going to find standard designs here. I have books that people can look through, but I have made train cakes and even a cake that was the replica of a home for a housewarming. This time of year, it's all about the desserts." Rhys pulled out one of the large iced cakes and set it on the turntable, then grabbed his piping bags of colored icing and got to work.

"You do all that by hand?"

Rhys got out his notes for this cake, made a few design marks for scale, and then began piping. "Yes. I know exactly what I want to do." He piped the outline of a Santa face on nearly the entire surface. The beard would fall down the one side. He returned to concentrating, while Gregory started the dishes behind him.

Usually he hated having other people in the kitchen—they asked a lot of questions and messed up his concentration. Gregory didn't do that. He worked quietly, cleaning and drying the pans. When the oven timer went off, Gregory used the mitts to take the last layers out of the oven and set them to cool.

Detailed cake decorating was the most time-consuming portion of making the cake. He sometimes took hours on one cake, and with the concentration it required, he sort of sank into the creative process and didn't even realize that Gregory brought him some water until the glass appeared near the edge of his vision. "Thanks." He piped the fluff of Santa's beard and stepped back to look at his work.

"That's really beautiful."

"Thanks." Rhys was pleased with it too, and put the finished cake in to chill. Then he iced the remaining cakes that had been crumb-coated and checked the clock and his order sheet. "I still have some items to be picked up, but thanks to you, I got that Santa cake done, and that was scheduled for tomorrow. So I'm ahead." Which was always a good place to be. His order book was full, and so were his days.

"I did?"

"Sure. I would have had to stop to handle the layers and wash the pans and all that." He checked his watch once again. "People should be arriving at any time, and then I thought that if you wanted, we could go get the ribbon and things we need for your sister's decorations, and maybe we can get some dinner, if you'd like."

Gregory seemed shocked. "That would be nice. I have no idea what kind of ribbon to get." It was pretty clear that Gregory was out of his depth, but Rhys had to give him credit—he hadn't given up, and he was really trying to do what he could for Annalise and her friend. That impressed him, because not many guys, gay or not, would be willing to plan a bachelorette party with decorations, food, and especially Santa-hatted penis baguettes.

"I need to finish cleaning up in here, and hopefully the remaining—"

The bell interrupted him, and he answered it, let in one of his customers, and helped her take the cake to the car. As usual, this time of day, when people got off work, was a popular pickup time. He also took orders for items later in the month and for New Year's. Soon there was only one order left to pick up.

"Do you wait all night?" Gregory asked.

"No. They are told when they place their orders that all pickups must be made by seven." Rhys finished his cleanup and checked his watch as the bell rang, just before seven. He had had a very productive day, and he locked the front door with a sigh after the last customer left.

"Do you always have people coming and going to your house?"

"Yes. The area here is zoned residential/small business, so I can operate the bakery out of the house. I had to have the entire place inspected, but that turned out to be no big deal. I'm a real neat freak, and everything in the kitchen is restaurant grade. I like working from home, and it keeps the business overhead down so I can do the things I really enjoy." Rhys turned off the kitchen lights and took Gregory's apron. "Ready to go?"

"Sure. Working around all that cake, I'm starved."

"There's a nice small diner down the street. They have good sandwiches." Rhys sighed. "After baking all day, I usually get something quick to eat and collapse. This is my hardest time of the year, but maybe instead we could go to a burger place I know. It's near the craft store."

"That would be awesome. And dinner is my treat." Gregory held his gaze, and Rhys's heart beat a little faster. He really did feel bad about what he'd done to Gregory in college. He'd been stupid, and Gregory was a really nice guy. And if he were honest, it had been quite a while since he'd spent time with a guy like that.

"Bring your file, and we'll see what we can get ticked off your list."

"Cool. I love a good burger. Do you want me to follow you?" Gregory asked.

Rhys nodded. He saw Gregory out, then locked up and went out the back and through the yard to the garage, where he got in his car and drove it around. Gregory pulled out in his Corolla and made sure he stayed behind Rhys.

The burger place was a chain, but they had really good food, and once they were inside and seated, the server took their drink orders.

"What are you doing now for work?" Rhys asked. They hadn't talked much about themselves during the afternoon.

"I always loved math and building things, so I work for an engineering firm. I apprenticed there during the summers, and they hired me on afterward. I didn't have to work today because it's Friday." Gregory drank some of his water. "Our office allows some of us to work nine, nine-hour days in a two-week period, so I get every other Friday off. I really like it, even if I don't often take the extra time." Basically he worked. It was what he did.

"So that was why you were able to help me today?" He liked it when Gregory smiled. Rhys had missed that and felt pretty lucky to see it again.

"Yeah. I would have gone over to see Annalise, but Jonathan is guarding her from any excitement or interruptions like a bulldog. It's actually kind of nice that he loves her so much." Gregory sighed loudly.

"What was that for?" Rhys asked.

Gregory shrugged. "I should just keep quiet. It's not something anyone can do for me."

Rhys nodded. "Loneliness is a real bitch sometimes."

"How did—?"

"Pretty simple, really. You were free on a Friday afternoon to help me in the kitchen all day. And I know what it's like to be lonely. Being alone is fine, but there are times when all I want is someone else's company."

The server returned, and Rhys ordered a bacon cheeseburger. Gregory got the same, with some ranch dressing for the fries.

"You're alone? I doubt that… really." Gregory seemed shocked.

"I work mostly by myself, and then… well… I haven't had a boyfriend in a long time. Guys don't want to date someone who works six days a week and falls into bed at the end of the day because he's been standing on his feet for nine hours or more and is just dead tired. Don't get me wrong—I love baking and what I do, but most guys don't understand. They want to go out on Saturday night, and I've been up since six and don't have the energy for that kind of stuff."

Gregory shook his head. "Well, I think that anyone would be lucky to have you and they should get over themselves." The way Gregory said it, like there was no argument, made him laugh.

"That's nice of you to say, but I know the life I have isn't really conducive to dating. I was thinking of getting a cat, but then I'd have to clean up after it, and the hair…. Or a dog, but I'd have the same issue, and I need the kitchen to be clean. So I live alone and pretty much work alone." He wasn't going to whine.

"What about your parents? I thought they were in the area?"

"Mom and Dad moved to Florida about two years ago. They wanted to retire, and six months later, my brother-in-law got a job in Tampa, so they moved there as well. So pretty much my family upped and relocated, and I'm still here." Rhys didn't want to make a big deal out of it. Things were the way they were, and he just needed to figure stuff out.

"Are you going to visit them for Christmas?" Gregory asked, and Rhys shrugged.

"They were going to come up here to visit, but Mom hates the cold, and they got the chance to go on a holiday cruise. They asked if I wanted to go, but I already had commitments and orders that I couldn't cancel. I told them to go and have fun with my sister and her husband." He was really thinking that decision had been a mistake, but it was too late to change it now. "It's okay. Are you spending Christmas with Annalise?"

"I hope so. This pregnancy is taking a lot out of her. She's due right at the new year, so things are really up in the air."

The server interrupted their conversation with their food. Rhys took a bite as food-induced silence took over. He was grateful for it. Rhys didn't talk about his family situation or his bouts of loneliness with most people. But with Gregory, he felt comfortable enough to give his feelings words, which was both nice and strange at the same time.

"This is really good." Gregory hummed around his food.

Rhys sort of lost himself in his lips and the delight in his eyes. Damn, he wished he'd been the one to put that there instead of the food. He stifled a snort when he realized he was slightly jealous of a hamburger.

"Yeah. The trick is to have the grill at just the right temperature. If it's too hot, the burger chars on the outside, and if it isn't hot enough, you don't get that 'grilled' flavor that makes it taste so good." Rhys took another bite. "It took them a little bit before they found that right temperature, but they have now, and the manager is really good about her food quality."

"Do you know everyone in food?" Gregory's eyes twinkled with a hint of mischief.

Rhys chuckled. "Pretty much. Once word got around about my baking, it seemed every foodie wanted to be a customer." He took another bite and swallowed before finishing his answer. "It isn't everyone who's willing to spend nearly a hundred dollars for a cake. But that's what it costs if you want one that's custom-designed and made. At first I wondered if it would be worth it, which is why I started at home instead of a stand-alone bakery. But people have responded, and I get a lot of business. But it was still a struggle. It takes a lot of customers to keep a place like mine going. I do wedding cakes, but that's only a single occasion. Everyone only has one anniversary or birthday a year. Let's see. So I get three cakes per customer per year... plus maybe some other order. It takes a large number of customers." Rhys had figured all that out before he decided to try to make a go of it. "Finish your dinner, and we'll go shopping." He was delighted when the mischief crept back into Gregory's eyes. Someone might not be much of a cook, but he was a shopper. That was awesome.

Gregory ate a little faster, and soon he had paid the bill, and they walked across the shopping center lot to the craft store. For as tentative as he was in the kitchen, he seemed to burst with energy once they entered the store, which was exciting and attractive as hell.

CHAPTER 4

"WE COULD use this for the centerpieces, and this ribbon on the favors. They coordinate, but don't look too matchy-matchy," Gregory said.

"I thought you weren't into this stuff?" Rhys asked.

"Oh, I can't *make* shit worth a damn, but I can coordinate color and things like that really well. I'm kind of klutzy, in case you didn't get that from the whole pans-on-the-floor incident, but I understand and love working with color." Gregory put the ribbon in the basket.

"Great. We have a theme for the party. Peppermint. We should get a number of bags of hard candy that we can use. Fill some glass jars, and we can use them as part of the centerpieces. We could use artificial flowers and greens, but they look flat." Rhys set down the fake poinsettias. "We could get real greens and put the decorations together a few days before the party. That way they would stay fresh, and the space would smell like pine and peppermint when the guests arrive."

"Sounds awesome." Thanks to Rhys, Gregory was getting into the spirit of this whole exercise more and more. He added some artificial berries to the basket, and they continued through the store, getting all the supplies they needed. Gregory consulted the list once again. "Chocolates for the favors."

"Order them from Wymer's. They have a two-piece truffle box. I've seen them in a red-and-white box, which will go with your theme," Rhys offered.

Gregory made a note. He would never be able to pull this off if it weren't for Rhys. "That will be the last of it for the favors. The decorations should be good, other than the baguettes." He couldn't help rolling his eyes at the idea, but if Annalise wanted them, then that was going to happen. "We have a plan for the food and dessert." That ticked off everything on the list, and Gregory felt so much better than he had a few days ago. "I guess all we need is the time to do all this."

"We can start on Sunday if you like, and then finish off next Sunday with the decorations. The food will need to be done two days before."

Rhys grinned. "But you got this." He put his hand up and Gregory slapped it, wishing they were smacking something else together.

He needed to stop thinking about Rhys's lips and the intensity in his eyes. Gregory wasn't nearly as sure as Rhys was, but his energy was catching, and Gregory liked it. Someone else having confidence in him gave him a jolt of it himself. "Let's pay for this stuff."

Rhys followed him to the registers, and Gregory put the purchases on a credit card. He always tried to be careful, and he figured that Annalise would pay him back when the bill came, so he wasn't too worried about it. But even now, he thought about it and wished he had the cash just to pay for it. He watched his expenses, because it would be so easy to get mired in credit card debt, and he desperately wanted to be able to save for a house of his own.

Gregory took the bags and carried them to where Rhys was waiting. "I really want to thank you for all of this," Gregory said, and Rhys smiled as they stepped outside into the cold and now-windy night air. He didn't really want to say goodbye, because in the back of his mind, if he did, then Rhys might disappear and…. Gregory sighed, needing to put this out of his head. They weren't in college any longer—they were adults, responsible ones from what he'd seen. "I'll see you on Sunday?" he asked.

"Absolutely. Come to the house at four. We can work at the table to get some of the preliminary things done and prepared, and this time I'll cook for you. We can try out some of the recipes your sister provided." Rhys grinned.

Gregory said good night and headed for his car. He put the bags in the trunk and closed it, then unlocked the car and opened the door to get inside.

"Gregory," Rhys said from behind him, and when he turned around, Rhys leaned closer and kissed him. It was quick and rather chaste, but it had happened, and Gregory smiled. "I just wanted to put that out there. I hope a kiss is okay." He shifted from foot to foot nervously, and Gregory nodded and smiled even bigger. "I remember that you were always the shy one, and sometimes I get impulsive, but I didn't want to let you go without… well, telling you somehow that, well, I still like you and I should have chosen you when I had the chance."

"I like you too, and the kiss was nice." Gregory touched his lips. "I'll definitely be looking forward to Sunday." He continued smiling, and his heart beat a little faster as he got into his car.

ALL DAY Saturday, Gregory kept thinking about Rhys and that kiss. It had taken some guts for him to do that, and Gregory had not only liked it, but it took away some of his nervousness about what Rhys wanted. Granted, it was only a kiss, but it signaled a lot of possibilities. Gregory tried not to let his head get too far ahead. But he had been excited all of Saturday, and the clock couldn't move fast enough toward four o'clock on Sunday.

"Come on in," Rhys said when he answered the door.

Gregory stepped inside, and Rhys stood just outside the hall area while he took off his coat. He could tell Rhys was nervous, so Gregory stepped up to him and returned his kiss from Friday. "Is that okay?"

"Yes. And here I was afraid I had acted like an idiot. I should have said something instead of just kissing you the other day. When I got back here, I wondered if I'd been assuming things, and then...." He took a deep breath. Gregory remembered that Rhys tended to ramble when he got nervous, and how cute it was, because at least he wasn't the only nervous one.

"You read things right." Gregory sighed and followed Rhys into the dining room, covered with Christmas craft stuff. "I brought the things we bought."

"Perfect. The party is in a week, so I thought we could make the favors for each place. We can then add the chocolates when we pick them up, and we'll be good."

Gregory sat across from Rhys and tried to keep his attention on the task rather than on Rhys. Now that he knew Rhys was interested, things took on a whole new light, and the heated looks he got in response only took on more meaning. Gregory definitely remembered how Rhys had been in college. Hell, it was etched on his memory, including the little mole on his hip, and the way Rhys—

"What are you thinking?" Rhys asked as he leaned over the table.

Gregory blushed but didn't turn away. Rhys clearly knew what was on his mind, but he refused to be ashamed of it. "Well...."

Now it was Rhys's turn to blush, and Gregory chuckled. Clearly the two of them had the same idea. Rhys cleared his throat, and Gregory pulled his attention back to the present.

"Okay. What are we doing?"

"Based on your sister's instructions, she envisioned something like this." Rhys lifted up an example with some crystals. "It's nice, but I was thinking we could make these." He held up a bow of about the same size, but made with more ribbon, that incorporated the crystals as well as the peppermint candies in a sachet. "We can put the chocolates here, and this will go with everything else we're doing."

Gregory wasn't sure at first, but then shrugged. "Let's go with the blingy one. We bought enough ribbon, right?"

"Yes. These are prettier." Rhys came around and took the seat next to his. "Let me show you to make them. It's just a matter of technique." He got some wire and demonstrated how to hold it and loop the ribbon. Then he finished it off and cut the tails. "That's all there is to it. We can make the bows and then attach the rest when we're done."

Gregory nodded, girded his loins, and dug in. It took them about two hours to make all the bows, and after the first couple, Gregory got into it and his turned out almost as nicely as Rhys's, who fluffed his and made them prettier. Then they finished up the embellishments and set all twenty aside in a box.

"Well, that's done." And Annalise was going to be so pleased.

"Yup, and I found some jars." Rhys lifted a box from one of the chairs. "None of them are really huge, but they're varying heights, and once filled with the peppermints, they should look great as part of the table centerpieces, which we'll make next Sunday. That should finish up the decorative items, and we can then do the cooking just before the party." Rhys stood, and Gregory followed him into the kitchen.

"What now?"

"Dinner—I'm starved. You know where the aprons are," Rhys said, and Gregory got one. "I thought we'd check out the quiche recipe of your sister's. It looks a little off to me, and I want to test it. I made the shell this afternoon, so I'm going to talk you through the filling, and then we'll bake it."

Gregory was nearing panic. "You have to be kidding."

"You can do it." Rhys put his hand on his shoulder. "We'll do it together." He got out the eggs and cream, and cut up some bacon to brown off. He also got some ham, spinach, and a chunk of cheese, which Gregory managed to grate without cutting his hand up.

"Awesome. Cut the ham in small cubes while I finish the bacon, and then we can start."

Gregory was so careful with the ham, it took forever. But when he was done, the bacon was drained and Rhys had squeezed the liquid out of the spinach. "Is this right?"

"Perfect. I put the ingredients out for you. Here's the recipe, and I'll let you do it while I watch." Rhys stepped back, and Gregory slowly went through the steps. Rhys showed him how to whisk and slowly blend in the wet ingredients. "Add an extra egg," Rhys said. "I think that's what's wrong. Does your sister get fresh eggs?"

Gregory nodded. "A friend has chickens."

"That's why. We'll need one more for extra body since ours are store-bought."

Gregory did as Rhys asked and finished whisking the mixture. He added the bacon, ham, cheese, and spinach and stirred them in the way Rhys told him as he turned on the oven.

"Go ahead and pour it into the shell… slowly. You want to keep from dripping over or it will stick to the pan."

Gregory poured and didn't spill anything. Rhys used a spatula to clean the bowl, and then once the oven beeped that it was up to temperature, Gregory slid the quiche in and closed the door. Rhys had him set the timer, and Gregory heaved a deep breath. It seemed like he'd been holding it the entire time. "I did okay?"

"I think it's going to be amazing. When I'm doing some other baking, I'll make the shells ahead, and you can finish them. I think your sister will be pleased." Rhys cleaned up the work area and opened a bottle of white wine. He poured a couple of glasses, and they sat, sipping and making a salad, while they waited for it to bake.

"What else do we do now?" Gregory asked.

"Hmmm," Rhys said as he wiped his hand and came around the island to where Gregory sat. "How about kiss the cook?" He leaned down, and Gregory closed the distance between them. This kiss was less chaste and more hot… a lot more hot. Rhys certainly hadn't lost his touch in the kiss department, and Gregory felt it all the way to his toes. "Damn. You were always so responsive." Rhys blinked, his face so close to Gregory's. "You always put your whole self into everything you did.

I forgot how attractive that is." Rhys kissed him again, and this time he was in no hurry to stop. Gregory slipped his hands around Rhys's neck, drawing him closer, increasing the pressure between them. Rhys parted his lips, and Gregory teased his tongue to Rhys's lips, moaning when Rhys sucked on it lightly.

"Damn," Gregory whimpered, not even sure if it was audible, but he didn't care. His head spun, and when Rhys pulled back, Gregory gaped and tried to get his bearings because... wow.

Rhys stood straight and took a deep breath. "I think I need to back away now." He went to the other side of the island.

"Did I do something wrong?" Gregory asked.

"Oh God, no. But if I don't put a little distance between us, I'm going to pull you up the stairs and pick things up where we left them off in college, quiche and house be damned, because if I get you upstairs, the place could burn down around us and I wouldn't be able to stop."

"Oh." He swallowed hard. "Okay."

"Yeah, and I think you and I need to get to know each other again before that happens." Rhys picked up his wineglass and drained it, then poured another. "You deserve that after what happened, and I want you to be able to trust me. I'm not the same stupid kid I was then, but you need to see that for yourself." He set down his glass and peered into the oven. "Oh, that looks beautiful. You did a great job."

"Thanks." Gregory had to drive home or he'd have pounded his wine as well. "I guess you're right, but...." Damn, he wanted that upstairs, bedroom... and maybe all-night thing. His entire body zinged with anticipation, but he forced himself to calm down. They were here for dinner and to help his sister because of the bachelorette evening.

"How is your sister doing?" Rhys asked, and it seemed they both had the same idea to cool things off.

"She's better, but still on bed rest. I hope this baby comes soon and is healthy." Gregory took another sip of wine as the oven timer dinged.

CHAPTER 5

IT WAS funny how things could change so quickly. He worked just as hard, but Gregory called each evening and they talked a while. Rhys's holiday was looking much brighter just from those calls.

The bell rang. He let Gregory in and received an excited kiss once he got his coat off.

"Are we making the centerpieces?" Gregory asked, and chuckled when Rhys didn't let him go.

"Eventually," he whispered, tugging Gregory down for another taste of his sweet lips. He loved Gregory's soft moans and the way he always seemed surprised at the instant intensity between them. It set Rhys on fire, and judging by the way Gregory gasped when he stepped back, the feeling was more than mutual.

Gregory's lips were red and his face flushed. "I...." He touched his lips with the tip of his finger. "I thought about that all week." His nervously sweet smile had Rhys doing the same. He had thought about Gregory a lot, especially when he was alone at night.

"Me too."

Gregory wrapped his arms around him, holding tight. "I got a call on my way over from Jonathan. It seemed he is taking Annalise to the hospital. She's been in some distress, and he thinks the baby is going to come one way or another. I asked if I should be there, and he said there was nothing I could do right now. The kids were staying with his mother tonight anyway." Gregory held him tighter. "What if something happens to her?"

Rhys held him in return. "Your sister is strong. She's going to have that baby, and then she'll be at the party that you put together for her." Rhys knew there was little either of them could do, and it was best if he tried to keep Gregory busy. "I cut some greens yesterday and got some green foamy floral oasis, so we can make what we need, and I thought we'd put them in the garage to keep them cool until the party."

"That sounds like a good idea." Gregory backed away. "I'm sorry I'm acting like such a dope. It's just that she's my only family and—"

"I know. And you're not being a dope. Now why don't we get to work and make your sister proud?" Rhys sat next to Gregory, and they worked together to fill the jars with peppermints and then build the arrangements around them. They needed five, according to the list, and used the greens and the same ribbon they'd used for the favors to tie everything together.

"They're beautiful," Gregory said as he looked over their finished product.

"You did an amazing job," Rhys said with a smile.

Gregory shook his head. "I didn't know anything about making these. That was your idea."

"No. You were the one who picked out the colors and put that together. This… the centerpieces… all sprang from that. And look at those bows and the ribbon work—you did that. I didn't." Rhys clasped his shoulder. "You came up with that. Give yourself credit. You're crafty." He grinned, and Gregory rolled his eyes.

His phone rang, and Gregory snatched it up off the table. He answered it and made a number of humming sounds and then sighed and smiled. "Oh my God, it's a girl! You had a girl!" he practically shouted. "That's amazing. And Annalise is doing fine? … Thank you so much, Jonathan. Thank you." He hung up and sighed hugely.

"I take it your sister had the baby."

"And it's a girl. No one in Jonathan's family has had a girl as far back as anyone can remember. Annalise figured she would never have a daughter, but she did." Gregory sat down, still smiling. "Jonathan said she's weak and will need a lot of rest, but Annalise is going to be fine. He asked me to come visit tomorrow so she can rest." Gregory looked like a wrung-out rag for a second and then bounded to his feet with a burst of energy. "Wow." He turned to Rhys and paled. "That means she'll definitely be at the party. Is it bad that I hoped she might still be in bed?"

"You wanted the pressure off?"

Gregory nodded. "Kind of. But now she'll be there, and…."

"Since these are done, why don't you and I go ahead and plan the rest of the food and how we're going to get everything done so this can be the best party ever? Then your sister will be so proud of the job you did that she'll want you to plan all the parties going forward." Both he and Gregory laughed, but seeing Gregory smile was always a beautiful thing.

Rhys slid his hand around the back of Gregory's neck, gently tugging him closer. He took his lips, and Gregory pressed nearer. Rhys deepened the kiss. He suddenly wasn't interested in menus, decorations, or desserts. All he wanted was Gregory. His instinct was to press forward and take what he wanted, but instead he gentled the kiss and pulled back.

"Rhys, I…." Gregory blinked a few times. "I want…."

"I know. Me too, but it's so soon." Rhys gazed into Gregory's eyes. "I've had crap luck with relationships, and I tend to rush in too early." He stroked Gregory's arm. "I'd rather wait a little, because I want this to work between us, and I think you're worth waiting for." He caressed Gregory's cheek, and Gregory closed his eyes, leaning into the touch. Rhys lightly pressed his fingers to Gregory's chin, and Gregory raised his face. Rhys kissed him. "I missed this as soon as I was stupid enough to send you away. I want you to know that sometimes life gives us each a second chance, and I don't intend to waste this one."

"Oh," Gregory said, sliding his eyes open. "So you do like me, then?" He was teasing, and Rhys nuzzled in closer.

"You're daft sometimes," Rhys retorted without heat. "Come on. I think I've figured out how to make the baguettes." He grinned. "Wanna go make some penises? I thought instead of actually making them edible—because they aren't going to stay super fresh anyway—we can make smaller ones, put them in plastic, and use them as ornaments on the tree. That should be fun and saucy. Then I can make a few fresh ones that we can put out as part of a bread plate."

Gregory chuckled. "Okay. Let's go make some penises."

IT HAD been a long time since Rhys had done something this fun in the kitchen, and so laden with visual innuendo.

"How do these look?" Gregory asked as he held up two globs of dough.

"Nice size and shape. They'll be quite a mouthful," Rhys retorted, and Gregory rolled his eyes. They had gone on like that for the last hour, with the bad puns and jokes, as they formed the loaves and got them into the oven. "Do you think cut or uncut?"

Gregory shook his head. "We can let nature and the baking decide." The two of them were definitely straining the amount of penis humor humanly possible as they worked and baked.

Once the baguettes were out of the oven and cooled, Rhys placed each into a plastic bag and set them in the freezer. "We can thaw and decorate them before the party. Do you think piped hats?" Rhys closed the door and couldn't help wondering at the fun he was having, and if it would continue with Gregory once the party was over.

"Yeah. Probably best." Gregory was grinning. "I can't wait to see Annalise's expression when she sees this… all of this. The cake is going to be stunning, and the food will be amazing. But the decorations and the favors are beautiful. Annalise is going to be impressed, and Cynthia will be so thrilled."

It was incredible to see Gregory happy and excited rather than down and fearful of the task ahead. That was so much like the Gregory he remembered from college, and it was good to see him back again.

Gregory's phone rang, and he pressed the speaker button, probably because he was up to his wrists in baguette dough. "Annalise, are you okay?"

"Yes. Jonathan is right here holding Victoria, and he's going to text you pictures, but I wanted to talk to you."

"It's great to hear your voice. I've been so worried about you." Gregory tried not to sniff, but it was pretty clear how relieved he was to hear his sister's voice. "How long will you be in the hospital?"

"A few days. They had to deliver the baby surgically, and she's just beautiful. Maybe tomorrow you can come up after work and we can introduce you to your niece."

This time Gregory did sniff, and Rhys took his hand, staying quiet but supporting and considering himself very lucky to get to be a part of this happy moment. "I'd love that." He lightly bit his lower lip. "I should let you get some rest, but I'll see you tomorrow after work."

She paused. "Am I on speaker?"

"Yes. I'm working on stuff for the party with…." Gregory paused. "Well… I got a boyfriend…." He looked over at Rhys, who smiled and nodded. "Yeah. While you were having Victoria, I got a boyfriend, and he's helping me with the party stuff for Cynthia. It's going to be great. I'll see you tomorrow," he added hastily and ended the call. "She is going to grill me no end when I see her."

"I bet. She sounds like a real drill sergeant kind of person."

"Yup." Gregory was still bouncy, but they got to work finishing up with the baguettes and getting them in the freezer. "So tomorrow I have to go to the hospital after work, but with the party on Thursday, I thought I would come over on Tuesday and Wednesday to help with the rest of the prep."

"Good. I'll bake the layers on Wednesday so they can cool, and I added the cake and other prep to my Wednesday and Thursday schedule. The party is at six, so we should be there at four to get everything set up. I contacted the venue, and they have a professional oven. So for the quiches, we'll take the ingredients and shells and bake them there. The rest will be done ahead of time. We'll get the tables set, room decorated, and then your sister and her friends will come in to an amazing evening, and you and I can duck out and have a pretty earth-shatteringly amazing evening of our own." Rhys leaned even closer. "I may even put on my own Santa outfit and do my best to take it off, really slowly." He swayed his hips, and Gregory whined.

"Okay. Now that's something to look forward to."

Rhys loved the raw desire in Gregory's eyes, and it would be so much fun to give in to it. But anticipation was the best increaser of desire that he knew, for himself and obviously for Gregory.

"Should we clean this up? Is there anything else we can do to prepare?"

"No. Right now, it's the cooking. I got the cheese and charcuterie items. We can put those together the day of the party so they don't dry out. I'll really need your help with the transportation and last-minute put-together, but we can do this." Rhys had done a lot of events and delivered a huge number of cakes, but this event and cake were special because they were for Gregory. "Everything is going to be okay. I promise. Something always goes wrong, but we'll handle it." He stepped behind Gregory, leaned down, and gently sucked at the base of his neck. "God, you smell and taste so good." His entire body thrummed with desire, but waiting would be worth it. At least that's what he kept telling himself, but Rhys wasn't sure he could last that long. "Let's clean up and we can get some dinner."

CHAPTER 6

GREGORY WAS both keyed up and nervous. After work for the past two days, he'd spent his evenings with Rhys getting ready for the party. They baked quiche shells, cake layers, and savory cream puff shells, and made dips that could keep. He had checked that all the arrangements were set and had hired a server to help make sure the food portion of the evening would go smoothly. Gregory closed his trunk and thanked his lucky stars that even though it was cold, it wasn't snowing, but that was in the forecast for that night.

"Ready?" Rhys asked.

"Yeah. I'll meet you there." Gregory got into the car and slowly drove to the venue, which was a private party space next to one of the lodges. He unloaded everything into the kitchen area and waited for Rhys. Once they were ready, Gregory went out front to where the tables had been set up with tablecloths and place settings. He got the centerpieces and favors placed before trimming the tree in the corner with the baguettes.

"They look sort of bawdy-cute that way," Rhys said when Gregory was just finishing up.

"Yeah, they do, and the room is spectacular. Festive and not overdone. The entertainment can be over there to do his thing. And I have a table for the cake right there."

"I'll bring it out." Rhys went back and returned with a stand. They had changed their minds, so Rhys had done a two-tier cake with smaller layers for height and dramatic effect. It was in the same candy theme as the other decorations.

"We have an hour before the party," Gregory said, as his phone vibrated. "Annalise is on her way. She's coming with the baby." Gregory smiled as he looked over the room to check that everything was perfect.

Rhys slid his arms around Gregory's waist and leaned in close. "Don't worry. Everything is going to be delicious, and the ladies will have a good time." He kissed his temple. "I need to go finish traying up the food, and I'll instruct Marcus on how he should serve. Come on back and get the breads so they can be on each table. We can also start setting out the trays on the buffet so you and I can see their reactions and then have a party of our own."

Gregory followed Rhys into the kitchen, got the cheese tray laid out, and brought it out as Annalise came in with one of her friends carrying the baby carrier. He set down the tray and watched as she scanned the room.

Her gaze paused on the tree, and her mouth fell open. "What the heck is that?"

"What do you mean?" Gregory turned to her. "We made them as ornaments instead of one for each place, but I thought it was cute. There are baguettes at each table." He turned and showed her what they'd done, but Annalise's expression didn't alter one bit. If anything, her eyes grew more thunderous.

"Was this your idea?" She stepped closer, and Gregory wondered if she'd lost her mind.

"What do you mean? It was on the list. I may have changed a few things because Rhys had some really good ideas, but I did all of the things you had on your list." He hurried away, his heart racing. He hadn't imagined the whole thing—he knew that. Rhys had seen the list as well. In the kitchen, Gregory got out the file and strode back. He handed her both pages of the list.

"See, this is my list." She held up the first page.

"But what about that page?" Gregory asked, and she pulled it out and read it over.

"Where did you get this?"

"It was in the folder you gave me. The baguettes were on the list, so Rhys and I made them as ornaments. I think they're sort of funny. We added the faces to give them personality." At this point he didn't tell her that as they were finishing them, they'd made up penis voices and had dick-to-dick conversations.

"That's Jonathan's writing." She pulled out her phone and began texting. She must have gotten an answer right away, because she raised her gaze to the ceiling. "Apparently my husband, who is going to get it when I get home, thought the idea would be funny, and he wrote up the item and stuck the sheet in my folder for me to find. He didn't know I was going to give it to you...."

"So the whole Santa-hatted penis baguette thing wasn't your idea?" Gregory asked, and when Annalise shook her head, he lost it completely. "Well, you have a dick baguette tree now, so you might as well make the most if it. The ones on the tables can be eaten, but these are just for decoration. They're a little old to eat."

Annalise was still scowling.

"Oh for God's sake, lighten up. The room is beautiful and the food is amazing, and I'll have you know that I helped make all of it."

That had his sister doing a double take. "You're kidding?"

"Nope. Oh, and your quiche recipe needs more regular store-bought eggs to work. At least that's what Rhys said." Gregory put his hands on his hips. "We worked hard to put this together, and look at that cake… and everything else."

She did and nodded, and then her lips curled upward. "It is beautiful, Greggy. And I love the candy theme you did. The centerpieces are better than what I would have done."

Rhys came out of the kitchen carrying trays of savory filled cream puffs and placed them on the table.

"Annalise, this is Rhys. He helped me get all this together, and he's the one who made the cake."

Rhys came over. "It's a pleasure to meet you." He shook her hand. "Gregory has done a great job with this party. I really hope you're pleased. Sorry to run, but I need to get the rest of the food out before everyone else arrives." He headed back to the kitchen, and Gregory caught her gaze, cocked his eyebrows the way he'd seen Rhys do on occasion, and waited for her response, almost daring her not to like it.

"It's beautiful, Greggy. It really is." Her gaze softened and her shoulders relaxed. "I'm just going to kill my husband when I get home." Of course, she wasn't serious and seemed to be seeing the humor in the situation.

"Nope. You're not allowed to do that. He was a tiger, making sure you got rest and standing guard over you and the baby. Speaking of which…." Gregory lowered his gaze to the carrier where the sleeping little girl rested. He reached down and gently removed her, cradling the little bundle to him. "You're so pretty. Such a sweet little one." He held her, the warmth seeping through his clothes and going right to his heart.

A click sounded off to the side where Rhys had his camera out and had snapped some pictures. Gregory crooked his finger, and Rhys came over.

"Isn't she precious?"

"I know. You want one of your own someday?" Rhys said, and Gregory thought for a few seconds before nodding. "More than one?"

"Two should be perfect, I think, and a house with a backyard for them to play in." He was having fun, and all wrapped up in seeing his new niece.

Victoria began to fuss, and Annalise took her to get her fed while Gregory helped Rhys get out the last of the food as the ladies began to arrive.

Cynthia squealed a little and was all smiles when she saw the room, and purposely gave Gregory a hug. "I love the tree," she whispered to him, and if Annalise had been there at that moment, he'd have flashed her a smirk. Instead, he hugged Cynthia a little tighter.

"I'm glad." Gregory introduced her to Marcus. "He'll be taking care of service tonight."

"You aren't staying?" She half pouted.

"Nope. You're getting married soon, and I have my own new man to spend some time with. I'm sure Annalise and Marcus can handle anything from here." His heart rate already sped up at the thought of some alone time with Rhys. "You have a good time, and I'll see you at the wedding, I'm sure." He kissed her cheek and went into the kitchen, where Rhys was packing up his things.

"I went over everything with Marcus, and he will handle it from here. The dishes and everything belong to the hall, and I have all my tools packed up. So I think you and I can hit the road." Rhys's smile was wickedly delightful and sent all kinds of blush-worthy thoughts racing through his mind.

"Thank you both," Annalise said as she came into the kitchen with Victoria sleeping on her shoulder. "Greggy, you did an amazing job. You too, Rhys. I know a lot of this—"

"It was Gregory," Rhys said quickly, interrupting her. "I guided him and helped, but he was determined to make this nice, and he put in the time to get it done." Rhys once again slipped an arm around Gregory's waist, standing next to him. It was amazing how much taller Gregory stood with Rhys next to him, knowing he had support and someone to watch his back. "He deserves most of the credit."

More voices drifted in from the other room, and Annalise went to greet them as Gregory and Rhys went out the back door and to their cars. "I'll meet you at the house?" Rhys asked.

"Yes." Gregory got in his car and drove the couple of miles back to Rhys's home, parked behind him on the street, and went inside, where he found Rhys putting his tools away in the kitchen.

"Were the baguettes really just a joke item your brother-in-law added to the list?" Rhys asked as he turned out the kitchen lights when he was done.

"I guess so. I thought Annalise was going to pop a gasket, but she came around, and Cynthia liked them." The hilarity of the whole thing was almost too much. "I have to admit, making them was one of the best activities we did."

Rhys came closer. "What was the best one?" he asked, his voice a little deeper and rougher. Gregory came closer, giving him his answer in the form of a kiss, which Rhys returned with energy and gusto. "I think we should take this upstairs." When Gregory nodded, Rhys took him by the hand to lead him up the stairs. "You're shaking."

"I guess I'm a little nervous," Gregory admitted once they reached the landing.

Rhys tugged him into his arms. "Why? This isn't the first time you and I have done this." He nuzzled a little closer. "Remember the night alone in your dorm room? You had that loft setup. It was like we were in our own little cave, and—"

"Yeah, I do. Things changed a week after that."

Rhys held him tighter. "I know, and that was my fault. But we're both older now, and we aren't stupid college kids. I know what I want." He gently guided Gregory's gaze upward. "I want you." Rhys captured his lips, and Gregory gasped at the ferocity, holding Rhys just as intensely. Rhys guided him out of the hall and into a warm bedroom with a huge bed.

"Oh my," Gregory said. The bedroom was luxurious, with thick bedding, and when Rhys gentled him down onto the mattress, its softness wrapped around him and he whimpered.

"Decadent, isn't it?" Rhys whispered in his ear.

"Uh-huh," Gregory moaned, and further discussion was cut off by Rhys's lips. There was something familiar about being with Rhys, but exciting too, like discovering a toy that you'd lost and never thought you'd see again, and suddenly it was there and you really missed it. Only in this case, the toy got better... oh so much, eye-rollingly, knowing-just-where-to-touch better. "I think I know what I want for Christmas this year." He groaned loudly when Rhys gave him his present early.

EPILOGUE

RHYS SMILED, nestled in a leather chair in Annalise's family room, with two boys sitting at his feet while he read them *The Night Before Christmas*.

"Boys, you've heard that story so many times already," Annalise said.

"He does good voices," Kevin, the younger of the two boys, said before turning back to Rhys.

Gregory held Victoria, sitting on the side of the sofa closest to him, with the Christmas tree twinkling. The wrapping paper had been cleaned up, the opened presents still under the tree. Rhys had been a little surprised that Gregory had invited him for Christmas, but maybe he shouldn't have been. They had been spending a lot of time together since the party. In fact, things between them had been going really well. So maybe his surprise was just his own jitteriness coming forward. And he'd been shocked that there were so many presents. Gregory's gift of an antique cake stand had been particularly thoughtful. But most of all, he'd been surprised at how welcoming and kind the entire family had been for him, and for his and Gregory's relationship.

Rhys went back to reading the story as the scent of a heavenly Christmas dinner wafted in from the other room. "Are you sure you don't need help from either of us?" Rhys asked once he had finished the story and the boys' attention had turned to the gifts they'd gotten.

"We're doing fine," Hanna, Jonathan's mother, said when she came in. "Dinner will be on the table in half an hour."

"All right," Gregory said, making no move to get up with Victoria asleep in his arms. He had been a regular baby hog all day.

"Do you want me to take her?" Rhys asked, and Gregory got up and carefully transferred her over. She didn't wake and slept on his shoulder. Rhys's mother chose that moment to call, and Gregory handed him his phone.

"Merry Christmas, Mom," he said quietly. "You aren't going to believe this, but I'm holding a baby. Gregory's niece, Victoria. I sent you pictures a few days go."

His mom chuckled. "I know you did. You're like a proud uncle."

The truth was that Annalise had asked the boys to call him Uncle Rhys, and that had nearly left him in tears. Yeah, it was too soon, but being a part of a family was something he hadn't realized he'd wanted until the possibility had landed in his lap.

"I think so." He chatted with her, wishing both her and his dad a wonderful Christmas. "By the way, I wanted to tell you that when I come to visit next week, I hope you don't mind—"

"You're bringing Gregory?" his mother asked with undisguised delight.

"Yes. They gave him the time off, and we were able to get a ticket." He was so happy, he could bust.

"Well, that's the best Christmas present you could give us. You know we only want you to be happy, and we've been worried with you there all alone. We'll have gifts for both of you when you get here, so leave room in your luggage." His mother always went overboard.

"We will." Rhys looked up as Annalise came in and gently lifted Victoria. "It looks like it's time for dinner. I'll talk to you in a few days, and we can finalize details." He told his mom he loved her and ended the call, then joined the others in the dining room. He sat next to Gregory as Jonathan brought in the platter of roast beef and set it on the table before sitting down. Annalise took her seat with an approving smile.

Gregory stood and gently clinked his glass. "This year has been very special. We welcome two new additions to our table this year. Little Victoria, the biggest Christmas surprise for all of us—"

"And Uncle Rhys, who reads really good," James interrupted, sharing a grin with Kevin.

"Yes. And there's one last surprise for all of you. The cake that Rhys and I brought, well, I baked it. He did the construction and decorating, but I baked it." Gregory grinned. "It's been a holiday season of firsts for all of us… including some interesting bread baking. But what makes it all special is that we can be here… together." Gregory took Rhys's hand and squeezed it gently.

"Does this mean that you are going to host the next holiday dinner?" Annalise asked.

Gregory turned to Rhys and then back to his sister. "How about we do it together? That's what family is about, helping each other and learning new things."

"Like baking bread shaped like penises," Kevin added, and every adult in the room turned to him. Both boys put hands over their mouths and giggled. "We seen them when Mama brought 'em home." No secrets in this house, that was for sure.

"Now, boys, settle down," Jonathan said, trying to be stern and failing miserably as Gregory took his seat once again.

"But, Dad. Can we make penis bread sometime?" James asked, and each of his parents looked heavenward for guidance.

"Uncle Rhys will show you how when you're older," Gregory whispered, and then held up his glass. "To getting the best Christmas presents ever this year."

The family turned to where little Victoria's carrier lay in its stand, her lips moving as she slept, but Gregory turned to him, his eyes filled with wonder and, dare he think it, love.

"Yup," Kevin agreed.

Rhys had a pretty good idea what Kevin was thankful for, and James too, for that matter: their little sister. But what Rhys was thankful for, and the best Christmas gift he would ever receive, sat right next to him, watching him as though he hung the moon. This was definitely a merry Christmas.

RUDOLPH THE RESCUE JACK RUSSELL

PROLOGUE

I STILL miss Mom Claire. She got me when I was just a puppy, and I remember her looking me in the eyes and smiling. I licked her face and peed on her because I was so excited to meet her. Mom Claire always smelled better than dog biscuits and even ham, though she didn't smell better than chicken, because nothing smells better than chicken. The breeder lady called me bad, but Mom Claire smiled and said it was okay. I licked her face again, and she held me close. That was when I knew she loved me.

Mom Claire took me home and fed me good stuff. She gave me a nice place to sleep right at the foot of her bed on a small pad of my own. I always thought of Mom Claire as special... and she was.

People came and went. Some were nice, and some, like her son Weasel—or Wesley, I'm not sure—were not nice and smelled bad. I knew I had to protect Mom Claire from him, even if she didn't know it.

I always thought Mom Claire and I would be together forever, but then one night, I was asleep and the angels came and took Mom Claire away. They didn't take the people part of her, just the love part. I missed her and stayed with Mom Claire because I didn't want her to be alone.

Then Weasel came and put me in a crate. I barked and snapped at him because I wanted to stay with Mom Claire, but she was gone, and now so was my home and everything. He drove and drove. I liked the car with Mom Claire. She used to stop at McDonald's, and she always gave me a bite of her hamburger. But Weasel didn't do anything like that, so I lay down in the crate, my head on my paws, watching the back of the seat. I didn't know what was going to happen, and I was scared. The car smelled funny, like old cheese and stinky feet. I love cheese, but this smelled yucky and gross.

Finally the car stopped, and Weasel lifted the crate out of the stinky car. I was happy for the fresh air and stood, looking out the crate door, wagging my tail in excitement. Was this my home? No, not home. *Shelter*. I heard that word a lot.

There were lots of other dogs. Some of them watched like me, wanting to play. Others were old and tired. Some were even sick, but Mitchell, the good man at the shelter, tried to make them feel better. Mitchell was nice and gave me treats. He also gave me a shot, which wasn't nice, but then he gave me a treat, so that was okay, and the shot didn't hurt *that* much.

Still, the shelter was loud, with barking dogs and stuff, and I missed Mom Claire a *lot*. I missed sleeping with her and the walks we took, and I missed looking out the front window to watch out for things. Mom Claire didn't have dog eyes, not like me. Mostly I missed the love.

People came and went, and a lot of them took dogs with them. For everyone, I put my paws on the door of the enclosure and wagged my tail, excited to see if they would like me and take me to a forever home. That was all I wanted—a forever home, like what I thought I had with Mom Claire. But I wasn't a quitter. Mom Claire had loved me with her whole heart, and I wanted that again, so I didn't give up, no matter what.

CHAPTER 1

"YOU KNOW you don't have to do this," Palmer said with his usual gentle expression. He had been Alex's therapist for the last few years, and Alex knew he was right. There was no real need for him to go to the shelter, except that he was determined to conquer one of his fears. The list of things he avoided was long: birds (they carried disease); heights (because he just knew he was going to fall); clowns (the damned things were scary); even rabbits (he just knew those beady eyes were judging him). And dogs. Every other kid he'd known growing up had a dog, and they had to shut them away every time Alex came over, which he didn't do very often because they didn't want to play with the weird kid who didn't like Fido.

So here he was standing outside a shelter near Carlisle, Pennsylvania, where he could hear the barks, yips, and howls of what sounded like a million dogs. His instinct was to get back in his car, close the door, start the engine, and peel the hell out of there, except that would involve another of Alex's issues—wasting his tires by spinning them. Instead he stood still, breathing in through his nose and out his mouth the way Palmer had taught hm.

"Are you Alexander?" a "stop the clocks and hold time still so Alex could take in the epitome of gorgeousness" man asked as he strode across the gravel path from the converted barn that held the shelter. Alex willed himself not to do something stupid as the man's lips parted and his mouth drew upward and deep blue eyes took on a sparkle. "I'm Luther. We talked on the phone a little while ago." Luther wore jeans that hugged his thighs just the right away. His coat was unzipped, so Alex got a peek at his lime green shirt, open at the collar to reveal the barest hint of golden skin before it disappeared behind the fabric.

He refused to draw into himself the way he usually did when he met people he knew were so far out of his league that he might as well not even try. The barks and yips drifted out of the building and into the cold early winter morning. Alex's fear threatened to rise, but Luther simply smiled more brightly. "That's me," he finally answered, proud his voice didn't crack.

"You said on the phone that you have an issue with dogs and that you were hoping to have a chance to face it," Luther said. "That's pretty brave."

"How many dogs are there?"

"We currently have fifteen. There are some larger dogs as well as smaller ones. We are working with a few to correct some behavioral issues. Those are not ones we're going to put with you. Since you said that you were trying to get over a fear of dogs, I thought of five that are really well-behaved. Can I ask what it is that you're actually afraid is going to happen?" Luther asked gently.

Alex liked that Luther didn't make a move toward the shelter or try to push him forward. Talking was good. That was what Palmer had told him. "I don't know. Maybe it's going to attack me or... eat my face or something." He could tell Luther was trying not to grin.

"Okay. First thing, we don't have any face-eaters here. All of the dogs I think I can introduce you to are sweet animals. They might try to lick you, and a few of them will bound around because they're so excited to see you. These are dogs who love attention and people."

Alex felt himself tense. "Are you sure?"

"Very much so," Luther said. "Why don't you come inside? All of the dogs are in enclosures. I thought you could just look around and see them. They can't get out, and you can take your time." He led the way to the door and opened it, then held it while Alex decided if this was truly a good idea or the worst thing he'd tried since those watermelon smoothies with vodka last summer. Yuck.

Making up his mind, he took a step inside. Enclosures lined both sides of the concrete aisle floor, some larger than others. The scent of dog was prevalent but not unpleasant. "There's a lot of them."

"Yes, there are, and we got a call an hour ago about a couple more that Mitchell is going to pick up when he finishes at the clinic. I volunteer here a couple days a month just to help out after work and on weekends."

Alex swept his gaze over all the dogs. Some of them looked like the embodiment of him: closed off, way back in their enclosures. One even shook a little. "So these are all alone?"

"Yes. We are trying to find each dog their forever home. Don't feel like you have to hurry. I know this is a big step for you, and the dogs are always a little energetic when someone comes in, but they'll settle down."

Alex nodded, his heart racing as he took a step toward one of the enclosures. "Is something wrong with him?"

"Her," Luther corrected gently, those big eyes going even softer. "Yeah. When we found her, she had three puppies and was giving them everything she had. Elsa here was so thin and malnourished that a lot of her hair had fallen out. The pups are weaned now, and we've been feeding her well, so her hair is growing back." Luther knelt by the cage, and Elsa came over to him. She was reddish brown, wide in her shoulders, but not too big. Luther opened the enclosure, and Elsa went right to him and rested against his leg.

"She looks strong."

"Under normal circumstances, she would be. But now she's a little weak. You can pet her if you want. She's a real sweetheart." The way Luther said the words almost broke Alex's heart. He could hear the hurt for her in his voice, but more than that, Alex saw the pain in those big brown doggie eyes, like she understood a hurt that went so deep, you didn't know how to climb out. "You don't have to."

"What will happen to her?" Alex asked, not ready to try touching… yet.

"Hopefully we can find her a home. Mitchell spayed her, and she's growing stronger. I've been thinking about adopting her myself," Luther said. "But I want to do that with each of the dogs, and Mitchell says I need to be sure." He lifted his gaze to meet Alex's. "I'm a big softie."

"It doesn't look like it at all to me," Alex said before clamping his lips closed.

Before Alex could die of embarrassment, Luther chuckled warmly, his gaze darkening for just a second. "I really am. If I could, I swear I'd take half the dogs home with me."

"You don't have one?" Alex asked. He found his attention drawn to Luther, his worry about the dogs around him abating somewhat.

"No. I've moved a couple times in the last few years, and I haven't been settled enough for a dog. I just got a job in the psychology department at Dickinson College, so hopefully I'm going to be here for a while. I just have to make sure I get the right companion." For a second

Alex wondered what kind of company Luther wanted, but then he was probably being foolish. Of course he meant one of the dogs. He wasn't talking about Alex, even though Luther made Alex's temperature rise. He gave Elsa a gentle pat, and she licked his hand. Then Luther guided her back in the enclosure and closed the door.

Alex followed him through the shelter, watching each dog as they passed. A few whined, and one barked, making Alex jump.

"That's Janie. She's just loud," Luther said as he approached the enclosure. The dog stopped barking and stretched, her backside in the air, tail wagging. "She's just getting my attention." He petted her gently, and Janie settled down. "Sometimes it's just a matter of seeing what they want." They moved on, and Luther opened another enclosure and took out a small dog that couldn't have weighed more than five pounds. "This is Dolly. She loves people." Luther held her gently. "Come on over. She's just a sweetheart."

"Okay." Damn it all, Alex felt like a kid. Hell, most kids did this all the damned time, and here he was ready to piss himself over a tiny dog. He reached out and lightly stroked behind her ears, half closing his eyes, ready to pull away at any second.

"She likes you."

Alex continued gently stroking between her ears, and Dolly looked up at him with beautiful eyes. "She's so nice."

"Yes, she is. Most dogs are. I know that some can be really energetic, like Rex over there. He has so much energy he doesn't know what to do about it, so he comes off as aggressive, but he just wants attention." Luther continued holding Dolly for him, and Alex kept petting her. Before he knew it, Luther had transferred Dolly to his arms, and Alex just petted her while she lay there.

Alex blinked when he truly realized he was holding a dog. "How did you do that?" he asked. "You just gave her to me and…." He could feel his tension rising.

"You were comfortable, and she's happy with you." Luther gently stroked his shoulder. "You aren't going to hurt her, and she likes you."

"She does?" All the dogs he'd met growing up had tried to jump on him to push him down. They barked and raced at him like they wanted to chase him away. Dolly was sweet, and she slowly turned her head, then rested it against his chest.

"She'll stay right there for as long as you want to pet her," Luther said quietly before taking Dolly and gently setting her back in the enclosure. "You realize you held a dog? And I think you liked it."

No one ever teased Alex, but Luther seemed to be. For a second, he wondered if Luther was picking on him, but that smile had returned.

"Okay. I guess I did." Alex smiled to himself. He and Palmer had been dealing with his anxiety issues for a while, and they had agreed that Alex should try working on just one of them to start. Alex had chosen dogs because he passed by the veterinary office and the shelter every day on his way to work at a grocery store corporate office, where he was in charge of store payouts.

"How about another?" Luther asked. "This is Rudolph. He's mostly Jack Russell terrier. He was brought in because his owner passed away. Her son brought him here to get rid of him."

Alex found himself almost unable to talk. "You mean he just threw away this little guy?"

"He did. From what Mitchell said—Mitchell runs the shelter and is the vet up the street—Rudolph here hated the son with a passion, barking at him and snarling all the time. So if we know nothing else, Rudolph has good people instincts, because the guy was a real jerk." Luther let Rudolph out, and he pranced right up to Alex and wound through his legs, happy and maybe a little jumpy, tail going a million miles an hour. Rudolph put his front paws on Alex's legs and looked up at him with what had to be a doggie smile.

"What do I do?" Alex asked.

"Just pet him. Rudolph is so wonderful. We've had some interest in him, but everyone seems to pick a different dog. He's really special, though."

Alex took a deep breath, and sweat broke out on the back of his neck. But he had just held a dog, so he could do this. Before he could change his mind, he leaned down and petted Rudolph, whose tail just wagged faster, if that was possible. Rudolph licked his hand, and Alex pulled back. "Is he tasting me?"

"Sort of," Luther said. "He isn't going to bite you. Dogs use their nose and tongue to explore the world the way we use our hands and eyes. So it's okay. He's just getting to know you." Alex tried again, petting Rudolph. He wasn't sure how much more of this he was going to be able to take. The dogs had been good and the experience was positive, but

Alex wondered how long it would be before something went wrong—because something always did.

"He's really sweet," Alex said to try to reassure himself. Palmer had said that saying positive things out loud so he could hear them when he was stressed might help him.

"Do you want to sit with him?" Luther asked. Then he led Alex to a chair. He sat, and Rudolph jumped onto his lap and balanced on his legs, tongue out, tail going, watching him with that doggie smile.

Luther said nothing, and Alex petted Rudolph, who sat down. "I think I like him."

"He sure likes you."

Alex kept petting Rudolph. "Do you get a lot of dogs at this time of year?"

"Christmas is a hard time for a lot of people. Mitchell says that the holidays are a time when lots of people get dogs. Some get them as gifts for others, but Mitchell discourages that. A dog is a personal choice. Last year he had someone bring a dog back the day after Christmas for a refund." Luther rolled his eyes, and Rudolph licked Alex's chin. Under normal circumstances, something like that would send his anxiety through the roof, but Alex didn't seem to mind with Rudolph.

"I really like him. You're a good boy," Alex told Rudolph, who leaned against his chest. "You seem to like me too." Alex took a deep breath, and to his surprise, some of his general anxiety began to abate. The world tended to be a source of worry for him. He and Palmer had talked through this a number of times. He was on medication and had tried yoga, breathing, meditation, and God knows what else. But this little dog soothed him in a way he never would have thought possible.

"Hello," someone called from the door.

"Should we put him back?" Alex asked as a man and a woman came inside. "You need to help them."

Luther smiled at him once more. "Just sit there with Rudolph and relax. I'm going to help these people. You can take all the time you want." He leaned closer, his breath warming Alex's cheek. "Maybe what you both need is a little attention and care, and there is nothing like a little puppy love." He went over to greet the couple and show them through the shelter while Alex sat with Rudolph.

He watched and petted the energetically sweet dog. Alex kept half an eye on the couple as Luther talked to them about various dogs. They took a few out, including Elsa and a dog named Tally, as well as Rex and Tipper, but they couldn't seem to make up their minds.

"I think I want a smaller dog," the woman said. She looked at Dolly and one other before turning her attention to where Alex sat. As soon as she looked at him, Alex's anxiety went wild. He had no idea why, but he didn't like the woman at all. Something got his back up, and he put an arm around Rudolph to shield him from her.

"Is that dog available?" she asked, pointing a manicured finger in their direction.

"That's Rudolph. He's been here in the shelter a few weeks," Luther said. He gave her Rudolph's backstory as the dog pressed closer to Alex, pulling his tail close. The wagging came to a halt. "He's—"

"Not available," Alex found himself saying in a rush. "He's being adopted. But I'm sure you'll find the perfect dog for you." *Preferably someplace else*, he added in his mind. "Isn't that right, Rudolph? You're coming home with me." That tail started going fast, like he understood Alex. Rudolph licked his chin again, prancing on Alex's legs even as Alex wondered if he'd made a huge mistake.

CHAPTER 2

ALEX CONTINUED petting Rudolph, looking halfway down toward his feet while Luther led the couple away. What had he done? Alex slowly realized that he had committed to a dog. He had to be out of his mind, and yet Rudolph sat on his lap, soaking up attention—and what was even more shocking, Alex *liked* having him there.

"Do you really think you're up to this?" Luther asked once the couple had left with Dolly cradled in the woman's arms. They seemed happy, and Alex hoped they were, but they weren't going to be taking his dog. Alex registered the thought and stifled a gasp.

"I really wish I knew. They looked at Rudolph here, and I just knew they weren't going to be taking him. Not that *I* have the first clue how to take care of him." Still, he petted Rudolph and realized he had done the right thing. Alex had no illusions that a few hours in the shelter had cured him of his issue with dogs—or his anxiety—but this dog seemed to soothe something inside him, and that was way too valuable to walk away from.

"Well, I can give you a list of things you'll need to get for him, and there are some forms you'll need to fill out."

"They didn't do that," Alex said, referring the earlier couple.

"This wasn't their first visit. They have been looking for a dog for a few weeks and stopped in before and registered. They actually saw Rudolph last week but passed him by." That explained why they were so methodical and kind of aloof.

"Well, they can't have my dog." Alex still didn't know how he was going to live with Rudolph, but the little guy seemed so happy, and that was catching. There hadn't been a lot of joy in Alex's life lately, and this dog seemed to have brought some light into it. That was precious.

"Luther," a man interrupted. "I'm sorry."

"Hey, Mitchell. This is Alex, and he's been sitting with Rudolph here. The Dobsons just left with Dolly, and she's happy. Alex here is interested in adopting Rudolph."

Mitchell narrowed his gaze. "Aren't you the man who called because he was trying to get over a fear of dogs?"

Alex nodded. "I have a lot of anxiety issues, and dogs are part of it. But Rudolph makes me feel better and less jittery and stuff. Nothing else seems to, and...." Alex stroked Rudolph as Mitchell smiled.

"You two seem to fit together," Mitchell said before turning to Luther. "I'm about to close up for the night. There's some snow expected in an hour or so."

"Then let me get these forms filled out." Alex didn't want to get up, but he had to get this done and home before the snow hit. Though he didn't have anything for Rudolph—Luther had said there was a list of things and.... The anxiety returned big-time. Alex liked to do things a certain way.

"Luther will help you with the forms, and I'll check over Rudolph one more time. There's a pet mart in town. They close in a couple hours."

"Okay."

"I'm finished here for the night," Luther said. "I can follow you to the store and help you get everything you need to make Rudolph feel right at home." His smile had Alex's belly doing little flips, and Alex nodded slowly.

"Are you sure?"

"Of course," Luther said as Mitchell lifted Rudolph off Alex's lap and carried him through to the back. Luther helped Alex with the forms. Then he went over how to care for Rudolph, how much to feed him, and how often he needed to be walked.

"Where does he sleep?"

Luther's eyes widened. "He spent four years with a retired lady before she died, so I expect he slept with her. You should get him a dog bed of his own anyway so he has a place that's his."

"Is him sleeping with me safe? What if I roll over and hurt him?" Alex was horrified at the thought.

"Rudolph will most likely sleep curled up near your feet. I don't think you have anything to worry about. Are you used to sleeping alone?" Alex narrowed his gaze, and Luther's cheeks colored and he cleared his throat. "Sorry. I wasn't coming on to you or anything."

Alex wasn't sure how he felt about that. Part of him wished Luther *had* been. It would be nice to know that all his anxiety issues hadn't driven away the entire male population of Pennsylvania. "I didn't think that exactly." It had been a while since anyone had bothered to try to chase him, with his bundles of anxiety and almost obsessive ways of doing things.

"This guy is in real good health," Mitchell said as he brought out Rudolph, complete with a little red bow on his collar. He looked so cute, and Alex pulled out his phone and snapped a picture. He still couldn't believe he was adopting a dog, and yet when Mitchell handed Rudolph to him, he snuggled right up against his chest and Alex calmed once more. "I have a leash for you, as well as a small seat belt for him." Mitchell walked Alex out to his Prius, and once Rudolph was settled in the back, Alex said thank you and waited for Luther to get into his car so he could follow him into town.

THE PET supply store was big and bright, and filled with fish, reptiles, and turtles. The animals in tanks didn't bother Alex at all, though he had no intention of actually touching any of them. He had Rudolph on a leash, and they stood inside by one of the windows, waiting for Luther. In traffic they had gotten separated. Rudolph's tail wagged harder when he saw Luther.

"This place has so much stuff," Alex said once Luther joined him. "How am I going to find what I need?" The anxiety rose once more, and he went through all the things he needed again in his head just so he wouldn't forget anything.

"Don't worry, I have the list of what I went over with you." Luther got a cart, and they started through the store. That is, until Alex nearly tripped over Rudolph's leash. At first Alex thought it was because he had been paying more attention to Luther than to where he was going, but as soon as he untangled the leash, Rudolph ran around his legs and got him tangled once more.

"What's wrong?" Alex asked Rudolph, who looked up at him, wagging his tail as though there was nothing amiss and Alex hadn't nearly fallen on his face.

"Dogs will do what comes natural to them. That's always their go-to. You need to remember that when Rudolph misbehaves, most of the time it's your fault. But you have good instincts. You didn't get mad at Rudolph just now, you tried to figure out what was wrong. That will do you well." When Alex turned to Luther, he got one of those gentle smiles, and Alex wondered what it would be like if maybe it was possible that Luther could sort of like him. God, that had to be the most roundabout jittery thought in history.

"I don't know about that. I spent my life afraid of them, and now I have one," Alex said after he transferred the leash to his left hand. Now Rudolph happily walked between them, occasionally looking at Alex and then at Luther.

They went up the various aisles, with Luther helping him pick out food and bowls, as well as a mat. Alex squeaked various dog toys and got a number of them that Rudolph seemed to like. Flea treatments and a bed, along with a few other items, completed the list. "Who knew a small dog needed so much," Alex said as Luther pushed the full cart to the checkout.

By the time Alex had paid for his purchases and they were ready to leave the store, snow was falling heavily. "Thank you for all your help," Alex said as they went out to the car. He got Rudolph in the back first to get him out of the snow. Then Luther helped him get his purchases stowed and closed the trunk lid. Alex stood across from Luther as snow caught in his dark hair. Neither of them moved right away, and Alex knew he was going to say something stupid at any moment just to break the tension he didn't seem to understand.

"I was wondering if you'd like to have dinner sometime?" Luther asked. "Or maybe we could meet in the park when you take Rudolph for a walk?"

Alex knew he was dense at times. "Are you asking me out on a date?" His social skills weren't the best, so he wanted to be sure. Except now maybe he was coming off as kind of dumb. He wished he had kept quiet.

"Yes," Luther answered.

"Oh, okay, then," Alex said before going around to the driver's side of the car.

"Alex…," Luther said as he opened the car door. "Was that a yes?"

Alex paused. "It was. I'm sorry. It's been a while since I've been asked out, and yes, I'd like to have dinner with you."

"Good. Give me your number."

Alex did, and Luther typed the number into his phone. Then Alex's rang. "Now you have mine. I'll call you." He waved and hurried through the falling snow to his car, and Alex got inside his, closed the door, and started the engine to give both him and Rudolph some heat.

"THIS IS your new home," Alex said after he brought Rudolph inside. The drive had been rough. The wind had come up, blowing around the increasing snow, making visibility worse by the second. He let Rudolph off the leash before returning to the car. Then he brought in all his dog purchases, set up Rudolph's feeding station, and put his dog bed on the floor in his bedroom. He fed Rudolph and gave him some toys before setting about making himself some dinner—but he only got halfway through before the power went out, plunging the house into darkness.

Since he cooked with natural gas, he finished making dinner and ate using a flashlight. Once he put his dishes in the sink, he got a blanket and pillow, then got comfortable on the sofa with a battery lantern on the table. Rudolph jumped up and settled on Alex's lap.

"There isn't much to do except wait for the power to come back." He petted Rudolph. A night like this would usually leave him feeling very alone, but Rudolph filled the room with life and energy. Rudolph eventually curled into a ball, and Alex reached for the book he was reading, but he had to give up because there wasn't enough light. Instead, he simply curled under the blanket to wait it out until the power came on.

A ding pulled Alex out of his doze a while later. *How is Rudolph?* It was a message from Luther. *The power is out here.*

Us too. Rudolph is keeping me company as we wait it out. He sent the message as Rudolph thumped his leg with his tail. *I think I need to take him outside.*

Bundle up, it's really cold, Luther messaged. *Are you free tomorrow for dinner?* the next message asked. *We could go to Café Belgie.*

"That would be nice." He had to work, but hopefully the power would be back on and he could work from home. Otherwise he'd have to go into the office because they had generator power. But then he'd have to leave Rudolph, and he didn't want him to be alone all day. Other people sometimes brought their dogs to work, which had always bothered Alex because he was afraid of them, but he had never said anything. Instead, he had avoided the dogs when they were there. Well, now he had his own, and they could work around Rudolph. Sometimes his mind went in too many directions.

Text me your address and I'll pick you up at six. Luther sent a grinning smiley face, and Alex sent his address and added his own excited face. Maybe it was too much, but it had been a while since he'd had an actual date. Setting his phone on the coffee table, Alex pulled the blanket up higher, petting Rudolph and letting his mind wander over thoughts of Luther.

"WHY?" ALEX asked the following morning when he found toilet paper all over the bathroom floor.

Rudolph stood in the middle of the floor, tail wagging, looking as proud as punch. "Did you want to protect me from the evil toilet paper monster, or were you just playing?" He began cleaning up the mess and got his answer. Rudolph chased after each piece that fluttered to the floor. Finally Alex finished disposing of the shredded paper and closed the bathroom door. Rudolph followed him through the house, and Alex wondered if he should take Rudolph into his home office, but decided to give him a few treats and see if he could settle down in his bed, which Alex had moved to the living room.

Instead, Rudolph followed him everywhere, a bundle of energy that never seemed to wane. When it was time to start work, Alex took Rudolph outside to brave the snow and potty. Once he had finished, Alex dried him off and brought Rudolph's bed into his office and tried to get to work. But Rudoph decided that his lap was where he wanted to be, making it impossible for Alex to get anything accomplished.

"You and I need to come to an agreement. If I can't work, then I can't afford dog treats for you." Alex's frustration level rose higher as his routine-driven existence seemed tossed out the window by his new four-legged friend. After setting Rudolph down on the floor for the third time, he carried him out of the office, along with the bed, and set Rudoph on it before closing the door. Then he sighed and got to work reviewing line drawings for various product assortments. That was when the barking began, following by a mournful howl that ran up Alex's spine. Then, as if that weren't enough, Rudolph scratched at the door.

He didn't want Rudolph to hurt himself, so he opened the door. His dog bounded inside and up onto his chair, tail wagging and tongue out like he had just won the doggie lottery. Sighing and at a loss, with his anxiety growing, he snatched up his phone, took a picture of Rudolph, and sent a description of his problem to Luther.

He expected a text, but his phone rang instead.

"I take it he's got a mind of his own," Luther said, his smooth, mellow voice wrapping around Alex, taking his worry down in a few seconds.

"What do I do? I gotta work, and...."

"It's cool. He probably has a little separation anxiety," Luther said, instantly speaking Alex's language. "His previous owner died and he was brought to the shelter, so he's probably worried you'll leave him too."

"Oh."

"Can you work in another room of the house? Maybe in a place where Rudolph can sit next to you?" It went counter to Alex's grain. He worked in his office and lived in the rest of his house, without mixing the two. Still, he had things he had to get done, and this might be a simple solution.

"I'll try." Alex unhooked his laptop from its larger monitor and regular keyboard.

Luther chuckled gently. "I can wait here to make sure it works. I have a few minutes."

Just knowing Luther was on the other end of the line helped. Alex brought his laptop to the sofa and sat down with it on his lap. Rudolph sat next to him, then lay down, pressed close to him.

Alex picked up his phone from where he had placed it on the coffee table. "He seems happy."

"Good. But the important thing is, are you happy?" Luther asked.

Alex looked down at the white and light brown face, smiling. "I am. Thank you for everything." He felt kind of dumb now that the solution was so obvious.

"Good. I have to go. But I'll see you tonight." The simple thought made Alex smile again, and his belly fluttered a little in anticipation before he ended the call and got to work.

"I THINK we're done for the day," Alex told Rudolph hours later, once he completed his last task and closed his computer. Rudolph had been really good all day, but as soon as the laptop closed, he jumped down off the sofa and raced around the room like he couldn't contain his happiness and had to burn off all the pent-up energy. Alex got a ball he'd bought and rolled it toward the kitchen. Rudolph chased after it, then raced around the room again in a game of puppy keep-away. Once he slowed, he set the ball at Alex's feet so he could do it again.

Alex played with Rudolph, fed him, refilled his water, and then took him outside. Then he went to change clothes, unsure what to wear on his date but refusing to get too wound up. He decided on a light gray pair of pants, a blue button-down, and a sweater in navy with a touch of white and red in it. He checked himself in the mirror as the doorbell rang. Alex answered it, and Rudolph greeted Luther like a long-lost friend, bounding around his legs until he petted him.

"Would you like something to drink?" Alex asked, trying to think what he had in the house.

"Just some water would be great. I called ahead to make sure we'd have a table," Luther said, taking the offered seat on the sofa. Rudolph followed Alex into the kitchen and watched as he filled two glasses from the filter pitcher in the refrigerator. When Alex returned, he sat down next to Luther, and Rudolph jumped up next to him, then walked over Alex's lap before scooching between them until Alex moved to give him room.

"He's goofy sometimes," Alex said, gently stroking Rudolph anyway.

"How do you like being a dog parent so far?" Luther asked, his gaze meeting Alex's in a way that gave his words more meaning and seeming important enough that Alex's temperature rose. He knew he was being dumb. This was one date, and yet the idea that Luther—with his beautiful eyes, full lips, high cheekbones, and dark hair that flowed to his shoulders—seemed to like him left Alex's heart racing.

"I think I do. Rudolph slept with me." He couldn't help smiling. "And I was calmer. It's been a while since I wasn't alone at night." Alex purposely left it like that.

"He sure seems to love you," Luther said as he stroked Rudolph. "Dogs are great judges of character. This guy loves people, and yet when he was dropped off by his previous owner's son, Mitchell told me that Rudolph hated the guy, nipping and growling at him nonstop. Mitchell said he didn't like the little turd either." Luther smiled. "I've come to trust the instincts of dogs better than my own."

Alex sipped from his glass. "You seem like a real people person to me."

"I am generally, but it's my instinct when it comes to guys that seems to be total crap." He tensed a little and continued petting Rudolph.

"We have that in common," Alex said. He hadn't wanted to discuss his past dating disasters, but Luther had brought it up. "The last man I dated lasted three weeks, and then he said that I was just too much work and effort to deal with. I wasn't any fun, and everything had to be done my way or else I'd ruin everything." He knew his anxiety got in the way, and maybe Dewey had had a point.

"How long ago was the breakup?"

"Two years. It was the impetus for me seeing my therapist. After that I decided that I really wanted to work on my issues. Palmer has been really good for me." He smiled down at Rudolph. "Heck, because of him I have a dog now." He was still going to be nervous around other dogs, he knew that, but Rudolph was quickly weaving his way into his heart. "I'm honestly trying to work on my other issues, and maybe I can be less... weird." He knew people saw him that way.

Luther brushed his hand over Alex's as they both petted Rudolph. Alex stopped moving, and Luther's hand rested right on top of his, warm and gentle. "You don't need to be anyone other than who you are. It's admirable that you're working on what you think you need to better yourself, but worry less about pleasing others and just be you."

Alex held Luther's gaze and smiled. No one had ever said something like that to him. Alex had never fit in. He was too jittery, worried too much, looked too geeky, skipped when the other boys didn't—you name it. He never seemed to do anything right. He'd worked hard in school but wasn't a gifted student. So he always felt like he was on the outside looking in... and he worried about it all the time. Hell, he obsessed about *everything*—but looking into Luther's deep, incredible eyes, all the other anxieties faded away as he wondered if something with Luther could be possible. Maybe he wouldn't mess this one up.

"My ex was just a world-class jerk. He drove trucks for a living, and I found out that he was very well acquainted with every truck stop from coast to coast and that the cab of his truck where he slept was very rarely empty."

"I see." Alex's anxiety rose again, only this time it was for Luther. Alex took his hand. Rudolph shimmied around to see what was happening and why he wasn't getting attention, but then settled down once more, resting his head on Alex's knee. "How long were you together?"

"That's just it," Luther said, confusion in his voice. "He and I had talked about getting a house and a dog. We were going to start building a life. Ken was starting to expand his business and was looking into starting his own company so he could stay home more and have others drive for him. We were making all these plans, and then...." He sighed, and Alex took a chance, leaning against him slightly, their shoulders touching.

"I'm sorry." He knew how much that had to hurt. "Maybe I'm lucky that none of the guys I dated ever stuck around for too long. I guess my quirks and weirdness scared them off before anything ever got to that point."

Luther straightened up. "Don't put yourself down like that. You're pretty brave. Most folks don't stand up to their fears. They let them rule their life. You decided to conquer yours, and look... you have a dog now."

"But he's Rudolph, the best dog ever," Alex said with a smile. Luther grinned and squeezed Alex's fingers. "Is it time for us to go?"

"We'll miss our reservation otherwise," Luther said, and they got up to a huff from Rudolph, who jumped down and hurried to the door like he was going to get to go too.

Alex made sure he had water and, since he had already fed him, a few pieces of kibble as a treat. He also brought out his dog bed and toys. Lastly, he got his coat on and then gave Rudoph a dog bone before he and Luther left the house, with Alex less nervous than he had been on his last date with his ex, and damned grateful for it too.

Chapter 3

"Is it strange that I miss Rudolph? Not that I'm not having a good time, because I am, but…." Alex could feel himself rambling and tried to rein it in. If he let himself fixate on things, he would blow it, so he concentrated on keeping everything breezy, not rearranging the silverware because the server put the knife in the wrong place, or worrying about how he moved Alex's water glass when he refilled it.

"He's new in your life." Luther sipped from his beer glass. "Besides, you're probably wondering if he's getting into mischief." He winked like he was kidding.

Alex smiled. "I wasn't until you mentioned it." He paused, widening his eyes. "Now I can't stop wondering if Rudolph is tearing through the house or using the coffee table for a chew toy." He gasped and then grinned.

"Damn, you really had me there." Luther chuckled, flashing Alex a bright smile. "Can I ask you something?" The server brought their dinners. Luther took the first bite of his chicken and hummed softly. "This is good. How is yours?"

"Wonderful." Alex had decided to be adventurous and ordered the duck. Usually he stuck to what he knew, but he decided to go for it. He took another bite and swallowed. "You wanted to ask something."

"Yeah. I noticed you don't have a tree," Luther said.

"I usually get a smaller one closer to Christmas."

Luther shrugged in response.

"What?"

"I guess I pictured you as an artificial tree kind of guy."

Alex shook his head. "Nope. Mom and Dad always had a real tree growing up. It always made the house smell like pine. I was going to get one this weekend, but with Rudolph I'm wondering if that's such a good idea. What if he gets confused and tries to pee on it or knocks it over?"

Luther shrugged again. "He's a dog, and he'll make mistakes just as the rest of us do. But that's not a reason to stop living your life or worry about it. If he does pee on it, then you clean it up and tell him no. As for knocking it over, he's a small dog. Rudolph is more likely to pick off ornaments to play with, so put them out of his reach. The likely scenario is that he's just going to ignore it altogether as long as no one wraps food to put under it." Luther laughed.

"I take it there's a story there." Alex took another bite of his amazing duck with raspberry sauce and leaned forward.

"We had a poodle mix growing up. Toni was a really good dog. I took her to obedience class, and she was always good. One Christmas morning when I was fourteen, we came out to the living room, all excited, to find a real mess. Wrapping paper littered the floor, as did packaging and bits of plastic. The packages from under the tree were all over the place. Dad was mad, and Mom was upset. I started cleaning up the paper and found a tag. It was a present from Aunt Vicky that she'd apparently put under the tree when they'd visited Christmas Eve. She later told us it was meant to be a surprise."

"What was it?"

"A Hickory Farms summer sausage gift box," Luther answered.

"Oh my God," Alex said. "So Toni was just being a dog and going for the food."

"Yeah. None of the other packages were damaged, just moved and pushed aside in her quest to get to the cheese and meat. Dad was mad at the dog, but it wasn't her fault. It was Aunt Vicky's for sneaking the food under the tree without telling us. At all times it's good to remember that Rudolph is just being a dog and that we are the ones who can think and adjust our behavior. Still, they were mad. Toni felt bad, you could tell, but she was just being a dog." Luther made a face, and Alex smiled. "And I didn't have to eat any of that summer sausage. Aunt Vicky always thought it was something special, but I never liked it."

It felt like he was sharing a secret, and Alex smiled. "So you're an only child?"

Luther nodded. "I was actually my parents' third child. The older two didn't make it, and that was hard on my mom. Do you have brothers and sisters?"

"I have a younger sister, Melody, who is a bit of a terror. She's six years younger than me and the spoiled baby of the family if there ever was one. I had to look after her a lot when we were younger." He didn't need to go into their dysfunctional family dynamics, at least not on a first date. Melody could do no wrong, so every time he'd had to babysit, she was out of control and Alex would get in trouble for what she'd done.

"Do you get along?"

Alex shrugged. "I'm on my own. I see my family once a month or so for dinner or something. But otherwise I try to keep myself busy. They aren't very conducive to my mental health, as Palmer has helped me see. Every time I visit, I'm anxious for days afterwards."

"Will you be seeing them for Christmas?"

Alex shook his head. "Mom and Dad have decided that they are going on a cruise for the holidays and taking Melody. They hinted that I could go along but never really asked me, and if I wanted to go, then I'd have to pay my own way and share a cabin with my eighteen-year-old sister, who would spend all her time trying to sneak out to get some time to herself. So if I went, I'd end up as the babysitter again, and that isn't a lot of fun." So he was spending Christmas on his own for the first time. At least he had Rudolph to keep him company. His parents had said that they would send him a Christmas box with his gifts.

"So you'll be alone?"

"With Rudolph. Maybe he and I will watch the other Rudolph together. I'll get us each treats, and we can sit on the sofa and eat until we both fall into a food coma."

Luther set down his fork. "Or you and Rudolph can come spend Christmas with me and my family. Mom loves to cook, and we usually have Aunt Vicky and a few other friends and family with us. Mom always invites people she knows will be alone for the holiday."

"I don't want to impose." While his words were polite, Alex wasn't sure he would be up to spending the day smiling with strangers. What if Luther's family didn't like him, or what if his mother didn't want more people for the holiday?

"It's not imposing. My mom will be happy to have you there, and so would I." That smile came again, and Alex was tempted to say yes. "I'll pick you and Rudolph up on Christmas morning."

That made Alex pause. He was inviting him *and* his dog for the holiday. Alex had already been wondering what he was going to do with Rudolph if he did come to Christmas dinner, and here Luther had not only answered the question, but extended an invitation to him too. "Are you sure about this?"

Luther leaned forward. "Of course." He said it as though it truly wasn't a big deal, but for Alex, it definitely was.

"Thank you." At least he wasn't going to be eating a frozen dinner or Chinese takeout on the holiday, and he was going to be spending it with Luther. Though he didn't want to read too much into that. Luther was probably just being nice. As much as Alex would welcome the idea that Luther might like him, he didn't dare let himself hope too much. Alex knew that his issues were more than most other people could take, and he didn't blame them.

"So you'll come?" Luther asked with a touch of excitement, and Alex nodded, trying not to get his hopes up but feeling truly happy for the first time in a while.

"THAT WAS a great dinner," Alex said as he and Luther went out to the car. The cold night air had stilled, and flakes of snow drifted through the air before settling in the wreaths that decorated the downtown lampposts. "Thank you." He had reached for the check, but Luther had gotten to it first and paid for their dinner.

Luther unlocked the car, and Alex settled into the passenger seat and closed the door. Snow had obscured the windshield, but the wipers brushed it away as soon as Luther started the engine to take him home.

At the house, Luther parked, and as they headed up the walk, Rudolph peered out of the window, his tail wagging. Once they got close, he jumped down, and Alex wasn't surprised when he opened the door to Rudolph bouncing with excitement.

"What did you do?" Luther asked.

Alex lifted his gaze to the stuffing strewn over the floor. He gasped and started checking over the sofa cushions and then the chairs. Then he bent down and picked up a bit of orange fabric.

"It looks like the carrot toy we got him." Relieved, he began picking up the bits of fluff. Rudolph jumped on the couch cushion, watching the proceedings with pride.

"Did you protect the house from the evil carrot monster?" Luther asked, giving Rudolph attention.

"I thought at first he had gone after one of the cushions or something."

"Nope," Luther said. "You have yourself a good boy here. He tore into one of his toys." He sat down, and Alex tossed away the remaining bits of dog toy before sitting next to him, Rudolph bounding onto his lap.

"I find myself tensing sometimes when he does that," Alex confessed. "Like I'm scared of him, and then I remember that I'm not." He petted Rudolph, who wagged his tail, mouth open in puppy happiness, before settling between them for a few minutes. But as soon as Alex began to relax, Rudolph jumped down and ran off, tearing around the room in circles. "I should let him out." Alex hurried out back, got the leash, and took Rudolph out in the backyard.

"You should fence this area come spring. Then he could run in back without you worrying about him getting out." Luther was close enough that Alex could feel his heat in the cold air. Alex inhaled and got a nose full of Luther's head-spinning scent.

"There are lots of things I need to do. Usually I try to do them myself, but building fences is probably beyond my skill set." This was his first house, and Alex was trying to put as much sweat equity into it as he could. "Still, that's what the internet is for."

"And friends," Luther added softly, sending a ripple of heat through him.

Rudolph did his business on one of the boxwoods and pranced away like he was proud of himself. Then he hurried over and raced around Alex's legs, tying him up in the leash.

"He has too much energy," Alex said.

"It's a trait of the breed. Just learn to go with it and take him on walks to let him work it off." Luther shivered, and Alex got Rudolph inside and the back door closed. Then he took off Rudolph's leash, and the dog raced onto the sofa and watched him over the back. Alex and Luther sat down again, with Rudolph taking his place between them, settling in for pets.

"We could watch a movie," Alex offered, not sure what he should do. This type of thing was hard for him. Did he offer drinks, a movie, snacks? What did he talk about? Was just being quiet okay? A million things raced through his head, and each time he had to admit he didn't know only increased his worry that he was being an idiot.

"That would be great," Luther answered. "I like comedies or action flicks. I can look to see what's available if you like." And just like that, Luther took away the worry.

"Cool. I have beer if you like, or some juice. There might be a soda or something too." Not that Alex drank beer, but his dad did, and he had left a few the last time his parents visited. At least he hoped so.

Luther smiled. "Whatever you're having is great." There was a smile, and Alex was so grateful Luther hadn't told him to just relax. His parents had tried to help him get over his anxiety more times than he could count, but their efforts more often than not involved them telling him to just relax or to chill—words that always had the opposite effect.

Alex went to get drinks, and by the time he had returned, Luther had *Lethal Weapon 2* up on the screen.

"Is this okay?"

Alex grinned. "I love this one." His parents had hated it when he watched this type of movie. His mom told him once that she thought movies caused his anxiety. Alex had rolled his eyes at the idea.

Luther started the movie, and Alex placed the sodas on the table before settling in to watch. Rudolph climbed onto his lap after a few minutes, and Alex stroked his back, tension slowly easing from him until the action on screen got his heart racing once more. About the time that Danny Glover was found sitting on the toilet bomb, Luther leaned closer until their shoulders touched.

Suddenly the sound from the television receded under the pounding of his heart. He turned to Luther, who leaned closer. Under normal circumstances, Alex would have worried about whether Luther was going to kiss him and if he was ready for it, but Luther just drew nearer, and Alex found himself responding. Without thinking, he deepened the kiss, sliding his eyes closed and just letting himself enjoy the way Luther tasted, the feel of his lips. It was wonderful... and over before Alex could wonder or worry.

"Was that okay?" Luther asked.

"Uh-huh," Alex said as Rudolph licked his chin. "I think he's jealous."

Luther chuckled before lifting Rudolph to the floor, where he went after another of his toys, and Luther leaned in again. This time Alex was ready, and he slipped his arms around Luther's neck and held him through a second kiss. Part of him wondered if this meant that Luther wanted to take things further, but Luther backed away and sat up straight as the movie continued. He did take Alex's hand, and they sat together as the house on the hill came crashing down. Not that Alex's attention was on the TV—instead, it was centered on his hand in Luther's.

By the time the credits rolled, Rudolph was on Alex's lap and Alex was leaning against Luther's shoulder. He was comfortable and kind of blinky. "I think I should go," Luther said softly.

"Oh, okay," Alex whispered, and then Luther's heat was gone as he stood. Alex saw him to the door, with Rudolph prancing to get Luther's attention for a goodbye pet. Then he hurried off to tear apart another of his toys, and Alex stood at the door. "I'll call you tomorrow. Maybe we can go tree shopping?"

"That would be fun," Alex answered, unsure what came next, but Luther kissed him gently and then left the house.

Alex stood in the doorway watching as Luther got to his car. Alex's heart was still racing, his lips curled upward, and the smile lasted well after he'd closed the door and started cleaning up the glasses. He refused to let his mind wander to what the evening meant and what was to come. Instead, he tried to let himself be happy—at least for a while.

Chapter 4

"What about this one?" Luther asked as he pointed out a tree on the lot of the Weis supermarket.

"Isn't it a little tall?" Alex asked.

"We could move the table in front of the window and put it there. The lights would shine through, and it would be festive." And just like that, Alex could picture the tree in that spot.

"It's perfect," he said quietly. He stroked the tree's soft needles and paid the attendant before he and Luther loaded the tree on top of Alex's car.

He drove home slowly, and once they were there, Luther hefted the tree off the car, and Alex hurried ahead to get the stand ready. Alex put the table in the spare room, and then they brought the tree inside and got it in place. Rudolph hurried over to check out the new addition, sniffing and poking around under it before prancing away and jumping onto the sofa, where he stood with his front paws on the arm to watch the proceedings like the prince he seemed to think he was.

"We need music," Luther said, getting out his phone. Instantly, "Sleigh Ride" began to play, and the room seemed to fill with cheer.

Alex already had the boxes of decorations and lights in the corner. He got out the first string of multicolored lights, which he had made sure still worked, and Luther bravely began winding them onto the tree branches. Alex's first instinct was to point out imperfections, but he held himself back. Once he had the lights strung, Luther stepped back and used the final string to fill in any holes. "That's better than I usually manage," Alex told him. "Thank you."

"Is there any pattern to the ornaments that you like?" Luther asked, interrupting his singalong rendition of "Jingle Bell Rock." Alex hadn't had this much fun in a long time.

"Not really. There aren't a lot of them." He was afraid his tree was going to look bare, but Luther seemed to have a way, and they placed the ornaments with enough space that by the time they were through, his tree didn't look completely pathetic.

Then the song changed to "Mele Kalikimaka," and Luther tugged Alex over and slowly danced him around the room.

"You're a nut."

"But a fun one."

Alex couldn't argue with that and put his head on Luther's shoulder. The two of them swayed through the rest of the song. Then Rudolph wanted to get in on the action, running in circles in his own happy dance.

The song came to an end and Luther kissed Alex, this time harder than before, with passion that rose between them quickly. Alex's head swam in it, and he sighed softly in Luther's tight embrace, holding him in return.

Alex cupped Luther's cheeks in his hands, returning the kiss with one of his own just as the doorbell rang. A knock followed, sending Rudolph into a barking frenzy.

"What is that? Are you expecting someone?"

"No. But I know who it is." The knock came again, more insistent this time. "It's my mother."

It was Luther's turn to tense. The way he held Alex shifted, and then he pulled away. What was it about his mom? "You'd better answer the door before she decides to break it down." His humor seemed gone, and in an instant, the holiday cheer that had filled the room evaporated like fog in the wind. Luther lifted Rudolph, calming him as Alex opened the door and let the whirlwind that was his mother into the house.

"I knew you were home. I could hear the music," she declared as she stepped inside. "Did you get one of those dog alarm doorbells?" Her question died as she saw Rudolph. "When did you get a dog? You were always afraid of them." She set her purse on the nearest chair and took off her coat. She usually draped it over the back of the chair, but now she held it like she didn't quite know what to do.

Rudolph growled, and Luther did his best to soothe him. Clearly he didn't like her.

"Can you hang this up for me? I don't want to get dog hair on it." She handed over the coat without even looking in Alex's direction, knowing he would do as she asked. "Who are you?"

"This is Luther. He's a friend, and he volunteers at the shelter where I got Rudolph. He helped me get the things I'd need for him, and the two of us have been seeing each other." God, why did he always feel like a teenager again when his mother looked at him that way?

"But you hate dogs," she said softly, as though she were dissecting everything Alex did. It was unnerving. "You always have. Remember the time the neighbor had that brown boxer and he snapped at you for no reason? And the time your cousin's chihuahua snapped at you when you went to pet it? Nasty little thing." She turned up her lip, and Alex's mind clicked on those instances and a chill went up his spine.

"Rudolph is a wonderful dog, and Alex has been courageous enough to face his fears." Luther came over and passed Rudolph to him. Alex cuddled Rudolph close, and he stopped growling, though he never stopped watching Alex's mom.

"What did you need?" Alex asked. "You don't usually just drop by." His mother was more the kind of person who called in advance like she was making an appointment to have her hair done.

"Yes. You made me forget. Your father and I were talking, and we can arrange for another cabin. There are a few left on the ship. We thought you should come with us for the holidays. I always thought it a shame that you wouldn't be with us. This way we can all be together as a family. You and Melody would have your own cabins next to each other." She said it as though it was the greatest idea ever and like she was doing him a big favor.

"Maybe I should get ready to go," Luther said softly. "You and your mom have things to talk about." He turned away.

"You don't need to go," Alex said gently.

"I think I should," Luther said, and Alex nodded. He couldn't make Luther stay, but he didn't want him to go. Hell, he wanted to beg him to stay. His anxiety was already going through the roof. His hands shook, and the tension in the room seemed to pull out all the oxygen.

"Don't," he managed to say, touching Luther's arm. He took a deep breath and closed his eyes, using a technique he had since he was a kid, trying to shut himself off from everything. Rudolph licked his chin and up his neck, making Alex smile a little, and some of the chill slipped away. "Mom isn't going to be staying very long."

"We need to talk about this cruise. If you're coming with us, there are a lot of things that I'm going to need so we can get everything filled out properly. I thought I could book the cabin using your computer, and then we can fill out all the passenger information. They're going to need it right away."

Luther gently squeezed Alex's arm gently. "I'll call you tomorrow." Alex nodded, and Luther leaned close. "I promise. You talk over what you need to with your mom." He got his coat, and Alex still held Rudolph as Luther reached for the door. Alex was well aware that Luther couldn't get out of the house fast enough, and he felt like if he didn't stop Luther somehow, he was never going to see him again. His nerves jangled, and he didn't know what to do. Luther opened the door and then paused. He returned to where Alex stood, leaned down, and kissed him gently. He also gave Rudolph a few pats and then left the house, closing the door behind him.

"Good. He's gone." She brushed off the seat of one of the high-backed chairs before perching on the edge of it. "Now you and I can talk about the plans for the holidays. Your father and I thought we'd make the cruise your Christmas present...."

As she went on with her plans, he stood there, barely listening as his mind clicked in a million different directions. For as long as he could remember, he'd always been nervous and anxious. "Mom," he said gently. "It's great that you, Dad, and Melody are going on a cruise for the holidays, but I don't want to." He really wasn't interested. "It's nice that you want me to go along now, but it's not what I want." Besides, she hadn't considered the fact that he had already told them that the vacation schedules in the office were set. "I can't get the time off at this late date anyway."

"Please. Like what you do won't wait until after the holidays." She rolled her eyes.

"Mom," he said more firmly. "If I go, then Jane will have to cancel her plans, and I won't do that to her. Someone from my department needs to be in the office, and I let the people who work for me have the time this year." God, he felt better standing up to her a little. She always steamrolled over what he wanted or thought.

"Still, your father and I think—" she began, the way she always did. Like what the two of them thought should hold sway over everything and everyone.

"No, Mom," he said more forcefully. "I can't do that. I appreciate the offer to join you, but I can't." He sat on the sofa, and Rudolph stood on his lap, his tail still, watching Mom without moving, which was rare for his energetic dog. "Was there something else that you came over to see me about?" She could have just called—that would have been easier.

But it was harder for him to tell his mother no in person, and she knew that.

"Can't I come to see you?" she asked.

"You can, but you don't usually." She kept watching Rudolph. "Do you want to hold him?" Alex asked. "Rudolph is really nice, and I'm finding that he's good company. Luther is helping me learn how to take care of him properly."

She shook her head. "I don't care for dogs. Never have. Melody kept asking for a dog all the time, but you were so terrified of them, so we told her no."

Alex leaned forward. "Except it was you who didn't like dogs. You never wanted Melody to have one either, so you used my anxiety as an excuse to tell her no when it was possible that if I got used to a dog, I'd get over my issues and come to love them." He'd certainly come to adore Rudolph easily enough.

"How was I to know?" she snapped, eyeing Rudolph like he was the devil himself. "It was best that you didn't get one. We were always traveling, and it would have been hard on any animal that we got, being left in a kennel or with a pet sitter."

Alex stood and brought Rudolph closer. His mom's eyes widened, and she sat back to try to get away.

"And you're scared of dogs. All those years you told Melody that it was me when it was really you." He sat back down. "So what else have you projected onto me?" After years in therapy, he had learned the lingo pretty well.

"You *were* afraid of dogs," she said. "I didn't do that." She sat up straighter, and Alex knew that expression. She would deny doing anything wrong to her last breath.

"No, but you used it." His entire childhood, he'd heard his mother tell Melody or her friends that they couldn't get a dog or that they couldn't go hiking because Alex was anxious around animals or that Alex didn't like the outdoors because there could be bears. And yeah, he had been worried about stuff like that, but his parents hadn't soothed him or tried to talk him away from the fear. Mom had just told Melody that they couldn't go camping or to Yellowstone because of him. "I like dogs. At least I like Rudolph, and I know now that they aren't going to bite or attack me. I met a number of dogs at the shelter the other day, and

I'm going to go back until I get over this fear. I'm tired of being worried all the time and anxious about everything."

"Well, that's good," she said gently and then sighed. "So you aren't coming with us." She never seemed to let anything go.

"No. I can't get off work, and I have Rudolph to look after. Even if I could take the time off, I wouldn't put him with a pet sitter or in a kennel. He and I are just figuring things out." He gently stroked Rudolph's wiry head. "You and Dad have fun with Melody. I already have plans for Christmas Day. Luther invited me to spend the day with his family, so none of you have to worry that I'll be alone." He glanced at the tree near his mom and smiled at what Luther had helped him do. "Is there anything else?"

She stood, and Alex got her coat. "I'll see you before you leave next week," he offered.

"Don't feel like you have to. I'm sure you're going to be very busy," she told him. He knew it was because she wasn't getting her way. The invitation to join the cruise was nice, and Alex appreciated it, even if they had waited until the last minute. But he wasn't going to let her make him feel guilty or anxious about not going. It just wasn't possible, and that was all there was to it. Maybe if they had asked him months ago, when they'd initially decided to go, he could have. But right now Alex had a good excuse to stay home, and that was the right thing for him.

Alex saw his mother to the door and kissed her cheek before closing the door behind her, then set Rudolph down.

His family was going away for the holidays, and he was staying home. A few years ago, the thought would have sent him into worries about loneliness and being left out. But now all he could feel was relief. It was best that he made his own way, and he was looking forward to spending the day with Luther… and even meeting his family. Now *that* was a surprise.

CHAPTER 5

WORK THE following day was long and boring. Alex kept watching the clock. A good share of the people in the office were either on vacation or getting ready to leave, which meant the place was growing quieter. A few times during the day, music drifted into his office, and Alex found himself humming along to various Christmas carols.

"You okay?" Wendy asked after rapping lightly on his door frame. She was the senior of the people who worked for him and probably had more experience than the rest of his team together. "You seem extra happy and un-jumpy. What's going on?"

"Nothing," he answered out of habit. "Well, I got a dog."

"Is that why you didn't jump down Renee's throat when she messed up everything for the fourth time? Maybe we should have gotten you a dog a year ago." She sat down. "Whatever it is, keep it up. It's nice to see you happy."

"Thanks. It's kind of nice not to be jumpy and wondering when things are going to go to hell all the time."

"Where is this dog of yours right now?" Wendy asked.

"At home. I went to let him out and check on him at lunch. Rudolph was tickled to see me. You know, it's great to have someone at home thrilled to see me when I walk in the door."

Wendy scoffed lightly. "What you need is a man to do that for you."

He swallowed hard and glanced down at the top of his desk.

"I see. There's one of those too. Did they come as a set?"

Alex rolled his eyes.

"They did." She grinned. "Now tell me how a man who practically jumped up on his desk when I brought Henri into the office last month ends up with a dog and a guy in his life at the same time. 'Cause, honey, I may need to go out and get me another dog if they're giving away cute guys as a gift with purchase. Maybe then I could trade in Herb for a newer model." Alex knew she was kidding. She and Herb had been married for thirty years, and he sent her flowers at work every once in a while.

"Luther is nice, and I met him at the shelter. He started off helping me get the things I'd need for Rudolph, but since then we've been on a few dates, and I really like him."

Wendy relaxed in her seat. "So what's the problem?"

"He met my mother yesterday. She wants me to go on the family cruise and offered to get me the passage as a Christmas present. I turned her down, but I think she might have scared Luther off." He hadn't called or texted yet today, and Alex was a little worried, but he was trying not to get wound up about it.

"Wow." Her expression clearly showed she thought he was kidding.

"I'm serious. He couldn't get out of the house fast enough. We had gotten a tree and just finished decorating it when she showed up."

Wendy tilted her head forward and looked at him over her glasses. "If that's all it took to scare him off, then he wasn't worth bothering with in the first place. Besides, he could have been busy. What does he do?"

"Teaches psychology at Dickinson."

"Then it's finals time, and he's probably really busy during the day. Give him a break and don't worry about it." She leaned forward. "Besides, I saw Joe walking down the hallway in this direction, so it's possible you may have something real to worry about." She stood and stepped out of the office as Alex's vice president peered in.

"Do you have a minute?" he asked and then sat right down. "I just got a request for a complete relay of store 340. Apparently they need to rework the assortment in the store. They have the new assortment, and they want to make the changes to the store layout in January." He sat back, and Alex could already see the writing on the wall. "They need this done right away so they can get it approved and start work." Which meant they would expect Alex to work through the holidays in order to be on time. "I told them that they were being too aggressive and optimistic on their timelines for this time of the year."

"And they don't care." Alex knew the drill as well as Joe. "I have the current layout for the store in the system. I can finish a proposed layout before the holidays, but then it's going to need approval, and shepherding that through takes time. You know that."

"I'm scheduling a meeting for between the holidays with all the parties. They can review what they need to, and we'll get their approval at the meeting. Then we can input the details and have the final layouts after the first of the year."

Alex already felt the pressure building. They did this to him every time. Alex was amazing at his job, and yet he was expected to do the impossible time and time again. "You know none of this will happen, right?"

Joe smiled. "Of course I do. But I put out the plan and stipulated that any deviation will push back their timeline. And I stipulated that all approvals had to be done at the meeting, no exceptions. So if you can get your layouts done before Christmas, we'll send everything out, and the departments have to be ready or they don't get what they want." He made it sound simple. "I know you can do this. I'll shepherd it through the approvals. I got your back."

Alex thanked him. He was a little relieved, but in the end he had been handed days of work to complete on his own. It would keep him busy, but he could do much of it at home, so he could work there the week before Christmas without anyone disturbing him. He already had permission to work from home. "Then I'll get it done." He just needed to make sure he had all the information he needed.

"Thank you," Joe said and stood. "Have a good holiday." He smiled and left, with Alex shaking his head. Joe was always careful to say the right things, but sometimes Alex swore he was the Grinch in disguise. He checked the time and made a list of things he would need to redesign the store layout. Then he finished his outstanding tasks and left. He still hadn't heard anything from Luther and was beginning to get a little worried.

ALEX HURRIED into the house and was greeted by a jumping Rudolph. He got the leash and took him out to potty right away. Then he turned on the tree, its multicolored lights livening up the room and adding some festive cheer. Alex settled on the sofa with a drink and turned on the television, trying to occupy his sometimes too-active mind. He thought about messaging Luther to see if he was all right, and he picked up his phone and stared at the screen. What the hell was he afraid of?

He sent off a quick message to see how Luther was and then leaned back on the sofa, Rudolph jumping into his lap. Alex ended up watching one of the myriad romantic holiday movies that seemed to be on, and he got caught up in it pretty quickly. This one was about a prince and a girl from New York somewhere. He swore he'd already seen this movie plot a dozen times, but he got into the story nonetheless.

His phone buzzing on the coffee table pulled Alex out of the story. He picked it up, smiling. *Sorry. Got really busy with exams and closing out the term.*

Do you want to come by? Alex sent and received a smiley face in response.

Be there in half an hour. It was followed by a bunch of Christmas emojis that made Alex smile.

"Luther is coming over," Alex said before jumping up. There were things he needed to do, and he quickly picked up the house and ran the vacuum. He also changed the sheets on the bed in a fit of wishful thinking. They had kissed, but Luther seemed intent on taking things slowly, which Alex liked. Luther seemed to understand that Alex needed a chance to process things.

The last thing he did was put on some Christmas music before answering the door. Rudolph bounded around Luther's legs like he hadn't seen him in days. Luther gave the little jumping bean pets and then stood straight.

"I'm sorry about my mom yesterday. She gets a little intense."

Luther tugged Alex closer. "No need. I thought maybe the two of you needed to talk, and well…." He paused. "I figured you needed to work out the details of your cruise, and you didn't need me to be here." The disappointment in Luther's eyes was unmistakable.

"I'm not going. I can't take off work at this late date, and besides, I was invited to Christmas dinner with my boyfriend." They had never talked about what the two of them were, and maybe Alex was jumping to conclusions and the ten minutes he'd just spent changing the sheets were wishful thinking.

"You're not going with your family?" Luther asked.

Alex shook his head. "My mother always thinks that everyone should just drop what they're doing because she wants them to. My job isn't important—only what she happens to want." He sighed. "And what she really needed was someone to watch Melody so she and Dad could go out and do their thing. I don't want that kind of trip." He drew closer. "I'd rather spend the holiday with you."

"With me, as your boyfriend?" Luther asked, and Alex nodded. "I like that." He kissed Alex hard, and Alex held him in return, energy building between them.

"I do too," Alex whispered as he pulled back. "But… how long before you get tired of me?" He had to ask. "How long before my anxieties become too much for you? My last boyfriend couldn't get away fast enough. He seemed to think that everything would just go away and…."

Luther smoothed his hand down Alex's arm. "And the more he pressured you to change, the more your anxiety intensified." It was like Luther had been there. "You are who you are, and caring for someone means that you love them for the person they are, not what you think they'll become or how you can change them. Besides, you have courage and strength. Rudolph is proof of that." Luther smiled as he leaned closer.

"But will you get tired of me?" Alex asked.

Luther shook his head. "Somehow I very much doubt it. You have this way of keeping me on my toes. You surprise me, and not many people do that." He kissed Alex once more.

"Still." Alex felt his hand shaking and tried to cover it up. Luther took it and gently stroked the back of it. "I worry about things."

"You don't need to. I'm not going to walk away because you get anxious or need change to happen slowly in your life. There are things that none of us can change, and there are things we can control. But the best parts of ourselves come out when we trust someone enough to place the things we get to have a say in in the hands of the people we care about."

Rudolph barked from where he stood on the sofa. Clearly he felt a little left out.

"Maybe we can test this theory of your upstairs?" Alex asked quietly, still uncertain what Luther wanted, but he got his answer with a heated smile and a gentle tug toward the stairs.

"This isn't the time for you to be up here," Alex told Rudolph as he barreled up onto the bed just as Luther worked his shirt off.

Rudolph perched on the edge of the bed, tail wagging, mouth open in that knowing doggie smile he had.

"Off the bed and go downstairs."

Of course Rudolph ignored him. Thankfully Luther lifted him off the bed and left the room.

Alex took the opportunity to remove the rest of his clothes while Luther clomped down the stairs and then returned a few minutes later, closing the bedroom door. "I gave him a bone." Luther stalked closer. "Damn, you're stunning." He kicked off his shoes and stripped off his pants, baring his built and honed body to Alex's gaze. Alex had imagined what might be under Luther's clothes since they met, but reality beat his imagination by a mile. Luther grinned as he climbed onto the bed, his gaze as hot as a summer day. He drew closer, his hands gliding up Alex's chest to his neck and cheeks.

"You're the one who looks great naked. I'm just a skinny guy who needs to gain a few pounds." Alex had no illusions about how he looked. Thankfully, body image wasn't one of the things he was anxious about.

"Nope. I'm not buying it." Luther caressed his sides before kissing Alex hard, probably so he couldn't argue. And who was he to tell Luther he was wrong? Hell, talking became unnecessary over the next hour as Luther took him to heights Alex had only dreamed about. Outside the house, the night air was cold and the wind whistled around the house, but in this room, there was heat, passion, and everything Alex could ever want, building up to a breathless pinnacle that left him satiated and panting.

He and Luther lay side by side, Luther's fingers entwined with Alex's. "Jesus," Alex whispered, not daring to move.

There was a scratch, scratch, scratch, followed by a sharp bark, then more scratching.

"I think your dog is done with his bone," Luther said and then laughed. Alex got a few tissues, and they cleaned up quickly, then opened the door before Rudolph could dig a hole through it.

"You know, we never did have dinner," Alex said.

"We had more important things to do," Luther breathed and patted the bed. Rudolph scurried between them and settled right down.

"You really are a naughty thing," Alex scolded lightly. "Do you mind that he's here? I can put him in his bed."

"It's nice." Luther stroked Rudolph gently and got a doggie kiss on the chin. "I really like the little ball of energy." Luther leaned closer, and he and Alex shared a kiss that threatened to reignite the fire they'd lit earlier.

This time Rudolph took the hint and got out of the room.

CHAPTER 6

ALEX SAVED his work and closed his laptop. He had gotten the store layout done and sent to Joe for his review. He had been determined to have it done before Christmas, and it was four o'clock Christmas Eve and it was done.

"Are you ready to start the celebrating?" Luther asked, slinking his arms over Alex's shoulders and down his chest.

"I had to finish this," he said. "I'm sorry I've been so busy this past week." He sighed and let some of the tension wash away. He was starting to get better at doing things like that. His main task was done, and Joe was largely going to take things from here.

"You know it's okay." Luther kissed the top of his head. "If you're done, why don't you put your work things away?" The tree was already lit, and at some point Luther had added cut greens with white lights threaded through them to the top of his fireplace. Those were on as well. Alex was happy to be able to leave work behind for a while, and it seemed Rudolph was too.

"Where did you get that?" Alex asked when he saw the red bow attached to Rudolph's collar. He practically jumped up into Alex's lap as soon as he pushed his chair away from the dining room table, where he'd been working the past few days. "Did Uncle Luther get that for you?" he asked and got frantic doggie kisses on the chin. He held Rudolph close, turning to watch happily as Luther dimmed the lights. Christmas music began to play, and Alex sighed, holding Rudolph and finally letting go of all the tension. It had been a long time since he'd been this content and, dare he say it... in love. It had only been a few weeks, and yet Alex was sure of how he felt. It seemed fast, but he was beginning to understand that when good things happened to him, he needed to embrace them rather than worrying them to death.

Luther bounded over as soon as he had the room the way he wanted. "Do you want to open our presents tonight or take them with us to my parents'?"

Alex shrugged, biting his lower lip and then releasing it. He wasn't going to worry about meeting Luther's family. After all, they raised Luther and he was pretty amazing, so chances were that they would be too. He had received an email from Luther's mom to say hello and how excited she was that he and Rudolph were going to come. Alex thought it pretty amazing that she included an invitation for his dog too.

"What do you want to do?" Alex teased, but the excited way Luther's eyes goggled every time he looked at the tree told Alex everything he wanted to know. "Let me guess, you shook every present when you were a kid, trying to figure out what it was." God, he loved Luther's playfulness. It made Alex want to play as well.

"Of course. Didn't you?" Luther asked.

Alex rolled his eyes. "You met my mother, remember? She knew where everything was. There were no 'Christmas shenanigans,' as she put it, in her house."

"Trying to figure out what your presents are is part of the fun." Luther sat on the sofa, his long legs stretching out in front of him.

"Would you mind if we waited until tomorrow? That way I won't be sitting at your folks' watching everyone else open gifts with nothing to do."

"Sure. Have you opened the stuff from your family?"

Alex shook his head. "I'll do it in the morning." There wasn't much—two presents and a card—which was fine. They were out having fun, and honestly, he was happy for them. Heck, he was happy right here.

He lifted Rudolph, and the two of them sat down next to Luther. Rudolph pranced over both their laps before jumping down to sniff the packages. "I put the things for him up in the front closet." Luther got up and returned with a chew bone squeaky toy that sent Rudolph into a fit of doggie rapture. He raced through the house with it in his mouth before settling under the table to try to rip it apart. "You got presents for my dog?"

"Of course I did. It's his first Christmas with his new daddy, and I figured that if he was busy, then maybe we could be too." Luther turned to Alex and kissed him as he pressed him down onto the cushions. "Are you sure you don't want to open your present?"

Alex chuckled and drew Luther closer. "You are the best Christmas present I've ever gotten. How could anything else compare?"

Rudolph raced over and jumped onto the sofa near Alex's head.

"Yeah, okay. You're the best present too." Alex smiled and got a doggie kiss across the lips.

"We can't both be the best present," Luther groused playfully.

"Sure you can. I got you both at the same time, so you're both the best Christmas present I've ever had." Alex paused, his belly clenching a little, but then he let it go. "Because love is the best gift of all."

For a second he wondered if he might have rushed in too soon, but Luther kissed him hard, showing Alex that he truly had both given and received the best present possible.

EPILOGUE

I WOKE at the foot of the big bed, listening for any sounds in the house. I heard nothing other than Daddy Alex and Luther breathing under the covers. I was a little cold, so I got up and quietly drew closer to Daddy Alex, then settled down right between the two of them where it was toasty warm.

Daddy Alex petted me gently and then went back to sleep. I closed my eyes again. It was what Daddy Alex called Christmas morning. I didn't really know what Christmas was, but there were packages under the tree and some that smelled like bacon and sausage in the closet. The ones under the tree in the house didn't smell like anything, so I left them alone. But I really wanted the ones in the closet. I saw them when Daddy Luther opened the door yesterday, and I'd dreamed about them all night. Daddy Alex had called him Uncle Luther, but I knew he was really Daddy Luther. I could tell that they loved each other, even if they didn't know it yet. Dogs can always tell. I wasn't sure if the treats in the closet or my daddies made me happier. I supposed it didn't matter what made my tail thump on the bed.

I didn't think about Mom Claire as much as I used to, but I missed her and hoped she would be happy that I found a forever home. She always loved me, and I would always love her in the depths of my doggie heart, but now Daddy Alex was there too, and I wasn't going to be alone. I would be loved, and Daddy Alex and Daddy Luther would always be there for me; I just knew it.

I closed my eyes, my doggie mind filling with the things I loved: bacon treats, my new squeaky bone, and my two daddies who petted me in their sleep. The best doggie Christmas ever.

REGRET ME NOT

THE MORNING AFTER....

THE EVER-PRESENT shush of the sea echoed in his ears. Even before he was awake, Pierce Atwater knew that sound had haunted him in his dreams.

He yawned and stretched, the familiar aches of healing injuries pulling at his skin and muscles and the unfamiliar ache in his backside waking him up fully. Oh, hey. It had been a while since that happened.

With a heave, Pierce sat up entirely, getting his bearings. The beach house he'd lived in since Thanksgiving glowed as bright and gold as he remembered—too beautiful. Almost pristine.

His body, on the other hand—that felt well-used.

He turned and looked at the bed he'd just vacated, noting that it was rumpled and sex stained; lovemaking and sweat permeated the room.

Oh wow. Oh damn. What had he done?

A piece of paper—the ripped-off corner of a brown grocery bag— caught his attention on the other pillow of the king-sized bed.

Please don't leave without saying goodbye—
—H

Pierce stared at the note, only marginally prepared for the giant ache that bloomed in his chest.

Aw, Hal—you deserve so very much more.

He looked around the room again, eyes falling on the clock radio. He was supposed to leave in an hour—he'd told his sister specifically that he'd be in Orlando by lunch so he could bake cookies with her kids.

He looked at the note again and tried hard to breathe.

THE MONTH BEFORE

"SO YOU have the Lyft app, right?"

"Yeah, Sasha—don't worry about me, okay?" Pierce regarded his younger sister fondly. She was made to be a mother—even if she came into being one a little young.

Sasha bit her lip, trying not to argue. She'd been such a sweet kid growing up—never saying boo to either of their rather domineering parents. She'd gotten pregnant right out of high school, and even though Marshall had stepped up and married her and they'd both managed to get their degrees, their parents... well, they'd never let Sasha live down what a disappointment she'd been. Or—their words—what a slut either.

Pierce had hated them long before Sasha got pregnant, but the way they'd tried to destroy her for a simple human failing had sort of sealed the deal.

But parenthood had made Sasha—and Marshall—a great deal stronger than they'd been as feckless teenagers, and while Sasha wouldn't *argue* with her beloved older brother, she would *discuss* things she disagreed with.

"Pierce, you almost died," she said quietly, her thin face suddenly lost in the pallor of anxiety and the cloud of fine dark hair she could never keep back in a ponytail. "I mean... I refuse to see Mom and Dad over the holidays because they're just... just...."

"Awful," he supplied with feeling. Yeah. He'd resolved not to put up with awful anymore.

"Toxic," she agreed, leaning back against her aging SUV. Darius and Abigail were sleeping in the back seat after playing out in the surf under Pierce's supervision while Marshall and Sasha moved Pierce into the condo. Pierce had worried—he couldn't move very well without the cane these days, and what did he know about kids and water?

But mostly what they'd wanted to do was run away from the waves and collect shells, and the one time Abigail had been knocked on her ass into the surf, Pierce had bent down and picked her up by the hand before the pain even registered.

The move had hurt—but it had given him some hope. His doctors kept assuring him that he could get most of his mobility back if he kept active and remembered his aqua regimen. Picking Abigail up and reassuring her that Uncle Pierce wouldn't let her drown gave him some confidence that his body might someday be back up to par. And the condo had a pool, which was why he'd taken his best friend Derrick's offer to let him use it over the winter months while Pierce got his life together. Pierce was definitely in a position to follow his doctor's advice.

So now, looking at his sister and thinking about how much self-assurance she'd had to grow to push a little into Pierce's state of mind, he couldn't be mad at her.

And he had to be honest.

"I'll be grumpy and pissed off and bitter," he said, letting his mouth twist into a scowl of disdain for the land of the living. He'd been fighting it off since Sasha picked him up at the airport. "It's a good thing you made me get the car app, because seriously, I may have let myself starve to death. As it is, the groceries are going to keep me going for a good long time."

Sasha's eyes grew big and bright, and he took her hand and squeezed.

"Don't worry, sweetie. None of it is your fault. You would have let me stay at your place forever, and I was getting in your way. This is good. I'll hang out here, find a little peace, and when I go back to Orlando, I'll be up for getting my own apartment and getting out of your hair, okay?"

"I'd never kick you out, Pierce," she said miserably. "You know that." She wiped the back of her hand across her big brown eyes. "You just… you got out of the hospital and—"

"And I was an awful fucking bastard," he said with feeling. *Oh God.* The defining moment for calling up Derrick to take him up on his offer was when he'd heard his father's words coming out of his mouth, telling his sister she was useless because she couldn't help him off the couch without pain. "Sasha, you deserve better than me. You deserve better, period. I'm not going to hang around you and get in your way again until I'm decent company for human beings, okay?"

Sasha shook her head, still crying. "You were in pain," she whispered. "And you were sorry right after. And you've done so much for me, Pierce. I can forgive you for being mean once when you did so much for me...."

He remembered the night she'd shown up at his apartment, in tears, practically hysterical, because she'd told the parents about an impending Darius and had been read the riot act about what a fuckup she was.

He'd taken her in—let her stay with him for a couple of months until she and Marshall scraped up enough money for rent and a car. She'd gotten a job, and Pierce had paid her tuition as she made her way through school. She had a career now—one she could work from home as a developmental editor of a small press. Marshall had his degree in software engineering, and together they made a good living—good enough to afford a guest bedroom and to put Pierce up for a month after the accident.

Pierce squeezed her hand now. "You listen to me," he said gruffly. "You don't owe me a thing. You're the only family I want to see—pretty much ever. So just let me work shit out in my own head, and I'll come back for Christmas a whole new man, okay?"

"I like the one you are right now!" she said staunchly, and then she threw herself in his arms and held on tight. "Love you, big brother," she whispered, and Marshall stood behind her, guiding her away.

"Love you too," he said belatedly, and Marshall turned and shook his hand firmly.

"Come back when you promised, okay?" Marshall was just as slight as Sasha—two small, mild-mannered people getting along in a bright, brash world. Pierce had always fancied himself their champion knight—he couldn't be that as he was.

He had to make himself better.

"Christmas Eve," Pierce vowed. "Don't worry, Marshall. Nobody likes being alone on Christmas."

Marshall shrugged. "We wouldn't be alone, Pierce. We just don't want you to be."

With that, the guy Pierce and Sasha's parents had driven off their property with a baseball bat guided a disconsolate Sasha into the old vehicle and piloted it away.

As soon as they'd left the parking lot, Pierce allowed his shoulders to sag and dragged his sorry ass to the back door of the condo.

He crawled into bed and stayed there until he absolutely had to get up and pee the next morning.

STAYING IN bed for sixteen hours had consequences—he almost didn't make it to the bathroom, he was so sore. After he'd taken care of business and washed down a granola bar, he realized he was going to have to be serious about that pool thing, or he really could end up curling into a ball and dying in a beach condo in Florida.

For a moment he contemplated it—he'd always been the kind of guy to consider all the angles—but eventually he decided he wouldn't go quickly enough and managed a pair of board shorts and a T-shirt. As he walked through the tiled hall of the condo, he realized the tile was going to destroy his body almost as quickly as the inactivity, and made a mental note to buy some rubber mats at the very least, so he'd have some padding for his joints. Derrick had said to make himself at home— ergonomic home decorating was a go!

Just as soon as he got into the… ahhh… pool.

Heated, of course, and a perfect counterpoint to a cool day in the high fifties/low sixties. He'd set his phone on a lounge chair, playing something disgustingly upbeat and perky, and went about doing the exercises he and his physical therapist had worked on.

Actual physical motor activity really did have magical properties— it must have. He was working up a head of steam, the resistance and buoyancy of the water supporting his body as he used active stretching techniques, when a voice cut into his workout Zen.

"If you don't straighten your back, you'll be in a world of hurt!"

Crap. Whoever that was, he was right.

Pierce adjusted his form and then looked over his right shoulder, from whence the voice—deep and sharp and young—had issued.

"Thanks," he said briefly, taking in the sprawled form of what looked to be a teenager wearing board shorts, a leopard-print bathrobe, and giant aviator sunglasses, lounging in one of the chaises. Dark hair, faintly sun streaked, was cut almost Boy Scout short around an adorable frat boy face. His hands were sort of a mess, loosely wrapped in gauze, but other than that, he was as untouched as a virgin's dreams.

"Dude, what in the hell are you listening to? This shit." The boy shuddered. "I'm saying. I bet you could work up a sweat if you had decent music."

"It's a mix," Pierce said weakly, feeling old and slow. "I just hit an easy button, you kn—"

"I'll get you a better sound," the kid said, picking up the phone. "What's your password?"

Pierce gave it to him and then stopped dead in the water and almost drowned. He was in the deep end, and he had to work to stay afloat and—

"Don't spaz," the kid said on a note of deep disgust. "My phone's in the condo, and I could give a shit about your passwords. Jesus, if I was a hacker genius, I'd be someplace warm, you think?"

Pierce took a deep breath, and suddenly Katy Perry came blaring out of his phone. Well, okay, so everybody had heard this song; it did make him want to work harder. Pierce was calling it a win.

"Thanks," he said again, panting now because he was moving faster.

The kid shrugged. "Don't worry about it. You gonna be here tomorrow?"

"Yeah, but—"

"Same time?"

"Yeah." 'Cause why not. Nothing better to do, right? No job, no wife, no life?

"Good. I'll see you here with better music. Now stop doing that water walk thing and do a mountain climber—come on—I know you can."

Pierce glared at him—and switched the move.

"There you go. Now follow my pace. You can go faster." The kid started clapping, and Pierce struggled to keep up.

"I can't... do... that...," he gasped. He expected attitude back, because the kid had given him nothing but, and he was surprised when the clapping slowed.

"Sorry. You just look younger than this pace."

Pierce had his back to the kid, but he had the sensation of a thorough visual once-over. He adjusted to the new pace and found his wind again. "Car accident," he managed, trying not to be offended.

"Aw... aw hell. I'm sorry. I'm being an ass. I should just leave you to your workout."

"No," Pierce called out, stopping to tread water and cool down enough to talk. "Sorry—just… I was getting a workout. I suck doing this alone." He kept his arms and legs moving and found the kid on the side of the pool again—he'd moved from where Pierce had first spotted him to stand right in front of the line Pierce was using to go back and forth.

"Yeah, well, being alone sort of sucks on all fronts," the kid said philosophically. "I'll try not to be an ass if you try to do a hard workout, how's that?"

Pierce found himself nodding, even though he'd only come out to the pool out of what he deemed necessity. "Deal," he panted.

"Okay, now back to mountain climbers. I'll set the pace, and if it's too fast, cry uncle."

"Groovy," Pierce breathed, positioning himself to go. "Now shoot."

The kid put him through a decently difficult workout, adjusting for the things Pierce couldn't do yet and pushing him hard in the stuff he could. After forty-five minutes, Pierce was starting to cramp up, though, and the kid had him stretch out.

Good stuff, really—the blue freedom of the water, the structure of the workout, and the congeniality of dealing with another human being without bitterness or backstory served as sort of a purge—some of the self-pity Pierce had wallowed in for the past sixteen hours was rinsed away.

But not all of it.

He was getting out of the pool when the damage in his calf and thigh screamed protest, and he groaned and grabbed on to the rail. The kid was right there, though, stepping into the water regardless of his pricey flip-flops and the hem of his leopard-print bathrobe.

"Uh-oh—overdid it. C'mon, let me help you to the hot tub. I'll give you a rubdown, okay?"

"No," Pierce grunted, suddenly aware of this kid. Lean and narrow but defined practically by muscle group, his body was a work of art, and Pierce didn't even know if he was of age. And even if he was of age, he was too damned young for Pierce.

"No hot tub?" the kid asked sharply. "Or no gay guy touching you?"

Pierce's face heated. "No hot teenager touching me?" he mumbled, limping toward the steamy goodness of the little spa and trying not to lean too much into the kid's strong arms.

The youngster's throaty chuckle didn't reassure him in the least. "I'm twenty-three, old man, so cool your jets. Besides, I'm"—his voice dropped sadly, and the suddenly vulnerable look on his frat boy face made him look even younger—"well, I'd like to become a massage therapist, but I've only got half the coursework and hours done. Seriously, though, I'm halfway a professional, and I'm pretty good, so maybe let me work out the cramp in your leg?" He smiled winningly and used his free hand to lift his shades so he could bat a pair of admittedly limpid and arresting amber-brown eyes. "After all, I did work you over pretty hard."

Pierce rolled his eyes at the double entendre, but as he reached for the rail of the hot tub, he had to concede that having his leg worked on would make the whole working-out thing feel like less of a mistake.

"Yeah, sure," he muttered, taking the steps creakily one at a time. "Sure, you can squeeze my muscles till I scream."

The kid chuckled again, inviting Pierce in on the laugh. "So you're happy to let me rub one out on you?"

Pierce groaned. "God, kid, I can hardly walk. No sex jokes until I can make it out of the pool without collapsing."

"So there can be sex jokes. Eventually. I just want to make sure." Very gingerly the kid lowered Pierce until he was sitting. After he straightened, he scampered up the steps and pulled off his sodden robe, laying it out on the chaise to dry, and kicked off his ruined leather sandals.

"Oh geez." Pierce thought of the massacre of perfectly good shoes and robe and was attacked by his conscience, which he'd assumed was dormant or dead. "Kid, I'm sorry about the clothes—"

"Don't be." He shrugged. "They're my old man's, and since he kicked me out of the house for Christmas, he can pretty much kiss off his super classy robe and huaraches, you hear me?"

Pierce wasn't sure whether to chuckle or be horrified. "Just for Christmas?" he asked, making sure.

He lowered the sunglasses over his eyes again, probably to help him look insouciant when he was—in all likelihood—wounded. "Folks were having important political friends over. I'm a gay embarrassment, so I got the beach house. Last year they were in Europe, and I got the beach house with my boyfriend and we fucked like lemmings. No boyfriend this year."

"The lemmings are safe?" Pierce asked, sympathies reluctantly stirred. Parents who judged their kids for sexual activity? He knew those assholes! Pierce and Sasha had grown up with their very own set.

Kid laughed, sounding young and happy instead of casual and cynical. Pierce liked the sound. "Here, let me rub your leg down—I promised."

Pierce grunted. "Kid—"

"Hal—"

"Like the computer?"

Hal stared at him, unimpressed. "Oh dear, a *Space Odyssey* joke. I've never heard one of those, given that I've had this stupid name since birth. Now give me your leg."

Pierce complied, startled by the venom. "Well, I could call you 'Prince Hal,' like—"

"King Henry the Fifth? Like in the Branagh movie?"

Pierce racked his brains, trying to remember. "I thought Branagh just did *Hamlet*," he said, confused.

Hal gasped and wrapped his hands around Pierce's ankle. "Heathen! How could you not know about the Branagh King Henry? He was young and still faithful and downright adorable!"

As he spoke, Hal worked his capable, agile fingers up Pierce's leg—between that and the hot, bubbling water, Pierce's entire body was melting like chocolate in the sun.

"The faithful part is important to you?" Pierce asked, trying to keep his mind on the conversation and not just tilt his head back and drool. Maybe his doctor was missing out on something here. The rubdown in the tub after the physical activity felt like an exciting new way to make a battered body feel whole again.

"Mm-hmm… wow." Hal rubbed careful circles around the network of scars on Pierce's knee. "What did you do here?"

"Car accident," Pierce told him again.

"I know that—but here?"

"The door buckled in and ripped up my knee and thigh," Pierce admitted reluctantly. "My arm and shoulder too."

"You were driving," Hal assessed. "What happened?"

Oh, Pierce didn't want to talk about this. "One of those super big trucks ran a red light," he said shortly, and then Hal started rubbing circles at the place where his knee was stiffest. Not the part with the scars, curiously enough—it was like Hal had magic fingers.

"Bummer. Were you alone in the car?"

Ugh. This was what Pierce didn't want to talk about. "My soon-to-be ex-wife," he said, unable to control the loathing.

Hal seemed to hear it anyway—but didn't stop working Pierce's calf and knee. Belatedly, the intimacy of the situation hit Pierce, and he felt stupid. Another human being was touching him, giving him pleasure that was unsolicited by duty or money.

It had been so long.

Pierce closed his eyes and groaned, waiting for Hal to ask the inevitable question.

"Soon-to-be ex?"

It hadn't taken long.

"We were fighting when the truck hit us," Pierce remembered. "When I woke up, Cynthia was hovering over my hospital bed. She said 'Pierce, I forgive you.'"

Hal grunted, eyebrows knitting as he worked on a particularly tough knot.

"That sounds... well, sort of bitchy. What did you say back?"

"I said 'Cynthia, I want a divorce.'"

Hal cackled—and his hands moved up to Pierce's thigh, one hand holding the inner thigh and the other working on the outer.

A charge of heat zinged from Hal's knowing, awesome hands straight to Pierce's groin, and he wondered how embarrassed he'd be if he didn't call a halt to this divine exercise in physical therapy.

Pierce tilted his head back and shuddered and then grabbed Hal's hand—but not hard. "A little personal, a little fast," he said quietly.

Hal grinned, seemingly not put off at all.

"My crowd tends to be a little fast," he said, waggling his eyebrows. Then he winked. "That's okay—taking your time has its advantages too."

Pierce groaned comically and relaxed when Hal went back to his calf. "You don't even know if I'm open for business," he said, trying not to be an asshole. He'd barely gotten out of bed that morning.

"You didn't sock me in the nose. I'm calling it a win!"

Pierce felt sort of a reluctant admiration. "An optimist," he murmured. "Rare species, highly endangered. Usually found in small family groups of quiet suburb dwellers." Pierce remembered Sasha and what an asshole he'd been. Gently he pulled his leg out of Hal's grip.

"What's the matter?" Hal asked as Pierce gathered his noodle-y muscles and rose to pull himself out of the hot tub. "I thought we were getting along so well!"

"We were," Pierce said, hating himself. "But I'm sort of toxic to nice people, and kid, you're just... just really nice. I'm giving you a chance to save yourself some prick burns."

"Huh."

Oh God, the concrete was hard on his feet and joints. He started a slow, determined limp to his chaise, but he couldn't resist. That word was just sitting out there, begging for banter.

"Huh what?"

"No one has ever tried to save me from their inner prick before. Harold Justice Lombard the Fifth is intrigued."

Pierce stopped by a table, catching his balance on the back of one of the chairs. "Is that really your name? And you're an optimist? Holy God, kid, run far away from me—you're like a unicorn or something!"

Before he could even think about moving on, Hal had hopped out of the hot tub and was sprinting for Pierce's stuff. He came trotting back holding Pierce's towel, phone, and oh sweet baby jebus, his padded flip-flops.

"Here." Hal set the flip-flops down so Pierce could step into them and then handed over his cane. While Pierce was getting into his shoes—and finding his balance—Hal wrapped the towel around his shoulders.

"Thank you," Pierce said reluctantly. "That's kind."

Hal came around in front of him and pulled the ends of the towel together, making sure he was wrapped tight.

"Now, I'll see you tomorrow, okay? And don't worry about bringing music, because I'm going to fix you right up. I'll bring Backstreet Boys—that's your generation, right?"

"I'm only thirty-two!" Pierce complained, not sure when he'd agreed to a second workout.

Hal's cheerfully salacious grin told him all he needed to about what he had just inadvertently done. "Excellent. That's truly the best news I've heard all day. I'll bring something good—trust me."

This close, Pierce could see the wickedly sparkling brown eyes behind the sunglasses—and the sudden swallow and slightly parted lips that indicated Hal wasn't quite as bold and brave as he was pretending to be.

It was the vulnerability that did it.

"Sure," Pierce said softly. "I'll be here tomorrow at ten."

And that was enough, apparently, because Hal gave him a toothy grin, then moved to the side and bowed with an elegant gesture. "Then carry on, good sir. We shall see each other in the yon."

Oh geez. What a little hambone.

"Of course, Sir Knight," Pierce returned, resigned to his fate. "Be careful of your unicorn horn, okay? I'd hate to see it broken or bent or anything."

"Will do."

Pierce made better time with the cane and the shoes, and his limp away from the field of battle had a little more dignity this time.

But he was not free from the wonderful world of social interaction—not just yet.

As he approached the back of his condo, he watched an older woman struggle to get her little foldable pull cart full of groceries through the back gate that led to the individual courtyard that was a feature of all the lower-level condos. The gates were tricky—they all had a really strong spring—and Pierce had been forbidden from even trying to wrestle his luggage inside, which was why Sasha and Marshall had done it.

But the elderly woman, dressed flamboyantly in bright magenta and sky blue, didn't have a Sasha and a Marshall, and Pierce figured what the hell—how hard could it be to reach over and hold the gate open, right?

He reached out and pushed, and she hauled her dolly up over the concrete step and into the little patio.

"Thank you," she said shortly.

"Anytime," he told her, waiting patiently for her to clear the gate so he could lower his arm.

"You know, you shouldn't spend too much time with that Lombard kid—he's trouble."

Pierce was surprised enough to let the gate slip out of his fingers, and he scrambled to keep it from crashing into the grumpy old hag and her absurdly stocked shopping cart. Seriously—she had five boxes of protein bars. If she didn't have some laxatives stuffed in that thing, she'd be in a world of hurt.

"I'm sorry?" he asked, trying not to wince as he strained all the muscles he'd just loosened up in the hot tub.

"That Lombard kid. He's—" She looked both ways, like somebody could hear her. "—you know. G-a-y. And he's not quiet about it either! Last year he brought his"—she wrinkled her nose—"boyfriend to the condo, and they were holding hands and snuggling. Perfectly awful, if you ask me."

Ugh. "I didn't, you snotty bitch," Pierce snapped, letting the gate close on her cart.

"Well, I never!"

"You should," Pierce told her, hobbling away. "And while you're at it, buy some laxatives—you'll feel better. Jesus, lady, he's a sweet kid. You really gotta gossip about him like that?"

He had to admit, he got a great deal of satisfaction hearing her swear at her cart and the gate and Pierce all together as he made it through the gate of his own apartment. If he was going to let his inner asshole reach out and touch people, telling that woman off was the way to go.

Besides.

He walked into his condo and leaned back against the door, letting some of the outrage seep from his body.

That sweet kid. Seriously—what had he done to deserve that old biddy and her bitchery? Pierce felt a surge of protectiveness swelling his chest. Yeah, the kid might make more advances, but Pierce was a grown-up. He didn't have to give in. What mattered was Harold Justice Lombard the Fifth didn't have to spend his mornings alone.

Pierce couldn't do much. No job, no wife, no life, right?

But he could be a willing recipient of all that chirpy goodwill.

What could it hurt? Seriously. What could it possibly hurt?

SLIPPERY SLOPES

"I'M DYING!" Pierce complained under the R & B stylings of Jay-Z. For one thing, Jay-Z hadn't been his thing in high school, but for another? He was sure if he did one more underwater leap, his stomach muscles would explode.

"You are not dying!" Hal laughed. "You just can't think of anything better to do!"

"Ugh... if you were older than a minute—"

"I'd still be kicking your ass, old man. Now come on. Your injuries suck, I get it, but we want you to have mobility in a month!"

Pierce stopped dead and almost drowned, then resumed the exercise at a slightly saner pace. "What's a month have to do with it?" he panted, underwater leaping for all he was worth.

"Well, you said you were here until Christmas Eve. I figure you came here to be alone and grumpy and pissed at the world, and you have a month to get over yourself. Mobility will help."

Pierce scowled because that was incredibly astute—but he kept exercising so he might continue to breathe. "Where in the hell did you get that?" he demanded, surly as fuck. He'd shown up that morning all willing to accept Hal's revoltingly happy goodwill and had, instead, been told to suck it up, buttercup, he was going to get his ass beat into the pool.

He'd had no idea such a darling child could be such a sadistic drill sergeant.

"Nine upper division units in psychology. Duh!"

Pierce managed a look at Hal's face and saw the snarky smile that had charmed Pierce in the first place.

"To be a massage therapist?"

"Well, that's just this year," Hal informed him loftily. "I am a man of many ambitions."

"You are a young flake with no direction," Pierce deduced and then felt bad.

Hal shook it off like the proverbial duck. "Well, the massage-therapist thing seems to be sticking," he admitted. "I got the certificate online over the summer, and I've been getting my practice hours on the guys on the sports teams at school. And I'm a personal trainer and aqua instructor. I like knowing stuff that'll help me help people."

"Ah, so I'm a project." Well, it made sense. Pierce had never been a looker—long bony jaw, narrow green eyes, sand-brown hair. The accident injuries just made his tall, awkward body look gnarled and misshapen. "It all becomes clear."

He didn't expect Hal to glare at him. "Yeah, well, like anybody over thirty, you can't see for shit. Now tuck and boogie—no, don't bend your knees, keep them straight and kick from the hip!"

Oh ouch. "What in the hell—were you a Roman general in a past life?"

Hal's glare lightened up. "Those guys got play. You realize that, don't you?"

It took Pierce a couple of moves to realize he was talking about sex. "Yeah," he said, remembering something about that in college. "But only the gay or bi ones. No women for them."

Hal crouched down at the pool's edge and took off his sunglasses. "What about you?"

"I may have mentioned an ex-wife?" Pierce was embarrassed about that, actually. The whole divorce was embarrassing. In fact, so was the entire marriage.

"Yeah, but you never said anything about ex-boyfriends," Hal wheedled. "Enquiring minds want to know!"

Oh God. Pierce could just put him off. He *should* just put him off. Or lie. Or not give in to his flirting. But all of Pierce's energy right now was going into keeping up with this goddamned song!

"He was a sweet kid," Pierce muttered. "An optimist. I was too cranky for him. Take a lesson."

But of course that's not what Hal heard. "I knew it!" he crowed, standing up and hopping on the edge of the pool. "I knew you were bent!"

As in "not straight." Of course. "Only a little," Pierce panted. "To the left." He should have hated himself for adding to the play, but Hal chortled, and he couldn't. So easy to make this kid smile. How long since Pierce thought he was capable of doing that?

A sudden shift in music caught Pierce's attention. "Oh thank God," he muttered to take the conversation away from sex. "Beastie Boys."

"I thought you said you were only thirty-two!" Hal protested, and Pierce would have rolled his eyes, but he might have gotten them wet.

"Beastie Boys are forever!" he proclaimed, and continued to work his ass off to the soul-sweetening strains of "Sabotage."

And then, to make life extra special, Hal gave him Coldplay for the cooldown.

It was like the kid cared.

Of course, Pierce should have known the grilling wouldn't just stop there. He'd hoped, but Hal had proved nothing if not relentless.

"So," he said slyly while working Pierce's leg over in the hot tub. "Bent?"

Pierce grunted. "College-try bi," he said flippantly, and Hal rewarded him with a thumb right in the middle of his arch. "Augh! Okay! Okay!" Hal fixed the cramp with his palm, and after a few moments, Pierce took a deep breath and closed his eyes. "Loren. Loren Simpson. We met in our senior year, and we were both between girlfriends, and…." And… he could picture Loren's face—blue eyes, earnestness, the fever flush that came over him when he came. "He was sweet," Pierce said simply. "For a little while, it was true love."

"Why'd it end?" Hal asked, his hands almost too gentle on Pierce's calf to do any good.

"He was premed. I was engineering." Pierce still remembered that day—the day they'd realized it wouldn't work out. The ache in his chest that hadn't quit for a month, the way Loren had kept wiping his eyes with the back of his hand.

The transported, almost ethereal expression on Loren's face as he came inside Pierce for the last time.

"So you broke up?" Hal sounded indignant, and Pierce opened his eyes and regarded his young friend with a sadness he couldn't shake.

"It was the grown-up decision," he said, and it sounded like a cop-out now, when it hadn't back in school. "I had a job offer already from Hewlett-Packard, Loren had been accepted to Stanford. His parents would have cut off his support if he'd come out—"

"What about yours?" Hal asked perceptively.

Pierce wanted to shrug, but he couldn't. "Oh, mine would have—most definitely. But I didn't really care about mine. They were assholes.

I cut off contact with them about a year later anyway. But Loren... it meant a lot to him. All of it. Med school, Stanford, Mom and Dad. I couldn't... you know."

Hal shook his head, looking angry. "You didn't fight for him?" he asked, sounding forlorn.

"Oh, kid. Is that what happened to you?"

Hal turned away, his hands completely still.

"We made a decision together. He didn't want me to fight for him. He told me himself." Pierce remembered how hard he'd fought that. The part of him that died when he resigned himself to the breakup. "But I wasn't happy about it," he admitted.

Hal had perched his sunglasses on the top of his head when they'd gotten into the hot tub, and now he lowered them again before turning back to look at Pierce. No doubt his eyes were red-rimmed.

"So, you would have fought for him," Hal said, like this mattered to him a great deal.

It was on the tip of his tongue to say "No, eventually we all give up." He hated to disillusion the kid. But he couldn't forget Sasha, showing up at his apartment a year after school, saying she was pregnant. Pierce had fought for her, hadn't he? Yeah, he'd apparently become a real festering cold sore since, but once, just once in his life, he'd fought for someone, and he'd made a difference.

"Yeah," he said, because here, under the gray haze of late November in Florida, he could remember wanting to fight. The need to be with someone he truly cared about had boiled in his blood then, no matter how thin that blood was now.

"Good," Hal said, nodding. Then he went back to Pierce's feet, but by now the nerves were too raw. Pierce pulled away.

"Sorry—my feet are about done."

"The tile floors, right?" Hal nodded like it was a foregone conclusion. "They're great because you can sweep all the sand out when you walk on the beach, but they're hell on your body."

Pierce grunted. Just getting out of bed hurt.

"Tell you what." Hal grinned perkily. "Tomorrow we'll do a light workout, mostly stretching, then we can go buy mats."

Duh. "Like rubber mats?" Hey, that had been his idea too!

"Oh yeah—the kind they have at the gym should do. You can cut them to size—they'll make walking on those floors so much easier, trust me." His melancholia over Pierce's apparent failure to believe in true love had melted, and damn. The kid was offering to do him a solid.

"Sure," Pierce said, because otherwise tomorrow was doing a whole lot of what he'd done over the last two days. "Maybe I can get a chair too." Derrick had a small work desk in the living room, but he apparently used a kitchen chair to work there. Pierce had taken one look at that setup and known it would break his fragile, healing body. "I can start... I don't know. Looking up jobs or something."

"Here in Florida?" Hal asked, sounding eager.

"Naw." Pierce shrugged. "I've got a house in Sacramento. It's small, but I got to keep it and most of the furniture after the divorce." He smiled a little, remembering the den that he got to outfit all on his own. "The bedroom is fucking pink, but the den is nice. All hardwood and paneling. A work desk and a big gaming TV." His smile faded. It was the first time he'd thought happily of home since he'd awakened in the hospital. Sasha had come out when he'd called her, after Cynthia had stormed out of his room, and she'd met him at discharge with enough pain pills to get him on the plane, along with all the luggage she could pack.

God bless his sister. He'd paid her back so poorly.

"Oh." Hal's shoulders sagged. Then he perked up. "I've never been to California. Maybe I could visit."

That suddenly, Pierce needed to know about Hal for a change. "Where do your parents live?" he asked, thinking the kid seemed to need to get away a lot.

"North Carolina," Hal muttered, like the state name was a dirty word. Well, when you were young and gay, maybe it was right now. "My father's a judge."

Yikes.

"A conservative judge?" Pierce asked, just to make sure.

"Is there any other kind?"

"I had a liberal judge let me off a traffic ticket once," Pierce told him, just to ease some of the bitterness.

Hal grinned at him. "In California?"

"Yeah. In California." Pierce winked and then sighed. "Well, the heat has effectively sucked all the energy from my bones, and it's time for me to go take my nap."

"Oh God—I'm sorry. Here—let me help you out."

Pierce didn't refuse his help per se, just tried to do most of the work himself. He leaned heavily on the rail and took solid, shuffling steps on his own, trying to get to the table. Finally Hal huffed in exasperation.

"I'm stronger than I look, okay? Just lean on me a little. Jesus, what could happen?"

"I could put too much weight on you, you could overbalance, I could land wrong and call you a horrible name that I'll regret for the rest of my life," Pierce snarled. "You seem to like me a little—at the moment, it's the only win I've got."

Oh dammit dammit dammit—way to go and injure the frickin' unicorn, Pierce!

But his unicorn wasn't looking cowed or wounded or any of the things Sasha had.

"Well, it's not much of a win if you don't trust me to hold some of your weight. Now come on—here!" Hal tucked his hand under Pierce's elbow, and Pierce had no choice. He leaned. Together they made it to the table, where his cane sat accusingly, as did the sandals that would protect his feet from the deck.

Hal helped him balance as he slid his feet into the flip-flops. "I really did put you through your paces," he said grudgingly. "You did it all like a champ, but you should carb up a little when you get back to your condo. What're you going to have for lunch?"

Pierce thought about the groceries Sasha and Marshall had brought over. "Can of soup and some crackers," he announced, because hey—he had enough of that stuff to last him for four more days if he ate it day and night, like he had been.

"Not good enough," Hal said grimly, handing him his cane and then wrapping his towel over his shoulders. "Lead me to your condo, oh emaciated one—let me see your stores."

Oh... hell no. No. "I know you have something better to do," Pierce told him, hating feeling this vulnerable.

Hal appeared to think about it. "Hm… meeting world leaders for lunch, solving hunger for dinner, penning my novel before I go to bed… but right the hell now, I really only have to go see if my neighbor has anything to eat before he starves himself to death because he's a stubborn asshole!"

"I have food," Pierce muttered. "You don't need to worry about me."

"Oh, but I do." Hal took off his sunglasses with his free hand and batted his eyelashes. They stood close enough that Pierce could see the true, remarkable gold-brown of his eyes.

His throat went dry. "I'd rather not be an object of pity," he said, knowing he couldn't be more pathetic if he tried.

"Then let me feed you so I don't feel sorry for you," Hal said sweetly, but he was standing very still and staring at Pierce soberly.

Pierce nodded just to break the moment—them, frozen, staring at each other. But nothing could erase the heat of Hal's skin as he continued to escort Pierce down the sidewalk.

"Nobody uses the pool," Pierce mumbled, realizing this was their second day alone.

"Later," Hal told him, surprisingly. "A few people come out to sun themselves later. But it's not prime condo season right now."

Pierce grunted and continued his trek. "The holidays."

"Yeah."

The word had the ring of loneliness in it, and Pierce looked at him in question. But this time it was Hal's turn to be looking away.

"You, uh… spending the holidays here—that wasn't your idea, was it?"

He shrugged. "Told you—too gay to be an asset."

"Is that, uh, just for the holidays, or is that for the rest of the year?"

Hal grimaced. "Let's just say that next semester, I am enrolled in fifteen credits of poli sci at UNC and leave it at that."

It was like watching the pictures on a slot machine whir and click… wanted to be a masseur or a fitness trainer—cherry. Too gay for the holidays—cherry. Twenty-three and not done with school—cherry and jackpot!

"If you don't do what they want you to do, they'll cut you off," Pierce muttered. "Charming."

"Whatever. I told them I'd come here and think about it."

Pierce remembered Hal's outfit on the first day and felt a chill in his stomach. "Don't you mean drink about it?" he asked kindly.

"Yeah, well, that. Except…." Hal kicked at a piece of gravel as they neared the gate of the condo.

"What?" Because now Pierce was curious.

"I hate getting drunk. Seriously. I like training and helping people and shit. You can't do that if you're going to destroy your body. So I bought, like, all this fucking vodka, and after the first three greyhounds, I trashed the place. I fell asleep. I woke up and decided to take a swim and… well, you were already here."

"Trashed the place? Do you need to clean up?"

"When I'm not so mad, I'll do it again, sure. But I'm not drinking any more vodka after that."

Pierce stepped forward to undo the lock on the gate and laughed. "Well, lucky for us both. You don't like to get drunk, and I'm not happy about drowning. It was kismet."

Hal pushed through the gate and held it while Pierce limped by. "You don't agree with my dad? That I should get my ass in gear and pick something?"

Pierce thought about it as he led the way through the back hallway, past the laundry room, the bedroom, and into the kitchen that opened up to the living room. He paused there—he always did—because the back door looked over a brace of rushes and off to the sea. While the sea in Florida was a little tamer than the sea in California, that didn't mean he couldn't appreciate having it right there at his window. Of course, he hadn't this trip—because pain and bitterness and general assholery, but that didn't mean he couldn't start *now*.

"No," he said, almost absently, pondering that view. He snapped to and answered with more conviction. "I think that whole 'your kid has to do what you tell them, even as an adult' idea is sort of… bullshit," he said. "I mean, you support them, sure. Hold them accountable. But you're obviously not partying the fuck out of UNC. How many units do you have?"

Hal grunted. "Well, if I had them in the right classes, I'd have a master's by now."

Pierce laughed and settled down onto one of the stools that sat at the counter. "I… I always wanted more time to think about it," he said, remembering. "I mean, I took a film theory class and some history classes and thought 'Hey! I'd like to do something with this!' But I was tired of eating soup and crackers five nights a week and driving a car that was writing its last will and testament. I mean, if I could have gone to school for another three years, I totally would have."

Hal's smile still had an edge of unhappiness to it, but Pierce didn't know what to tell him. "Here—let me see what's for lunch," he said. He began poking around the pantry and the cupboards, clucking when he came up with english muffins and lunch meat. "You were going to have tinned soup? Here, let me make you a sandwich. You even have a tomato and pickles. And butter! Geez."

Pierce stood up and tried not to groan theatrically. "Hal.... Hal... bubby... the reason I was going for canned soup was that I didn't feel like making anything. I can't ask you to—"

"I'll make myself one too," Hal said mildly. "Now sit there and talk to me about something stupid."

"Something stupid?"

"Yeah." Hal looked up from his food preparation, and Pierce realized he wasn't kidding, even a little. "Something that doesn't hurt."

Oh. Well, at least Pierce wasn't the only one not comfortable with all the soul baring they'd done in the last two days.

Pierce bit his lip, trying to remember something, anything, whimsical that he could talk about. All he had in his arsenal was stuff from when he was a kid.

"So," he said, feeling foolish, "have I talked to you about my deep and abiding love for the old Looney Tunes cartoons?"

Hal shot him a look of such naked hope, he felt like an absolute hero for even thinking about it. "Bugs Bunny or Daffy Duck?" he asked.

"Wabbit season, naturally."

Hal's smile turned wicked. "Duck season," he returned.

"Wabbit season."

"Duck season."

"Duck season!" Pierce remembered this game.

"Bang," Hal told him with a smile. Derrick had a widescreen TV on the far wall, and Hal gestured with his chin. "I bet you could find some of that on a premium channel. Go, sit—I'll bring you food, you eat and fall asleep."

"I'm not—" Pierce yawned. "Dammit!"

"Yeah, well, I really did work you hard." Hal bit his lip in an expression that was starting to look more and more vulnerable. "Thanks for letting me. Like I said, tomorrow we'll do something lighter, and we can go shopping."

"That's sounds...." Oh wait. Shopping. And it was getting close to Christmas! "Hey—can we get more than rubber mats and a chair?"

Hal crossed his expressive brown eyes. "No, then I'll have to dump your ass at the store. Why, what did you have in mind?"

"Well, you know. Christmas is coming. I'd like to sort of spoil my sister's family a little. She's got kids. They're not bad. Maybe get her an espresso machine or something. She and her husband power up with Mr. Coffee—it's horrible."

"So, rubber mats, Legos, Barbies, and a Keurig? It's a good thing I've got a CR-V—if I'd gone for the Tesla I'd wanted, you'd be fucked."

Pierce blushed, feeling exploitive. "I'm sorry—you know, we don't have to do that. I can order their stuff from here—it'll even show up gift-wrapped—"

"No," Hal said, like he was surprised the idea pleased him too. "Don't do that. I mean, even if we don't get to everything tomorrow, it will... it will give us a quest." His full and beaming smile emerged, the one that made Pierce think he was an invincible unicorn. "Even if we are thwarted in our first sally, Sir Knight, we shall continue to assail the indomitable fortress of consumerism until we have achieved... uh, gift-tasticness?"

Pierce shrugged. "Or redemption. You know, either-or?"

"Redemption?" Pierce could practically see Hal's antennae rise up. "For what?"

Pierce stood and managed the trek across the tile to the coffee table. He didn't want to talk about it—not today, when they'd discovered some neutral ground.

"I thought we were watching cartoons," he said gently.

"Yeah." Hal swallowed, and his smile dimmed. "You're right. Cartoons—we need to figure out which season it is."

Pierce made himself comfortable and welcomed the sandwich and glass of milk when Hal walked it over. They watched cartoons for the next hour, laughing like children at the basic slapstick humor. As Pierce dozed off, slumping sideways onto the pillows of the couch, he couldn't remember the last time he'd felt that young.

He woke up to late-afternoon shadows, cuddled under a throw in a chilly, empty apartment. The sound of the sea washed hypnotically through his bones like it did every minute of every day here. A note sat on the marble coffee table in front of him.

Thanks for the company—I'll give you a Hal break tonight, but see you bright and early tomorrow.

—H

Pierce sat up, feeling unexpectedly refreshed, and pondered the note.

A Hal break? Who said he needed a break from Hal? He was starting to sort of like Hal. Why would he want a break?

He shivered and stood up, dislodging the chenille throw as he went to turn on the lights in the living room. He stared at the thing, trying to place where it had come from, and then he realized—

Derrick kept his spare blankets in the linen closet between the bathroom and the bedroom. Hal had needed to go looking for that. He'd done it on purpose, to make sure Pierce was comfortable, after he'd made Pierce a meal and entertained him.

Pierce couldn't stop looking at the throw as it lay crumpled on the floor.

What season was it?

It was denial season.

HE GOT up eventually and made himself a can of soup and then settled back down in front of the television, remote in hand. His phone buzzed, the sound so alien of late that he barely recognized it before he remembered to pick up.

"Derrick?"

"Are you dead?"

"Oh God. No." Pierce sat up from his sprawl and stretched carefully. "I'm sorry—I got here two days ago. I should have called."

"Yeah, well, I was in a turkey coma until yesterday, so you're doing okay. How are you?"

Pierce grunted. "Better," he confessed. Derrick knew why he'd come here—had been the one to calm him down after Pierce had blown up at Sasha. Derrick had told him then that it wasn't unforgivable, but Pierce—he still felt the shame down in his gut.

"As in no longer suicidal?" Derrick asked sharply.

Pierce flushed. "I wasn't that bad," he mumbled. "It was just… I was an asshole. I didn't want to expose her to me being an asshole to her in her own house. Wasn't her fault. How's Miranda?"

Derrick's wife, bless her, should have divorced Pierce's best friend a long time ago, because she was way too damned good for him. "She's fine. Or she will be when she recovers from the humiliation. Apparently she forgot to put enough sugar in one of the damned pies. Her family won't let her live it down. If one more jackass calls me with an offer to bring over a cup of sugar, I'm gonna go fuckin' ballistic."

Pierce grimaced. "Ouch. Family."

"What a fuckin' bag of dicks."

Pierce had to laugh. "Yeah, well, witness."

"Shut up. You and Sasha give me hope. None of these assholes would have let a thing like that slow them down."

Well, there was a reason Derrick was his best friend. That and—

"How's work?" Pierce asked before he could stop himself.

Derrick cackled. "Missing the hell out of you, that's for sure. Speaking of assholes…." Well, layoffs had been coming, and Pierce had the bad luck to crash his truck about a week before they arrived. He'd been pretty sure he hadn't been on the list before he'd been taken out of commission, but who could prove what?

Pierce gusted out a breath. "Yeah, well, sadly it's mutual." He'd liked his job designing graphics chips for video game players—he and his team, Derrick included, had worked really well together.

"Well, I know you're doing okay for money," Derrick said frankly, because he'd gotten a year's worth of severance at the layoff—and both Pierce and the guy who'd hit him had good insurance that had paid out. "But I also know you, and that's the whole reason I called."

"Besides making sure I wasn't dead," Pierce said dryly.

"Well, that too. Anyway—there's a smaller company out here putting out feelers. Young, hot, fresh—willing to blow you if you promise to come, that sort of thing. Anyway, I gave them your card. They're going to be emailing you in a couple of days. Try not to fuck this up."

Pierce gasped, suddenly almost tearful. "A job? You got me a job?"

"No, I dropped your name. Don't be dramatic. And I told them you wouldn't be back until March of next year too, so don't blow the first vacation you've had in years."

Pierce gave a rusty laugh. "I'm still rehabilitating," he reminded his friend. "No promises I'll be 100 percent ever, you know that."

"Can you walk?" Derrick demanded. "Can you use a computer?"

"Yes and yes," Pierce told him promptly, thinking about the range of motion he could feel in his legs after two days of decent aqua therapy.

"Then the rest is improvement. Anyway—you'll have time."

"I will." Pierce felt his throat get thick again. "Thank you. Just, seriously, thank you. That's... that's awesome."

"Just tell me you aren't rotting at my beach condo eating canned soup and trying to die alone."

"No." Pierce felt the corners of his mouth turn up without meaning to make that happen. "In fact, I think I made a friend."

"Hm... promising." Derrick was sort of a midsize man with a thatch of blond hair and a goatee, and Pierce could picture him stroking his goatee. "Would this be a friend with tits that you can sleep with?"

Pierce grunted. "Doesn't need breasts—you know that."

Derrick grunted back. "I forget. I'm a straight white male who tries not to have entitlement issues—pity me."

Oh God. Derrick and Miranda probably gave 10 percent of their income to liberal causes. "I refuse to pity you now that I've been repressed," Pierce told him grandly. "But seriously, a friend. That's all I could ask for, and I'm calling it a win."

"But is it a cute friend? That's all I'm asking," Derrick needled, and Pierce gave in.

"He's really sort of adorable."

Derrick's cackle was all he ever wanted in a buddy. "Excellent! I see good things in your future, my man. I shall leave you alone so I can go impregnate my wife!"

Pierce blinked. "Was that, uh, something you'd planned on doing?"

And suddenly the joking fell away. "We're hoping," his friend confessed. "Are you happy for us?"

"Only if I'm invited to the birth." Pierce waited a moment to see if he'd gone too far, but Derrick's howl of mock outrage reassured him.

"Oh, you dickhead! I love you so! Yes, I'll tell Miranda right now that's a priority!"

Pierce's laugh surprised him—two days ago he would have said it was beyond him.

What a difference a Hal made.

"Don't tell her that or you'll never conceive. Now go! Be nice to your wife." His voice dropped. "And good luck, man. You guys... you're the best."

"So are you. Come back to us, 'kay? If I take Miranda to one more Kings' game, she'll divorce me."

"Understood."

Derrick hung up, and Pierce was left in the empty condo again. But his laughter still rang on the cold tile, and Pierce could hear Hal's reaction to the conversation he'd just had.

Hey, Hal—I have friends! We're actually funny together!

He suddenly wanted his young friend to see him when he wasn't angry and bitter.

He wanted Hal to know he could be fun too, and not just when Looney Tunes was on.

PUBLIC WORKS

"HEY, HAL—WHO'S that?"

Hal looked up from the rack of jeans he was perusing—in Pierce's size—and glanced in the same direction Pierce was. "I have no idea."

The kid—um, young man—Hal's age sported a brownish man bun and a scarf around his white T-shirted neck and had been cruising Hal with raised eyebrows and a predatory gleam since they'd arrived at the outlet mall. Now as Hal looked over his shoulder, the guy winked and smiled coquettishly.

Hal rolled his eyes and turned back to Pierce. "Now see, if we weren't in Tommy Hilfiger, he wouldn't have seen us, and I wouldn't have to scrape him like a barnacle. So you need to just concede to the inevitable and let me buy you pants that don't look like dad jeans."

Pierce let out a little whine. "I thought we'd be at Target or something—at least for the rubber mats and the office chair."

Hal looked at him unhappily. "Crap. Would you believe I forgot that's why we came? I was just so damned excited to go somewhere with you."

Oh no. Pierce grimaced. "Look, I don't want to piss on your parade, but—"

"But you don't want to waste time doing something not practical. I get it." Hal snapped his sunglasses on over his eyes and turned toward the exit, self-recrimination etched in every line of his body.

"No!" Pierce laughed, wondering where that wound had come from. "Not at all. I'm actually having a really good time, even if you apparently think I look like hell."

"Really?" Hal turned back and slid the sunglasses up to the top of his head again. "Then what is it?"

Pierce shrugged, embarrassed. Hal had kept his promise about giving him a light stretching workout that morning—Pierce had felt invigorated as he'd clumped to the condo, showered, and put on a pair of jeans and a Hawaiian shirt—by far the dressiest things he owned. Hal's good-natured ribbing about the dad jeans had prompted Pierce to offer to buy some more clothes—and then Hal had offered to buy them for him.

They'd had fun until just this minute. "I… I've got maybe two stores in me," he said apologetically. "If one of them is here and the other one is Target, I'm going to have to get a Lyft into town to go Christmas shopping." *Ugh.* "Sorry—I'm just trying to get as much as possible out of my freeloading here."

Hal smacked his forehead. "Doh! Okay—good. I mean, not good that I totally forgot your agenda like a punk, but good that you made that clear. Gotcha. Tell you what. Let's get you some clothes—because… dude."

"Understood," Pierce said dryly. Cynthia hadn't liked the way he'd dressed either—but then, she hadn't made him laugh when they'd gone shopping. If she'd tried to make it fun, even a little, talking about movie stars with consummate bitchery or joking about how a yellow shirt would make him look like Tweety Bird, Pierce might have stepped up his game.

"Then we'll go out to lunch—they've got the best café here. I'm dying to take you. Afterward we'll go to Target. I know where the rubber matting is—I bought a shit-ton for my place a couple of years ago, and you can find the office chair of your dreams. Then, you work out heavy for the next two days, and we try this again after that?"

Pierce smiled, flattered. "You wouldn't mind taking me back? I'm, uh"—he gestured to the whole store—"I'm sort of a clod, you know."

Hal winked. "Yeah, but you're willing to be trained up. That's my favorite sort of clod. And seriously, I'm having fun. Just let me know if your leg or your hip gets too stiff. I'll go look for stuff and bring it to you in the dressing room, okay?"

"That's… that's really nice." Suddenly Pierce wanted to cry. "You're really good at this planning stuff, you know? Babying my weak ass? It's… it's nice, that's all."

Oh! He'd never seen such preening. But since Hal was preening as he held up decent-looking shirts in his size, Pierce was going to call it a win.

He tried on two pairs of jeans and three shirts, awkwardly taking things on and off in the cramped dressing room while his semi-abused body ached. He held out the one pair of jeans that fit and said, "I'll get these, okay?"

"What about the shirts?" Hal asked, taking the jeans and scrupulously not looking at Pierce's bare and scarred body in the cubicle.

"Well, the blue one fits and looks pretty good, the red one is too tight, and the yellow one…. Tweety Bird and me should not be friends."

"Gotcha. I'll go get these—"

"No, no." Pierce waved him off. "No—this was a good idea, and it was fun, and I'm the one getting the clothes. I'll get them."

Hal *hmm*ed noncommittally. "Just get dressed," he said mildly. "I'll meet you at checkout."

Pierce met him at the cash stand, where Hal presented him with the bag of already purchased items—plus another pair of jeans and three shirts in the same size.

And a belt.

"Aw, man!" Pierce said, looking through the bag's contents. "That's not—"

"It was my choice," Hal said, only the faintest bit of rebellion in his tone. "Here—let me carry the bag. We can go eat at the spicy seafood place, and you can promise that next time we go out, you'll look less like a suburban dad and more like a hot guy in his thirties."

Pierce wrapped both mental hands around his misanthropy and asked patiently, "Why? Why is it so important to you that I don't look like a suburban dad?"

Hal scowled—and the look was surprisingly effective on him. "'Cause that guy scoping me out was shady, that's why. For all he knows, we're on a date, and I don't like anyone throwing shade on you."

"You did see him!" He knew it!

"Well, yeah. But it's rude. People used to do that to Russ and me all the time."

"Try to poach you from your boyfriend?" Pierce was lost.

"No. Try to poach Russ. He's sort of a model, and he's really frickin' beautiful. And he used to laugh it off, like it was no big deal. And then…." He shook his head. "Here. The spicy fried fish is to die for. I'd do that."

Pierce was just grateful to hobble through the outdoor mall into the bar-style restaurant and sit down. Lord, it was sixty degrees outside, but the humidity and the glare of the sun made it feel about eighty. He really hated the trickle of sweat that crept from his neck to between his shoulder blades to disappear under the waistband of his jeans and haunt the crack of his ass.

A perky waitress with thick blonde hair in twin french braids seated them and took their drink orders, leaving Pierce to look around, grateful they'd arrived in the afternoon lull.

"Mm…," he said, closing his eyes and turning his face toward the fan. "Air conditioning."

Hal laughed, some of his earlier bitterness fading away. "You Californians—you're easy to please," he said, and Pierce waggled his eyebrows.

"Yup. You have no idea."

"Maybe someday." Hal winked and looked at the menu. "So, the spicy fried fish—"

"They've got a fish and chips plate with it?"

"Yup—right there. It's big enough for two if you want to split it."

Oh perfect. "You read my mind."

They set their menus down, and Pierce wondered whether or not to break their little bubble by asking the hard question.

Then Hal said, "Yes, he cheated on me. A lot. And the thing is, I believed him when he said it wasn't personal. He just got… lured. I mean, it was his fault, but he was like a dog chasing a cat and running into the street. Just never saw the bad thing coming, not even when it was fucking him, you know?"

Ouch. "I'm sorry." Pierce meant it with all his heart.

Hal shrugged and fiddled with his water glass. "You didn't do it. You wouldn't do it, either, would you." The surety in his voice was flattering, and for once Pierce didn't have to worry about disillusioning him.

"Nope. Cynthia and I did not have that problem." Odd how it had never occurred to him, not even when things were really bad.

"Then what was the problem?" Hal asked.

The waitress arrived with their iced teas—Hal's sweetened, Pierce's unsweetened with lemonade added—and they gave their orders. Hal added an order of fried calamari because he said it was really wonderful and not on the platter, and then she left and they were alone.

With that question hanging between them.

For a breath, a heartbeat, Pierce thought about refuting the question. Claiming it was too personal. Asking to talk about something stupid.

All he had to do was say "Wabbit season," and this convo never had to happen.

But Hal had bought him clothes. Not because he didn't think Pierce was presentable, really, but to defend his honor.

What an absurdly sweet thing to do.

Pierce would have rather paid for the clothes—especially since Derrick's contact had gotten back to him that morning and practically slobbered all over the cyberwaves at his expertise. He had a settlement from the insurance company, a settlement from the old job—and a new job in the works.

He could have bought his own goddamned clothes.

But Hal apparently had money of his own. What he wanted—what he really wanted—seemed to be friendship.

And that came with telling embarrassing stories about where you decided to draw the line.

"She was judgy as fuck," Pierce said boldly.

"So that's a deal breaker?" Hal asked, cringing. No doubt he was thinking about his earlier celebrity bitchery, but that wasn't what Pierce was talking about.

"You know how you said your ex didn't mean it personally? About cheating?"

Hal nodded, looking troubled. "Yeah. I mean, he meant it every time he said it was the last. I sort of felt bad for him in the end, but I couldn't do it anymore."

"See—she would never have forgiven like that. I mean, you broke up with him, and good for you—but she wouldn't have been okay with it inside. She would have told her mom and her sister and her entire extended family, talking about the cheating again and again and again, and how awful it was and what a horrible human being the cheater was, and then she would have pulled out a Bible verse or quoted some prominent writer or politician and… and never, not once, would there have been an acknowledgment, I guess, that the guy was human. Not once."

"But you didn't cheat," Hal said, confused. "So why is this a deal?"

"Because it wasn't just cheating!" Pierce burst out. "It was…." *Oh hell.* "See, my sister, who is the sweetest woman in the world and lives with her equally sweet husband and two adorable kids—she got pregnant at eighteen. And it wasn't easy. I mean, Sasha and I both stopped talking to our parents about it because, dude! They were horrible to her. And I'd just gotten my job at Hewlett-Packard, and I supported her while Marshall worked on getting them an apartment, and we tried to get them cars that worked. She could have gone home, I guess, but they were just hell-bent on making her 'pay.' Like having to deal with a kid while you're getting through college isn't payment enough?"

"Yeah, that'd be rough," Hal said, nodding. "And she had another one?"

Pierce shrugged. "You know, they were married by then and had jobs, but even if they didn't—whose business is it to say it's a bad thing? It's like you and your parents. Why should they get to tell you that you're too gay for Christmas? I think that's horrible. And Cynthia— she just didn't let it go. So I'm talking to Sasha over the computer, and I say something about a business trip I might have to take to Korea, and Sasha... she's never been out of the country, right? She gets really wistful, like, 'Oh yeah, I'd love to do that,' and Cynthia—who is just walking around behind me, putting away laundry—goes, 'Well, you shouldn't have gotten knocked up!'"

"Oh ouch!" Hal stared at him with wide horrified eyes. "What. A. Twat."

"Right?" Oh, Pierce had been wrong. This wasn't something that needed to be hidden. This was something he needed to get off his chest! "And I managed to get off the call with Sasha, but Cynthia and I— well, we fought for the next two days. We fought over dinner, and we fought while we showered. And all I was saying was, judging people is a really shitty way to go through life. And all she kept repeating was that if people didn't want to be judged, they shouldn't fuck up."

Hal cringed again, and Pierce felt a surge of affection for him that had not a thing to do with his warm brown eyes and lush pink mouth or the new clothes leaning against Pierce's calf as he sat. "I'm not wrong, am I?"

"Not from my view," Hal said sincerely. "But—and I'm not being judgy—"

Pierce smiled, appreciating him.

"—but this didn't occur to you before you got married?"

Pierce blew out a breath. "She was my first relationship after Loren," he said simply. "And I was so damned lonely. And she... she could be really kind. I just never saw the strings attached until it was too late."

"Was that the only reason?" Hal asked after a pause. "Because divorcing someone for just one flaw, that seems sort of…."

"Judgy?" Pierce finished, then grew thoughtful. "There was more. There was… I guess there was just this sort of… I want to say superficiality, but that's not the word. Like I said—she could be kind. Her best friend in the world was a big girl—plain and shy—but whenever she came over, I watched Cynthia just light up, and I could tell that when she looked at Wendy, she was seeing an angel from heaven, you know? So she had depth, and she was capable of really nice moments. But it was like she needed a list—she needed someone to tell her what was right and what was wrong, and if she had permission to think it was wrong, boy, did she do that shit up right, you know?"

Hal nodded, looking thoughtful. "I do." He flashed a smile. "Father's a judge, right?"

"Yeah. It was that kind of thing too. The law was the law was the law—but there was no… no understanding that the law could be changed. It's like…."

Pierce searched hard for a simile—it was just such a hard idea to pinpoint.

"Like, when I was in high school, my best friend, Derrick—the guy whose condo I'm currently freeloading in—his older sister got pregnant right when her husband was deployed."

Hal grimaced. "Is it just me, or do you know a lot of pregnant women?"

"That kid just turned sixteen, give me a break. Anyway—Derrick's sister called the school and begged him to take her to the doctor when she went into labor, but he didn't have a car, and I did. So we left school—just left. I didn't call my folks, he didn't call his, 'cause we were kids and hey, lady with a baby."

"Well, yeah." Hal took a pull of his iced tea. "They scare me too."

"They're not so bad—seriously. Derrick and his wife want to have kids. I'm rooting for them. I'll get to play with kids that I don't have to take home with me. It'll be brilliant."

"But about leaving school at seventeen?" Hal was good at keeping up with him.

"We got her to the hospital, and we were even in the room with her until their parents got there. And the next day we go back to school, feeling like heroes, and—"

"You got detention for ditching out on school."

Pierce stared at him. "For two weeks. How did you guess?"

"Because. It was a story about rules and why some of them are stupid. And I got it. I mean... I get it. It's a good analogy." Hal was gazing at him now with a sort of softness in his eyes.

Pierce's face heated. "Sorry. Just... haven't been out with a friend in a while. I... I was talking too much."

"No," Hal said. "You... it's just, I saw the end coming, and I felt bad. You were a unicorn once too."

And that flush wouldn't quit. "I had my moments," he mumbled. Oh God, he really had talked too much.

Hal's smile went quietly blinding. "You'll have more."

Pierce's throat went dry, and he was sucking the dregs of his Arnold Palmer when the waitress came by with the food and two plates.

The mood, successfully broken, lightened up with discussions of amazing spices in the breading and other great things to eat. By the time they were done, Hal had Pierce nodding his head and saying yes to chicken and waffles when they went out again in three days, and that sudden bolt of intimacy between them was forgotten.

Or over.

Maybe not forgotten.

THE TRIP to Target didn't take long, and they emerged victorious with a box of the rubberized mesh mats and an office chair. By the time they got to the car, though, Pierce was limping fiercely, and the arm holding the cane was cramping too.

"Oh man," Hal muttered as he piloted his CR-V over the skyway to the outer beach. "I'm so sorry. All you asked was for stuff to make your condo not awful. I didn't mean to break you."

Pierce let out a weak laugh. "Don't apologize," he said, meaning it. "It was my best day in a long time."

Hal darted a look at him before looking back at traffic. "You mean that?"

"Yeah. Why wouldn't I?"

Hal just shook his head. "Tell you what. We get back, you sit and watch television while I put the mats all over the place. Then I can make us some dinner while we watch TV."

It was such an easy plan—simple and domestic. Hal made him put on sleep pants and a T-shirt and watch the TV in the bedroom with a prop behind his back while he ran around and put the mats down. Dinner was an english muffin sandwich again, and Pierce started dozing off not long after, but he pulled himself awake long enough to say, "You don't have to leave. Watch as much TV as you want."

"I need to look some stuff up on my computer," Hal said. "If you give me the keys, I can go get it and come back."

"Sure. They're on the counter." Sometime after that, in his dreams, he felt the brief touch of fingertips on his temple as he slept, but he was too tired to open his eyes and see if it was real.

He woke up in the middle of the night to use the bathroom and realized Hal had taken him at his word. The bed—a giant king-sized pedestal affair that made Pierce think of sleeping on the divan of the gods—was big enough that Pierce hadn't even realized that sometime in the night, Hal had just stretched out in a pair of sweats, covering up with the throw he'd pulled out a few days before. He was huddled under it now, like he was cold.

After Pierce hobbled to the bathroom, he took a mild painkiller—the cramping in his leg and arm hadn't eased up, and he had to concede he'd overdone it. The good news was, the rubber matting under his feet softened the impact against the tile, and what used to feel like a death march without his flip-flops was now just averagely uncomfortable. After the painkiller, he went to the linen cupboard and grabbed one more afghan.

He paused on the way back to bed. He hadn't drawn the blinds in front of the sliding glass door to the beach, and for a moment he stood, mesmerized by the view of the moonlight, bright against the black sky and luminous on the water.

"Whatcha doin'?" Hal mumbled from the room behind him.

Pierce turned and smiled, because he sounded sleepy and dear. "Nothing. Taking an Advil. Get under the covers, baby—you're cold."

"Mm'kay."

Pierce walked back into the room and laid the throw at the foot of the bed in case they got cold, then crawled in. He turned toward Hal, wondering if he'd feel anything about having a man in his bed again, but Hal was on the edge, not even close enough for Pierce to feel his body heat.

He closed his eyes, letting the painkiller do its work.

In that honest moment between sleeping and dreaming, he was brave enough to admit that it would be nice to roll over and snuggle that hard young body, to bury his nose in the hollow of Hal's shoulder and see what he smelled like when he was warm and soft in the dark.

HAL TOOK Pierce's rehabilitation damned seriously.

He'd upped the workout—Pierce was at an hour and a half now, much of it stretching, with more stretching in the hot tub.

Hal always got in and rubbed him down, hands solicitous and impersonal.

Pierce was starting to… twitch every time Hal stopped at midthigh or his glutes. The rubdown felt incomplete, he sulked to himself.

He didn't even want to admit to the vague ache of arousal that plagued him when they sat and ate lunch or dinner in front of the television. He tried to justify it to himself. He and Cynthia hadn't been having sex before the accident—it had been a while.

Hal was cute—by anybody's standards—and he'd been kind and generous with his time.

He was entertaining—he kept up a constant stream of snark and banter when they were together, and after that moment in the café, he'd kept it light—stupid things that occupied their time and made them smile but didn't tap too deeply into the heart muscle.

He had good hands, Pierce thought. Good, long-fingered, competent hands that worked deeply into his calf or his thigh or his instep or bicep or forearm, and he could take care of every sore part of Pierce's body.

Even his psyche.

Even his heart.

That was it.

It was his hands.

Right.

The next "light" workout day, they put off Christmas shopping again and went grocery shopping. Pierce insisted on paying, buying enough groceries for both of them since Hal seemed to be staying more at Pierce's place than his own.

Pierce hadn't even seen Hal's condo. For one thing, it was on the top floor, and that was a pain in the—literal—ass. All he really knew about the place was that it must have an amazing assortment of clothes, because Hal wore something different every day.

The day after grocery shopping, Pierce doubled down after his workout and proclaimed it laundry day.

Hal helped him pull the linens off the bed, neither of them mentioning that he'd been sleeping on the far end, only returning to his place to work out and shower in the morning before Pierce's time in the pool. After the load started, Pierce turned to him.

"So, go up to your place and get a load of undies or something. We'll put it in next." He knew Hal had his own washing machine— he must, because the unit above Pierce's place did laundry almost constantly, it sounded like.

Hal cocked his head, and for a moment Pierce expected him to say "Naw—I'll go run a load upstairs," which was way more logical.

Instead he looked Pierce in the eye and said, "Okay. I'll bring my toiletries here too, and some clothes."

For a moment it felt like a dare. "If you want to, why not?"

Hal's usually expressive face closed down, like he was playing poker and Pierce had just made an unexpected bet.

"Won't you be afraid someone will think the worst?"

Pierce blinked. "What's the worst?" he asked stupidly.

Hal's jaw dropped. "That we're, uh...."

Oh. Heat—sticky, sweaty heat that had become closer and closer to Pierce's skin in the past week—suddenly washed his face, his neck, his back.

"Why—" he squeaked and then cleared his throat. "It doesn't matter to me," he said, wishing he could move from the hallway, grab a soda from the fridge, a glass of water, anything. His throat felt like baby powder, the old-fashioned talcum kind with extra grit. "You're a friend. Lots of people stay in a beach house with friends."

Hal's expression opened, and what Pierce saw didn't reassure him in the least. He looked... sly and vaguely predatory. He raised his hand and feathered his fingertips across Pierce's scarred cheekbone. "Sure, Pierce. You and me, we're friends."

Pierce closed his eyes and wished....

For what?

A palm on his cheek? Hal's breath against his face?

A simple kiss?

When Pierce opened his eyes, Hal had stepped back, smiling cockily. "I'll go get the next load of laundry," he said, practically whistling. "We can go for a walk after we shove this one in the dryer."

"Wait—didn't I just work out?" Pierce demanded, although, in fact, he felt better, looser, and more mobile than he had a week and a half earlier. He had to admit, the rubber mats were a simple solution to walking on the tile, and the office chair helped him not wreck his back when he communicated with what appeared to be an office behind an exciting and lucrative job offer.

Hal paused and turned his head, winking. "Just ten minutes, my man. It won't kill you, and geez—aren't you a little interested in seeing the ocean?"

His words hit Pierce in the guilt center. "I love the ocean," he said wistfully. The ocean was one of those places in Sacramento people claimed they loved but never went to visit. Here he'd been staying, the ocean just out his back window, and he hadn't so much as opened up the sliding glass door.

"Yeah, well, we better go take it in now, you know, because the next two days we're supposed to have rain."

Pierce frowned. "I thought hurricane season was over?" Because people from Sacramento also were afraid of pretty much every type of weather—rain, snow, drought—it was all frightening.

"Well, yeah—this is just a storm. You know, raindrops? It'll be fine. Besides—why do you think the window is built with those serious blinds?" He winked. "What's the matter—think we'll be locked in here while the world ends and I'll be the only person you'll have to fuck?"

Pierce rolled his eyes and prayed the sudden zoom of his heart rate didn't show. "You're all talk," he said, trying hard to be casual. "If you need to get laid before the apocalypse, I'm pretty sure all you have to do is open your door and you'll have a line down the staircase and wrapping around the condo."

Hal's sudden sucking-a-lemon expression told him the conversation didn't take quite the turn he'd expected. "If I wanted to fuck those losers, I wouldn't be moving my toothbrush down here. Now please tell me you have tennis shoes and not flip-flops, 'cause those things are good to get out to the pool but they're crap in the sand if you're injured."

Pierce nodded, trying hard not to think of the implications of things like loads of laundry and toothbrushes. "I can do that."

Hal nodded like it was a done deal, but as soon as he'd left the condo and shut the door behind him, Pierce limped back to his suitcase, pulled his long-neglected tennis shoes out as well as his socks, and positioned himself on the bed to try to put them both on.

The socks were... difficult. He had to hold a sock in one hand so he could balance himself against the bed, then slip a toe in before grabbing the elastic with the other hand and pulling it on. By the time he'd done that twice, he was sweating a little and feeling sore and stupid.

How—oh how—could he have fooled himself into thinking that his body was 100 percent? When he'd gotten there, he'd been at 40 percent at the most—that sort of pain, stiffness, and muscle loss didn't reappear in a day!

Or a week.

By the time Hal got back with the laundry, Pierce was sitting on the bed and staring at his feet. Yes, he'd slipped the tennis shoes on—but tying them was going to be a challenge.

"Oh, there you are," Hal said, poking his head in. "I set the basket on top of the washer so we don't forget to keep the parade moving. How are you—oh!" And God, he sounded so natural. "Would you like some help?"

"Augh!" Pierce voiced, because the frustration had been breaking him into a sweat for the last ten minutes. "How do you stand me? I'm worthless! I can't even put on my shoes!"

Hal paused on his way into the room. "There's got to be a Shakespeare quote in there," he said, like he was thinking about it hard. "About how a man's worth is more than his ability to lace his boots. Now you sound like you're in asshole mood—you're not going to kick me in the face if I squat down to tie those, are you?"

"No," Pierce told him—but sulkily. "I try not to hurt the people who help me. Usually."

"So that means there's some danger," Hal said, just to make sure. "That's good to know. You can protect yourself if you know the dangers."

Everything in Pierce's brain backed up and fountained out his ears. "You can't," he said fervently, because this suddenly seemed important.

"You can't. A relationship isn't like that—you can't protect yourself, even if you know the dangers. You protect yourself and you'll just… it's like a circuit. You can't make a circuit with the vinyl still on the wires. You either strip the protection off to make the circuit complete and hope it doesn't explode, or nothing ever happens."

Hal paused, kneeling at his feet, his hands warm on Pierce's calf. "That's… well, off topic, actually. And I'd love to know where it came from. But for right now, I just need to know if you're going to kick me in the face."

He rubbed Pierce's calf absentmindedly, his hands warm and strong and capable. The taut panic wire that had been zinging up Pierce's spine since he'd realized that no, he couldn't really bend far enough to put on his shoes yet, and how embarrassing that was when this young, attractive man was… was putting himself at close range—that panic wire stilled, muted, the charge of embarrassment dampening until Pierce could breathe again.

"No," Pierce whispered huskily. "Wouldn't dream of it."

Hal blinked a couple of times, looking up at him. "How do you strip the wires?" he asked, the absentminded rubbing turning into a caress.

The question made Pierce's eyes burn. "I have no idea."

The corners of Hal's mouth turned down, and he stopped touching Pierce and made quick work of the laces. "We'll figure it out," he promised. He stood, offering Pierce a hand up, and Pierce took it, then accepted the hated cane so he could make his way through the house.

Once he got outside, the cold and humid breeze took his breath away. He kept walking, expecting Hal to catch up at any moment, but he was surprised when he'd gone nearly a hundred yards before Hal trotted up to his side. Hal zipped up a windbreaker of his own before handing Pierce a zippered hoodie.

"It's frickin' cold out here!" he called, and Pierce grimaced.

"You guys are a little spoiled," he said through the wind. He remembered going running in the chill of a Sacramento winter, when it got down to the thirties.

"Yeah, well, humor me." Hal stood solicitously and helped him on with the hoodie; then together they soldiered through the loose sand that formed a pathway through the rushes toward the harder sand of the beach. Hal's hand hovered under his elbow for a few steps, and Pierce, eschewing his pride for once, paused and took his hand, putting it firmly under his arm.

"People will think we're a couple," Hal said, and he had to talk over the sound of the surf, so it was hard to know if he was flirting or embarrassed.

"I don't mind if you don't."

Hal squeezed his elbow in response, and they hit the harder-packed sand of the beach proper.

Pierce swung toward the pounding surf and paused. The waves were decent-sized but still small compared to high tide in Monterey or Half-Moon Bay, and the horizon tinted toward gold instead of gray-blue.

But still, it was a great unfathomable deep, and since he'd hauled his limping ass out here, he wanted a good look at it.

"Why are you stopping?" Hal tugged on him, and Pierce bit his lip, standing still.

"Because," he said, having trouble raising his voice. "It deserves our respect, don't you think? If you don't respect the ocean, or time, or fate, or the big things in the world, you sort of have it coming when they knock you on your ass."

Hal stopped tugging and drew up even with him. Shyly, with tentative little pauses and jerks, he put his arm around Pierce's shoulders. Pierce let him.

"Does it make you feel alone?" he asked, voice throbbing with a loneliness he rarely showed but Pierce had guessed at.

"Yeah," Pierce said, wrapping his arm around Hal's waist. Comfort, right?

Maybe.

"Then why do we keep coming here?"

"Because it's great and vast and holy," Pierce told him, unexpectedly moved by having it right there, in front of him, when he'd ignored it for the better part of two weeks. "And it lets us touch our toes to its surf and play."

"Do you think you'll ever be able to strip the vinyl off?" Hal asked quietly. "Let your wires touch?"

Pierce swallowed, although the question wasn't unanticipated.

"I have to know I'm strong enough to take the charge," he answered. Oh, he liked this metaphor. It was another layer of vinyl between him and the pain of the divorce, and his bitterness, and of loving someone enough for the love to hurt.

"I'll test it gently," Hal whispered. "When you're ready."

Eventually they turned and took off to the north, letting the wind and the late-afternoon shadows batter at them. They walked carefully, dodging the big bits of broken shells that were sharp enough to cut through old tennis shoes if the traveler were unwary. When Pierce's leg began to complain loudly instead of nag subtly, he turned around and let Hal escort him home.

Pierce was older, and supposedly cynical and bitter, but he found himself clinging to the younger man's promise for the rest of the walk, even through the steady rain at the end. They returned to finish the laundry and remake the bed, talking quietly under the sound of the rain driving against the sliding glass door and the roar of the pounding surf. It made Pierce feel small, like the brightly lit condo was a quiet fortress of possibility against the bleak elements, and that feeling of intimacy lasted long into a quiet evening of eggs and chips for dinner before giggling their way through *Bob's Burgers*.

For once, Pierce didn't fall asleep on the couch. At eleven o'clock he stood and stretched and reached for his cane. Hal stood at the same time and turned off the television.

"I'll turn off the lights," he offered, yawning. He blinked and looked quietly at Pierce. "If you, I don't know, wanted to roll a little closer to the center of the bed tonight, I wouldn't grab your ass or anything."

Pierce smiled. "I never thought you would."

The wind gusted hard against the glass and they shared a look, haunted, searching for protection and companionship.

Two people under the covers—maybe tonight they'd be close enough to share warmth.

Pierce had just slid into bed and was setting his phone in the charger when it buzzed.

"You have friends?" Hal joked, although he'd seen Pierce take brief texts from his sister, checking in every day to make sure he wasn't dead.

"Apparently not," Pierce said grimly. "It's Cynthia."

"Does she not know about the time change?" Hal eyed the phone with distaste—it was after eleven.

"Nope," Pierce said cheerfully. On that thought, he hit Connect and yawned directly into the phone. "Evening"—yawn—"Cynthia. Nice of you to call."

"You're not in bed yet. You don't go to bed before twelve," she said flatly over the speaker.

"I'm still recovering," Pierce told her, stung. "And I was just going to bed after a rather busy day for me. Can I help you?"

He heard her blow out a breath, which was usually her cue for remembering the social niceties. He hadn't been kidding when he'd told Hal she needed a checklist. He used to think it was her way of making sure she didn't offend anybody. It hadn't been until this last year that he'd realized she'd used the checklist in the same way zealots bombing other countries used the dogma of their faith—as a crutch to support her hypothesis that she wasn't a bad person.

"I apologize," she said civilly. "You're right. There's a time difference, and I was thoughtless."

He skipped the part where he said "That's okay" because it wasn't. "What can I do for you?" he asked politely.

"Did you file for divorce already?" she asked.

"I've been in the hospital or Florida," he said, stomach sinking. "Remember, Cynthia? The hospital? I was wrapped in bandages, and you said, 'Pierce, I forgive you.'"

"And you said you wanted a divorce. I still don't understand." Her voice lowered, and the brittle exoskeleton of bitch grew a little softer. "I don't understand why that was the final straw. You never did explain it to me."

Pierce sighed, part of him wanting to claim the easy way out and pretend exhaustion, but part of him knowing that he was ending a seven-year relationship, and he owed her better than that.

"Cynthia, what did my sister ever do to you?"

"Your sister? I don't know—nothing, I guess. What does she have to do with this?"

"You kept saying she deserved to be poor, deserved to not get nice things, deserved to have to work when her husband had a good job. She'd earned that, you said. All the time. 'Welp, if Sasha didn't want to struggle, you know what she should have done.'"

"Well, she got knocked up, Pierce—you know that—"

"Yeah, but she's a good mother. She's kind. She's a better sister than I've ever deserved. Why doesn't she deserve a good life? Why does every struggle she has have to be… some sort of bill God hands her for a mistake she made a million years ago when she was a stupid kid? When does that term of service end?"

"Pierce, I don't know what this has to do with us—"

"Everything," he said quietly, pretty sure she would never get it. "What if I made a mistake? What if I invested in the wrong thing or trusted the wrong accountant? How long would I hear about that? What if someday I vote for the wrong politician and he screws up the world? Do I ever get to fix that with you? Because marriage is based on trust, sweetheart—and I finally got to the point where I couldn't trust you to forgive me if I so much as bought the wrong pair of tennis shoes."

"But… but I never said any of those things about you," she said, her voice wobbling.

"Yeah. But you said them about somebody. Somebody I cared for. And when I tried to explain it, all you could tell me was that she should have known better. Everybody makes mistakes, hon. Everybody. Holding a mistake like that against somebody—it makes you not a very good person, that's all."

"That's all?" she asked, and it wasn't his imagination. He'd hurt her. Deeply. He hadn't thought it was possible—but then, until these last two weeks, talking to Hal until he became another chamber of Pierce's heart, he hadn't found the words.

"Maybe it was just that way for me," he soothed. "Maybe somewhere out there is someone who will take the same sort of joy you do in finding that line in the sand."

"You're judging me, you bastard!" She was trying to pull her bitch on again, but he'd left her crying, and he hated that.

"You're right." Unwelcome and unbidden, he remembered when he'd first seen her. She'd been tall, healthy—a broad-cheekboned face and thick dark hair and eyes, with the sort of smile that sparkled. "I'm sorry," he said, his voice choking. "I am. I couldn't deal with it anymore. I should probably have been gentler about it, but… but you were there. I almost died. And when I woke up, I thought, 'Right now, we can say we're sorry, and we can make it better. I don't want to live like this anymore.'"

"And I said...." She breathed deeply, obviously trying to control her own tears. "I'm sorry, Pierce," she whispered after a few hard breaths. "I'm... I still don't get it all. But I'm starting to see I fucked up."

"I should have found better words." He hauled in a big lungful of air. "But my body hurt and my heart hurt and...."

"And you didn't trust me not to hurt you again," she whispered. "Okay. Okay. This isn't what I called for, but okay."

Pierce wiped his face with his palm, and Hal reached over to his side of the bed and grabbed a few tissues, handing them to him while he pulled himself together.

"What did you call for?" he asked after one of the worst moments of his life—including when the fire department had to use the jaws of life to peel him out of his destroyed pickup truck.

"I... I was going to file the papers," she whispered. "I just wanted to make sure they hadn't been filed yet."

"You do that," he said. "I won't stop you. Send them to my sister's house. I'm coming home in January. We can be divorced by the early part of next year."

"I... I was... I found somebody," she said, half laughing. "I didn't expect to, so soon. I was hoping for a June wedding."

Pierce paused, waiting for the impact, but he was apparently in the right position, because the blow flew right by. "I'm glad," he said, meaning it. "I am sincerely glad you found someone. I... I never wished you ill."

"Pierce?" she asked, her voice aching. "Why didn't you ever ask to have children? I... I want them. I didn't realize how much until I... I met this other guy. Why not us?"

Pierce thought about it. Hal grabbed the box of Kleenex and scooted close. Closer. Until their hips and thighs were touching under the covers. Part of Pierce was distracted by the warmth of the body—of Hal's body. But most of him was still putting this part of his past to bed.

"I was afraid to ask you," he said, his heart aching too. "You... you were so mean to Sasha, Cynthia. I... I was afraid you'd judge me too."

Her voice caught in a sob. "I... I'm sorry. I'm so sorry."

And now he could say this with a clear heart. "Me too. I'm so sorry. I... this was not how I saw us."

He'd imagined them once having children, being the kind of parents he saw Sasha and Marshall being. He hadn't realized, day after day, week after week, the fear of what she'd say, what she'd do—how that had built into a shell around his heart.

"Me neither. I… I filled the paperwork out already. You've got the house, like I promised. I hired a gardener to keep up the outside. Call me before you get home. I'll have someone come in and freshen the place up." Her voice stabilized, now that she was being practical. She'd always been good with details. "I took the bed, so if you send me a link to one, I'll order the replacement and be there when it's delivered."

"That's kind. You don't have to—"

"I do." A deep shuddery breath. "I… I guess I don't have as much kindness in me as I always thought. I should probably practice before I screw up another relationship, right?"

"It took two," Pierce admitted. "I… I should have found better words."

"It… you accused me. That's what it felt like," she confessed. "I…. God. Why didn't we have this talk years ago?"

Work. Promotions. Parties. Trips. Every moment, Pierce thinking they could work through it, he could live with her another week, another month, because he loved her, right?

Until all that resentment smothered the love. Dead. No resuscitation, no more love.

"I'm sorry. Just… so sorry."

"I still care for you," she said softly. "But… but we're better off over, aren't we."

It wasn't a question. "Yeah."

"I'll send the papers to Sasha's. I… I need you to know, I never wished her ill either."

No. She hadn't. "I know."

"Take care. I'll…. Can you call me on New Year's Eve? I… I'm going to miss you, okay?"

New Year's had always been them, alone, in a cabin in Tahoe. It had been special. "Yeah," he said on a sigh. "I'll call you."

The line went dead, and Pierce fumbled the phone into the charger. *God.* Hal was there. Their bodies were touching, and Hal had heard everyth—

"What's this?" Pierce asked softly, because he had a sudden armload of Hal, weeping softly on his T-shirted chest. "Oh, baby…. Hal… what's wrong?"

"You were really nice to her," Hal sobbed. "So nice." The rest of it was lost as Pierce wrapped his arms around Hal's shaking body, but Pierce heard the word "unicorn" in there somewhere.

He reached to turn off the light, wincing a little because it had been an active day for him, and his body had stiffened up. In the darkness, Hal seemed bigger somehow, warmth and weight, collapsed against Pierce's chest.

Pierce wrapped his arms around Hal's shoulders and rocked him, keeping him safe from the storm outside and whatever raged within.

They fell asleep tangled, Pierce curled around Hal, Hal's head pressed against his chest.

Pierce dreamed about a sunny day and Hal, dressed in a white linen shirt and dark cotton trousers, offering him a flower and a kiss, in an almost perfect world.

STRIPPING THE VINYL

PIERCE GOT up in the middle of the night to pee, like he usually did, untangling himself gently from Hal, who slept like the dead—or an exhausted child.

He crawled back into bed, and Hal burrowed up against him again, tangling their legs and scooting down so he could rest his cheek against Pierce's chest. Pierce, drowsy and uninhibited, stroked his back gently.

A warm human being in his bed. The joy of that event staggered him.

What're you doing, Pierce? You leave in two and a half weeks!

Leave? Not see this absurdly pretty kid day after day? Not have Hal urging him unmercifully in the pool and chattering about Looney Tunes and *Bob's Burgers* in the meantime?

Unconsciously, Pierce tightened his arms around Hal's shoulders. He fell asleep dreaming of a giant hole in his house at home and how nobody seemed to notice that if you walked into the bedroom, you'd fall into an enormous black pit without boundaries or bottom.

When the dark was still fathomless, he woke up to feel somebody—Hal—moving his lips down his bare stomach.

Pierce grunted and pulled at his shirt—it seemed to have rucked up in the night—and Hal gently but firmly pushed the shirt back up. His lips kept traveling down, down, then up, spending a moment on Pierce's nipples, until the haze of sleep and arousal made him groan.

Words... Pierce had to make words....

Words like... ah, God, hands everywhere... nipples... nibble just... oh, nip? Lick? Suck... no, no, different words.

No words?

Should there be "no" words here?

"Hal...," he whispered, raising his hands to Hal's thick hair to maybe pull him off... or knead his fingers in it, silky, and massage fingertips against Hal's scalp.

Hal pulled up long enough to say "Shh...." and hold his fingertips against Pierce's lips.

Okay. Hush. That was the only word.

Pierce closed his eyes against the darkness, seeing the pressure and pleasure of his body as bright white clouds against his eyelids.

A cloud at one nipple, under the play of Hal's tongue, and then at the other. Hal skimmed his fingers through the decently thick patch of hair on Pierce's chest, and Pierce breathed deeply and arched his hips, trying not to flail, trying to decide if he was dreaming.

The strobes of light danced behind his eyes. Bongo drumbeats of visual sensation, nipples, played to explosions of light, soft thrums of caress, down his ribs, across his soft stomach.

A hesitation at the waistband of his shorts, a flicker of lights as they were dragged down.

More tickling lights along his shaft, and a wafting pulse of breath along the head.

Pierce moaned, the actual sound in the quiet of the storm shocking.

"Hush," Hal breathed, and that one word anchored him in the present.

The rest was sensual stimuli, his harsh breathing overshadowing the rain beating on the windows and that watercolor firework behind his closed eyes.

Rough tongue, wet heat, a hot cave of pressure—Pierce sighed loudly, afraid to make more noise, afraid that if he even blinked, the moment would disappear. He threw his arm over his eyes and arched into Hal's mouth, his breathy moans growing but not breaking the bubble of silence over two men on the bed in the dark room.

He lost himself in the wonder of his body, the same body that had felt mostly useless, a betrayal of flesh and blood, over the past five months.

His body did amazing things.

Sure hands tugged gently on his balls, and that was it. "Coming," he managed, but the heat and the pressure didn't let up.

I should say something. About being HIV negative.

But he was coming, ejaculating, that part of his body working with amazing coordination considering it hadn't been used in more than half a year.

He came forever, until he felt pumped from the inside out, collapsing on the bed and pushing feebly at Hal's head when he became oversensitized.

"I… uh… neg—"

Hal covered his mouth with a sloppy, spit-covered hand. "Hush…."

Pierce moaned, his eyes closed of their own volition. Tired. So tired. Wrung out by emotion, by exertion, by oh-my-God sex! He curled into a ball on his side, only peripherally aware that someone was wiping at his groin with Kleenex and pulling his sleep pants and underwear up over his hips.

The rustling around his body stopped, and Hal backed carefully up against his front. Pierce flung his arm over that slim, taut waist and pulled closer, until they were spooning.

Warm and safe, content in a way he didn't know he could be, he fell asleep.

When he woke up in the morning, Hal was toasting bagels in the kitchen, singing Barry Manilow to himself. Until Pierce went to the bathroom and tried to peel his underwear off his come-sticky pubic hair, he thought the whole thing had been a dream.

"It's still raining and thundering!" Hal called from the living room. "You may as well shower—no pool today."

"Bummer," he muttered. The cleansing of the pool—that felt like something he needed right then.

"I'll give you a yoga lesson and a rubdown," Hal said, his voice coming right from the door. "So don't hop in the shower just yet, 'cause yoga will make you sweat."

"Okay—should I stay in my sleep pants?"

"Those'll work fine. Now hurry up and eat—I need to work you out so we can go shopping today."

Oh yeah. "Christmas shopping," Pierce said, the thought actually comforting him. Christmas. His family. His plans. Things not derailed by what may or may not have happened in the heart of the night. "You want we should get decorations? I mean, I'm not leaving until Christmas Eve. Some tinsel might be nice."

The breathing on the other side of the bathroom door grew awfully damned still. "Sure. Yeah. Let's do that. It'll be the only Christmas I get."

Pierce sucked in a breath full of mostly razor blades, and Hal padded back to the kitchen.

By himself?

Pierce would leave and Hal would be here by himself?

Because it's perfectly sane to ask this guy you've known for two weeks to come with you.

Alone?

Pierce may have only known the guy for two weeks, but he was pretty sure Hal hated to be alone.

But what sort of asshole asked a guy he barely knew to drop his life in Florida and come to Sacramento on a whim?

Pierce washed his hands and padded on the new rubber mats into the kitchen, where Hal had dished up two bagel sandwiches with some orange juice.

"This is awesome," he said, heart giving a big throb in his chest. "You're... you're really good at taking care of me."

Hal grinned sunnily. "See, that's excellent to hear, because my parents think I can barely take care of myself."

"They're deluded," Pierce said shortly, sitting down and unfolding his paper napkin onto his lap. "They've never woken up to bagels and orange juice with you."

He expected Hal to add "And blowjobs!" and maybe broach the subject—but that didn't happen.

"Well, maybe they were never as kind as you were," Hal said, smiling shyly.

Pierce's stomach knotted. "Kind?" God, that's what he'd said the day before too, after Pierce had gotten off the phone with his ex-wife.

"Yeah. The way you talked to Cynthia—that was... I mean, I was prepared to hear you hate her. I thought she sounded like a real bitch—but you didn't. You were... kind. And in the end, I think she got it. She got why the divorce. She understood."

Pierce looked away, feeling uncomfortable. "I'm not always nice," he said, suddenly desperately afraid of letting Hal down. "You know that. I was a grumpy bastard two weeks ago."

"You were in pain," Hal said simply. He beamed up at Pierce, showing no regret about the things they'd done in the night—hell, almost no knowledge of it. Just simple, uplifting forgiveness.

Pierce nodded and tried to give Hal something real. "Less pain every day," he said brightly.

"That's what I like to hear." Hal wiped his face and nodded decisively. "Okay—I'm going to go get my yoga mats and an area rug from upstairs—I don't want you trying yoga on the tile."

"I could do yoga in your place," Pierce said, and Hal's furtive look from under his lashes made something in Pierce's stomach twist.

"I, uh, need to clean up there," Hal told him. "It's just easier for me to go get my stuff."

Pierce nodded, wondering again what sort of damage Hal could have inflicted on his apartment in the two days after Thanksgiving and before he'd come down to the pool and seen Pierce struggling to do water aerobics to his iPhone.

In a dim, sort of distant way, it was starting to dawn on him that Hal had been very much alone in his life before he'd sprawled in a lounge chair and started bossing Pierce around.

Hal deserved more than that.

"So," Pierce said, resolving to talk about the blowjob in the room. "About—"

"Christmas shopping? I figure Target for decorations and toys, you think? And you should be able to get an appliance there for your sister, right?"

The desperation in his voice hit the raw edge of Pierce's nerve, and Pierce finally got it. They weren't supposed to talk about the blowjob in the night.

And for a moment he struggled against that—because he wanted to talk about it. Hell, he wanted to reciprocate it. But, oh God. He was leaving in two weeks. Whatever happened in those spare, breathless moments in the dark, how much could it mean?

Everything, you fucking coward. It means everything.

But Pierce had been locked in the silence of his own head since… well, not even before the accident. Since before Cynthia, really.

Since Loren.

Since he'd last believed in unicorns.

"What, uh," Pierce struggled to articulate. "What, uh, would you like for Christmas?"

Hal's full mouth—*had been wrapped around Pierce's cock*—quirked up at the corners. "A teddy bear," he said with satisfaction. "Something… something furry. To hug in bed."

Pierce remembered Hal's fingers petting the silky hair on his chest as he sucked on Pierce's nipples. "I can do bears," he said, fully aware of the innuendo and unable to stop it.

"You can do otters too," Hal said with a wink. "But I really only want a bear."

Pierce blushed and took a big bite of his bagel. "Mm'kay," he said through a full mouth. "'M brrrr."

Hal burst out laughing, and they finished breakfast in peace.

AN HOUR later, Pierce was stretching awkwardly, trying to attain the warrior's pose, and Hal was grabbing his sweaty body everywhere at once to help him find the position.

"Ouch!" Pierce complained after a particularly hard crank to his knee.

"Oh shit—I'm sorry! Okay, you know what? You work so hard in the water, you had me fooled. I'm going to go back to very basic moves—like kids' moves. They'll be good for your coordination, and if we increase the speed, they'll help you with cardio. You game?"

Pierce's body hurt—a lot—and those warm fuzzy thoughts he'd had about Hal that morning had become sort of thin and meshy over the last fifteen minutes.

"Yeah," he admitted, pulling his feet under him and putting his hand out to try to find balance. Hal caught his hand and pulled up behind his elbow. "This isn't working."

"Okay. I'm going to help you sit down, and I need you to spread your legs. Let's start there."

Pierce let himself be stretched and wondered again who had told this kid he couldn't make a living doing what he was doing. Yeah, sure—he made mistakes. But no teacher started out perfect. And Hal had such a good heart, such a willingness to try what he needed in order to make his plan work.

How could you say no in the face of that raw enthusiasm?

Pierce obviously couldn't.

But the thing was, when he said something funny and Hal turned those laughing brown eyes on Pierce's face, Pierce didn't ever want to try. He wanted to tell Hal yes to absolutely everything, anything, as long as he could make this young man that happy.

And as Hal squatted at his feet and pushed his toes toward his nose to help with his dorsiflex, Pierce was finding fewer and fewer reasons he shouldn't do that.

Hal was honest about the workout being more intense than he'd anticipated—so he kept it to forty-five minutes and did lots of therapeutic breathing at the end. Pierce was grateful—and even more grateful that at the end he felt refreshed and not destroyed.

And then Hal helped Pierce stand up, and they were standing chest to chest, with only the memory of the hallucinogenic midnight blowjob between them.

"I'm negative," Pierce blurted.

Hal raised his eyebrows and smirked. "Yeah, but we're working on that." He said it with a little shake of the head, and Pierce heard the *Please, please don't talk about it* in that movement and took a deep breath.

"Forewarned is forearmed," he said, letting that have two meanings.

Hal's eyes widened for a moment, as though the thought surprised him. "Very true. And I've now been warned of your negativity."

He gestured grandly then, breaking the heat between them, and Pierce hobbled to the shower.

The rest of the day seemed to be spent in that dual state of awareness, though. On the one hand, they were the two guys who had spoken frankly and slyly for the last two weeks.

On the other hand, every time they touched, whether it was when Hal offered him a hand out of the car or bumped his shoulder as Pierce leaned his weight on the shopping cart, was like shaking a bottle full of lightning.

Sparks everywhere.

"Hm… throw pillows, what do you think?" Hal asked, looking at some brightly colored Christmas pillows with trees and holly berries on them.

"I think Derrick will be surprised," Pierce said, and then, remembering that Derrick and Miranda were supposed to be there on New Year's Day, said, "Throw them in, with some of the dark blue too. It'll be like a thank-you gift."

"That's really nice!" Hal said, with that surprising excitement for "niceness." "Also, it's really convenient, since we can use them too!"

"Well, if Derrick didn't like gifts that served double duty, he wouldn't have gotten me a PS4 with three extra controllers last year," Pierce told him dryly.

For a moment Hal looked blank, and then it hit him. "So he could play at your house," he said, nodding in approval. "But why three extras?"

"For our wives." Pierce shrugged. "Miranda liked to play but Cynthia didn't, so Miranda, being a better person than any of the rest of us hosers, pretended not to want to play so Derrick and I could have the game room to ourselves and she and Cynthia could go buy decorating stuff at Target."

"Hm…." Hal glared at the throw pillows like they were responsible for irony. "I am not sure how to feel about any of that. I mean, on the one hand, Derrick sounds like my kind of guy—"

"You'll love him," Pierce said, thinking that Derrick and Miranda could… could look after Hal, after they got there. "He's, like, ultra-super cool."

"Describe ultra-super cool," Hal said, eyebrow cocked skeptically.

Well. Here was an embarrassing story. "Like, he walked in on me and Loren before he knew about the bi thing. Took one look at Loren on his knees—"

"Oh my God!"

"Yeah—embarrassing, right?"

It could have been. It could have been horrific. But Derrick really was the best.

"What did you do?" Hal asked, entranced.

"It was more like what did *he* do. And what he did was take one look at Loren there and said, 'Oh my God, you're bi!'" Pierce ignored Hal's bark of laughter and continued. "And I said, 'Is this a problem?'" And Pierce left out how terrified he was, because he and Derrick… well, inseparable since grade school, which was why they'd roomed together in college. "And he said, 'It is when you don't leave a sock on the bedroom door, asshole! I don't care who you're with, I'll never unsee you having sex!'"

Hal laughed, ducking his head and then looking back at him with a softly bitten lip. "Poor man," he said, but his apple cheeks were popping with the force of his grin.

"Yeah. I'd be worried it scarred him for life, but he met Miranda about a month after that, and suddenly our apartment was made of socks on the door, so I think he'll be okay."

"That's… that's sweet." Hal's grin faded. "So they've been together since college?" he asked, suddenly uncertain. "Over ten years?"

"Yeah. Hey—this little wooden Christmas tree. Don't hate me, but I think this could go on the end table by the window, don't you?"

Hal looked at it and nodded, swallowing hard. "Yeah," he said. "It's perfect. I… I thought Russ and me were going to do that," he blurted. "Like… like your friend and his wife."

Pierce almost dropped the Christmas tree into the cart from about two feet up. He barely managed to lower it so it rested awkwardly on the throw pillows, and wondered if maybe he shouldn't have visited the kid's section first.

"Is this the guy who cheated on you?" he asked, because he knew that name now.

"Yeah." Hal's eyes cruised restlessly, and he reached out to a wooden dreidel, colored blue and white. "My mother has one of these," he said, pleased. "I… I mean, I have no idea what it's for, because we did Christmas like my dad's family, but—"

"We'll put it by the Christmas tree," Pierce told him, setting it carefully next to the tree. "Do you want a menorah?"

Hal frowned. "No… 'cause, again, I have no idea what it's for. But I do want a tinsel banner, so find that aisle, quick!"

"Yeah, sure. When did you and Russ break up?" Because Hal was avoiding two questions today, and if Pierce didn't get to, Hal didn't get to.

"Valentine's Day, this year," Hal told him, rolling his eyes. "So no, I'm not all sentimental about him now because he broke up with me before Christmas."

"Glad to know that," Pierce said dryly, and then he stopped and sighed. "Hal?"

"What?"

For a moment, they looked each other in the eyes, the bustle around them of a zillion people on a holiday mission making the painful personal moment a little easier to bear.

"If you ever want to tell me something… you know. Real. I could be that guy for you. Now. I mean, I couldn't have been that guy for you right after Thanksgiving. I was too pissed at myself. But I could be that guy for you now if you want."

A faint smile pulled the corners of Hal's mouth up.

"I'll... I'll keep that in mind." But he turned away quickly, reaching onto the shelves and coming back with an exquisite holiday star, a combination of fiber optics and plastic filigree that managed to look enchanting in spite of what should have been very tacky beginnings. "Don't hate me, but I love this."

Pierce grimaced, oddly let down. "Throw it in the cart," he said.

"But we don't have anything to put it on."

"We'll get some cord and hang it from the ceiling. It'll look avant-garde—no one will have to know we just made it up as we went along."

Hal laughed, but there was no joy in the sound. "Apparently that's all of adulthood."

"Yeah, well, adulthood has some surprisingly awesome moments, so don't knock it," Pierce snapped, trying hard not to be heartbroken. He stalked through decorations a little faster, wanting to get to the kids' department before the weariness in his legs became a problem.

Hal caught up with him easily and placed his hand on the back of Pierce's elbow. Normally Pierce didn't need this unless he was using his cane, and right before he shook off the hand, he recognized it for what it truly was:

A peace offering.

"Some dinner after we get the presents and get out of here?" Hal offered as a treaty.

"Sure. What do you want for Christmas, though?"

"I already told you—a teddy bear!"

Pierce grimaced. "Oh, dammit! Speaking of things in the kids' department—"

Hal smacked his forehead with his palm. "Yeah. You have short people to spoil. Where to, hoss?"

God, Target was huge. Past the linens and a rockin' discussion of whether it was okay to have lavender-scented dreams when you slept on purple sheets, and on through towels, with more arguments about whether pretty patterned towels meant someone was douchey—Hal said yes—or just Californian—Pierce was on that boat.

Finally, just before Hal came to the conclusion that all Californians were inevitably douchey—which Pierce would have argued against to the death—they found the toy department.

And Nirvana.

"Oh. My. God." Hal swung around the Lego shelves like Julie Andrews did a helicopter twirl on a mountain in the alps. "Legos? Seriously? This is what Legos look like these days?"

Pierce looked around, comforted by the fact that he was pretty sure Darius only had about half these sets. "What? You never got Legos as a kid?"

He got a scowl in return. "My cutoff date for Legos was twelve. Some asshole put a little number on the box that said they were good from eight to twelve, so my dad the judge and mom the helicopter parent started getting me foreign language lessons and science camp memberships after that."

"You know, you're not making a case for money making a good parent," Pierce said, truly dismayed. "Do you *see* the Millennium Falcon? That thing's good 'til you're sixteen!"

Hal smirked at him. "How old were you?"

"Well, Sasha and Marshall gave it to me three years ago—remember that study I'm crazy about? It's got a Lego Millennium Falcon in a glass case on the shelf. Took Derrick and me three days, but man, it was worth it."

"So, what? You and your sister just swap Lego sets?" Hal picked up a giant Lego Batman scenario that cost a hundred dollars easy.

"You forget," Pierce said patiently. "My parents were douchebags too. So basically, all *we* got for Christmas was Sunday school clothes and Bible study coloring books—"

"Yuck!"

"I'm saying. We got older, and it was mostly wooden chess sets for me and sewing kits for Sasha. So when I was twelve, and we could walk to the store together, we would save our allowance and buy each *other* gifts. She always bought me Legos, because—dude? Can you see?"

"I'm sold," Hal said seriously, grabbing a big bucket of assorted parts and looking at it with lust in his eyes.

"Well, I would buy her Barbies. And now that Abigail is, like, four years old, I promised Sasha I'd keep that kid eyeballs-deep in Barbie dolls and Monster High and whatever else is current and pink and awesome." Pierce gestured grandly. "If she wants Legos, I'll get them. Pink Legos? I'm on it. Those kids are getting more toys than they know what to do with—Sasha and I made a pact."

"Word," Hal said, nodding like he was now the choir and Pierce could preach. "But, about this bucket of Legos—don't you think we could make an awesome Christmas tree with this?"

"Put it in," Pierce said, liking this plan. "And grab the giant *Guardians of the Galaxy* one behind you." He grinned, feeling magnanimous and evil. "And go find two teddy bears—one for you and one for Sasha."

"Wait—I thought you were getting your sister a Keurig?" Hal asked suspiciously.

Pierce remembered his sister as a child, all big brown eyes and dark hair, pale and afraid of pissing off Mom and Dad. "A coffee maker to wake up her inner adult," he said with dignity, "and a teddy bear to comfort her inner child."

Hal grinned. "Okay—you look at Barbies, and I'll go cruise stuffed animals. Meet back in five."

Pierce thought about family planning and wondered if he could sneak lubricant and condoms into the cart and get back in time to find Abigail's present. He cursed his range of motion, because he knew he wouldn't make it, and being... overt about it might just frighten Hal off.

Dammit.

But he owed his niece a present and had just decided on the Monster High Mansion when Hal came around the corner, one giant stuffed pink bear under one arm, and a giant stuffed bear with green eyes and light brown fur held against his chest with the other.

Pierce looked from the bear to Hal's face and back again. "Is that supposed to be me?" he asked dryly.

"Do you let me cuddle you like this?" Hal asked, waggling his eyebrows.

"I might." Pierce waggled his back, wondering how long they could flirt without actually mentioning the damned blowjob-in-the-dark-room thing that had happened the night before.

"Then yes," Hal said archly, putting both bears in the laden cart. He paused for a moment and looked at the cart again. "And we're going to have to stop debating on which bear I'm going to sleep with and check out. This thing's full and"—he raked Pierce's body over with a critical eye—"unless I miss my guess, you're getting tired."

"No I'm—" Pierce yawned. "—not."

Hal raised an eyebrow, looking bored.

"Fine. And I'm starving. Let's go."

The line was damned long, and by the time they got through it, Pierce was limping badly. Hal made him go sit down in the CR-V while he unloaded the cart, and when he got back into the car, he sighed like he'd made a big decision.

"Okay—here's what we're going to do. I'm going to call a chain restaurant for takeout, we'll go park in the takeout spot and I'll run in and get it, and we'll take it back home with us. That way you can eat and crash, and I can start immediately on making a Christmas tree out of Legos because honestly, it *is* all about me, and that sounds like the most fun *ever*."

Pierce laughed—because how could he not. "Yeah," he said, wishing he was a woman with ibuprofen in her purse or something. "That sounds awesome."

Hal's hand, warm on his shoulder, surprised him. "I'll take care of you," he said softly. "I'm young, but I can train up quick."

And Pierce, tired, confused, and in need of some reassurance, took it for what it was. "You'll do a great job," he said. "I don't know why you worry."

Hal looked away. "Yeah. Yeah, you do." He pulled out his phone and started tapping into it without looking up. "So, Applebee's—what's your favorite item there?"

Pierce ordered a sandwich, and they were both quiet on the drive. Hal parked, and Pierce leaned back against the seat, eyes closed.

"It'll be a minute," Hal said softly. "I'm going to run next door to get something before getting our food."

Pierce kept his eyes closed and nodded. He wasn't even sure when Hal came out, takeout bags rustling as he put them behind the driver seat, and he tried hard not to drool on the way home.

HE WOKE up for takeout at Derrick's little glass-topped table, the Target bags sitting accusingly in the corner of the room.

"We forgot wrapping paper," Pierce said, halfway through his sandwich, and Hal smacked his forehead with his palm.

"D'oh! God, we suck at this!"

"Right?" Pierce couldn't help the shocked laughter. "We're, like, epically bad. We'll have to learn to make lists."

"Either that or set up a little minicamp at Target. 'Hello, we're the eternal shoppers. We go home between trips, but we have a cot for the times we forget half the shit we came for.'"

"That would totally work," Pierce agreed. "Like in those apocalyptic movies, where people gather in a shopping mall or Target. You've got years' worth of canned goods and all the clothes in your size you could ask for."

"And they've got video games and probably their own generator," Hal said, because maybe when you were twenty-three you remembered the important stuff.

"And sleeping bags and futons—" *And condoms and lubricant and privacy.* "—and we, uh, you could be totally comfortable there for quite some time." Oh God. Pierce had just remembered why he was the bear and why Hal would rank videogames as a postapocalyptic necessity.

But Hal didn't seem to think there was anything amiss. "We," he said, eyes to the side like he was imagining something pleasant. "*We* could be happy and comfortable for quite some time."

"Okay," Pierce mumbled, not sure what he was agreeing to. Suddenly he didn't care. "*We* could be happy and comfortable in Target after the apocalypse. It'll be our destination place when we're running from the zombie hordes."

They finished dinner, talking about the best strategy for defeating the vicious undead, and Pierce got up to help clear the table while Hal raided the bags.

"You can throw the pillows on the couch," Pierce instructed, rinsing silverware and cups. "That's where they were meant to go anyway."

Hal started to laugh, all evil. "Throw pillows. Get it? They're *throw* pillows, and I'm throwing them."

Pierce stared at him. "Oh dear God."

He repeated his evil cackle and sailed the next pillow across the room like a Frisbee. The next one went too far, and Pierce stuck his hand up and caught it before it could hit the refrigerator.

They both stopped and stared at Pierce's game hand and arm in shock.

Pierce met Hal's grinning countenance with fierce triumph of his own, and then Hal pumped his fist, dancing on the hard tile of the living room with undisguised glee.

"*I* am going to be the best massage therapist/personal trainer on the *planet*! I'm rehab therapy *king of the frickin' world*!"

Pierce dried his good hand at the sink, then grabbed the pillow to chuck it at Hal's head. Hal didn't even duck, he was enjoying his celebration too much. And why not? Pierce grinned at him, not quite ready to mambo—or so he thought.

"You don't get out of this that easy," Hal told him, dancing into the kitchen. "Here—turn toward me—conga line! You're the big spoon!"

Oh wow. Hands on slim hips, Bugs Bunny moves ready! There was only the music in Hal's head, and he slowed it down enough for Pierce to keep up. *Bum-bum-bum-bum-ba-BUMP, bum-bum-bum-bum-ba-BUMP,* together they conga-trained into the living room. Hal grabbed his hands and turned them around so Pierce's back was toward the couch, and Pierce, caught up in the madness, wrapped his arms around Hal's waist as he fell backward, pulling Hal down on top of him.

He turned at the last moment, depositing Hal sloppily next to him, while the two of them laughed like children. Then they both seemed to take a breath at the same time, and the moment grew long, stretched breathlessly between them, a taffy moment with no end.

Pierce broke first, biting his lip and looking down at Hal's chest, heat stealing over his cheeks. *Kiss me, Hal. Please.* Hal leaned forward, and Pierce looked up into his eyes. For a moment, while his heart beat in his ears, they stared at each other, and Hal's plush mouth pursed, came closer, and…

…veered to the right to gently buss Pierce's cheek.

Come on!

Hal pushed himself up to his feet, bouncing like the moment never happened.

Oh. Maybe last night was a fluke. Maybe he's just really kind and doesn't want me after all. I'm older and have scars, and I was pretty fuckin' average anyway. Maybe he just wants to be friends.

He is *a pretty amazing friend.*

"Are you ready to do the Lego thing?" Hal asked, and Pierce nodded bemusedly, trying hard to keep his disappointment to himself.

THEY WERE deep into the intricacies of making rectangular Legos turn into a round shape when his phone buzzed with Sasha's nightly text—and then rang, because apparently the text was a warning shot.

Pierce answered the phone saying, "Hey, Sasha, what's up?"

"You sound happier," she said, but *she* didn't, and Pierce's antennae went on high alert.

"I am. What's wrong?"

"They're coming," she said, voice crumbling. "Pierce, I didn't know what to do. They called up and said they were coming for Christmas—they didn't ask or anything. I mean, I don't even know how they knew my number. I wasn't even living here the last time I talked to them."

Pierce blinked, trying not to freak out. "Wait. You mean—our *parents* are coming?"

"Yeah. What am I going to do?"

Oh Jesus. "Do you want them in your house, Sash? Be honest. I was the bastard who told them not to talk to you at all if they couldn't be nice. If you want them back in your life—"

"No!" Her voice cracked into tears. "No. Pierce, I can't even.... My kids just watched me cry, and Marshall had to help me breathe after they hung up, and he was going to call them up and tell them to go to hell but... but he's not a... a *warrior*, Pierce. You are." And now she sounded like she was crying quietly, like when they were kids. "You are. Please, I know you're mad at yourself now, because you got mad because you were hurt. But... but that's just because you're used to being on the making-it-right side of things. That's why you and Cynthia, I think—I mean, for all her faults, Pierce, she kept trying to make the world better."

"Don't worry," he said grimly. "Sasha, don't worry. Where'd they call from?"

"I'll text you the number," she said, sniffling. "Please don't let them come to my house on Christmas. I'm sorry I'm such a... a fucking *mouse* about this—"

"Stop," he said, making sure his voice was firm. "Sasha, you are strong. You walked out of their lives and you... I was an asshole when I was there, but even *I* could see what a good life you made for your kids. So don't... don't be mad at yourself because you don't have the asshole gene, okay? I guess it's all I'm good for."

"No," she protested. "No—that's not why I asked you."

Pierce's mouth twisted—he couldn't help it. But he kept the bitterness out of his voice when he talked to his little sister. "Honey, I'm going to go call them now, okay?" He pushed himself up off the couch, where Hal was looking at him with big eyes.

Well, Hal didn't want him at all—he might as well show Hal who he really was.

"Thank you," Sasha said on a sigh. "Thanks, Pierce. I'm so grateful."

"Love you, Sash," he said quietly. "I'll take that info now."

He disconnected and grimaced at Hal. "You don't want to hear what's going to happen next."

"You're not an asshole," Hal said staunchly.

Pierce sighed. "You're such a sweet guy. You wouldn't know an asshole if...." *He came in your mouth in the dark.* "If he threw a pillow at your head." And with that, Pierce limped to the bedroom, just as his phone dinged with Sasha's text and a number he thought would have changed by now.

He hit the link with a sigh.

"Hello, Atwater residence, Diana Atwater speaking."

Oh hell—his mother hadn't changed in the least.

"This is your son, Pierce, Diana. I've called to ask you very nicely to stay the fuck away from Florida."

"Pierce?" For once his mother sounded startled. "Pierce, why on earth would you be calling?"

"You called Sasha, right?"

"Yes, but you made it very clear that you never wished to speak to us again. We honored your wishes. Your sister, on the other hand—"

"Is the same person she was eight years ago, except happy. Why in the hell would you call her up out of the blue and fuck that up?"

He waited for something to happen inside him, something that would relent, some scrap of decency that would let him feel bad about the way he was speaking to his mother. But all he could remember was a rigid back in the front of the car as his mother taxied him and Sasha around town, six days a week, to the relentless activities that he and Sasha had been enrolled in pretty much since preschool. Derrick would get to soccer practice singing Led Zeppelin at the top of his lungs with his father or hanging out for one last bit of conversation with his mom. Pierce would slingshot the fuck out of the back seat like all the demons of hell were on his ass.

Or at least one big freezing demon with perfectly coifed hair.

"I really don't know what this has to do with you, Pierce—"

"I'm going to be at Sasha's for Christmas. Did you let her tell you that?"

There was a shocked silence. "No—we didn't think—"

"What? That Sasha and I talked? I wrecked my car, Mom. Wrecked my car, lost my job, almost died, and got a divorce. And Sasha stepped up to take care of me like I took care of her. I'm staying at a friend's beach house right now, but you know what? I *promised* to come back. And Sasha wants me back for Christmas. So I'm going to be there, and Sasha wants me there and not you. Live with that."

"But… but, Pierce." And for the first time in his life, Pierce heard his mother's voice waver. "Our grandchildren. You'd deprive… your father and me of meeting our grandchildren?"

Pierce took a deep breath and thought of forgiveness. "You really want to meet your grandchildren? Start with a card on their birthdays. Start with presents. Start with a phone call once a week where you get to know them. *Don't* call your daughter up and bully her into something she would rather not do."

"You really don't think much of us, do you?"

It was not his imagination. She sounded hurt. The last time they'd had this conversation, she'd sounded pissed and superior and smug. She'd told him that his interference would be immaterial—Sasha would come crawling back eventually.

Shit.

Just like Cynthia. Someone had fucking learned.

"No," he said, his voice dropping. "I don't. But you still have a chance with Sasha. Not this Christmas you don't. This Christmas I'm going to be there, in all my pissed-off glory—"

"We could see you too, son," his mother said hesitantly.

"I'm bisexual. I'm seeing a man right now. No."

Yeah, he'd always wondered if he should come out to his parents— why would he need to if he was married to Cynthia? If Loren was going to break up with him? His mother's harshly drawn breath was all the reward he'd ever needed.

"Why would you even tell us that?" his mother asked, her voice breaking.

"Why would it even matter?" he shot back. "See? You're the same people. You're the people who screamed at Sasha until she broke. You're the people who drove her boyfriend—the one who'd proposed, by the way—away with a baseball bat. You're the same judgmental, disapproving assholes you've always been—and you just proved it all over again. You want a relationship with your grandchildren, go ahead and send a card and some presents. Just remember, I've got an eight-year head start spoiling them rotten, and they are *always* going to love me best."

"Does Sasha even know who she's exposing her children to?" Diana asked, voice all venom. "Does *she* know about your... your... *perversion?*"

"She's known since I was in college. See, you were never really interested in us as people—but we always had each other's backs. Still do. So, are you coming to Christmas if I'm there?"

"No. I'll have to discuss this with your father to see if we want to come at all."

"Just say no. Neither of us want you back in our lives. If you can't do the work, don't bother."

It was as good an exit line as any, so he hung up. Pierce set the phone in the charger and sat heavily on the bed. He heard a noise in the doorway and turned his head, unsurprised to see Hal there.

"Sorry," he rasped, hating himself so badly in that moment.

"Why?" Hal asked. He reached behind him and switched off the hall light. Pierce realized the bedroom was the only room in the house that still had a light on. Well, it was pretty late. Suddenly wiped out, he pulled his feet out of his flip-flops and pulled his mostly clean sleep pants out from under the pillow.

"That wasn't... pleasant." Pierce sighed. "Hold on a second." He grabbed his phone off the charger and texted *I told her I'd be there and I'm bisexual. Make sure Marshall knows.*

Pierce set the phone down and wrestled with his cargo shorts. After he won, he laid them on the dresser and grabbed the sleep pants.

"You can just wear boxers," Hal said. It sounded like he was tripping over his tongue.

Pierce didn't even look at him. He felt... numb. And sad. And unwanted.

His phone pinged. *Marshall's always known. She just texted and said she'd be in touch, but they wouldn't be coming for Christmas. Thank you.*

He swallowed. God, he still couldn't look Hal in the eyes. *Love you, Sasha. Night.*

Love you back. Night.

His fingers were still fairly nimble. He'd realized that in the past two weeks—his arm had been broken and sustained muscle and nerve damage, but his hand and fingers worked just fine. He unbuttoned his overshirt and laid it down next to the cargo pants before setting the phone down one last time.

He felt Hal's weight depress the bed and stretched forward to turn off the light while the comforter under his ass got yanked down. Nice. That was a nice thing to do.

He was unprepared for Hal's heat at his back or the hands at the hem of his T-shirt in the dark.

"What are you—"

"Shh...." Hal breathed into his ear. "Just... hush."

This again?

But he could feel Hal's lips his neck, his ear, down his shoulder. *This* again didn't seem like a terrible thing. Hal lifted his T-shirt up over his head, and Pierce could raise his hands up to help him out—a thing he couldn't have done two and a half weeks ago.

"Thank—"

Hal kissed the back of his neck, and he grunted, all senses going on overdrive. Then Hal put his lips almost touching the whorls of Pierce's ear. "You are *not* an asshole."

Pierce moaned, his entire body going boneless. Hal moved and pulled him backward until he was lying face up in the darkness. He stared at the ceiling while Hal kissed his way down again, thinking *Dammit, no. Not... not... ah....*

Hal's mouth, dreamy, insistent, wrapped around Pierce's cock through the cotton of his boxers. Pierce massaged his head as Hal mouthed him. Pierce grunted, his hips bucking, his libido getting the hint that last night's activity had *not* been a fluke.

He was going to say something, give a direction, ask if he could reciprocate—*something*—but then Hal tugged at his boxers, and he was naked under the cool air of the ceiling fan, his knees spread before the world. Hal repositioned himself between Pierce's legs, and Pierce lifted his head, watching Hal suck his cock, bare now, over Pierce's long body.

Hal's eyes gleamed wickedly in the dark room, daring him to say anything. *Daring* him to actively engage.

"Harder," Pierce whispered. "Faster. Oh God, *yes!*"

Hal took him down, all the way, grabbing his shaft as he pulled his head back, and Pierce urged him on unashamedly. If this was what Hal wanted to do, Pierce wanted it—oh God, how he wanted it.

"That's so good," Pierce rasped. "So… oh God. Hal…. Hal, I'm going to…."

Then Hal slid his fingers, slick with spit, down Pierce's crease, and Pierce almost sobbed. One finger, penetrating, just a little, just enough….

"Come!" Pierce cried, tugging on his hair.

But like the night before, when Pierce had been able to pretend it never really happened, Hal sucked hard on the bell and swallowed.

"Thank you," Pierce chanted. "Thank you, thank you, thank you…."

Hal moved off his cock and pulled up his shorts, sliding up the bed to rest his head on Pierce's chest.

And Pierce wanted more. With another tug on Hal's hair, Pierce held his head back.

"Kiss me," he ordered gently.

Hal's mouth, glazed with spit and come, swollen from sucking on Pierce's cock, parted. "But—"

Pierce kissed him, the kiss as sensual as the blowjob. He fell into Hal's mouth, plundered it, tasted his own semen and swept his tongue in for more. Hal groaned, and Pierce turned his body so Hal was lying on his back in his underwear.

Oh Lord—he was so beautiful. Cut muscles, golden skin—tiny flat caramel-colored nipples. Pierce wanted to taste it all, but Hal's mouth was too delicious to leave.

He kissed and allowed his hand to roam, playing with the tightened ends of the nipple candy and gliding his palm down the smooth skin of Hal's stomach.

And still that kiss went on, Pierce's replete body howling for intimate knowledge of the man who had so pleased him.

He slid his hand under Hal's waistband and groaned at the decadence of the hardened flesh under his palm.

"Jesus, Hal, you're huge," he breathed, squeezing the base and tightening his grip over the shaft.

Hal half sobbed into his mouth. "Ah... oh God... just... keep... oh please...."

Pierce pushed up to move so he could taste too, remember the feeling of a cock down his throat, luxuriate in the taste of another man's spend. Hal shook his head and captured Pierce with his hands, holding him there for more kisses, intimate and blistering, while Pierce grasped him hard and stroked.

The first spill of hot precome from the head was torture. Pierce *wanted* it, *craved* the feel of it spurting down the back of his throat. But Hal kept up with the kisses, so Pierce kept stroking until Hal cried out, "Slow! Hard! Squeeze the... ohmigod omigod omigod.... *Pierce!*"

Ah! Pierce bucked against Hal's hip, spilling a little bit himself as the first thick spurt oiled the rest of that amazing member. Pierce kept squeezing, touching, fondling, until the final spend, and Hal whimpered a little, sore.

Pierce pulled his hand up to his mouth, but Hal stopped him, eyes anxious and searching in the darkness.

"I need to get tested," he whispered, head turned like he was ashamed.

"Do," Pierce told him, wiping his hand off on the sheets and going in for a kiss. "I want to—"

Hal took his mouth hard, clinging, pulling back right when Pierce's entire brain was about to obliviate. "Why?" he asked while their harsh breathing returned to normal. "Why did you...?"

"I wanted it to be real," Pierce told him, his voice a faint rumble and not a whisper. "I wanted us to touch."

Hal closed his eyes, like that hurt, and swallowed. "I'll get tested tomorrow," he promised.

"Did you think I wouldn't understand?" Pierce's turn to lay his head on Hal's shoulder. "Did you think I'd judge you?"

"I wanted you to... to think I was a grown-up," Hal confessed, voice breaking a little. "All your talk about being old and cynical. I... wanted to be a grown-up and still a unicorn. So you'd know...."

"Shh...." Pierce's turn to silence the roaring in Hal's heart. He rolled a bit and kissed Hal, taking the sadness and the worry away. "Shh...." He kissed him again, just the slip of a tongue, not arousing but kind, healing. "You'll always be a unicorn," he promised. "You'll be forty-five and a unicorn. Or sixty. Just because I'm not as strong as you are doesn't mean I don't believe in you."

Hal shook his head and buried his face in the hollow of Pierce's shoulder. "You are," he hiccupped. "You are a unicorn. You just won't see…."

Pierce didn't know what to do with that. He nuzzled Hal's temple until his breathing quieted down some and Pierce could close his eyes and fall fast asleep.

FUTURE SHOCKS

"YOU CAN wait out in the car," Hal said, fidgeting with his key fob. "This'll take—"

"Anywhere from ten minutes to an hour," Pierce gauged, looking the medical clinic over grimly. "Anything hospital inclined is a crapshoot."

"I can drop you off at Walmart—it's right down the road." Hal still wouldn't look at him.

"Dammit!" Pierce snapped. "Hal! This isn't the end of the world! It's an HIV test—I got my first one in college." *Oh God—Ass. Hole.* Pierce took a deep breath and tried to be a unicorn, which was hard since Hal had been an evasive sprite all damned morning about the HIV test thing.

"I hate making you a part of my bad decision making," Hal said after a moment, and oh holy crap and pass the potatoes, something *real*.

Pierce took a deep breath. "Forgetting the rubber happens." He let out a laugh. "Ask my sister. I wasn't joking when I said shaming people for sexual activity is high on my list of douchebag things to do."

"But it wasn't just once," Hal muttered, staring out the window. "I broke up with Russ, and Russ called me all sorts of… you know, prude and baby, and I was a stupid dumbass kid about it and set out to…." He flailed, avoiding Pierce's eyes like Pierce was a red-eyed dragon who hypnotized his prey.

"Set out to fuck everything that moved to prove him wrong?" Oh Lord, college.

Hal looked at him sideways—but at least he looked at him. "After Loren?" he said softly.

"After Katrina," Pierce said with a grimace. "First relationship. Freshman year. True love always, until Derrick found out she'd done everybody at school while we were going out."

"Ouch!"

Pierce shrugged—distance gave perspective. "You know, everybody has their damage. Whatever happened to *her* to make her need that? And I really do believe it was something she felt compelled to do—breaking up hurt her, mostly because she felt like she couldn't help herself. But yeah. I went out to prove I could bang all the things." Pierce did the unthinkable then—they'd had sexual activity and they'd even had kissing, but they hadn't yet done this.

He reached out and grabbed Hal's hand and brought the knuckles to his lips.

"I had a friend," he said, smiling a little before holding Hal's hand to his cheek. God, tenderness. He wanted to give Hal *all* the tenderness. "Derrick came to clubs with me and fucked all the things too. I forgot rubbers left and right and pretended I was hip and devil-may-care. Derrick forgot once and had a panic attack. So I… I said, 'Hey, let's just go check it out together, so we can not freak out about it,' right?"

"You were both negative, right?"

"Right," Pierce said, nodding. "I wouldn't bullshit you. But I had blood tests run in the hospital anyway—I would have told you that first night, Hal." He frowned. "Although I wish you'd asked."

Hal swallowed and tugged at his hand. Pierce let him go with some disappointment, but then Hal turned his palm and cupped Pierce's cheek.

"I'll get tested now," he said, stroking Pierce's lower lip with his thumb. "And… and I'll remember to ask the… if… uh, if I ever need to again."

Pierce kissed the inside of his palm and moved away so he could open the door and climb out with his cane. He avoided saying the obvious thing, the thing neither of them were saying.

They had less than a week and a half. Unless they decided to make this a long-distance thing, he was getting tested so they could share a handful of nights together.

The thought left a terrible ache, an empty void in the center of Pierce's chest.

Today. I'll be with him today. And tomorrow. And the next day. It will have to be good enough.

FIFTEEN MINUTES later they came out of the clinic, Hal looking disgustedly at his phone.

"They'll call me in one or two days?" he asked, upset.

"That's what they said," Pierce said mildly.

"Two days."

"So they said."

"We have to wait two days?"

"I hate to tell you this, but I can still give you blowjobs. You heard the guy—the risk of HIV through swallowing is—"

"Too big to risk," Hal snapped, glaring at him. "Handsies all the way."

Pierce glared at him, making diabolical, slow, and sensual plans that would make "handsies" look like a gift from the gods. "Sure," he said. "Handsies. 'Cause we're fourteen-year-olds grabbing each other in the locker room. Handsies."

Hal unlocked the doors with a gentle beep, hiding a smirk.

"What?" Pierce asked, swinging into the CR-V and cursing the stiffness left over from his morning workout. Dammit—he was seriously going to have to keep swimming if he ever wanted to move again.

If he ever wanted to possess Hal, completely, or pull his knees up to his chest and let Hal take him.

"Thirteen," Hal said, closing the door and starting the car. "I was thirteen, old man. What? Did you save your hand job cherry for college?"

"Graduation," Pierce muttered, embarrassed. "Some of us were *not* that cute in high school."

Hal paused in the act of pulling his seat belt on. "What makes you think some of us *were*? Cute in high school, I mean."

Pierce rolled his eyes. "Do I have to say it?" he asked, mortally embarrassed. "Are you really going to make me tell you this?"

Hal stared at him through those big amber eyes. Pierce had noticed, this last week, how lush his black eyelashes were, how strong his nose was, straight bridged and not too big. What a strong jaw he had, and how his smile was as innocent and bright as his mouth was sinfully wicked.

"Tell me what?"

Truth was a compulsion. "You're beautiful," Pierce said, embarrassed. "You... I was so embarrassed, that first day, because you were so pretty—so beautiful, and you were talking to me, and I was at my worst in my entire life. I couldn't even see your eyes then. And your eyes are beautiful. And your mouth is beautiful. I don't know how you could have been anything but beautiful in high school. I... I just don't understand."

It was his turn to look away, avoiding Hal's eyes.

Hal fumbled for his hand, but Pierce still couldn't have looked at him.

"I *so* would have blown you when I was in high school," Hal said fervently.

"And that would have made me a creepy old guy molesting an underage boy."

Hal laughed shortly. "Look at me. We're wasting gas."

Pierce turned reluctantly because he was right. "What?"

"I'm twenty-three."

"I *know* that."

"I'm only a little stupid."

Pierce couldn't help the faint smile. "Aren't we all."

"I wanted you from that first day. Hurt and pale—it didn't matter."

"Because you're crazy," Pierce said slowly, like you spoke to crazy people so as not to set them off.

Hal dragged the knuckles of his free hand down the side of Pierce's scarred cheek. "Because you're a unicorn," he said. Then he kissed Pierce, one of the softest, most tender kisses Pierce could ever remember. Aching with gentleness, it undid him, leveled everything in his heart, in his mind, that could have stood against Hal's incursion into his soul.

Hal pulled away and stroked his lower lip again. "Don't try to deny it," he whispered, and while Pierce was looking for words that wouldn't shatter either of them, Hal pulled away from the clinic. "So—should we try for wrapping paper this time?"

"How about rubbers and lube," Pierce muttered, unsettled and vulnerable. "We could start there."

"Sure. Zombie Apocalypse Central, here we come."

THEY REMEMBERED wrapping paper, ribbon, condoms, and lubricant.

They forgot scissors and tape.

"I don't even believe this," Hal said as he stared at the paper on the table in disbelief. "This is… this is *epic*. I'm, like, if I never see another Target for the rest of my life, it will be too soon for me in my next life and the guy I bang after that!"

"How can Derrick not have any scissors?" Pierce asked, rifling through the drawers. "I mean, we bought ribbon—if I just had, you know, scissors, I could cut the ribbon and wrap everything and use the ribbon to secure it."

Hal turned his head to gaze at Pierce in disbelief. "So you admit to being a Boy Scout, but you're going to deny the unicorn thing?"

Pierce wrinkled his nose. "Fine. Yes. Whatever." He flopped down in the love seat, which was where Hal usually sat when they watched television. "I'm at a loss," he said, shaking his head. "I say I skip Christmas at my sister's, turn down the job, and start living at the beach. You can throw me money when you visit from college."

"That's not a plan!" Hal told him, horror coloring his voice.

"It is too," Pierce insisted. "It's a plan. It's very much a plan."

"Well, it's a *shitty* plan. How about you stay here, watch some TV, and let me go get scissors and tape at the little drugstore up at the corner. They're crappy for Christmas shopping, but scissors and tape they can handle."

Pierce gazed at him in naked gratitude. "I would do unmentionable things to and for you just so I didn't have to go to Target again."

Hal rolled his eyes. "Same here." He handed Pierce the remote control and bent down, squeezing his shoulder and nuzzling his temple. "Nap. I'll get takeout. We'll work out double tomorrow, how's that?"

Perfect.

PIERCE JERKED awake about an hour later, looking around the condo muzzily. He'd fallen asleep watching a rerun of *2 Broke Girls* and now a rerun of *Castle* had taken its place. Hal had opened the shades over the sliding glass doors, and the sun, which had been sulking behind clouds and haze when he'd first sat down, was now glaring at him on the horizon.

He yawned and stretched, trying to remember if he'd heard Hal return.

Takeout boxes sat on the table—unopened and still steaming—so he must have been there somewhere.

Pierce stood, shivering, and made his way over the rubber mats toward the bedroom, wondering if Hal had gone down for a nap of his own. He approached the doorway, which stood dark, and heard Hal's voice.

"No, I haven't decided. I told you that ten minutes ago." He paused, and in the darkness, Pierce could see him stretched horizontally on the bed, facing the window and not the doorway. "You said I had until after New Year's—why is this a problem?" He grunted and swung his feet over his bottom, the gesture absurdly young. "What do I *want* you to do? Well, maybe not kick me out for Christmas—that would be a start. But how about letting me get my massage therapy certificate—I mean, I could go for sports medicine if you want, but I've been trying to get that done between my coursework for two years. You have to know I mean it by now!"

Whatever the reply, it was *not* what he wanted to hear. He groaned and rolled over to his back. "Yeah! I get it! I'm not good enough to be your kid anyway—you've made that clear!" He spotted Pierce and held out his hand.

For a moment, Pierce thought about retreating into the living room to give him his "space," but two things stopped him.

One was that Hal had been there—two of the worst phone calls of his life, and Hal had been there, holding, supporting—making love. Pierce couldn't just leave him to work out his own shit.

But Pierce didn't *want* to leave him—that was the second thing.

He stepped into the room and threw himself lengthwise on the bed next to Hal, then rolled over on his side and slid his hand up under Hal's T-shirt so he was touching bare skin.

Hal captured his hand and clung.

"No, I'm not being overdramatic—and it's not a gay thing. You don't want me home because I'm gay—excuse the hell out of me for being gay. You don't want me to leech off your fortune unless I'm doing something worthwhile. Like be a lawyer. And only be a lawyer. And be nothing else but a lawyer."

The next thing over the phone made him sit up explosively, and Pierce had to scramble to sit next to him.

"How do I know that? Because I've been telling you. Yes I have. Yes I have. No, yes I have! I've been *telling you for years* that I want to do something else. Well, maybe if you'd have let me take the general ed I wanted to instead of the prelaw, I would have had a better idea sooner, but I know now!" He took a deep breath through the next flurry of conversation—from a woman, it sounded like, so Mom, probably—

REGRET ME NOT 211

and then blurted, "If you guys cared at all about who I *am* instead of who you *want me to be*, maybe this wouldn't sound like drama to you!"

He listened for another minute and then burst out, "I'll tell you after New Year's like I said I would! No! *Don't* call me on Christmas Day, because I don't give a fuck what you're doing, just like you don't give a *fuck* about me!"

He hit End Call, but that apparently wasn't satisfying enough, because he cocked his arm back, and Pierce had to rescue the phone.

"Oh oh oh! Hold up there, Chief—if you're thinking about going solo without backup, paying for a phone is a bad way to start."

Hal let go of the phone and threw himself back onto the bed, scrubbing his face with his hands. "Augh!"

Pierce lay down next to him again, keeping that bare skin contact with his hand to the soft skin of Hal's taut middle.

"I'm so pissed!" Hal raged. "Called me up right when I pulled in, and it was all, 'Why haven't you signed up for classes?' and I was all 'Because you gave me extra time!' and they were all…." He took a deep breath and shook his head. "Like it was all predetermined. That I would go be this thing they wanted me to be and I wouldn't argue with them, and it would all be okay."

"They *really* don't know you very well," Pierce said, pulling air from the hollow of his neck and shoulder.

Hal turned so quickly their lips touched before he had a chance to decide. Pierce went with it, parting his lips, delving into his sweet mouth for a few breaths, a few heartbeats. Hal pulled back, and he almost keened.

God, he wanted all the time he could possibly get.

"Why do you say that?" Hal asked softly.

"They don't know you?" Pierce frowned. "Because… you're not… docile. You… you push back. You fight. You make decisions. I… I know you're young." He grimaced. "But God, Hal, do you think we'd be… do you think I'd… I mean, I wouldn't be having a relationship with you if you didn't know who you are."

A slow smile spread over Hal's godsbedamned beautiful face. "I was a pushover with Russ," he rasped. "I've been a good kid all my life. When push came to shove, I think they just expected me to…."

"Bend over and take it?" Pierce said throatily. There was no question at all—none—who would top between them. Who would have his hands most comfortably on the reins, who would gauge the situation, the heat of their bodies, the susceptibility of flesh, more competently of the two of them.

Pierce could top, was comfortable doing so—but Hal was *made* to be in control.

Hal blinked, slowly, expression turning sultry in the dim light of late afternoon. "I will *take* you," he promised. "I will... I will shove myself so far inside you that you'll taste me coming when I'm in your ass."

Pierce closed his eyes, hard, painfully hard, at the sound of Hal's voice promising dire things. "That will happen," he promised rashly, because what if he couldn't? His body was looser now, but still—not 100 percent. Creeping past 50 percent. He leaned close to Hal's ear and whispered, "I want you inside me so bad...."

Hal's sound—raw, wanting, primal—did things to Pierce's body that actual sex had missed. Oh man—how could he have lived this long and not known what it was like to be wanted like that?

With a feral growl, Hal rolled over, lying on top of Pierce and claiming his mouth in a hard, wet mauling of a kiss. His tongue swept inside, and Pierce's defenses disintegrated, his good sense annihilated at the hard pressure of Hal's groin against his.

Pierce yanked at his shirt, wanting that chest—golden, soft-skinned, hard muscled—under his hands. He was *starving* for touch like this, for Hal's mouth slanting over his again and again and again.

Hal moved faster than he did, and he pulled back to haul his shirt over his head and shove his jeans and underwear down off his feet, finishing before Pierce could even unbutton his own shirt.

Hal took over the task with shaking fingers.

"You"—button—"are trying"—button—"to kill me." Button, button, button.

Pierce opened his arms so Hal could help him struggle out of the shirt, and then his T-shirt.

"I need you alive," Pierce told him as Hal yanked at the waistband of his cargo shorts. Pierce lifted up his ass and let them be hauled down.

They paused for a moment, naked in the twilight, vulnerable and wanting.

Hal groaned and crashed his mouth down again, his hand going straight for Pierce's cock.

Well, two could play at that game.

It was a rough, rocky race to the finish line, a carnal stroking of each other's cocks while their mouths never stopped the mutual ravishing. Hal's hand was a rough, strong wonder on Pierce's erection—no finesse, no titillation. Pure hand-fucking that made the phrase "handsies" even more juvenile—a diminishment of the power knotting Pierce's belly, his thighs, his taint.

He groaned into Hal's mouth, brought abruptly to the edge of a spinning climax, and Hal bucked and spurted, apparently hitting his own peak just that fast.

"Ah!" Pierce broke off from the kiss, wanting to revel in the feeling of come over his fingers. Hal bit his neck, hard enough to leave a mark, and again, lower, and again, sucking the flesh in his mouth without apology.

Pierce gave Hal's cock one more frantic, expert stroke, squeezing at the head, oiling the whole member with the precome. Hal bit his shoulder and growled, bucking, coming undone in Pierce's hand while Pierce let the white light and tumbling surf of climax crash over them both.

When their bodies had stopped convulsing, they were left in a trembling, chilly aftermath, breathing harshly into the shadows of each other's flesh.

"Eventually," Hal panted, "we're going to need condoms."

"Sure," Pierce said. He thought, *Once you're inside me, I don't know if I can ever leave you.*

Oh hells. Oh God, oh hells, oh damn.

Hal, a week and a half isn't going to be enough.

THE NEXT morning, Hal really did double down on the workout to make up for their laziness the night before. Pierce went along with it—well, he grumbled about slave drivers and torturers and fucking sadists until the older couple who had been thinking about coming to the pool toward the end of the workout looked at each other in alarm and retreated—but by God, he did it.

He still had the idea that maybe he'd be up to using the condoms and the lubricant by the time he left for Sasha's.

Artificial deadline, you fuckwad.

Yeah, his inner voice was bitter, but it was hard to talk it off the ledge when he was pushing so hard he could barely breathe.

"Okay, slow that down a little," Hal said. "We're doing the open-gaited run—not so fast, but active stretching. Make sure you stretch a *lot*, because—" He paused in his torture and grinned lasciviously. "—well, just because."

Pierce wanted to roll his eyes, but he also wanted to do more of what they'd been doing at night, so he refrained.

The overbright *ting* of Hal's phone cutting through the music it played made them both pause. "Don't stop!" Hal snapped, and Pierce *did* manage not to roll his eyes—but he didn't stop.

"Hello. Hal Lombard." Suddenly Hal went very still. Pierce paused to look at him in concern, and Hal didn't stop him. "Yes? Yes. Negative?"

The slow smile across his face told Pierce the negative was exactly what they'd been hoping for. He caught Hal's eyes and smiled.

"Thank you. Yes—happy holidays to you too."

He hit End Call and the music resumed, but Pierce didn't head toward the other side of the pool. "Negative?" he asked softly.

Hal bit his lip and nodded. "Yeah."

"Good."

Hal frowned. "*You* need to get moving again or you're going to cramp like a guy kidnapped in the trunk of a car. Now go!"

"Sadist."

"Whatever. Do you want a rubdown in the hot tub?"

Yes. I want a rubdown in the hot tub, and in the bed, and all over my body.

"Maybe."

"Then move your ass, Pierce—thataboy!"

Pierce finished his workout with a minimum of fuss. He'd seen the soft smile, the pleased relief. He'd been a part of that.

He'd be a part of the celebration too.

THAT NIGHT Pierce wrapped presents while Hal finished the Lego Christmas tree.

"Do you want me to wrap your bear?" Pierce asked, just to make sure.

"It's the only thing I'm going to have to open," Hal told him without self-pity. "Of course."

"Okay, then. Just remember the Legos are yours too."

Hal grinned at him with the glee of a five-year-old. "Yeah?"

"Of course they are!" Pierce grinned back. He would have to give Hal Legos for Christmas every year.

Shit. Crap. Whatever.

Pierce would get his address and send him Legos for Christmas every year, even if that was the only time ever after they talked to each other after Pierce left on the twenty-fourth.

That was a promise he made himself. Legos for Hal Lombard, forever. It was a deal.

Hal was concentrating on putting details on the tree, though. Teeny-tiny corner pieces in red, blue, and yellow served as Christmas tree lights. Pierce was very impressed.

Pierce, clumsy this year but still able, wrapped the Keurig and the two giant teddy bears and the big boxes with glee. He wanted to give Hal something else, he thought as he arranged the gifts on the floor near the end table, where the Christmas tree would go.

"What do massage therapists *need*?" he asked himself.

Hal didn't even look up. "We need a certificate," he said promptly. "From a reputable school or apprentice program, and about 500 hours of practice. In some states it's 1100. Who knows."

Pierce grimaced cheerfully—you couldn't say his boy wasn't focused. "I mean materially. Is there a kind of massage oil you like? Do you need a folding table? What *things* do you need to be a massage therapist?"

Hal shrugged. "A sturdy table—the kind that can hold up to 500 pounds but wheels in on its own. Massage oil. An internship. It's pretty simple, but it takes dedication. And, you know, not being a dick with people's bodies. I mean, I took a couple summer classes and have about 300 hours, but it's not close yet."

"Okay," Pierce said, thinking hard. "Okay."

"So, what do you think? Should I add non-Lego touches? Ribbon? Cotton balls? Tinsel?"

Pierce looked at it critically. "I think non-Lego touches would be awesome. Come on, raid the stash pile—let's see what you can do."

"Yeah, well, thank God for tape. Okay—here we go."

Pierce finished stacking his gifts and sat down at the laptop desk while Hal worked away, industrious and absorbed. Some of the fury of their lovemaking the night before had abated, but the underlying tension, that continual need, was gnawing away at Pierce's stomach.

He was going to *need* Hal again that night. He was going to *need* him in the morning. Pierce had been mildly paranoid about becoming addicted to pain pills when he'd been released from the hospital—he'd had no idea his most frightening addiction would be the body of the pushy aqua instructor who had just sort of bossed his way into Pierce's life.

How did you recover from that?

He started searching the internet for massage tables, not even batting an eyelash at the prices. He could do it. He *should* do it. He should buy Hal a massage table, so when he decided not to take his parents' prefab life, he could have a head start into the life of his own.

Two things stopped him from just pushing the button.

The first was that delivery wouldn't be until after he left for Sasha's. He imagined Hal, sad and alone—and possibly hungover—the day after Christmas, getting the massage table from the lover who'd wandered into his life and then wandered out again.

He imagined him trying to set a world record for bingeing on greyhounds. He imagined the headline "College Student Dies of Alcohol Poisoning After Receiving a Really Expensive Gift from a Thoughtless Bastard."

Imagined smashing his own head against his keyboard until the computer didn't go anymore.

But that was only the first thing.

The second thing was that, even if Hal got it and loved it—took it and became a world-class massage therapist who catered to the stars and owed it all to Pierce and his fabulous gift and the faith he had such a short time to impart—it wouldn't be enough.

It would feel like a real expensive tip to a therapist—and that's not what Pierce wanted to give him at all.

"Ta-da!"

Pierce had no idea how long he was lost in an agony of indecision, but he turned around, and Hal stood holding the Lego Christmas tree out in front of him with all the aplomb of an excited twelve-year-old.

Pierce's heart almost throbbed right out of his chest.

"Let me get a picture," he said, his smile hurting his cheeks. "C'mon, stand right there—" He motioned to the light, and Hal moved to the optimum spot, a proud smile on his face.

Pierce took the picture, and then another one, and then three more, before Hal snatched the camera out of his hand.

"Jesus, nobody needs that many pictures of me!"

"I do," Pierce defended grumpily. "It's important."

"Whatever. Here—selfie with the tree!"

"That's not gonna—"

"Ugh."

They both stared at the picture, with Pierce's eyes half open and a Lego Christmas tree sprouting from Hal's mouth like a deformed tooth.

"Okay—just us." Hal set the tree down and looped his arm over Pierce's shoulder, and both of them smiled at the phone with such optimism and hope, Pierce almost didn't believe it was him in that picture. Hal snapped it, then grabbed the phone.

"Here," he said, and his voice dropped like he'd realized, hey, this might be the only evidence that both of them ever existed in the same space and made multiple trips to Target and dominated the pool in the morning and sometimes took halting, pointless, beautiful walks along the beach. "Let me send it to my phone."

"So I have your contacts," Pierce said, which sounded obvious, but they hadn't done that yet. Exchanging numbers would mean they were thinking about beyond this moment.

Hal looked up at him sideways. "So I can look at your smile," he said.

Pierce nodded, his throat tight. "I can text you the next time I go to Target."

Hal's laughter sounded false to his ears, but Pierce didn't have the heart to look him in the eyes. "Here," he said quietly. "Set it on the end table—I'll text Sasha. She can show the kids."

The neighbor made a Christmas tree—we're both very proud.

He sent one of the ones with Hal and one with the wrapped presents, both looking festive and out of place in the bright bold and white of the condo, and then sent the same thing to Derrick.

Neither responded, but as Pierce looked up, he realized something.

"Hey," he said, musing. "Don't you have a bestie? A buddy? A girl you wish you could marry? Something?"

Hal shrugged, ambling away from the Christmas corner, looking embarrassed. "I, uh, lost my peer group in the divorce," he said, trying to look like it was no big deal. "And... well, I took a lot of different classes. No time to hang out with the other biology majors or history majors because... you know...."

"You were taking six other things," Pierce said, getting it—but only a little. The answer hit him then, and his stomach knotted. "Tough being a judge's son?"

Hal screwed his eyes shut and flopped on the small couch. "You have no idea."

"All the kids in high school were—"

"Affluent, white, and shitty to other people," Hal muttered. "Yeah. I mean, the gay thing, fine. The massage-therapist thing?"

"Not so fine," Pierce said, getting it. "I went to a commuter school. If you weren't in the same major, you just didn't meet that many people."

Hal cocked his head. "Why a commuter school?"

Pierce shrugged. "Not much money, I guess." He thought about it, suddenly feeling like a crappy human being. "I had to help Sasha through school, but I guess I wouldn't have gotten through without my parents."

Hal looked like he wanted to say something—desperately. But he bit his lip and grabbed the remote instead.

"Wabbit season," he said softly.

"Duck season." Suddenly all Pierce wanted to do was kill time until they could be bodies moving in the dark.

THAT NIGHT, as they stood up to go to bed, he moved quickly enough to wrap his arms around Hal's waist and whisper in his ear.

"Go in, get undressed, lie naked on the bed." At Hal's indrawn breath, he added, "Turn off the light and close your eyes."

He heard Hal's swallow and let him go ahead while Pierce got the lights and locked up. On his way, he grabbed the lubricant off the table, where it had sat, chaste, in its little bag with the condoms.

He left the condoms on the table—his body was sore from the extra workout that morning, and cramping up in the middle of sex was not attractive.

Besides. He wanted to take care of Hal tonight.

When he got to the room, he paused to let his eyes adjust to the dark. And because he wanted to see Hal, legs splayed indecently, naked and vulnerable.

And for that night, his.

He undressed as quickly as he could, leaving his boxers up near his pillow to make them easier to find when they were done, and then, without saying a word, positioned himself between Hal's knees.

He heard the little gasp that meant Hal felt him, and then ran his hands up and down Hal's calves. Hal groaned softly, so Pierce followed through on the caress, behind the knees to his inner thighs. Pierce didn't know anything about massage, but he did know about the wonders of skin against skin.

He ran both hands to Hal's inner thighs, where he could run palms around the soft flesh of his legs and his thumbs down the juncture of leg and erogenous zone. When he extended the caress to part Hal's asscheeks, Hal's groan almost rocked him off the bed.

Pierce stretched out on his stomach, putting most of his weight on his good side, and bent his head, tracing a path with his tongue where his thumbs had been.

"Killing. Me."

Hal's voice, loud and demanding in the dark, startled Pierce badly enough to slip, face-planting with his mouth over Hal's balls.

Disgruntled, he sucked one into his mouth, pleased when Hal's feet came off the bed and he made a happy, turned-on sound.

"Okay, okay, okay," Hal whispered. "No talking."

Pierce sucked a little harder in acknowledgment and positioned himself again, this time with his hand on Hal's thickening cock.

He licked a line between his fingers and his thumb—because there was a space between them, because damn. He got to the bell and played, excited because tonight was his turn. He widened his mouth and lowered his head, letting his lips barely brush the head, his tongue flutter around it, while his hot breath promised the cave of wonders was *right there*.

Hal grunted and tried to buck but held himself back.

Pierce repaid him with a lick over the head, while his other hand fumbled for the lube bottle. Hal groaned, and Pierce gave another butterfly lick, and another, tasting precome.

"You know what that means," Pierce whispered into the darkness.

"You want to swallow?"

Just hearing the words was dirty enough to make Pierce hard.

"Sure." He tightened his mouth then and lowered his head, putting pressure all the way down to the root. Hal moaned and massaged Pierce's scalp through his hair while Pierce wiggled on the bed and tried to remember his plan.

Oh yes.

Lubricant.

He one-handed the bottle while he worked, his weaker arm trembling for the seconds it took to make his fingers slick and snap the top back on.

But once that was done, he could explore, sliding his fingertips down the center of Hal's warm cleft, finding the pucker in the center. A part of him yearned for sunlight and an entire day to make love, but most of him knew that his body had maybe a half an hour in it.

He would make it count.

He slid a fingertip inside and played the edge of Hal's bell with his tongue and the very delicate edge of his teeth. Hal let out a deep shudder and hunched down on the finger, taking Pierce up to his second knuckle.

"Getting cheeky," Pierce whispered, making sure his breath ghosted over the wet skin of Hal's cockhead.

"Not. A. Virgin," Hal graveled from a constricted throat.

Pierce grunted and took Hal's cock all the way down to the back of his throat—and added another finger.

The sound Hal let out was not quite human.

Oh, he was tight. His ass clamped down hard on Pierce's fingers, and Pierce thrust them in deeper and then pulled them out. Hal planted his feet farther apart and lifted his hips, giving Pierce free rein, and Pierce took it, lowering his mouth to the root and shoving his fingers in harder.

Hal moaned, shaking, and spurted just a little bit of pre.

But he didn't come. Not yet.

Pierce added a little more lube—and then he added, very slowly, another finger.

Hal screamed into his forearm, and Pierce thrust hard, digging his tongue into the slit at the top and widening his fingers at the root on the bottom.

Pierce knew himself, knew he'd be gibbering by now, begging, *needing*, but Hal—Hal kept more inside. He grabbed his thighs, spreading himself wider, and Pierce fucked him harder, sucking him, swirling his tongue for all he was worth.

Hal let out a groan and let go of his thighs. He banged his hands into the bed as he chased his elusive orgasm, and Pierce changed tactics.

He kept his fingers in the searing heat of Hal's body but started to move them *slowly*. He pulled his head back to torment the head of Hal's cock, but he used his other hand to squeeze and stroke *slowly*.

He continued to tease—tongue and the faintest edge of his teeth— but he went *slowly*.

Hal lost his mind.

His arms went first, flailing and pounding the bed on either side, and Pierce stopped for a moment, fingers still fucking, and issued an order. "Your nipples, Hal—pinch them!"

Hal did what he suggested, and Pierce kept up the slow pressure, the caress, the driving Hal out of his mind.

He kept squeezing the head of Hal's cock whenever he got to the end of the stroke and... one more time... and another... and another... and....

Hal screamed, his chest lifting off the bed like he was being hauled up by strings, his head tilted back as he cried out. Pierce didn't stop, not even when his mouth flooded, and he had to swallow, and again.

Hal collapsed against the bed in a limp heap, whimpering, "Done. I'm done," and Pierce finally stopped. He wiped his fingers on a washcloth he'd brought, and wiped his mouth on his bare shoulder while Hal curled up on his side self-protectively and caught his breath.

"Pierce?" he said, voice quavery in the moonlight coming from the window.

"Yeah?"

"Come here. I need to kiss you."

Pierce didn't ask if he'd mind tasting his own come—that was part of the celebration, he figured. He scooted up to lay his head on the pillow, and Hal took his mouth, sweeping his tongue in, taking over again and again and again. Pierce kissed him back, aroused, but just as happy to neck in the dark until they fell asleep.

But Hal had words for him before that happened.

"That was amazing," he whispered, and Pierce smiled, justifiably proud.

"You're fun to make love to," he said. He couldn't remember another lover—not Cynthia, not Loren—who would have abandoned himself so thoroughly. "I could suck your cock for a month."

Hal laughed weakly, but he was apparently thinking about something else. "I'm... I think tomorrow I'm going to go get you a gift. Is that okay?"

Pierce smiled, though, darkness and all. "Okay but not necessary," he said, nuzzling Hal's sweaty chest.

"I... I need to do something else, though, up in my condo." Hal grunted. "Just, you know, some housecleaning stuff. I haven't really been living there. I should...."

Pierce frowned. "You don't want to move ba—"

"No! Not... not until I have to." Hal let out a frustrated puff of air. "Just... tonight, I took care of my old business, and you did something really awesome for me. And I just want to take care of my old business again. But I don't want you to have to—"

Pierce shoved up on his good elbow. "You've done nothing this month but deal with me and my old business," he accused. "Why wouldn't I want to help you with—?"

Hal kissed him, hard, demandingly, until Pierce was an amoeba, melting into the mattress. "Please," he whispered. "I don't want you to see me like... like the condo would let you see me."

Pierce scowled, but he had to admit—he'd been out-bossed. "I could take it," he protested, feeling young and protected and not liking it. "I actually *am* older than you."

Hal laughed and kissed his cheek. "Believe me, Captain Recovery, I am aware. Just...." He licked the corner of his own mouth delicately, where a shiny drop of come threatened to trickle down. "You let me be the boss between us," he said after a moment, running his hand over Pierce's naked chest.

"Maybe I'm just naturally submissive," Pierce admitted, feeling like that was a big step.

Hal's raucous laughter told him maybe he hadn't said anything that insightful after all. "You think?" He ran his hand to Pierce's groin and began to tickle. "It's why we need you stretched and mobile, my friend—you have the makings of a sexual dynamo, and we just need recovery to free it. Like letting the Tasmanian devil out of his cage."

Pierce chuckled weakly and allowed Hal to fondle his cock.

"Feels like you came already," Hal said, nuzzling Pierce's bicep.

"I did, a little." Pierce smiled complacently, so happy in this moment he was surprised he had the wherewithal to speak. "I... this here? Us. You in my mouth? It's perfect."

Hal dropped his head to rest it on Pierce's shoulder. "Yeah."

They didn't mention the deadline or the things they might not get a chance to do.

It was the only time in Pierce's life that he was content to let "perfect" just exist, even if it might not be "permanent."

'TWAS THE NIGHT BEFORE

TRUE TO his word, Hal disappeared for a few hours the next day, right after their time at the pool. Pierce used the time to talk with his new employers and to take a look at the projects he'd be starting in March. He readily admitted to himself that the job would be a lot more fun than his old one—he seemed to have landed on his feet there, and another layer of the depression that had dogged him when he'd arrived at the condo peeled away.

I'm a provider again. I can even provide for... a college student. Or a massage therapy student. Or a dog. Or whatever.

Oh, the things he didn't want to think about.

He spent two hours writing a research-and-development plan for something he wasn't supposed to do for two months, just to avoid the thing he might have to do in slightly more than a week.

Hal showed up in the late afternoon, teeth chattering and lips almost blue with cold.

Pierce greeted him, holding his fingers and rubbing. "What in the hell?"

"Power's off at the condo," Hal muttered. "Wish I'd known—had to throw out all the frozen food."

Pierce frowned. "Wait. Power's off? It's not off here?"

Hal turned away, jaw locked grimly. "My parents had it turned off in their unit. Told the manager it wasn't supposed to be occupied."

Pierce gaped. "Uh...."

Hal shrugged. "Yes, they knew this was where I was. Yes, it was a tactic to get me to cave. But when I told the manager I was here, he recognized me, assumed it was a mistake, and told me he'd have it back on tomorrow."

Pierce shivered and wrapped his arm around Hal's shoulders, wanting to warm him up from the inside out. "Did you get all your shopping done?" he asked hopefully.

REGRET ME NOT   225

"They canceled my credit cards," Hal muttered glumly. "But I've got a bank account they can't touch. I'll go into town tomorrow and get cash."

Oh hells. "Oh baby," Pierce murmured, holding him tighter. "I'm so sorry."

Hal shook his head—but sank into Pierce's hold. "I'm not," he said fiercely. "If they wanted to show me who they were, they couldn't have picked a better way to do it."

"But... but... what will you do... you know. After?" *After I leave. After I ride off into the sunset to be with my family when you've just realized you don't have family to speak of.*

"I have power until New Year's. I've got money. I've got a car. Don't worry, Pierce, I won't be homeless." Hal pulled away, not looking at him, and started hunting around the kitchen. "Did you cook?"

"We bought a roast—I threw in some onion soup and some carrots and some stewed tomatoes. It wasn't much."

"You cooked!"

Pierce had to smile, although he wasn't sure he could breathe. "Sure. We'll call it cooking."

Hal turned to him, face alight. "For me? You cooked *for me?*"

Come home with me. I'll cook for you forever.

Pierce almost said it out loud, which was ludicrous because he only had four or five things, tops, that he could make without embarrassment. One of them was ham. "Yeah," he choked. "Of course. You'd tell me, right?"

"Tell you what?"

Hal poked the contents of the slow cooker with the wooden spoon next to it and breathed in rapturously. "The meat's falling apart. Can I eat? It looks great. Let's eat!"

"If you were going to end up homeless. If you had nowhere to go. You'd tell me. You'd say, 'Hey, can I have some help here, 'cause we're friends and lovers and I know you don't want me to be alone and homeless and alone.'"

Hal looked over his shoulder. "You'd tell *me*, right? If you were going back to Sacramento to be alone and not homeless but still alone."

"It's not the same thing," Pierce rasped. He could see himself clearly, in his little house with the big yard, with no Cynthia, working until the wee hours of the night, until his body knotted up and he could barely move, all to avoid the sound of his house when there was nobody there.

Hal left the roast alone to kiss his cheek. "Sure it is," he said softly. "But I've got more than enough to rent an apartment and live on my own, so don't worry about it. Let's eat."

Wabbit season.

Duck season.

Lonely season.

Fuck season.

Wanting season.

Suck it season.

Crying season.

Denying season.

Pierce was beginning to see why that bit always ended in "Bang!"

HAL'S WHIMPERS woke him up at 4:00 a.m....

"Wha—?"

"Sorry." Even in the dark, Pierce could hear his teeth chattering. "Bad dream."

Pierce rolled over and pulled him close. He'd put on boxers after lovemaking that night, but Hal was still bare and naked, vulnerable under their little blanket fort. Pierce wrapped his arms around his shoulders and tried to be his human shield.

"Shh. It's okay, baby. Don't worry. Nobody's going to hurt you."

Except you, Pierce, you cowardly coward who cowers.

Hal didn't say it—maybe he didn't even think it. But it was there, drifting between Pierce's ears, even as Hal settled down and fell asleep.

THE WEEK passed so quickly. Aqua, rubdowns, walks that grew longer and longer. Pierce had always assumed that a vacation with nothing to do would be a death sentence of boredom—but not with Hal. Sitting in front of the television was a treat. Surfing the net or working was a treat.

Just hearing him breathe in the same room was a treat.

And after his mysterious trips to clean out the condo—and how much damage could he have done in two days? Pierce was starting to be seriously concerned—greeting Hal as he walked in the doorway was like Christmas and his birthday rolled into one.

Except on Christmas, Pierce would be gone, and Hal would be here, in his condo. With parents who could turn the heat off at any moment.

December 22, Pierce got a text from Sasha:

You're coming, right? Have you booked a car?

Pierce looked at the text and grimaced. Yes, he should probably try to book a car ahead of time.

Not yet.

Why not!

Busy.

With your friend?

Pierce sighed.

I don't want to leave him.

Invite him to come.

It's complicated.

Coming over for Christmas? So easy. I'm making ham. Feeds everybody.

Oh Jesus. Pierce's sister. Best. Human being. Ever.

If I invite him for Christmas, I'll invite him forever.

There was a pause, and Pierce wondered if he'd even mentioned he was sleeping with the neighbor.

THAT kind of friend?

Yes.

Good enough for forever?

Yes.

He stared at the word. Felt compelled to add:

He's young. He's just starting out. He's getting his massage certificate. What would he do with me, Sasha? I'm grumpy and divorced.

And still that incriminating silence.

And his whole life is here. And mine is in Sacramento.

He stared at the phone and willed his sister to text something.

And it's been a shitty year. Why would he follow me 3000 miles when there's other people here? I probably still can't drive. I don't want him to pity me.

And… nothing.

What if he said no?

He'd be almost as stupid as you are.

Sasha!

I'll book the car for twelve. If you cancel it for whatever reason, let me know.

He's TWENTY-THREE.

I love you, Pierce, but Jesus, you worry too much.

He was in the middle of typing "I love you too," when she texted again.

I don't feel like arguing either. If you show up here heartbroken I'll need my strength. TTYL

And that was that.

PIERCE WOKE up the morning of the twenty-third feeling the sort of despair in his stomach he hadn't felt since the hospital, except reversed.

In the hospital it had been *Oh shit, I'm in the hospital, and I'm trapped here until they say I can go home, and then I'm with Cynthia and I'm trapped there, and then I'm home, and that's worse.*

Now, the day before Christmas Eve, it was *Oh shit. I'm going to have a wonderful day with someone I love, and then I'm going to have to leave forever because....*

Why again?

Because grown men who knew how the world worked didn't fall in love in a month? In a week? In a day?

In the first hour, when I was pissed and he was hungover, and he helped me first and came on to me second?

"Hey," Hal said at his side.

Pierce rolled over to smile at him, holding the sheet up in front of his mouth because he'd caught himself snoring once or twice the night before and his breath could give dragons a run for their money.

"Hey," he said back. "Happy Christmas Adam."

Hal grinned and pulled the sheet away. "The day before Eve," he murmured, then touched lips with him.

Pierce gave up on protecting Hal and opened his mouth, all the things he wanted to say shorting out like a neon sign in a windstorm.

The kiss went long and deep, and Pierce moaned, needing.

Hal pulled away and smiled shyly. "So, you need to take a hot shower—"

"No workout?"

He shook his head. "No. No workout. Today is better than a workout. I'm going to get my massage table from upstairs—"

"You have a massage table?" Well, it was a good thing Pierce had chickened out, wasn't it!

"Yeah. I thought you knew that—you asked me what I needed. Anyway. I'm going to bring it down here and heat up the oils." He grinned as he swung out of bed. "That's going to be my Christmas present to you," he said, proud of himself. "A full-body massage, and then we'll make Christmas cookies—"

Pierce frowned. "You bought ingredients?" Hal had gone shopping the day before, while Pierce had been answering some questions with the new bosses online.

"I did." Hal grinned smugly. "And I bought a ham and some asparagus too, so we'll make cookies and then cook Christmas dinner and then...."

He grinned at Pierce with a predatory quirk to his eyebrows.

"What?" Pierce asked, actually breathless.

"We'll see how far you can stretch," Hal hummed. He twisted in the bed, leaned forward, and placed his lips right up against Pierce's ear. "I want inside you so bad."

Pierce's eyes honest to God rolled back in his head, and his chest tightened with the need to breathe.

"You want it too," Hal said, those amber eyes lit up from inside with lust and hellfire and unholy desire.

"So bad," Pierce moaned breathily.

"Merry Christmas to us."

Pierce nodded, completely helpless, his heart full of words that meant forever, his brain full of that light from Hal's smile.

THE MASSAGE table didn't seem like much—it came in folded, on wheels, with a little latch to hold it closed. Pierce got out of the shower and watched as Hal set up the table and put one sheet down on the bottom.

"I'm supposed to do this with two sheets," Hal said, sounding very professional. "Because not everybody wants to be all naked and stuff in front of someone who's just going to rub their muscles." He glanced up at Pierce and winked. "But I've seen all you got, so we only have to use it if you get cold. The one on the bottom is to sop up the extra oil so you don't slide around the table like a pancake on a griddle."

Heat rose up from the balls of Pierce's feet to flush across his neck. "I, uh, take it I'm the only one who gets the optional top sheet."

Hal laughed. "Yeah. I mean, people make a big deal about massage therapists and happy endings, but the fact is, getting a full-body massage is really a whole big… thing. A lot of people practically go into subspace when they're getting a body rub—muscles in their necks and back that haven't released in years suddenly don't hurt anymore. It's pretty euphoric."

"No sex necessary," Pierce said—he'd known this before, although he'd never gotten a massage himself.

"Oh, it's necessary," Hal purred, waggling his eyebrows. "But that's just because I want you. Really fucking bad."

"Again," Pierce said softly.

"It's not getting any less urgent," Hal agreed calmly. He swallowed and bit his lip shyly. "It's just this… this massage thing. It's different. It's not sex. I… it's something I do really well, and I wanted to… to *give* it to you."

Pierce got it. "It's my Christmas present," he repeated, delighted.

Hal nodded. "Exactly! I couldn't…." And now his bit lip seemed vulnerable. "I couldn't find anything good," he said finally. "Everything I found was an 'us' thing. I needed a 'you' thing. This thing—I mean, there's sex tonight, but it's ten in the morning. This thing is all about you."

Pierce studied his bare and bony feet for a moment. "Jesus, Harold. I just got you a teddy bear."

"And Legos," Hal said softly. "And you."

Pierce opened his mouth—not sure of what he'd say next—but Hal called him over. "If I was with a client, I'd leave the room, because, you know, privacy and professional. But here—give me the towel, I'll put it down where your crotch is supposed to go. Now lie flat, facedown—yeah, face in the face cradle when you get settled."

Pierce complied, taking his time because Hal was right. They *did* know each other—he *wasn't* self-conscious about how long it took to get situated, to place his limbs so they wouldn't hurt, to be in a position where touching would be okay.

"Now I'm going to put some music in—I'm going to use movie soundtracks, because most of the time those don't drive people bugshit, okay?"

Pierce had to smile. "Okay." He put his face in the face thing, and Hal adjusted it so it didn't feel like his neck was going to drop off, and then....

Transported was the only word.

Hal was right—it wasn't sexual, even though Pierce and Hal were sexual creatures to each other.

But it was *amazing*. Hal's cheerful, kind patter and his hard, no-bullshit hands just sort of... pushed all of the tension, all of the pain out of Pierce's body. They talked, like they always did. Telling stories, bullshitting, zinging one-liners, but the whole time Hal's hands, his careful, caring, marvelous hands were ridding Pierce of every angry toxin that had knotted his muscles from his toes to his tingling scalp. Toward the end, the conversation died, and Pierce was only vaguely aware of himself, floating, the euphoria of pain and stress release suspending his busy, doubting brain, putting a hold on all the words, the obstacles Pierce tended to put in his own way.

There was only peace.

"Here you go," Hal said, sitting him up. He must have gone into the other room for clothes, but Pierce didn't remember him going. "I'm going to put on your sleep shorts and your T-shirt. If you feel like dressing up later, that's fine, but until you're a little less floaty-pants, that'll do."

"Floaty-pants?" Pierce asked, bemused.

"Yeah. Dude—that euphoria thing is strong within you. I've got over 300 hours, and I don't know if I've *ever* massaged anyone that tense." He looked down, worried. "I... I wish I'd done it sooner, but you didn't seem that excited about the idea."

Pierce was too stoned on holistic pain relief to lie. About anything. "I didn't want to take advantage of you," he said baldly. "Because you're young. And pretty. And you could be spending your time with hipsters and cute college students and you spent a month making a bitter old guy feel like sunshine."

Hal paused in the middle of slipping his shorts on. "Like sunshine? No, don't get up—I'm going to put your sandals on or you're going to kill yourself on the tile."

"My feet are slippery," Pierce said wisely. Hal had spent twenty minutes on his arches and between his toes and… mmm….

"Yes, they are. I made you feel like sunshine?"

"Like the light from the sea through the sliding glass door," Pierce said, gesturing vaguely to the view. Hal had pulled back the blinds that morning, and the whole world glowed gold. "I hated it when I got here. But you make my heart feel like that. And I'm like the storm. All grim clouds. And how do I ask for more sunshine?" Pierce smiled benevolently. "I don't know how I'll even see the sun again when I can't see you."

Hal blinked hard and stood Pierce up on his sandals while wiping his eyes off on his shoulder. "That's…. God, Pierce. You're really saying these things to me. Do you even *know* what's coming out of your mouth?"

"Speaking of my mouth, are there cookies?"

Hal's laugh sounded a little bit hysterical. "Just sit here, big man, and I'm going to clean up and make you such amazing Christmas cookies, I'll ruin you for Christmas forever unless I'm there to cook for you."

"That would be amazing," Pierce said benevolently. "The having you to cook for me. And the Christmas. And the forever. I'll have to ask you sometime."

"About what?" Hal whispered, wrapping his arm around Pierce's waist.

"About forever."

"You do that," Hal said. "Whenever you're ready."

Pierce pouted. "But I'm leaving tomorrow. I'll have to text. Texting's no good. Can't smell you then. You smell like sunshine and cookies."

Hal sat him down in one of the kitchen chairs and cupped his cheeks. "You ask me whenever you're ready. Don't worry, Pierce. I'll always be there." And then he bent forward and took Pierce's mouth. For a moment the sunshine went away, and they were gliding over big fluffy clouds in a starry sky.

Not storm clouds at all.

For a moment Pierce hoped Hal could see him just like that.

And then Hal was gone, doing things with the massage table and washing his hands and starting work in the kitchen, and Pierce was left staring out into space, dreaming about a starry night above the clouds while lost in the smell of sunshine.

And cookies.

IT TOOK him about an hour to come down, and that was only because the sugar high from all the cookies gave him the kind of jolt needed to cut through all those lovely endorphins.

Finally, though, by the time dinner was done, he was completely in the moment. His body felt loose and functional, and his mind was thrilled to be following Hal's perky banter through ham and potatoes to biting the heads off the reindeer-shaped cookies and letting the headless bodies thrash around spouting pink frosting blood.

And then pelting each other with M&M's they were supposed to be using as decorations.

When they'd stopped laughing—and Hal had swept up the candy—they retreated to the living room to watch Christmas movies.

Pierce stared at *Love Actually* thoughtfully. "Weird."

"What?" Hal was a cuddler—he pushed aggressively into Pierce's arms, and Pierce wrapped himself around Hal's shoulders.

"It's... it's hard to know it's Christmas here. I mean, the stores were all decked out—and the Christmas tree helps." On one of Hal's last trips, he'd strung lights along the valance for the blinds, and that helped too.

"It's not cold enough," Hal said moodily. "Not like places that snow. I hate Florida."

"No—I mean, it's in the sixties, so it's a little warm. It's...." Pierce grimaced, feeling foolish because it had taken him a month to figure this out. "It's the sun. It's in the wrong place. And it feels like it can't be Christmas when the sun is in the wrong place."

Hal squinted up at him. "Are you still on your massage high?"

Oh God—how embarrassing. "No! It's... it's just odd. That's all. Odd."

"Sure. Whatever. Besides—tomorrow's not Christmas. It's Christmas Eve."

Pierce grunted. It felt more like D-day. "You know, you *could* just come with me to my sis—"

"Wabbit season," Hal snapped.

It was the first time they'd had to use the personal safeword that day.

"It is not," Pierce argued. "It is not Wabbit Season. Why would going to my sister's be—"

"Wabbit season," Hal insisted, scowling up at him. "We'll talk about it tomorrow."

Pierce could have pointed out the whole car situation, but he didn't. This felt bigger than having to cancel a Lyft an hour before it showed up at his door.

He squeezed Hal—hard. "You had better not disappear from my life tomorrow, you idiot duck," he muttered.

"I promise, no boom."

Pierce sat up like he'd been stung. "Was there? Was there ever going to be a boom?"

Hal rolled his eyes. "Cool your jets, panic man. I was going to *drink* myself to death—and I told you how that ended. No. There was not going to be a boom."

Pierce settled back down into the couch, but now his hands were shaking and clammy, and his pleasant Christmas doze felt shattered.

Hal sighed, took his hand, and kissed it. "Shh... it's just this night, baby. Just you and me and this movie and Christmas. Watch the movie. Hold me tight. You'll feel the Christmas thing—I promise. And the sun is exactly where it's supposed to be. I swear."

Pierce nodded, soothed by his words, by his soft kiss on the palm of Pierce's hand—and by the sweet movie that both of them quoted as it played.

"Did you hope?" Hal asked toward the middle of the movie.

"Hope for what?"

"That the guy from *Walking Dead* would find a guy instead of a girl?"

Pierce chuckled. "Well he found Daryl!"

"I meant in *this* movie."

Pierce thought about it. "No," he answered at last. "I was too busy hoping the girl with the brother didn't answer the phone."

Hal grunted. "Why?"

"Because the people you love should never get in the way of the people you love."

Hal was quiet for a moment, lying sideways with his head on Pierce's lap. "You could be the best person I've ever met," he said.

Pierce stroked his hair back from his face, his heart so full in that moment he couldn't hear the incessant crashing of the surf. "Not even close—shh… it's the part with the Dido song…."

They watched the movie, entranced, and then Hal stood up from the couch and offered him a hand up. Pierce stood, and Hal cupped his cheeks, giving him a brief kiss.

"Go undress," he said, giving orders naturally. "Pull down the duvet and lie on your side. I've got an idea."

Pierce shuddered, thinking he might know what this particular idea entailed. If he was right, it was a *good* idea, and he wanted to be a part of it.

He walked his newly loosened body into the bedroom, stripping out of his sleep shorts, boxers, and T-shirt, and unlike getting the massage, he suddenly felt *very* naked, and *very* sexual.

And in spite of the scars on his body, the silver strands of hair on his head, the lines in the corners of his green eyes, he didn't feel old and wrecked, as he had when he'd arrived here.

He felt young and desirable and in desperate need of whatever Hal wanted to dish out tonight.

He lay down on the bed on his side—not facing the end table, like Hal probably expected, but facing the center of the bed.

Hal finished turning off the lights and locking up and walked into the bedroom shucking clothes, dropping them in his usual pile next to the bed. He looked up and caught Pierce's eyes on him.

"What?"

"I was remembering that first night. In the dark. How you didn't even want to talk about it."

"I was afraid," Hal told him quietly, crawling to the middle of the bed so he could talk to Pierce eye to eye. "I wanted you so bad—so bad. But you were so… so angry. Closed off. Hurt. I thought maybe if we just kept it us, in the dark, you'd let it happen."

Pierce closed his eyes and savored how far they'd come. "I don't want you in the dark," he said. "I want… I want to walk down the street with you. I want to introduce you to everyone I know. I—"

Hal put two fingers on his lips. "I want you," he whispered. "All of you. Now roll over and turn off the light."

Pierce did, staying on his side and facing away from Hal's amber eyes.

Hal's hands—his magic hands—skated over Pierce's shoulders, his arms, his side, and Hal pressed up against Pierce's back, aggressively naked. The thought of him—all of him—lined up against Pierce's bare back sent a shiver of recognition, of arousal zinging through Pierce's body.

Hal pulled the longish hair from Pierce's ear and started talking dirty. "You like my hands?"

"Yes."

"Where do you want them?"

"Everywhere."

Hal bit his earlobe softly. "Be specific."

"Nipples," Pierce said, aware that his were tingling, needy, wanting attention in the worst way.

His was rewarded with a soft scraping of Hal's nails against the ridge of flesh, and he whined.

"Not enough?" Hal tormented.

"Pinch!"

"Sure."

But he was so greedy for the pinch, it arced through his body, electricity seeking all his erogenous zones, and he cried out and thrust his hips back and forth, immediately aching and needy.

Without prompting he propped his knee against the bed, opening his groin and his back end up for all the most exciting play he ever needed.

"Want something else?" Hal asked, laughing.

"Touch me," Pierce begged, shameless. "All the places."

"Sure."

Oh, he was wicked, this boy. He touched Pierce's flanks, the outside of his thighs, the very edge of Pierce's crease.

"You're teasing me!" Pierce accused, whimpering and not caring.

"You're being vague," Hal said, laughing. "Now be specific—"

"Stroke my c... inner thighs." Pierce loved the tantalizing touches—he would ask for them.

"Ooh—I like how you think."

Hal palmed his inner thighs, both of them, sliding the sides of his hand down the juncture of his body, feeding his wants while keeping his needs just hungry enough.

"My balls," Pierce panted. "My taint…."

"Teasing yourself!" Hal purred, thrusting up against Pierce's buttock, his cock leaving a patch of wet against Pierce's skin.

"You're doing such a good job for me!" Pierce moaned. Hal cupped his balls, scooting down a little on the bed to get access and leverage, and Pierce moaned again, breathily.

"You want more teasing?" Hal urged. "What else do you want?"

"Lick me," Pierce begged, unafraid. This was Hal—he wouldn't leave Pierce hanging. Hal moved all the way down, leaving a string of kisses down Pierce's spine. When he got to Pierce's backside, Pierce's propped knee still holding him open and accessible, he parted Pierce's cheeks and dove in.

And Pierce almost cried.

"It's so good," he panted, forgetting how this thing was supposed to work. He reached down to stroke his cock, and Hal punished him by stopping with the tongue action.

"But… but…."

"That's going to make it over too soon," Hal told him. "Just for that, roll over on your stomach."

Pierce didn't hesitate—but he *did* have to adjust himself to make sure he didn't squash his dick against the bed and tweak it forever.

Hal got between his legs, spread his cheeks, and stuck two slick fingers inside. Pierce bucked into the intrusion, driving them deeper.

"More," he begged. "Are you happy?"

Hal kept thrusting them and pulling back, and Pierce's body ached with need, hot and cold sweat popping out on his brow, on his back. Oh *God*, he needed the whole reaming act. He pulled his knees carefully under him, feeling some stiffness, some pulling on muscles, but thanks to the work he'd done this month, thanks to the massage earlier in the day, no pain.

And he sat there, spread and vulnerable, and begged the most intimate of acts from a kid he hadn't known a month ago but couldn't imagine not knowing tomorrow.

"Cocky, aren't ya?" Hal asked, thrusting his fingers in harder and faster. A cool slick drizzled down the fingers, and Hal spread it around. Pierce groaned, welcoming the stretch, the invasion, wanting more.

"You're the one with the cock," Pierce taunted back. "Are you going to do something with it?"

Hal bit his asscheek delicately, the tiny needles of pain driving Pierce higher.

"You think you're ready?" Hal asked, voice muffled in Pierce's flesh.

"I am," Pierce begged. "I am. I so am."

Hal moved from the vee of his legs. "On your side again," he ordered, then changed his voice. "It's good you can do this for a little bit now, but I don't want to take you like this—it might rip some things that just got stretched, okay?"

"Deal," Pierce mumbled, rolling to his side and propping his knee up again. "Now are you gonna—*yes*...."

There was something irrevocable about someone's cock in your ass.

Hal's cock was sized generously, but it was more than that. It was flesh inside your flesh, it was giving somebody a pass to your body and hoping they respected you enough to not hurt you.

Hal's body could have hurt, but it didn't. It filled Pierce, stretching him more, destroying his guards, the shelters Pierce had hidden in, the barriers he'd erected, swearing that he and he alone could exist behind those walls.

Hal battered them down and took their place, and Pierce cried out, not in pain, not even in pleasure, although he was aroused beyond endurance, but in surrender.

Still, Hal kept thrusting, kept *fucking*, and Pierce cried out again, gibbering, begging, needing more, and more, and more—

"*Now*," Hal panted. "*Now* you can grab your cock! C'mon, Pierce, stroke it. Squeeze it. Thumb on the top, dig it into the pee slit—that's right... tighten for me, baby. C'mon... you're almost there... oh God... you're so warm. So hot. So good. Come, baby... come for me.... *Come!*"

Pierce shouted, the orgasm contracting all his muscles, even the ones wrapped around Hal's cock. His cock spurted, his hand growing hot and sticky. Hal gave a strangled cry behind him, and Pierce felt it, Hal's spend, scalding a path inside.

Claimed. Marked. Wanted.

Pierce moaned softly as come trickled from his backside, his entire body trembling with reawakened arousal—and more.

He belonged to somebody. Somebody in his life wanted him, had staked a claim, body and soul.

The thought was annihilating—and it spiked his desire like nothing else in the world.

Hal's turn to moan, and he bit the juncture of Pierce's neck and shoulder.

"Again," Hal whispered.

"Oh God yes."

"Again," Hal chanted, snapping his hips so they bounced off Pierce's backside. His cock had hardened already, gotten, if anything, fatter and more demanding.

"Please."

"*Again!*"

And Hal fucked him hard, without mercy, without hesitation.

Again.

Christmas Eve Morning

PIERCE STARED at the note, feeling again the deliciousness of his used body.

The amazing vibrancy of his reawakened heart.

He'd packed the day before, and he didn't even stop to shower before pulling on his clothes.

He wasn't sure what he was going to say, but he wanted to be wearing Hal's sex on his skin and inside his body when he said it. He barely stopped to splash water on his face and brush his teeth.

He knew which condo belonged to Hal's parents—had seen Hal disappear into it those first days—and it had always loomed, tall and unapproachable, the stairwell daunting to his wounded limbs.

The walk wasn't easy—he used his cane and the rail—but every step felt like he was ascending a tower, maybe to battle for the prince inside.

He didn't even wait to catch his breath before banging on the door.

He heard sounds inside—scurrying—the slamming of drawers and a muffled "Oh dammit!" before the door opened.

Hal stared at him, surprised and joyous.

His eyes were red-rimmed, like he'd been crying.

"No," Pierce snapped, rubbing under Hal's eyes with a gentle thumb.

"No?"

"No, I'm not going to talk to you before I leave. I'm going to take you *with* me. Come with me. Don't stay here." Pierce took a deep breath, and before it could hit him that he'd said the words, he kept going. "And it's not pity. I mean, it is, but for me. Without you. Without you I'd feel so sorry for myself I'd curl up and die. I almost did, and that was before I knew you. But now that I know you—now that"—he shivered—"now that I feel you inside me, forget about it. I can't go on. I can't go home. I can't… can't just pretend that it's Christmas unless you're there with me. Stay with me. We'll visit my sister—she'll feed you ham. We'll drive to Sacramento, and you can be a massage therapist there. I'll take you to the mountains and the ocean, where the sun's in the right place."

He paused, and Hal just gaped at him, mouth open, eyes stunned.

Pierce's voice broke. "Just stay with me. I love you. And it's stupid and idealistic, and I don't care. We can be that couple, the one who was never supposed to meet but who stayed together forever. I just know—" He took a deep shuddering breath and wiped his cheeks on his shoulders. "—I just know my life won't be good—not the job or the house or the friends or the family—none of it will be good without you in it."

He took another deep breath—or sob, actually—and wiped his eyes again, getting a good look at Hal.

Who was smiling and crying at once.

"What?" Pierce demanded. "You're just standing there—what? C'mon, say some—"

Hal opened the door and showed the two neatly packed suitcases next to him.

"Do you think I was going to let you go?" he asked. "I was gonna stalk you to Orlando and *make* you love me."

Pierce laughed, shaking, and opened his arms. Hal went—oh, so easily. He fit, like he should be there all the times forever.

"Achievement unlocked," he rasped, burying his face in Hal's hair and taking comfort from his smell. "Stalking unnecessary. Come home with me."

"Yeah."

"Be a massage therapist."

"Yeah."

"I'll love you so hard, nobody'll care that you're a kid and I'm a grown-up."

"You're not a grown-up," Hal said against his chest. "You're a unicorn."

"Unicorns are the best," Pierce agreed.

"We should know."

He'd be a unicorn for the rest of his life—forever—if it meant Hal could be there next to him, snarking, believing, playing, for every Christmas—and every day thereafter.

IT TOOK them less than an hour to be ready to leave.

Pierce locked up the condo regretfully—it had been a good home for a month. It had, in fact, been witness to some of the happiest moments of his life.

"Where're we going again?" Hal asked, checking the Lego Christmas tree carefully, surrounded in its bed of teddy bears and brightly wrapped gifts.

"Orlando," Pierce said, holding up his phone. "I've got the directions here, because I can't remember for shit."

Hal nodded, like he got that. "And afterward?"

Pierce dared him with his eyes. "North Carolina," he said, wondering if this would get him left on the curb. "To tell your parents to forward your mail to Sacramento."

Hal jerked back. "That's a terrible idea."

"Indeed it is. Gonna fight me on it?"

"Mm…." Hal gnawed that lush lower lip. "No. No—it shall be terrible and uncomfortable and irritate the crap out of them. They'll loathe you."

"Excellent. I *like* this plan!"

"And after that?" Hal prodded.

"New York," Pierce said grandly. "I've never been. I don't have to be home until February. Let's enjoy this shit."

A dreamy smile took over Hal's face. "Really? Adventures?"

"Two knights riding a CR-V unicorn," Pierce told him grandly.

"Two unicorns with opposable thumbs," Hal corrected.

"We'll conquer the world," Pierce decided, hopping in the car and getting this road on the show.

He slammed the door with a satisfying *thunk*, and Hal hopped in and hit the ignition.

"As long as in the end we end up in the same stable." Hal's eyes were big and limpid amber, and Pierce got it.

"Yeah, unicorn," he said gently, squeezing Hal's knee. "There's home at the end of the rainbow. I promise."

Hal's face lit up, like he'd needed to hear it one more time. "Then into the great wide yonder it is!" He gestured grandly into the unexpectedly bright, crisp day, and hit the ignition.

They had relatives to visit and cookies to bake and grand adventures before them.

And a life together at the end of the quest.

There had never been happier unicorns.

Stay tuned for the adventures of Hal and Pierce, continued on Amy's blog.

LATE FOR CHRISTMAS

WATCH OUT FOR THAT TREE

CASSIDY HANCOCK hated being late—loathed it. Spent his entire life waking up early, setting alarms, and passing up invitations on the off chance a trip to the park with a friend would make him late for a Zoom meeting he had in two hours. What if something happened? What if he sprained his ankle? What if he found a dog and absolutely had to get it back to its owner? What if he didn't *want* to get it back to its owner? There was always that. Cassidy really did long for a dog—but dogs were messy and unexpected and he was afraid they would make him *late*.

A life in foster care had made him dread the sudden placement in someone else's house, made him dread the new schedule, the sudden left turn, the unexpected *anything* that might make him miss an appointment. Missed appointments meant bad grades, bad grades meant getting put somewhere else, getting put somewhere else meant new schools—it was all bad if you were late.

The minute he'd moved out of transitional care and into his own apartment with his own job and his own space, he had set out to become the Boy Who Wouldn't Be Late.

And now, at twenty-eight, that hard work had paid off. He had a good job that he enjoyed, and he'd managed to buy his own house in the cul-de-sac of a cute little suburban neighborhood, and while his house looked a lot like the house next to it and the one after that, he didn't care. He'd plant flowers, trim the tree, mow the lawn, and he would be the Man Who Wouldn't Be Late with the House That Fit In.

As one of the few teachers who had really seen him in high school had said, it was important to have goals.

Unfortunately, goals didn't mean jack when a drought-ridden tree cracked in a windstorm and took out all the power lines in the area. Cassidy's alarm didn't go off, and his phone was charging in the kitchen. He slept through the phone alarm, the coffee maker didn't go off, and by the time he woke up, he had half an hour to get to his daily morning meeting with his boss.

The meeting he never missed.

The meeting he was always ten minutes early for because Cassidy was *never late*.

He'd worked his way up from receptionist for the editor/owner of Folsom's most prestigious lifestyle magazine—in both print and electronic formats—to personal assistant, contributor, and part-time editor by being always on time, always impeccable, and always polite.

And now he was late!

He was hurrying outside into the blowy gray December day when he caught sight of the new neighbor.

Or rather the old neighbor's college-age son, who had moved into an apartment over his mother's garage this past year. He was escorting a ridiculous dog that had a pit bull head with the smooth, hypoallergenic brindle fur, and a corgi body.

Cassidy sort of craved that dog. He had, in fact, been having a really nice dream about that dog curled up at the foot of his bed, making whuffling sounds in his sleep, when he'd reached out to pet his imaginary dog and realized that not only was the dog not there, but the sky was much lighter outside than it was when he usually woke up.

So there went his neighbor, running after Gus-Gus the dog—Cassidy knew his name because he frequently did the corgi hop off-leash and waddled down the sidewalk with unabashed glee—wearing pajama pants and a homemade sweater in vibrant green, his longish, unkempt dark blond hair swirling in all directions, his pleasantly scruffy face twisted in sheepish annoyance, and Cassidy was forced to stop for reasons that had nothing to do with being late and everything to do with…

Reasons.

The young man really did wear the crap out of the sweater his mother had crocheted him, Cassidy thought with a lump in his throat. She'd even made a matching sweater for the dog.

Cassidy was so busy watching the young man that he didn't notice the tree in the neighbor's yard leaning precariously in the wind, the recent rain making the powder-dry earth unstable but not wet enough to hold together. He'd gotten to his car, which sat in the driveway because he'd converted much of his garage to a woodworking shop, when he heard the ominous *crack*. He looked up just in time to miss the tree crashing down on his head, where it would probably have killed him, but as he stumbled back, he fell on his ass, and when the tree landed, a solid branch impaled his leg and broke his fibula and tibia instead.

As he fell against the pavement, he was aware of two things.

One, the dog had run back and was licking his face, which was nicer than he'd thought it would be when he'd dreamed of owning the dog.

The other thing was the neighbor's college-age son was crouched down by him, telling him he was going to be okay while he talked into a telephone using the crisp diction and vocabulary of someone who knew exactly what they were doing.

Cassidy's leg was on fire, and he couldn't reach his pocket to find his phone to call his boss and tell her he was going to be late. He squinted up at the neighbor's son and said, "Which college are you going to, anyway?"

The boy smiled gently. "Stanford School of Medicine—I'm a resident of Mercy San Juan Folsom, orthopedic unit. Lucky you, Mr. Hancock—my boss is probably the guy who will set your leg."

Cassidy stared at him. "But you're not that old," he whispered, and then his eyes rolled back in his head and he passed out completely.

PROXIMITY

MARK TAYLOR—NOT to be confused with Chuck, he often said—was surprised to see his parents' stodgy neighbor, who never met a dress shoe he couldn't spit-polish or a hair he couldn't smooth back, was only twenty-eight.

But passed out and medicated, Cassidy Hancock was not only much younger than Mark assumed, he was also a lot cuter.

He had pointed features, which, when his brows were drawn down and his mouth pursed in disapproval, could appear severe and nearly fortyish. Relaxed with the medication, the skin was smooth and the mouth was actually softer than it first seemed.

Cassidy didn't look disapproving so much as he looked vulnerable, and Mark wasn't prepared for that. In spite of the praises his mother sang, Mark thought the guy was some sort of neighborhood sour plum, scowling at everything, talking to nobody.

And then Gus-Gus had licked his face and he'd smiled.

Mark loved the big tube-of-weird himself, but to see this guy, who was as buttoned-up as anyone he'd ever seen, including his ex-boyfriend, succumb to that charm—that was interesting.

Mark stood over Cassidy's hospital bed, studying his chart, when he heard a rustle behind him. "Isn't this your day off?"

He turned around and smiled. Holly Jacobsen was in her early thirties, with two children and a husband who was a delivery driver for UPS. She wore her thick blond hair in a short pixie cut and even had sparkly blue eyes and dimples. If she didn't have the slight crow's feet that indicated experience—and humor—she would definitely not look old enough to be the charge nurse on the orthopedic floor.

"It is," Mark said, shrugging. "I'm barely on the schedule until after Christmas." This had been on purpose. He was a senior resident at Folsom Medical Center, but he'd served his junior residency in the Bay Area. His father's passing and a bad breakup had given him a reason to apply for the senior position. He'd lucked out—Harry Chu, his boss, also happened to be one of his best friends coming up through Stanford and had given him a chance.

Mark didn't have the best record on paper.

His grades were great, yes, but he had a real problem with time management. Harry had known this, but he'd also frequently said Mark was one of the best doctors he'd ever worked with, and that was long after the internship they'd served together in the Mission District in San Francisco.

"You care, you listen, you pay attention—you catch things other doctors don't," Harry had said when he'd given Mark the job. "But you have got to learn to get your ass in gear!"

"Harry," Mark had ventured—carefully, of course, because he'd wanted the job and he hadn't wanted to piss his old friend off, "has it occurred to you that the reason I catch things other doctors don't is because I'm taking the time to pay attention?"

Harry grunted. "Yes. I completely get that. But you can't be Dr. Superman—everybody needs your time, not the first people on your roster, okay?"

So Harry gave Mark the job in a probationary way, with a light schedule before Christmas so he'd have time to help his mom fix up the house and get settled in the area and perhaps learn to arrive punctually more than 50 percent of the time.

Mark had managed about 80 percent so far, and Harry was pleased, but that didn't mean the rest of the staff wasn't rooting for him.

But then, the 20 percent of the time he'd been late had been to stop and get them donuts. Mark wasn't stupid. Keep the nurses and PAs happy and you could pretty much rule the hospital.

"So," Holly said now, laughing, "what are you doing here?"

Mark shrugged. "This is my neighbor. There he was, walking to his car while I was chasing Gus-Gus down the sidewalk, and suddenly a tree falls on his head."

"I thought it was his leg that was broken?"

Mark grimaced. "Well, he paused for some reason as he was walking toward his car, otherwise it would have been game over and lights out. Anyway, they got him free of the tree—and seriously, the branch impaled his leg, poor guy. Broke his tibia and his fibula, and isn't he frickin' lucky it wasn't his femur—and as they were loading him up in the ambulance, they said, 'Is there somebody you'd like us to call?'"

"And he said...?" Holly made a get-on-with-it gesture.

"Nobody," Mark said. "He said, 'No one.' And I felt awful for the guy. My mom came and got Gus-Gus, and I got in the ambulance with him. While Harry was operating on his leg, I showered up and put on a coat so I could look official in scrubs, because seriously, I'm just here for him."

"Aw," she said, actually looking at Cassidy as he lay dozing under the anesthetic. "Good-looking guy. Is he nice?"

"I have no idea," Mark said. "My mom seems to think so. I know he's obsessed with not being late because he's always looking at his watch." It was an old-fashioned timepiece too—not a Fitbit or a Garmin but a gold watch on a leather band, like something a father would give to his son.

She gave a snort. "Didn't you say that's why you broke up with your boyfriend?

"Well, he was obsessed with being on time *and* he was a dick," Mark said, although, like with most things, there was more to it than that. "But this guy gets a chance to prove he's not a dick, at least. Besides, my mother would never forgive me. Apparently he's been mowing her lawn along with his, and raking her leaves too, since Dad passed. He did it for *months* before she noticed, and when she went over to say something, he looked mortally embarrassed. She said about all he got out was 'I'm so sorry about your husband,' before he excused himself and closed the door. But he kept doing her chores for her—including cleaning her gutters. Not expecting thanks, just, you know, doing nice things."

"Oh," Holly said. "So he *is* a good guy."

"Either that or he's a plant from the HOA," Mark joked, and Holly laughed as he expected she would. But in truth, he was curious about the guy. His mother seemed to think he was just a little shy, but Mark wondered if there was more to it than that.

"Well, I'll leave you to ponder," she said. "Let me know if you need anything."

Mark shook his head and pulled up a chair, yawning. "Thanks, Holly. I'm going to wait until he wakes up and see if he needs anything." He'd been up late the night before, studying new grafting procedures so he could be ready if it came up, and he wouldn't mind a nice little doze in the comfy guest chair now.

She left, and he'd just gotten settled in, with his eyes closed, when a tired and surprisingly deep male voice said, "She brought me muffins when I moved in."

Mark blinked awake. "Who—"

"Your mom. She brought me muffins. I wrote her a thank-you note, but it didn't seem like enough."

Mark smiled fondly. "Well, my mom's like that. Nice, nice lady."

"You're lucky," Cassidy Hancock said. He squeezed his eyes tight. "I need to call my boss. Tell her why I'm late."

Mark grimaced. For a moment he'd been so human. "Buddy, I hate to break this to you, but you're more than late—you're going to be stuck at home for at least a month, and you'll need in-home nursing and someone to stay with you overnight too."

Cassidy closed his eyes tightly. "No," he muttered. "No, no, no, no, no...."

"Hey," Mark said gently. "It's okay. You have insurance and even the extra work insurance—I saw your card as the nurse was admitting you. I'm sorry. They can't fire you for this—"

Cassidy shook his head. "I can work from home," he said. "I don't always, but... I just... I don't know anyone. I... I live alone. Who's going to come stay with me? I'll be late!"

Mark was going to laugh at him just like he'd laughed at Brad, his ex, but he couldn't. Something about the half-panicked, almost tearful note in his voice when he said *I'll be late!* really tore at Mark's chest. This wasn't just a quirk of being uptight, was it? This was something deeper.

"Well, we can make some modifications to your house to help you," Mark said. "First, though, let me get you your phone, and you can talk to your boss and explain. There's got to be *someone* at work who can help you out."

Mark listened unabashedly to Cassidy's phone call and was even more mystified when he was done. Cassidy's boss, Rose McCormick, seemed like a real nice lady. She was not, in fact, a fire-breathing dick.

"Honey, don't worry about it. We'll miss you, for sure, but you're laid up! We'll make do until you get your computer and your house set up, okay?"

Cassidy nodded, looking miserable. "I should be able to be online tomorrow—"

"The day after, at the earliest," Mark said, appalled. Cassidy sent him a tortured look, and he shook his head sternly. "It would be better if you took a week," he said, not sure how much he could get away with.

"A week it shall be," Rose said. "You haven't taken any time off in years—practically since I hired you, which was when?"

"Five years ago," Cassidy said.

"That's terrible! Take a week off! Don't worry, Cass—the job will be here when you get back."

Cassidy looked stricken. "You promise?" he asked in a small voice.

Rose's face softened over the phone screen, as though she knew something about Cassidy Hancock that Mark did not. "Of course, sweetie. You don't just forget your assistant—and your friend—because he got hurt."

Cassidy nodded into his phone, looking lost and sad—and definitely younger than fortyish, and even younger than twenty-eight. "Okay. If you're sure—I can do online if you need me—"

"Honey, relax," she said. "Let this nice young man take care of you for a little while. He seems capable."

"Oh—he's not taking care of me," Cassidy said, as though he'd found his footing again. "He's my neighbor. And a doctor—but not mine. He was nice enough to call the ambulance and check on me and—"

"My mom and I will help him set up his house," Mark said, barging into his video call. "He's going to need a little help and looking after."

Rose—who looked to be in her fifties but spectacularly in her fifties, with smooth skin, short auburn hair, and cheekbones to die for—nodded, frowning. "Will he need help renting the equipment? We had to set up my mother's house when she broke her ankle. Does he have anyone to order for him and open up his house before he's discharged?"

"Rose, I can handle that—" Cassidy began, so Mark tugged gently on the phone until he had it to himself.

"I can help him set up the delivery," Mark said, "and my mother will be there to help him set up the house. We both work, though. I've got a light schedule, so I can check in a lot, but if we could coordinate tomorrow? He's going to need things like meal prep and housecleaning help for the next six weeks at least. I guess he doesn't have any family in town?"

"He doesn't have any family at all," Rose said, her voice dropping with compassion.

Mark turned his head to see Cassidy studiously looking away from this conversation, like it didn't have anything to do with him.

"Well, that's going to change," he decided. "No man's an island—particularly not with a cast that sticks out from the wheelchair."

"He's got insurance," Rose said, "but you're right. He's going to need help. Go ahead and take down my number from his phone—you seem like a capable young man. Between the two of us we should see that he's taken care of."

"And don't forget my mother," Mark said. "Believe me, once Yvonne Taylor gets her hands on a project, it's a lock."

"Wonderful. Well, between us, Dr. Taylor, let's see if we can't take care of Cassidy. He's a very sweet boy, and my office can't function without him for too long." She gave him a wink that let him know Cassidy was more to her than just her assistant. "Call me as soon as you have the details for setting up his home."

And with that she signed off, leaving Mark to smile encouragingly at Cassidy. "See? She was lovely. You can rest today; we can get you set up in the next few—you'll be fine."

Cassidy nodded, but he didn't look happy. In fact, his big hazel eyes were red-rimmed and shiny, and as Mark watched in dismay, he leaned back against his pillow and closed them, forcing the tears to spill over.

"Hey, hey," Mark soothed, wondering if this was just shock and exhaustion. Poor guy had, in fact, had quite a day. "Don't worry—you've got people. We'll take good care of you."

"I don't have people," Cassidy whispered. "And in the end, it's only me."

Mark opened his mouth to protest, but Cassidy's eyes were closed and he looked like he was probably falling asleep, so all Mark could do was look at him in surprise and wonder what had happened to this man before the tree had fallen on him.

Something had obviously left bigger damage than a broken leg.

MARK LEFT soon after Cassidy fell asleep, feeling bad about leaving him alone in the hospital but needing to get started on the retrofitting of the one-story ranch-style house now, before they took Cassidy home.

He also *really* wanted to talk to his mother.

He grabbed Cassidy's keys from his belongings, feeling a little like a thief, and tiptoed out of the hospital room with more stealth than was probably necessary. On his way out, he met Holly, who was standing by the nurse's station and charting on her tablet.

"You off?" she asked.

Mark glanced back to Cassidy's hospital room, troubled. "Tell him I'm going to set up his house," he said. "Tell him I'll be back when I can make it."

"Anything wrong?" she asked.

Mark shook his head. "No... yes... maybe?"

She laughed a little. "That's clear."

"He's... sad," Mark said, not sure why this should bother him so much, with the possible exception that this nice, handsome, vulnerable man had been kind to his mother when she'd needed it most. "I set his phone up to charge, but let me know if he needs anything, okay? And tell the next shift to do the same."

"Sure," she said before grinning at him. "I'll make a note on his chart."

"You're very cute," he said dryly and then left.

THE NEXT day, Mark visited Cassidy on his morning rounds, taking five minutes to reassure the man that he hadn't been forgotten.

The way Cassidy's face lit up—and then that light dampened as quickly as possible—as Mark walked in stuck with him. He kept Cassidy's key—this time with permission—and promised to tell Cassidy how he and his mother planned to modify the house so Cassidy could come home.

"Can I call you Cass?" he asked as he pocketed the key.

"I guess my boss does," Cassidy replied, looking disconcerted.

"We'll feel it out and see if it works," Mark promised. Something about that confusion twisted in his chest a little, and he was determined to solve the mystery of Cassidy Hancock if he did nothing else that day.

Later, as afternoon shadows stretched long across his tree-lined residential street, he opened the door to the neighbor's house for his mother. They ventured inside a little bit timidly—it felt alien and wrong to be there without the mysterious and reserved Cassidy Hancock, but Mark knew it had to be done.

The house had a partially open floor plan, the kitchen widening to a small dining room with a table obviously set up as an office space. There was an office chair set at a slightly off angle on the side of the round table, with the other four matching chairs crowded a little to accommodate it.

"Why is this crooked?" his mom asked herself softly.

The answer came immediately. "He can look out the window!" Mark supplied. From that chair, the large picture window of a breakfast nook peered out into the neighborhood. "We're in the corner lot. He can see the whole cul-de-sac from here—see?"

He pulled his mother to where he was standing, and she looked around as though pleasantly surprised.

"It's the whole neighborhood," she said. "What a lovely space."

"Unless you wanted to do something untoward on the table," he said with a wicked grin, because he would and he had, but also because he wanted his mother to react.

She smacked his arm and said, "Stop that!" and they were both satisfied.

The breakfast nook and dining room table were on one side of the foyer, and on the other side, still sharing space, sat a living room area that consisted of a couch and a love seat at right angles to each other but turned toward a television. He had gorgeous bookcases—hickory or oak, but hand-finished—filled with books on every subject from history to science to literature, all of them dust-free and, he noted in surprise, organized in alphabetical order according to author.

"Wow," he muttered, looking down the hallway toward the bedroom. He wondered if something in there indicated a human lived in this space, because standing in the foyer, he couldn't see it. The hickory picture frames over the mantel were spotless and dust-free, the diplomas on the wall behind the television in the same shape. Mark ventured closer to read the diplomas. Sac City High School, American River Junior College, CSU Sacramento—all local schools, but he'd been in the National Honor Society in high school and summa cum laude for his AA, BA, and MBA. He saw no pictures of Cassidy himself on the walls—which was reassuring, really, because the guys Mark had dated that lived alone but had their portraits on the walls were really sort of douchey—but the pictures on the brick mantel of the gas fireplace in the corner looked promising.

He'd just taken a step toward them when his mother spoke.

Her first words were not encouraging. "This is psychotically clean," she said, horrified.

"You like a clean house!" he protested. "You haven't stopped nagging me about my room since I was five!"

She gave him a droll look. "That's because you think three-quarters clean is all-the-way clean. Your room isn't clean if you've got a pile of moldy socks under your bed and you have to sniff the seat of your jeans to see if they've got one more day of wear."

"Who told!" he asked, embarrassed.

She rolled her eyes. "Oh, Mark. We knew."

"It was Dani and Keith," he said, naming his siblings without compunction. "They lie, Mom. They lie to get out of trouble—you know that."

"Yes, honey, and you tattle. It's a good system. Now this looks pretty accessible. The refrigerator and counter have a lot of space between them, and he can probably maneuver that in the chair, but he may need some help with the dishes because the sink and the counter are high. I think if we put a small table over here"—she pointed to a space between the refrigerator and the far counter—"and put the microwave on it, he can open the fridge, get a meal, and heat it up here. So that's a small modification. Now, refrigerator. Let's take a look."

"He likes fizzy water," Mark said. "And salads in a bag."

"And making his own sandwiches," Yvonne said, looking at the jar of pickles, the tomatoes—one of them sliced—and the processed cheese slices, all lined up neatly. The meat drawer held cold cuts, and there was a loaf of bread in a breadbox on the counter, as well as a box of granola to match the milk on the door.

"Well, not exciting," his mother began, but Mark suspiciously opened the freezer drawer.

"Ice cubes and five frozen dinners," she finished, her voice dull. "Oh, baby. I'm gonna feed this kid if it kills me."

Mark had to admit, it made perfect sense. Cereal every morning, a sandwich in the afternoon, a frozen dinner when he got home. Self-sufficient and methodical, but not... happy.

"Let's take a look at his bedroom and bathroom. That's where we usually need help." His mother sounded desperately optimistic, but he had to agree. Yvonne Taylor was an occupational therapist—she specialized in helping people work with disabilities or injuries. Whether she said, "We need a small table to set up the microwave," or "Hey, a jungle gym in the bathroom would be good," Mark would take her at her word.

"The hardwood floors are good," she said, and then paused before adding, "and very pretty. I mean, Mark, you can't deny he's got good taste."

Dark wood—hickory, leadwood, stained acacia—dominated the living room and dining room furniture pieces, but the floor was redwood. The upholstery was beige or cream, and so were the rugs, but the effect, with all of the different tones of wood, was striking and warm.

"It is a nice house," he agreed. "A little... well, like you said. Oddly clean."

"Let's see if he has skeletons in his closet," she told him with a smile that made her look younger than her nearly sixty years.

"Or bodies in the bathtub," Mark added grimly. Nothing about this house or its occupant seemed healthy.

"You are being cynical," she reprimanded and then grinned. "Or jealous because he's mastered the art of cleanliness and you haven't."

"Ha!" But Mark had to laugh. His mother was so very resilient—and not afraid to put her children in their places.

Mark, at twenty-seven, was the youngest, Keith was the oldest, and Dani was the pampered middle princess, which she readily admitted. Their mother still kept her hair dyed a wheat-colored blond, and her wide brown eyes were both lovely and wise. She may have gained a few more wrinkles after her gentle husband passed, but she was still luminously beautiful—at least in her children's eyes.

But as they ventured down the hallway, Mark got a sinking feeling that the lack of dust bunnies was even worse than skeletons.

He liked the guest room, complete with a queen-sized bed that had never been slept in but had been made up with a white coverlet and white throw pillows, and was almost showroom pristine. There was also a small den, which had been converted to a weight room with a stationary bicycle and a Bowflex, both of which explained the fact that Cassidy Hancock was not squishy around the middle—but he wasn't jacked to the nines either.

"We'll need a set of parallel bars in here," his mother said thoughtfully. "He's going to have to work to walk after his cast gets taken off. But otherwise, this is perfect."

"Too perfect," Mark grumbled. Everything had been wiped down. He even saw, gym style, a little rack with towels and a spray bottle of disinfectant in the corner. A hamper, which in Mark's room would be filled with dirty towels and probably some stinky gym clothes, was empty and smelled of Lysol.

"Mm," his mother said, mind obviously on her job. "I don't see any room back here for a washer/dryer, which means they're probably in the garage. They might be inaccessible—we'll need to see."

They got to the end of the hallway, with a perfectly cream-tiled bathroom and a large shower but no bathtub. "This might be perfect," she said. "There is plenty of room for him to maneuver, and if we put a lift on the toilet seat, he should be able to use the facilities on his own. We'll have to help him the first couple of times—it'll be awkward."

"Well, it's only being naked in front of your neighbors," Mark said, and her lips quirked. Making his mother laugh was one of his favorite life goals.

"That might be worse for him than the tree through the leg," she said seriously, and Mark felt a sigh welling up.

"There is something about him," he murmured. "Something... damaged."

She nodded. "Yes. I got that idea too. I tried to thank him for all his hard work with muffins once and... the look on his face. You had to see it. Like he'd been stabbed."

"Did he take the muffins?" Mark asked. His mother was a decent cook, and her Christmas cookies were to die for, but she was not a fabulous baker. Maybe Cassidy had known the perils of pumpkin muffins that could be thrown through a glass window.

"No," she said sadly. "He blushed and stammered and said he didn't want to go. Which was odd."

"He didn't want to go?" Now Mark was *really* surprised.

"Yeah. I told him he was welcome to stay, and we liked him in the neighborhood, and I was going to try with something else, but, you know, you moved in and God dropped a tree on him."

"The wind dropped a tree on him, Mom," Mark said dryly. "Maybe God kept it from dropping the tree on his head."

His mom's peal of laughter surprised him. "Oh my God—Mark! I was watching the whole thing from the window! *You* kept the tree from dropping on his head. He was just standing there, keys in one hand, briefcase in the other, staring at you as you ran after Gus-Gus. It was the damnedest thing!"

Mark remembered that moment, chasing after the damned dog and seeing those wide hazel eyes fixed hungrily on his face. For a moment, the "hurry-hurry" had dropped from Cassidy Hancock, and what had been left was interested man.

"Well, maybe not the *damnedest* thing," he said modestly.

She looked at him in surprise. "Really?"

Mark lifted a shoulder and threw some swagger into his smile and raised eyebrows. "Really-really."

His mother gave an unladylike snort. "Well, that would be awkward. I have the feeling you two might drive each other crazy."

Mark let his eyes drift around the hallway—long and straight and perfectly crème, with hickory moldings running along the floor, at waist level, and at the ceiling. "Hey, this house needs a little crazy," he said. "Let's take a look at the bedroom."

The bedroom was pretty much exactly what Mark expected. Eggshell-painted walls with a bedroom set of complementing and contrasting wood. The comforter was a surprise, though—a deep and soulful blue, with a patterning of white droplets over it, like rain. Mark felt a little bit of hope looking at it. It didn't match, and it looked worn and loved.

Then he saw the print on the wall, what looked like a lithograph of a piece of artwork that had been created with—surprise!—a patterning of different shades of wood. In this case it was a sunrise, with the sun made of something blond like ash and casting shadows of cypress and hickory.

"Pretty," his mother said, looking around. "Well, we've got a decent mattress, but we may need to bring some props in for his leg. The bedroom set is so nice—I'd hate to replace it with a hospital bed. Let me see what I can do." She turned and ventured into the adjoining bathroom, and he could tell by her sigh that there were no surprises there either.

White tile—the barest and whitest. This was the one room that obviously hadn't been remodeled when Cassidy moved into the house.

There was a shower/tub assembly, white and cast-iron, and a white-painted vanity that showed a lot of wear, splintering in places. A hamper sat in the corner. Mark looked inside out of sheer curiosity.

Briefs, socks, a tattered T-shirt, and a pair of sweats with holes in the knees sat inside, and Mark shut the lid with a sigh of relief.

"He's human after all?" his mother asked.

"It was starting to creep me out," he said.

"Me too." Without shame, she swung the mirror out on the vanity and peered inside the medicine cabinet. Shaving kit, electric shaver, ibuprofen, extra soap, and a couple of medications sat in militarily neat lines along the shelves. The medicine bottles were arranged perfectly, labels out, and Yvonne nodded like something made sense.

"Scary?" he asked.

She turned sad eyes to him. "Institutional," she said softly. "He's spent some time in a hospital or an orphanage or a mental facility—even children from foster homes do this sometimes. There's so much regimented time and so little personal interaction. It's like a person's entire self-worth becomes centered on the details like how neat your medicine cabinet is, how perfect your hair is done, how—"

"On time you are," Mark murmured.

Her eyebrows went up. "Oh yes."

Mark swallowed, wanting to go back and look at the pictures on the mantelpiece again. "Do you think? I mean, maybe we're just writing a mystery when there isn't one."

His mother pulled in a breath. "Or maybe he's just been sitting at the kitchen table, looking outside the front window, and seeing the lives and the families he's always wanted passing in front of his eyes."

Mark swallowed hard against the tightness in his throat. "Wow," he muttered. "That sucks. That really sucks. That...." He took a deep breath and remembered he was a doctor. "That is nothing more than conjecture."

Yvonne Taylor's luminous eyes peered at him, and that protective armor of doubt softened substantially. "Now that you've met him, do you really think so?"

He let out a hurt sound. "I think," he said, "that I am very interested in making sure our new neighbor is going to be okay. I mean—" He looked around. "—it's the first week of December, and I don't see a single holiday decoration—of *any* sort of holiday. If nothing else, we should help him put those up, don't you think?"

"Absolutely," she said. "But first let's get to work. My office can lend us the pillows and props for the bed, and we've got some stuff in the garage that can help for the rest of this. All we really need is some rails installed in the bathroom. I think we can have this place ready for Cassidy Hancock in *very* short order."

As they wandered into the front room, his phone buzzed in his pocket. "It's Holly," he said before hitting the little green button. "What's up, beautiful?"

"He's up," she said. "I just ended my shift. Is there anything you'd like me to ask him?"

"Mm… favorite foods, allergies, and what holidays he celebrates in the winter."

"Uhm…."

"Trust me, it's all need-to-know."

Holly gave a short laugh. "Wow, that's hush-hush. Hold on a sec, I'll go talk to him." She hung up, and Mark looked at his mother, eyebrows raised.

"So," Yvonne said softly. "Are we going to do this? Make this guy our project? I…." She looked around the house helplessly. "He seems pretty self-sufficient."

Since they'd moved to the front of the house, Mark wandered to the mantel. Something about those photos had been bugging him.

The first one he spotted was a group shot, a little out of focus, with a lot of people with red-eye, including Cassidy, who was standing at the end of a line, looking wistfully at the ten or so people in the center of the shot. One of those people, Mark could see, was the woman who had been talking to Cassidy about taking time off from work—Rose, his boss.

"Work," he murmured. And then he turned to the next photo, an outdoor shot of two children, more than professional quality. In fact, airbrushed. With a little price tag in the corner. "Stock photo," he said, frowning, but underneath, a neat, cramped hand had written *Katie* and *Joshua*. He swallowed and looked at the next picture. Another stock photo that came with the frame—this one a laughing young teenage girl in a bright red shirt, dancing in a clean hallway. *Sister Diane.* Oh God. This was going to break him. Another stock photo, an older couple, silver-haired, blue-eyed, with laugh lines, smiling at the photographer over coffee with an ocean background. *Mom and Dad.* And a final stock photo, a handsome adult male posing on the front lawn in shorts and a T-shirt with a handsome young Labrador retriever as an accessory. No caption on this one—but the implication was clear.

Mark stood staring at the clutter of Cassidy Hancock's dream family and tried to master his breathing. In his pocket, his phone rang, and his mother, who had moved to look over his shoulder, bumped him gently.

"Get that," she murmured.

His voice came out artificially bright. "Talk to me, Holly. I need your help, oh wise one."

"He's allergic to strawberries," she said, "celebrates Christmas but hasn't put his decorations up yet, and he says his favorite food is homemade lasagna or chicken casserole. How'd I do?"

"Perfect," Mark said, trying to get his balance. "I... I think we can work with that."

"So," she asked, her voice sinking conspiratorially, "what's his house like? A freak show? Are there bodies in the closet? Spiders in cages? What?"

Mark had to smile, but it was sad. "It's a lovely place," he said, meaning it. "Just needs some finishing touches." Like other people in Cassidy Hancock's life.

"Well, that's disappointing for the part of me that watches television mysteries, but as someone who's been his nurse all day? It's good to know. He's... haunted, if that makes any sense. I'm glad it's not too bad."

Mark couldn't tell her about the pictures or the institutionally arranged refrigerator and medicine cabinet. He was afraid to look in the garage and wondered if he arranged his laundry products in neat little rows like the books on the shelves.

"Friendly faces and voices might be really important to him," Mark said. "Make sure you tell him goodbye and that you'll be in tomorrow. I just... even if it's temporary, I think he needs to know you're coming back."

"Oh. Okay. I can do that. He seems like a sweet guy—not a problem. He was asking for you."

Mark swallowed. "Cool. Tell him we'll be setting up his house tomorrow—and not to fill up on hospital dinner tonight. I'll bring him takeout."

"Aw, that sweet. Well, gotta go—glad there weren't any bodies!"

She signed off, and Mark was left trying to wipe his eyes on his shoulder without alerting his mother. Her warm hand on the small of his back told him he'd failed.

"So that's a yes," Yvonne said when he'd pocketed his phone.

"About what?"

"About making him a project."

"Yes and no," he told her.

"What's the no?"

"Maybe I just want to know him a little better."

Her eyebrows arched. "Honey—"

"Look, he deserves more than to be a 'project.' But there's also the possibility he's a dick. Let's start with being his friends and work from there," he told her.

"Sure," she said. "Now let me go make some calls and we can bring him takeout."

"*I* was gonna bring him takeout!" he protested.

"Yes, but honey, I'm curious about him now. And hungry. And I don't want to cook. Also, we should ask where his Christmas decorations are, because you'll be breaking them out tomorrow."

Mark laughed. "Understood. We need you there. I get it."

"Get what?"

He hooked his arm around her shoulders. "I get that you're a nosy old broad and I'm at your mercy."

She laughed and leaned into him. "Yes on both counts. Shall we go?"

They went.

BIG EYES IN THE CORNER

CASSIDY WASN'T exactly sure how he happened to have this nice woman and her handsome son in his room, but he was terrified he'd say something to make them leave.

When he'd been in college, on scholarship, he'd stepped in a pothole, fallen, and broken his wrist. He'd not only had nobody to take him to the hospital, he'd had to summon a rideshare to take him back to his dorm and then show all his professors proof that he'd really broken it. His dormmates hadn't noticed, none of his classmates had cared, and God, he had wanted someone to talk to about the stupid misstep in the worst way.

Now he had a tree fall on his head—or well, his leg—and he got the nice lady from next door and her son, who was obviously *not* college-age now that Cassidy had seen him in a lab coat and scrubs, and they were eating with him like they were old friends.

It was surreal, and while he didn't want to question his good fortune, he was *really* interested in knowing when it would end so he could prepare himself for the letdown.

"You were in my house?" he asked through a mouthful of Chinese food. It wasn't lasagna, but then, takeout lasagna was harder than Chinese.

"It's lovely," his neighbor—Yvonne—said. "Where did you get the idea to decorate with all those different wood tones on top of cream upholstery?"

He smiled shyly. "My magazine did layouts for a couple of homes that used natural fibers and colors. I liked the idea, so I sort of ran with it when I bought my own house."

"Your magazine?" she asked, her eyes flicking to her son. "Which one do you work for?"

"*Gold Country Homes*," he said. "It's local, and we come out every month, online and paper." He couldn't help beaming. "I was part of the group that made it interactive online, with links to all of the contractors used in the layouts and the lists of materials. That was my idea."

Oh, how boring. He was talking about his job, of all things!

"What exactly do you do there?" Mark Taylor asked, and Cassidy worked hard not to let his heart swell in his throat. God, he was good-looking. Yes, his dark blond hair was curling over his collar and he hadn't shaved in a couple of days, but his eyes were the same warm brown of his mother's, and his jaw was square under all that scruff. He had high cheekbones, a slightly Roman nose, and his lean mouth was almost always quirked up at the corners, even when he was chasing his dog down the street in his pajamas.

"You're not wearing your sweater," Cassidy blurted. "The one your mom made you. Why?"

Mark blinked, and his ears—bare because his hair was tucked behind them—turned scarlet. "She made it for me in college," he said. "It's falling apart. I still love it, but you know, I only wear it over my pj's."

"Well if you ask nicely, maybe the yarn genie can make you one for Christmas," she said dryly.

"I *did* ask nice, and I happen to know it's already wrapped," Mark returned. "And if you tell me it's for Keith, I'm holding my breath until I pass out."

"That's a terrible trick," she admonished. "And don't tell Keith—he'll get jealous."

"I'm wearing it all the time," he replied. "I don't care if you made it lime green and pink. Let him get jealous—he needs to not give you crap about spending money on yarn."

They were standing on either side of the bed. Cassidy swung his head back and forth like he was watching a tennis match as they bantered. The moment was delightful, like unexpected chocolate, and he wanted to see it all.

"Keith can give me all the crap he wants," she said smugly. "He's got a chest like a barn and three kids—if he wants Mommy to make him a sweater, he's gotta *beg*, because otherwise Grandma's got other priorities."

Mark chuckled. "As you should." He looked at Cassidy, still smiling. "My brother and his kids live in town and shamelessly swarm my mother's house, particularly around Christmas—you'll get to meet them."

Cassidy's brain blanked out over "meet them." This would continue? He would still talk to these people after he was competent in his house, alone? The idea was boggling—and too wonderful to contemplate—so he stuck with questions. "What about his wife?"

Mark and Yvonne both sucked air in through their teeth. Before Cassidy could ask if he'd said anything wrong, Yvonne said, "Sure. She'll be around. It's fine."

Mark grimaced. "That's 'fine' in the ironic sense," he reassured Cassidy. "Mom, Dani—that's my sister—and I sort of loathe her. But we love Keith, so, you know, you put up with the things you can't change."

Cassidy swallowed, not sure he wanted to hear more. "Why do you.... What's wrong with her?" For a moment he'd been safe, but if they could dislike someone in their own family, that safety might not mean much.

"She's mean," Mark said on an exhale. "She's constantly yelling at the kids to keep it down or to stop talking when they're just being kids. She yells at Keith—in our presence, which makes it worse—to be a man and make more money. She doesn't have a job—never wanted one—and Keith probably makes plenty to support his family, but not the way she spends it. She's...."

"Awful," Cassidy said, surprised.

"And we're telling tales," Yvonne said firmly, flushing.

Mark shrugged. "I just wanted to warn him. If we plan to be up in his business, he's gonna run into Tanya, and I don't want her to scare him off."

"Good point." Yvonne turned toward Cassidy and patted his hand as it lay by his side. "Judge us not by how bitchy we are about Tanya. Judge us by how much we love Keith."

Cassidy felt a slow smile blooming. "Sure," he said, resolving to do just that. Then, hungrily, "What are the kids like?"

"Perfect," Yvonne said sunnily.

Mark snorted. "That's what she said about *us* when we were kids, but we were awful."

"You were spirited," Yvonne defended, and then she gave a wicked laugh. "And awful. Remember when you stranded Dad on the roof?"

Mark grimaced. "I was *trying* to clean up the yard! I thought he was done mucking around up there!"

She laughed outright. "Yes. To this day I don't know what he thought he knew about fixing roofs. I think he was trying to 'assess the damage,' but I'd already called the roof guy."

Mark's shrug was eloquent—and sad. "I think Dad wished he was more of a DIY guy, but he was a history teacher guy and couldn't so much as unblock a sink." He sighed. "But he was a pretty good dad, so it didn't matter that he couldn't build a treehouse or fix a tire."

Cassidy swallowed and looked at the plate on the tray above his bed. He'd eaten a little of the takeout—it had been so good—but he was suddenly too tired to eat.

"You about done there?" Yvonne asked gently.

Cassidy swallowed and went to take another bite and yawned instead. "I don't want to leave it on my plate," he said. "It's wonderful."

"Well, we can save it for tomorrow." Yvonne started to clean up. "The nurse's station has a refrigerator—they get the most wonderful tapioca that they keep there."

"Am I really in for one more day?" Cassidy asked fretfully.

"Getting restless already?" Mark asked, and he sounded so kind!

"Feeling worthless," Cassidy mumbled. "Can't work, can't take care of the house—dead weight."

"Nonsense," Yvonne said softly, and something about the way she'd lowered her voice told Cassidy she knew something he didn't. "You're pleasant, you're kind, you're good company. And the nurses say you have needed the sleep. Don't forget, pain is exhausting, and so is being medicated. One more night after this one and we can take you to your home and keep an eye on you. Don't worry."

Cassidy felt his face turn a dull red. "I'm sorry to be such a bother. You're both being more than kind. I... I don't know how to thank you or pay you back or—"

"Oh, honey," Yvonne told him. "That's not how friends work. Don't worry about it. You mowed my lawn without even asking for a thank-you when I could barely find my own shoes." She took the last of the paper containers and thrust them in a plastic bag. "Now I'm going to go put this in the fridge so you have it for tomorrow."

She disappeared into the bright corridor, leaving Cassidy alone with the handsome, warm, smiling, *out of his league* Mark Taylor.

Cassidy felt like he had to come clean. "I'm.... I haven't really done that much," he said, looking at that appealing narrow face. Mark was scruffy today, but Cassidy had seen him clean-shaven as well, and he couldn't decide which profile he liked more. They both made his chest ache—but in a good way.

Mark cocked his head, regarding him carefully. "I'm not sure that's true," he said softly. "We were all pretty wrecked when my dad died last year. It was so unexpected—one doctor's appointment and suddenly he had cancer and a month to live. There was hardly time to say goodbye. I got the resident's position here and transferred as soon as I could, but it still took nine months. Keith and Dani both made time to stay with Mom, but none of us could be there like we wanted. In the middle of all that, mowing her lawn or cleaning her gutters or trimming her trees—these were all things that needed to be done but none of us could do for her, and she was in no shape to do them herself. So it may not have felt like a lot to you, but it was *everything* to my family. This is more than a chance to pay you back, you know."

Cassidy's face was so hot, and he was so tired. He tried not to close his eyes as a way to chicken out of this situation "What is it, then?" he asked.

Mark's smile was so sweet—*so* damned sweet. "It's a way to get to know someone who helped us when we needed it," he said. "I know my mom tried and you got super shy and ran away, but you're trapped now." He emitted a mock-evil laugh that made Cassidy chuckle in spite of himself. "There is no way to escape the Taylor family trap—we've got our hooks in you now!"

Cassidy nodded and then tried one more time to be honest. "I.... It was so nice of her to bring muffins. I just.... Sometimes muffins mean that's the end."

Mark frowned. "What?"

"Muffins or cupcakes. 'Here, we know this is the end and you can't live here anymore, but have a muffin and you can know how much you'll miss a place that makes you muffins.'"

Mark's brown eyes honed in on his face. "Who did that for you?"

Cassidy couldn't meet his eyes. "Lots of places," he said softly. "First try at adoption, my first job—places will give you cookies and say, 'I'm sorry, we can't love you.' It happens all the time."

Mark breathed in hard through his nose, like he was having trouble coming up with words to deal with that. "We... we wouldn't do that to you," he said after a moment. "We only give you muffins if we want you to stay." He gave the doorway a quick look and bent down to murmur in Cassidy's ear. "But don't eat my mom's muffins. Pretend to—say they're great—but really, I'm telling you. You'll probably live longer if you don't."

Cassidy stared at him in horror. "That's a terrible thing to say!"

Mark checked the doorway again. "Which is why I'm whispering! She's the world's greatest woman, and you'll love her lasagna and kill for her Christmas cookies, but I'm telling you, no muffins. It will make you like us more."

He was standing so close, and he smelled so good. It had been so long for Cassidy—so long, and he couldn't recall if he'd ever had a moment like this.

"I already like you," he said, knowing he sounded besotted but unable to stop himself. They'd had dinner with him. It was the first time he'd eaten with anyone in months.

"Good!" Mark grinned at him but didn't move farther away, and Cassidy was flushing now from his nearness and not embarrassment. "This way you'll live to like us for a long, long time."

Cassidy couldn't help it—he stifled a laugh against his hand, feeling like a child with a secret. He'd never been that kid—the feeling was *enchanting*.

"That's better," Mark said, brown eyes twinkling. "Maybe next time I can get you to laugh outright."

Cassidy sobered and shook his head. Hard experience had taught him that things people knew you had could easily be stolen—and that included anything that made him laugh, or made him happy in any way.

A brief moment of frustration passed over Mark's handsome features, and then he gave a sigh of patience. "You're a tough nut to crack, Cassidy Hancock," he said, eyes narrowed. "But we'll do it."

"Why?" Cassidy asked again. "Why is it so important that you hear me laugh, or make me smile, or bring me dinner?"

"Because all evidence suggests you could be an amazing person to know," Mark said. "And very much worth the extra effort."

Cassidy couldn't help it. "I've never been in the past," he said gently.

"Oh, you have," Mark contradicted. "I just suspect people haven't taken the time to see. Now tell me, do you have Christmas ornaments in the garage, or do I get to clean out my mother's collection?"

"I have lights but no tree ornaments," Cassidy said. He felt a little sheepish. "I, uh, bought the house in June of last year, and it's the first time I've had a space for more than a tiny little potted plant. I was going to get a tree and maybe some ornaments this weekend."

"Ooh. That *is* unfortunate timing," Mark said, nodding sagely. "Well then, Mom and I can get you set. You're being released the day after tomorrow—leave it to us."

"That's an awful imposition—"

"Wait!" Mark actually hopped where he stood. "No! Even better! We'll get you set up to get home, and then this weekend, Keith is leaving the kids with my mom to do Christmas things. We can *all* come decorate your house—it'll be great! Your kitchen is huge—Mom can make cookies, which she does *way better* than muffins. Dani won't be there, but you'll get to meet Brandon, Kennedy, and LizBet—it'll be *great*."

"Uhm—" Cassidy gaped. "Those are a lot of names," he said weakly, and it almost hurt to watch Mark visibly restrain all that enthusiasm.

"Unless, I mean, you don't *want* us there in your house," Mark said penitently.

Cassidy had a sudden vivid memory of the family and the house he'd always dreamed of having when he was a kid. He might have had foster mothers who enjoyed baking cookies, but by then he'd been too scarred by the ones who hadn't even liked children to invest himself in their care.

This man was offering to drop that entire vision of childish hope into Cassidy's lap, and Cassidy, tired, overwhelmed, and in pain, suddenly wanted it, and wanted it so badly that any protests he might have offered were drowned out by the roaring in his ears.

"I do," he said, biting his lip. "No, it sounds wonderful. I've, uhm, never made Christmas cookies before. But I'm not, uhm, good with kids," he said. "Or I don't think I am. I don't have a lot of experience."

Mark cocked his head, and suddenly that exuberance that had seemed to make him deaf to anyone else in the room faded and was replaced by an astute evaluation. "You just have to remember your own childhood," Mark said. "Unless, of course, you never got to be a kid."

Cassidy looked away. "Not always an option," he rasped.

"I am aware."

Cassidy's eyes flicked quickly to Mark's, because it sounded as though Mark *knew* about Cassidy's childhood in a way Cassidy hadn't revealed, but at that moment, Mark jumped as though poked in the ribs.

"Shit," he muttered, checking his phone. "Scheduling snafu—they need me to pick up more shifts and I wasn't gonna! I gotta go talk with my boss!"

And with that Mark hurried out of the room. He must have passed his mother in the hallway, because she came in next.

"There—all squared away," she said. "Mark ran off to talk to his boss, so it's just you and me." She paused. "And you are looking sleepy. How about I turn on the TV and you can fall asleep? No need to entertain the freeloader who barged into your room."

"You brought me dinner," Cassidy protested, but she just laughed and turned on the set in the corner.

"Anything you like to watch?"

He named a family-friendly sitcom, and she made an approving sound.

"I love this one," she said, settling in daintily. Her voice dropped to a place between sadness and nostalgia. "Right after Harv died," she said, mouth twisting. "We hadn't seen the show and I wanted to, but he really loved something on at the same time. I found back episodes on a streaming service and...." She laughed a little. "Mark lived in the Bay Area at the time, and I begged him to come up on his day off to help me get the streaming service so I could catch up the entire series. He was so good. He didn't even ask questions, you know?"

"A good son?" Cassidy asked, because he'd always wondered what it took to be a good son. He'd tried—always neat, always clean, always on time—but nobody had seemed to want the job of being his mother.

"The best." She laughed, the sound soft. "A terrible child, really—a hot mess. Used to be able to run in from soccer, change his clothes for band, grab a snack, and run out of the house again and it would be like we got hit by a tsunami. In the morning Keith and Dani would be up on time, eating breakfast, and he'd be like the Flash. We'd be calling his name because he was going to be late and he'd zoom around the breakfast table and beat us out to the car—but everybody would be wearing their breakfast, right?"

Cassidy had to laugh with her. "How did you stand it?" he asked. He'd assumed those were deal-breakers for having parents that loved you.

"He was so sweet," she told him. "Like, the reason he overslept was because he'd been helping a friend with a paper, or the reason he was doing soccer and drama and debate at the same time was because people asked him and he couldn't say no. He always apologized after making a mess—he was just moving too fast to see his damage path, you know?"

Cassidy thought about the guys in college who had always seemed to know everybody, to do everything. He'd assumed they were superheroes, because he knew he wasn't like that. He could only do so much and be on time and neat and perfect.

"He's lucky you loved him anyway," he said, and she made a sound like a gasp, but he was starting to fade out.

"No, honey," she said gently. "We were lucky he whirled into our lives."

Cassidy swallowed. *What's wrong with me that I can't be loved?* But the show was on, and the mother was sarcastic but kind, and the father was clueless but warm, and the kids were misbehaving but not in terrible ways, and it was the life he'd always wanted but couldn't have, and he fell asleep to the familiar ache in his chest.

He couldn't say how long he'd dozed when the television switched off and he heard soft voices.

"How's he doing?" Mark—definitely Mark—asked.

"Sad," she murmured. "But kind."

"Well, the kind we knew. Let's work on the sad."

And then he felt a soft, sweet-smelling touch on his forehead, and the press of lips. "Night, sweetheart," Yvonne said. "We'll see you for dinner tomorrow. Don't forget to ask for your leftovers for lunch."

"G'night," he mumbled. "I can't believe you came."

"Well, you deserve someone who will show up in your life," she said, and then there was another kiss.

And then, when he thought she'd moved aside, a brief touch of a hand on his—but not Yvonne's.

"We'll work on the sad," Mark said softly. "No need to be sad."

Not when you're here, he thought, but he really couldn't stay awake another moment.

THE NEXT morning his boss visited—without flowers, but that wasn't her thing.

"Oh look," Rose said, spotting the vase of bright daisies Mark and Yvonne had brought the night before. "You're so solitary—I was afraid you'd be here all by yourself."

"My neighbors brought those—I was surprised," he said, comforted by her tactlessness. That was just the way she was, really, but she was also smart, a brilliant businesswoman, and surprisingly kind. She and her husband had thrown Christmas parties every year, insisting he attend. Since he'd aged out of foster care and graduated from college, they were pretty much the only celebrations he'd ever known.

"Well, they certainly seem to have taken you under their wing," Rose said approvingly. "This is the young man who spoke with me the other day?"

"Mark," Cassidy said, nodding. "I'm afraid he watched the tree branch fall on me—I think he feels bad."

"Oh?"

Cassidy let the skepticism roll through the room before he answered. "Oh what?"

"Well, he seemed to be more interested than that," she said, and then batted her eyes at him in her time-proven way of getting more information when she was interviewing someone for her magazine. *Gold Country Homes* had started out as a blog, but it had grown in popularity and prestige. Rose McCormick's opinion became highly sought-after, and ad space on her blog went at such a premium she could turn the blog into a full-fledged zine.

And then she'd gone for a print version, taking the best articles every two months and putting them into a full-color layout. Cassidy had been working for her for five years, arriving just when the print expansion had occurred, and while in the beginning it had been a struggle—particularly because they were working on the interactive links at the time—he felt some serious pride about helping to move Rose's talent, her vision, her joie de vivre into the world.

And, as always, the kindness.

"You met them today?" he said, surprised, because of all the things Mark and Yvonne had talked about in his room the night before, the meeting with Rose hadn't been one of them.

"Oh I did," she reassured him. "They said your house was spacious enough that we didn't need too many modifications, but Yvonne went over what they'd done. I think you can work from home just fine when you're feeling up to it." She swirled around his hospital bed as she spoke, her impeccable maroon pantsuit with its winter-white jacket making her look improbably like a fashionable Christmas elf. "I do love what you've done with the place, Cassidy. You should have shown me pictures or something, because it's really so improved."

Rose had helped him find the house, looking for square footage, location, and property values. He'd told her he wanted to decorate it himself, so she hadn't quibbled over the awful yellow-printed wallpaper and chipped kitchen and bathroom tile or even the terrible stained rugs that had dominated the place. Rose paid well, and Cassidy had lived so frugally to decorate the house of his dreams—he'd worked hard for the two months prior to moving in to have the place up to his specs.

He would never forget that feeling, walking over the threshold of his own home, the smell of new carpeting and paint sharp in his nose, his furniture already in place.

He had so few possessions to move in that day. His books, his clothes for work, his computer, a few things for the kitchen. But it had been *his*.

And then he'd realized the house's most unspoken attribute, its best benny.

That front window over the breakfast nook. He could see *everything*. The whole neighborhood had been *his* to observe. He'd seen families—happy families, busy families, quiet families. Some days when he worked from home, he would take a coffee break just staring out his window, watching children get on and off the bus for school, watching parents go jogging in the morning or walk their dogs at night.

And one day, watching a funeral procession arrive at the house next door. He'd seen them—from afar, of course. Mark, although Cassidy hadn't known his name. Yvonne. Even Keith and Dani and the infamous Tanya—and their children.

And they'd all been so sad.

Cassidy remembered the mild middle-aged man he'd seen cleaning gutters and raking leaves that fall after he'd moved in, and realized with a pang that he was seeing a family lose a key member, and the sight had affected him more than he'd known it could.

He'd come to feel protective over this family. Sure, they didn't even know his name, but he watched them *all the time*. And now they were missing a someone they loved—and it didn't seem fair.

He'd watched the lawn grow too long, and had mown it. He'd seen the branches and leaves fall from the tree and had raked them. He'd even trimmed the shrubs on the side of the house, because he remembered the lot of them walking, heads down in the cold March wind, looking devastated by the loss of a balding, average, apparently perfectly wonderful parent.

Cassidy had mourned a parent like that all his life. He felt like they were connected, this family and himself, and he wanted to make their grief easier.

It was unexpected and mortifying that they felt like they had to return his kindness, but they seemed so happy to do it.

And none of this gave him the words to explain to Rose why Mark Taylor made his heart beat just a little bit faster in his chest.

"Thank you," he said in response to the nice things she'd said about his house. "I'm sorry to be such an—"

Rose turned to him, an unusually stern expression on her lovely face. "Cassidy?"

"Yes?"

"I know something of how you grew up. You told me when I asked for your references, remember?"

"Yes." Cassidy's cheeks burned.

"And over the past five years, I've seen what that can do to someone like you—someone with more heart than self-defense. And it's a shame. You've got so much to give the world, and you try so hard. But sometimes you need to take some risks to get the bennies, you know what I'm talking about, Cass?"

"No," Cassidy said, completely lost.

She sighed and sat down next to his bed, much like Yvonne Taylor had the night before. "Honey, those people currently fixing up your house seem really nice—and they're working so hard to get to know you. You might try letting them in."

Cassidy's eyes burned and he let out a growl. "You have *no* idea what you're asking," he said, hoping maybe his tone would let her put herself back into her boss box and they would stop having this conversation.

She patted his hand. "Did I ever tell you about my son?" she asked, her voice dropping softly. "Justin?"

Cassidy was suddenly pulled out of his own misery. "Only that he's passed away," he said, voice low and respectful.

She nodded. "He was a little like you—quiet, self-deprecating. Worked so hard to be a nice boy that he missed out on some of the joy of just being a kid. His father and I didn't know any better. We had no idea that most children could be—and *should* be—raucous and loud and excited. And his sister came along, and she *was* raucous and loud and excited, and we were so busy chasing her we didn't see... didn't realize...."

Her voice broke, and Cassidy found it suddenly hard to breathe. "What happened?"

"He was sick," she said. "So sick. We didn't know until he started passing out in class, and by high school, he'd probably been sick for a year. By then, the cancer had spread and... and we had a month to say goodbye, and I didn't know how to tell him how sorry I was that he never got a chance to be loud and exciting. I could just hold his hand, like I'm holding yours, and cry."

She was crying now.

Cassidy tried hard to find a breath and couldn't. "What... what can I do?" he rasped.

She used a dainty finger to wipe under a mascaraed eye. "I've tried to mother you, Cassidy—and you... you took it. But so much like Justin. You just stood in one place and took whatever water and sunshine fell your way. You're not a plant, Cassidy. You're a person. If someone is looking at you like they want to love you, walk toward it. Even plants turn their faces to the sun and stretch out their roots, but be more than that. If these people are inviting you into their family, laugh like a child. Have friends. Yvonne Taylor is a lovely woman—I want to invite her to my poker night. Be like *that*. If someone makes you laugh, make plans to laugh again. If someone offers to do a kindness for you, accept it. Can you do that for me?"

Cassidy had so many doubts. *So* many doubts. But besides being kind and giving Cassidy the benefit of the doubt when he'd been new and had made mistakes, she was walking the talk. Yes, she was asking him to open himself in the way that had most terrified him since he was old enough to know that his hand of cards was shitty and he had very few options to win the game—but she was also showing cards she'd held close to her vest for a very long time.

"I can try," he promised rashly. "I.... It's so hard." And even that admission cost him.

"I know, honey." She held his hand to her lips and kissed the back of it tenderly. It came away briny. "We've tried at the office. We've gotten you to come to lunch with us, and get-togethers, but you're always so quiet. You must be having fun—you keep coming—but I would love to see you not just show up but laugh."

"What if I laugh at the wrong thing?" he asked, feeling at once pitiful and surprised he said it out loud.

She blinked in shock. "There's a wrong thing to laugh at?" she asked.

"Laughing at funerals *is a thing!*" he told her, agonized. It had always been one of his greatest fears. Laughing at the wrong thing or saying the wrong thing—one slip could cost him everything. One slip, and any friendships he'd had could be washed away.

"I know, baby," she said softly. "Hannah, my daughter, laughed all the way through Justin's. She was three, and she'd never seen so many people in black before. She kept us sane throughout the whole horrible affair, and then when it was done and all the people were gone, she asked if Justin could come out and play now. And my husband and I got to cry and cry and cry, and so did she. We still loved her, you understand? She gave us what nobody else could."

Cassidy let out a sound of frustration. "You're not going to let me out of this, are you?" he asked, wounded.

The look on her face was like sunrise. "No," she said. "Yvonne Taylor and I are going to gossip about you and tell tales, and we're going to find the Cassidy who could come up with that house, do you understand? The Cassidy who could comb through wood scraps and would cut down and buff out the ones that would make a sunrise."

Cassidy felt his face flush. "How did you know that was me? I only kept the lithograph."

"Because I've seen you do it before, remember? You made my husband and me those picture frames, and puzzles for Hannah's daughter. What we don't understand is why you didn't keep the original."

Oh, now he was squirming. "When the furniture makers saw what I'd done with all the scraps, they offered to have prints made and sell them for me as long as they could keep the original for their showroom. And they said in return I could root through their scrap pieces all I wanted, and they'd sell any other puzzle portraits I gave them." Oh, this was embarrassing. "The prints go for a *lot*," he whispered, like this was shameful. "When they're all framed and mounted, they go for almost $200—and I get half!"

Rose's expression was part delight and part hurt. "That's *amazing*, Cassidy. Why didn't you tell us? I love that you do that. We could put one of the prints in one of our photo layouts and get you *so much business!*"

He bit his lip. "That feels like cheating."

She hid her face in her hands for a moment and let out a sound between a moan and a cackle. When he could hear her talking, she was saying, "There is no bad laughter, there is no bad laughter," over and over again, and he was at a loss.

She finally left after patting his cheek one last time and making him promise to call her tomorrow after the Taylors got him settled, and he was left alone with his thoughts.

Usually this was a bad thing. He tended to think lonely thoughts about being left in corners so often he was finally comfortable there, but not this time.

This time the events of the past couple days, along with the pain medication, led him to think about his puzzle art, as he called it, and the people he'd just met.

He started planning portraits. A portrait of his boss using redwood for her hair and pale pine for the sharp cheekbones, ebony for her penetrating eyes. A profile of Yvonne using white ash for the hair and the sweetest cedar for the eyes, and of her son using....

And by then his attention wandered from materials and shapes to give a specific impression to create a caricature to Mark's face in general, and he fell asleep thinking about the high cheekbones and the warm brown eyes, the sensual mouth and the way he was always just about to laugh.

Natural Habitat

MARK'S MOTHER had traded in her minivan from his youth for the SUV of her middle age, which was fine because it still held the wheelchair perfectly, and the four doors made sitting Cassidy in the back with his awkward cast set at a slight angle but still extending from the hip just a little easier.

Still, Cassidy was obviously in pain and so *very* glad to be wheeled into his own home. He looked around appreciatively and made happy noises when he saw the modifications Yvonne had made.

Yvonne and Mark had rented a table that could hold the coffee maker, a couple of plates, bowls, and glasses, and even some basic supplies like granola bars, coffee, and creamer at Cassidy's height. It also held a microwave.

The shower seat was set up with the same idea, with a net bag that held shampoo, bodywash, and a body sponge. The long plastic sleeves to keep his cast dry were in the cupboard under the sink. They'd moved his basic toiletries into the larger bathroom and made sure the bathroom rug was tightly velcroed to the floor.

"The Velcro is there with an adhesive," Yvonne confided. "We did little test spots to make sure the adhesive remover won't stain the tile."

"Wow," Cassidy said, awed. "I wouldn't have thought of that."

"Bathrooms are tough," Yvonne told him. "We need you not to slip, and your tile gets a little dicey when it's wet, so we can't take away the rug. But rugs bunch and slip too, so we put that tight Velcro to all the edges. If you like it, you can leave it." She gave a rather wicked little giggle. "I'll be honest, I've got it on *my* bathroom rugs because they make me crazy!"

Cassidy gave a little head bob. "I never would have thought of it." He sounded sincere, but Mark was standing behind him after having wheeled him down the hall, so he couldn't see his expression. They'd removed the hall runner from the hardwood floor to make the wheelchair go easier. "Is there anything I should know about my bedroom?"

"Pillows," Mark said. "Or props. There's a whole... *thing* she'll probably have you go through when you're ready to nap." He had, in fact, been impressed by all the small pieces that his mother could bring to the situation to make Cassidy comfortable.

"I have to nap?" Cassidy said peevishly, and then immediately yawned. "I have to *nap*," he acknowledged in wonder. "Why do I have to nap?"

Mark couldn't help his laughter. Cassidy reminded him of Gus-Gus sometimes, particularly when the dog acknowledged he was too short to get somewhere he really wanted to be—like the counter, to sneak food. "Because a) you're still on pain meds, and they do that, and b) you just had surgery and it knocks you out, and c) you're still in a little bit of pain. Have I covered everything?"

Cassidy yawned again. "I'm sorry, I couldn't hear you. I was yawning." He followed it up with a sly look to see if the joke landed, and Mark rewarded him with a snort.

"Nice," he said approvingly. "But I guess you're ready for that nap now."

Cassidy surprised him, shaking his head. "I, uh, thought maybe we could have some lunch," he said, all in a rush like he was trying to get it out.

"Yeah?" Mark couldn't help it. His heart was doing a tiny fluttery happy dance, because this was the first time he could remember that the man in the wheelchair hadn't said, *Oh no, you can't, I don't mean to be a bother*, or something along those lines.

"I, uh, well, sandwiches are gonna be awkward," Cassidy said, "but, uhm, takeout or—"

"I've got Thai food on speed dial," Mark said happily. "Do you have something you like?"

"Never had it—"

"Green curry," Mark decided for him. "You'll love it. Green curry with chicken. It'll be great. And dumplings. Everyone likes dumplings. And chicken satay—I'll go ask Mom."

He was so excited he almost shoved Cassidy's wheelchair into the wall.

"Wait, hold on." He straightened the chair and called out, "Mom! Do you want Thai food?"

"I've got to go to work, honey," his mother said, coming out of the bedroom. "But you go ahead and order some for me and I'll come over and have it for dinner."

"Oooh, good idea," Mark said, pulling out his phone. His mother was staring at him. "What?"

"Maybe get poor Cassidy out of the hallway first?" she said delicately.

And Mark felt stupid. He was a *doctor*—was it too much to ask that he lost some dorkiness?

"Uhm, forward or backward?" he inquired.

"Well, if you push him into the bedroom, I can show you how to prop his leg," she said. "In fact, Cassidy, one of our little rentals in here is one of those trays on wheels like they have at the hospital, so we can get you situated *and* feed you. You've got your TV wall-mounted across from the bed, so that'll make your life easier in the next month. Come see."

Mark heard Cassidy sigh.

"What?" he asked, wondering if he had railroaded over the poor man for the final time.

"I was looking forward to eating at the table with you," he admitted. "But your mom's right. I *might* make it to when the food's delivered. I'm sor—"

"No." Mark couldn't help it. "No *sorry*. No *bother*. Mom's taking off, and you and me will wait for takeout and watch TV or play cards or Parcheesi or Monopoly or Trivial Pursuit. No sorry. It's fine."

And then he heard the most blessed of sounds. A choke/snort—a snort of laughter that Cassidy Hancock had by no means, by no measure whatsoever, wanted to slip through.

"What?" he asked.

"You... you just sound so excited to watch me sleep!"

Yvonne chuckled. "And that's not creepy at all! Now c'mon, we'll get you situated and then—"

And then Cassidy blew Mark's mind—and, he was pretty sure, his mother's as well.

"And you can bring over the dog?" he asked.

"The dog?" Mark repeated, not sure he'd heard right.

"Yeah. The, uhm, dog. Gus-Gus. I... I mean, I can't be late for anything today, right?"

Mark and his mother exchanged glances.

"Nope," Mark replied. "Nothing to do but get in bed and eat Thai food. And maybe wrestle you into the bathroom together, which will be embarrassing for both of us, but I for one vow to forget it."

Cassidy made that snort sound again and then got hold of himself. Mark could hear that noise all day. "Well, I'll pretend I can forget it too," he said weakly. "But if I don't have anywhere to be, I'd... I mean, if you think he'll be okay, I'd really love to pet the dog."

Mark and Yvonne met eyes again, because the wistfully voiced hope was so damned modest. "'Course," Mark said, keeping his voice casual. "Let's get you situated first."

TWENTY MINUTES later, Cassidy was set up on the bed, Mark had ordered, his mother had left after kissing Cassidy on the cheek the same as she did for Mark, and Mark had run next door to get Gus-Gus from his cozy doghouse in the backyard. The day was bright and only a little chilly, and Gus-Gus had a *lot* of energy, so they let him run around their backyard. Yes, he barked at the occasional bird, or cat, or a child playing in the yard behind them, or the mailman, but the vet called these activities "hobbies" and said all animals had them. Gus-Gus, she said, was a very active dog, because he had a *lot* of hobbies.

Running back and forth along the fence line, shouting curses and threats to the nine-hundred-pound gorilla he suspected might be delivering the mail, calling out cats for being assholes—these were all highly entertaining for Mark's weird-looking dog. Since the pit-wiener (as Mark's ex-boyfriend had called him, completely leaving out the corgi part of his lineage!) was also loyal and affectionate and adorable and only drooled a little, Mark figured that as long as his mother's HOA didn't object to Gus-Gus having hobbies, he would have nothing against them either.

And letting him run the fence line on those stubby little legs eventually tired him out so he wouldn't make an ass of himself inside.

Mark wanted the big goober to be civil and well-behaved, since his presence had been so specifically requested.

"You are not to jump up and lick his face," Mark admonished as he wiped him down, clearing some of the mud off his paws and the dew off his tummy. "There is to be no eating of his food and no leaping on his bed. This man is an entirely different fish than you're used to. You thought Brad was uptight? Well, he was—and he was a prick. This guy isn't a prick, but he's not used to dogs. I mean, he seems to think *you're* okay, but you furry people come with mud and slobber and fur and... all this!"

Gus-Gus wriggled in his arms in a half circle to lick Mark's face.

"Yes, that," Mark confirmed. "I'm just saying, you're a little much, Gus. Maybe tone it down."

Gus-Gus licked faster, and Mark tried not to think this entire enterprise was doomed.

He got back in time to watch his mother leave, bending to pat Gus-Gus on his smiling broad head before disappearing down the hallway and letting herself out.

Cassidy only had eyes for the dog.

"Gus-Gus?" he said, and his face was a sunrise of excitement. For his part, Gus-Gus wiggled and tried to jump up on the high queen-sized bed, but he was too damned short. Mark thought in a panic that even if he *did* make it up, he'd probably land right on Cassidy's leg, and that would be bad, but Cassidy turned to the empty side of the bed and patted it. "Gus-Gus!" he called. "C'mon, baby. There's a stool on that side— you can make it!"

And the dog got it. Before Mark could protest, the dog had run around to the other side, and in a moment he'd bounded up onto the bare space on the side of the bed and right into Cassidy's arms.

"Oh, who's a good boy? You are! What a good boy! You're so smart! Yes you are!"

The dog licked his face in an ecstasy of enthusiasm, and Cassidy, hair falling forward on his brow, hazel eyes wide and lit with joy, hugged Mark's dog like he had a kennel of his own.

God, he was beautiful.

The thought hit Mark not quite out of the blue—Mark had already known he was surprisingly handsome, especially when his expression was open and pleased—but right now, as he lavished what looked to be a lifetime of hoarded love on Mark's wriggling pit-wiener who was actually a corgi, he was just luminous. Stunning.

And then he looked at Mark shyly from under his lashes, and Mark's chest and groin gave an in-tandem throb.

And given the picture on the mantelpiece, he played for Mark's team—or would consider an at-bat, at the very least.

Gus-Gus, for his part, had settled down and was resting with his head on Cassidy's lap, gazing at him adoringly while Cassidy fondled his ears.

It was then that Mark realized he was in real peril of losing his dog. But then, if he could get Cassidy to unleash that torrent of affection on Mark like he'd unleashed it on Gus-Gus, well, the trade-off might be worth it!

"Wow. You like dogs?"

Cassidy nodded enthusiastically, but his gentle ear rub stayed the same. "I've always wanted one," he said softly. "Since I was a little kid. I've looked up care and breeds and training, and I pet the ones who let me."

"You couldn't get one as a kid?" Mark asked carefully. He and his mother had already guessed, but he wanted Cassidy to confirm it so it wasn't a subject they danced around.

"Foster homes," Cassidy said, his face pinking up. "I… I was left at a fire station when I was just born."

Mark stared. "Seriously?"

"Yeah." Cassidy sighed and lifted a shoulder. "Those are the babies that usually get thousands of offers, but I was sick. I had a strep infection for months. By the time they knew I was going to live, everybody had forgotten about the baby in the firehouse, and nobody wanted to adopt a sick toddler."

Mark's throat was suddenly sore and tight. "So, uhm, foster homes?"

Cassidy nodded. "Yeah. My first foster placement was nice, or so I'm told. But the foster parents were older, and they didn't have the energy for little kids anymore. I guess they thought someone would adopt me sometime." He spoke the words mostly to the dog, but Mark could hear the parts he wasn't saying.

Nobody wanted me. Nobody.

"It didn't happen," Mark said gruffly.

"It almost happened." Cassidy gave a slight smile. "There was an event with foster families. They brought kids to the park, and adoptive parents came and hosted games and played with the children and interacted. It was a chance for us to fall in love with each other, I guess."

"Did you fall in love?" Mark asked, but either way Cassidy answered, he knew this story didn't have a happy ending.

"Didn't get a chance." Cassidy let out a laugh that was probably supposed to show he was grown now and had gotten over it. "The, uh, foster family van broke down on the way. We never got a chance to see. And after that there was another family. And they were all pleasant, I guess. They all tried to be kind. They just never really... wanted me. There was a lot of 'Be neat! Be clean! Be on time! Get along!' but no...."

"No 'you will be part of our hearts forever,'" Mark whispered.

"I guess it doesn't really happen with boys like me," Cassidy said, trying to shrug it off.

For a moment Mark couldn't breathe. *Boys.*

"Well, you seem to have grown into a good man," Mark told him.

Cassidy smiled faintly. "I'm always on time," he said. Then he looked down at Gus-Gus. "That's why I can't get a dog," he said in apology. "You might make me late. You can miss a lot when you're late."

"You can miss a lot of life worrying about being late," Mark said, the epiphany so bright it hurt to look at.

Cassidy nodded and stared adoringly at Gus-Gus some more. "I can't seem to make myself find out."

He was quiet then, sinking into the pillows and the stillness of the house, and Mark searched for something to say.

It wasn't until Cassidy's breathing evened out that Mark realized he hadn't waited for Thai food after all and had fallen gently asleep. With a sigh, Mark covered him with a throw from the bottom of the bed and, after cautioning Gus-Gus to stay, ran over to his room above the garage for his tablet and some of the paperwork he'd brought home from the hospital.

The chair by the bed was really very comfy, he thought as he settled into his routine. This wasn't a bad way to spend an afternoon.

But every now and then as he worked, he would look up at Cassidy's sleeping face and wonder what it would be like to see him unleash the same unbridled affection on a person that he'd unleashed upon Gus-Gus. What would it be like to see him get so engaged and passionate over something that he allowed himself to be late for something, anything at all? What would it be like to watch him drop his guard and just be in the moment with Mark or his mother, or anyone in the family?

He'd tried. Mark could tell that the invitation for Thai food had been an attempt to do just that. Talking about his childhood had been rusty and unusual for him—Mark could hear it in his voice. He'd been reaching out, trusting Mark, a veritable stranger, with the most tender and painful parts of his life.

Mark just hoped he was worthy.

And a little part of him wanted Cassidy to love him as unconditionally as he'd loved Gus-Gus the super-weird dog.

Thai food got there about forty-five minutes later, giving Mark a chance to yawn and stretch before he ran to pay. He set it on the counter, used the bathroom, and went back into the bedroom to find Cassidy, eyes open, smiling widely at Gus-Gus like they were in the middle of a scintillating conversation.

"Food?" Mark asked, his voice cracking. Oh, this was too much—he *had* to get over being jealous of the damned dog.

"Starving," Cassidy admitted. He looked at the solid mass of fiberglass extending out from his hip and sighed. "How long again?"

"Eight weeks," Mark said in commiseration. "But in the meantime, you've got me to go fetch food."

He used Cassidy's plates to serve lunch, impressed by the heavy stoneware, even if there was only a service for four.

"These are nice," Mark said. "My God, you've got amazing taste."

Cassidy set the plate down on the serving tray and smiled in appreciation. "I've been working for Rose for five years now. You learn things about taste when you're working for a magazine about, you know—taste."

Mark chuckled and took a bite, closing his eyes to appreciate before continuing. "Well, my mom probably wishes I could take lessons from you. I went to college, moved in with my boyfriend, got my residency and moved home, and still had the same crap I'd had when I left home. She was like, 'You didn't even have dishes?'"

"You didn't even have dishes?" Cassidy prodded.

Mark nodded, impressed by the spar. "Well, don't tell *her*, but I did. I even picked out a new comforter and, holy crap, furniture, but I left all the new shit with the old boyfriend when I moved home."

Cassidy cocked his head. "Why'd you do that?"

Mark made a sound of frustration, because this still pissed him off. "Well, Brad was sort of an ass," he said frankly. "I mean, I thought he was awesome at first, but God, he was a prick."

"What made him a prick?" Cassidy asked curiously.

"Oh no, you got me started," Mark said. "So, like, we used to have to estimate how much time we each spent using lamps so we knew who had to buy the lightbulbs—*that* made him a prick. And worse than that. He was a doctor too, and while I was a resident in the same hospital but a different department, he was chief of surgery in pediatrics. You're like, 'Oh my God! What a saint!' because someone doing something that important *should* be a saint, and don't get me wrong, if I had a kid who was sick, I'd want Brad, hands down, to operate on them. But if I was called in to work an extra shift and God forbid Brad had made plans for us, I had to hear about how I should just pretend to be sick because it's not like I was saving a child's life or anything. I just set bones, right?"

"Wait, there's elitism between doctors?" Cassidy asked, sounding dumbfounded.

"Well, there shouldn't be!" Mark exploded. "But it was even more than that. I found Gus-Gus wandering in the park on a run and brought him home—he was just a puppy, and oh my God, did he look *weird*. I mean, the proportions were all wrong. I wasn't even sure he was a dog!"

Cassidy laughed like he should have, but he also fondled Gus-Gus's ears. "He's kidding," Cassidy said to Gus-Gus. "Your dogness is written all over you."

Gus's tail thumped on the coverlet, and he continued to gaze at Cassidy with a reverence he'd previously reserved for steak.

"Well, yes—and it was written all over our apartment too," Mark said ruefully.

Cassidy grimaced. "Gus-Gus! How rude!"

Gus's adoration didn't let up one bit, and Cassidy sent Mark a bit of a cheeky grin. "I don't see the problem," he said.

Mark chuckled—oh, he was delightful. "I didn't either," he said frankly. "But Brad did. I did my best. I took all the responsibilities— walked him, fed him, got him defleaed, and paid for his vet checkups— and the whole time I was getting an earful about how irresponsible I was to own a dog and why would I want to put my energy into an animal that confused food and grooming with love and how I'd better not let him sleep on Brad's side of the bed."

Cassidy made a wounded sound and put his hand protectively on Gus-Gus's head.

"And I get it. I was inconsiderate bringing the dog home without asking. But I was, at the time, looking for someone to take the little goober, and Brad kept telling me to take the dog to a shelter instead. Now I wanted him—my God, I wanted him—but I'd saddled Brad with him too, and even if he wasn't my boyfriend, he was my *roommate*, and I get that it wasn't cool. But when the only shelters that would take him were kill shelters that would give him a week before he was euthanized and Brad still wouldn't give me time to place him, I started to think the whole thing was a bad idea."

"What did you do?" Cassidy asked, looking enthralled.

Mark felt himself deflate. "Well, we were having rip-roaring fight after rip-roaring fight when my dad passed away. When I decided to take the second-year resident's position up here, Brad shook my hand and said it was probably for the best."

Cassidy winced. "That's… awful."

Mark sighed and set down his half-eaten plate of pad thai. "Yeah. It didn't really reflect well on either of us, you know? He thought I was reckless and irresponsible, and I thought he was inflexible and stone-fucking-cold. And he probably would have forgiven me for being irresponsible if I could have given him a break for needing to dot every *i* and cross every *t*."

"Mm." Cassidy took another bite of his food, and Mark smiled secretly to himself. He apparently liked green curry very much.

"Mm what?" Mark hadn't told his mother much about why the relationship ended. He had just said that things had started to cool before Mark decided to move in over the garage. Cassidy was, in fact, the first person he'd confessed the gory details to, and the move felt oddly freeing.

"I think he tried to get you to kill the dog," Cassidy said simply. "I mean, I know you're trying to be responsible and talk like someone who is trying to learn and grow from a situation, but the fact is, the dog was important to you. If he'd really cared about you, he would have understood that. A dog *is* a big responsibility. I mean, that's why I've been afraid to get one. But it's not like you didn't make it through med school." He smiled a little and looked Mark in the eyes, his stunning features thrown into relief by the late-afternoon shadows coming in through the window. "I see you walking the dog every day—or, well, sometimes he walks you. And look at him. He's so affectionate—so open. He trusts you'll take care of him."

"Or he wants one of your dumplings," Mark said dryly, recognizing that look in Gus-Gus's eyes.

"Chicken is probably better," Cassidy said, slipping Gus-Gus a tiny piece of chicken satay. Gus-Gus took it delicately, with the manners of a maître d'.

"Wow," Mark laughed. "You guys are a match made in heaven."

"I'd love it if that were so." Cassidy gave him a sweet smile and then took his own bite of chicken satay. "I'm just saying that just because you sort of, I don't know, fly by the seat of your pants, that doesn't mean you're 'reckless and irresponsible.'" He sighed, the melancholy so palpable it almost blocked the sun. "It just means you're… confident, I guess."

"Confident?" Mark had never thought of his propensity for rash decisions as confident.

"You have faith that you can handle the repercussions of your actions," Cassidy rephrased, and Mark smiled, impressed.

"Well done," he said. "You managed to make my worst quality sound almost bearable! Now do you!"

Cassidy shook his head with such heartrending seriousness that Mark almost ran, right then. So much quietly subsumed ache in that one gesture. Mark wasn't sure he could have fixed it if it had been a broken bone—he was definitely unsure about a broken human.

But he'd seen such promise in this day. Cassidy had tried, more than once, to show he liked Mark's company, to be present in getting to know each other. Mark felt like he had to try to draw him out.

"C'mon," Mark urged. "I know you don't have any bodies in the garage—we checked to see what your Christmas decorations looked like in case Mom had more in *her* garage. By the way, you've got a *lot* of woodworking tools in there. What do you use them for? I mean, besides the bookcases."

"You liked the bookcases?" Cassidy asked, his cheeks growing pink.

"They're gorgeous. But there was more stuff in there—really fine small tools, and an entire bench dedicated to using them. What do you use that for?" Mark and his mother had been fascinated. Keith liked to do woodwork—he made toys for his kids that Mark secretly coveted. They'd gone into the garage looking for decorations and the washer/ drier and had found, instead, Santa's workshop.

And now Cassidy's eyes went unconsciously to the lithograph on the wall, and Mark felt like he was missing some of the wonders of the chief elf. "It's beautiful—did...?" His eyes popped open wide as he made the connection. "Did you make the *original*?" he asked, stunned.

Cassidy nodded, obviously pleased. "Some of my furniture was made custom, but I'd taken shop classes in high school. I wanted to do some of it myself, and the bookshelves seemed like the place to start. The shelves turned out so well, I asked for their chips and cast-offs because I thought it would be sort of cool to make a picture with all of the scraps from the house. The furniture place wanted to see what I was doing, and they were so impressed they bought the original from me and made lithographs. I get a commission from the sales—and all the scraps they can give me."

"Wow," Mark said, his heart stammering in his chest. "That's... that's *gorgeous*. Have you done any other pieces?"

A casual shrug. "A couple, for people I work with. I... uhm, was working on one to finish, to sell before Christmas."

"That's amazing, Cassidy! How... how do you have this hidden talent and you don't even brag!"

Cassidy concentrated on his food for a moment, and Mark watched as his ears turned red. "It's just pictures," he mumbled.

"It's *art*!" Mark countered, genuinely surprised. "Do you have any idea what my mother would have given to give birth to a child who had even a *little* artistic ability? It's like your house—it's a showcase! The world should see it."

"I don't know anybody to invite," Cassidy said, still concentrating on his curry.

"My family," Mark said, and then he let out a self-deprecating snort. "Even though we've already invited ourselves."

"They're welcome," Cassidy mumbled. "I'd love to have your mother here baking cookies and your brother's kids here too."

"We'll try to keep them from wrecking the joint," Mark said, mostly kidding. At Cassidy's horrified look, he tried to explain. "They don't destroy property," he said, hoping it was true. "They're just...

Tanya's kids. If they get bored, they get into mischief so they can get people's attention."

"We should lock the garage," Cassidy said, completely sober. "I wouldn't want them to get hurt."

Mark cocked his head.

"What?" Cassidy went studiously back to his curry.

"I thought you'd be worried about the house, but you're not. You're worried about the kids. How awesome is that?"

Cassidy's expression was genuinely puzzled. "Furniture can be repaired," he said. "Upholstery cleans. Kids are... kids. They're important. They need to know they're more important than the furniture."

His intensity would have been unnerving if Mark hadn't had some idea where it came from. "You're right," he said softly. "That's something Brad never got, by the way. He refused to let Keith's kids visit, and it hurt."

"That's too bad," Cassidy said. "I mean, I can't promise I won't need to take a moment—I, uhm, you know, don't put a lot of wear on the place myself. But at least in theory I think the kids are more important."

Mark chuckled. "Well, I like your theory," he said. Then, sensing an opening, "But I still don't know what your worst flaw is."

Cassidy looked away. "It's dumb. It's obvious. It's stupid and I... I can't get past it. I almost had a boyfriend once, and we were supposed to go out on a date. I had my whole day mapped out—when I would get home, when I would get ready, when he would get there, when we would leave. He was late. And by the time he got here, about half an hour after he was supposed to, I was a wreck. I was almost in tears. I can't be late. If I know I have a meeting online, I need to be home an hour before it starts. Two if I can make it happen. I panic if I'm running so much as two minutes past when I usually run. I practically have an anxiety attack if I'm held up in traffic. I get to work half an hour early, and Rose doesn't open the office until nine on the dot. I've wasted hours of my life parked outside, drinking my coffee, because I can't... I can't be late."

His voice had risen as he'd spoken, his breathing growing harsher and more uneven, until Gus-Gus was searching his face worriedly from his perch on Cassidy's lap. In an effort to calm him down, Mark reached out and covered the hand resting on his tray with his own, breathing evenly, until Cassidy matched him breath for breath and met his eyes.

"That's not stupid," Mark murmured. "And it's not a flaw."

"It's a psychosis," Cassidy said savagely, his voice breaking.

"No," Mark murmured. "It's… it's a reaction, is what it is."

"To what?" But Cassidy couldn't meet his eyes. He knew. Mark knew.

"To things that happened a long time ago but feel like they were yesterday. To when a little boy really, really hoped for parents who would love him absolutely unconditionally. He hoped so hard, he pinned all his dreams on an event at a park, and his transportation broke down and he was late, and what should have been one of a million chances passed him by. And the only thing he could think of to control about his life was being on time."

Cassidy's next breath came harsh and shuddering, and Mark squeezed the hand under his. Cassidy was staring out the window behind him like he was wishing he was anywhere but there.

Mark was fiercely glad he was there, safe, in his own home with Mark by his side.

"That's stupid," Cassidy muttered, wiping his eyes with the back of his hand.

"It's human," Mark said, squeezing his other hand again. "You were a kid, and you were probably told to be clean and neat and on time, and you told yourself that's how you'd be loved. If you were the cleanest, neatest, most on-time boy in the world, somebody would love you. Am I right?"

He *heard* Cassidy swallow—he didn't even need to see his head bob.

"It's not the only reason you'd be really easy to love," Mark whispered. "But you wouldn't know that yet. Because nobody told you that when you were a kid."

Cassidy nodded reluctantly—probably as much to get Mark to stop probing so deeply, where all the wounds were, as to agree.

"They should have," Mark said. "You've got more to offer the world than being on time."

Cassidy didn't say anything, and he kept his face turned away. Mark moved his hand and began eating to give him a chance to compose himself.

They both pretended they didn't see it when Cassidy removed his glasses to wipe his eyes on his shoulder.

Mark spoke into the silence. "Hey, I bet I could find something fun to watch. Christmas movies abound right now. Wanna look?"

"Yeah," Cassidy croaked. "Sounds great. Thank you."

"My pleasure," Mark murmured. He picked up the remote and started channel surfing, but inside he was wondering what it would be like to climb into bed on the side Gus-Gus was sprawled out on. He would take Cassidy Hancock into his arms and hold him, hard and unapologetically, while the man purged himself of the last of his demons.

And then Mark would kiss him, sweeping all the bad memories away and building good ones, memories that had nothing to do with being on time and everything to do with *taking* their time, memories that proved to Cassidy once and for all that he had more to offer the world than being clean and neat and punctual, and that his goodness had nothing to do with punching a clock.

The Dark and the Light

Turned out, Cassidy *loved* kids.

Or maybe it was LizBet, Brandon, and Kennedy—he loved *those* kids.

LizBet was three, the baby, and Brandon and Kennedy were twins at seven. Kennedy was, in her words, a "girly girl" and came with a literal suitcase of dolls with doll parts and doll cars and doll clothes. Brandon had a similar suitcase, but with action figures.

LizBet had a diaper bag "just in case" and a couple of toys of her own.

For half an hour, as Mark and his mother set up for cookie baking, they played on Cassidy's living room floor. Cassidy was content to oversee as the kids asked him questions. *So* many questions.

"So do you get to *race* in that chair?"

"No place to race," he told them, not wanting to admit that he needed to build up his upper-body strength a *lot* more in order to be a proficient racer. His arms and chest had been sore for the past two days—and he'd been grateful not only for the nurse who came by in the mornings for a few hours, but also for Mark and his mother, who came by in the afternoons. Mark had spent the past two nights in his guest room with Gus-Gus, although Gus-Gus, apparently guessing there might be snacks in his future if he sucked up enough, had taken to sneaking into Cassidy's bed in the middle of the night, and Cassidy had no objections.

"Aw." Brandon, in particular, looked crushed.

"But your uncle Mark pushes me super fast down the block sometimes," Cassidy told him, chuckling. "Gus-Gus runs alongside us, barking. It's almost like a parade."

Brandon's expression brightened, and he pulled out a blank pad of recycled paper and some crayons. "I'm gonna draw a *parade!*" he said excitedly.

"Did a tree really fall on you?" Kennedy asked, quietly stealing one of her brother's dinosaur toys. When he didn't notice, she put a

Barbie on its back and started galloping them both around the house-shaped suitcase she'd brought all her stuff in.

"Yes," he said, still unable to believe it himself. "I was walking to my car, and it came crashing down and poked through my leg."

Her eyes got really big, and she grabbed a Lego block from Brandon's suitcase and sent it crashing down on Barbie's leg. "Like that?"

"Yes, but with more wind and more branches and less Barbie."

She giggled. "But this is Barbie's adventures with the tree. You have to live your own."

He nodded. "Well, I'm done with mine. She can keep going."

LizBet squealed and snagged one of Kennedy's Barbies, then sucked on its foot.

"LizBet!" Kennedy stared at her little sister, taking in the Barbie she had—obviously an older one—and the fact that LizBet might be drooling a little but she wasn't chewing. "Oh, fine. Just don't pull her hair out."

Cassidy caught sight of a bald Barbie near the bottom of the pile. "She's done that?" he asked delicately.

"No!" Kennedy retorted. "Of course not. I gave her a haircut. But she might. I need to be careful."

"Of course," Cassidy said, nodding gravely.

"Little sisters can wreck a lot of toys," Kennedy said.

"I did not know that." Cassidy found himself nodding a lot when he talked to them. He wasn't sure why that was.

"Did you have little brothers?" Kennedy asked. "Because Brandon *could* wreck my toys, but Dad won't let him."

"I had foster brothers and sisters," Cassidy said. "We didn't really know each other well enough to get into wrecking each other's stuff." He'd had quite a bit of his *stolen*, but he didn't want to tell her that. They'd all had so little, him and the boys and girls he'd grown up with. Stealing each other's toys had been a way to get some control over that. He hadn't really begrudged the other kids what they'd taken, although he would have liked some things of his own.

"Why did you have that? Where were your mommy and daddy?" Kennedy had big brown eyes, a lot like Mark's, and they grew particularly limpid.

"I don't know," he said simply. "They left me with people who would make sure I had food and a roof over my head and would get to school on time. I'm pretty sure they thought it was the best thing for me."

Kennedy squinted at him as though the words coming out of his mouth had nothing to do with the language she knew. "*You* need an action figure!" she said emphatically. "Uncle Mark! Your boyfriend needs an action figure for Christmas! And dinosaurs! And a Barbie! He didn't get any as a little kid—it's your job to make sure he gets some now!"

Mark came into the living room, wiping his hands all over one of Cassidy's brand-new kitchen towels. Cassidy didn't care. Mark's dark blond hair was rumpled around his eyes, his blond stubble was coming in patchily because he hadn't shaved in two days, and he was wearing the tatty crocheted sweater that had made Cassidy think he was a wayward college student when he'd first moved into his mother's garage.

And he had flour on his nose.

He looked delicious, and if he wanted to wipe his hands all over Cassidy's walls and then his cream-colored carpet, Cassidy was totally fine with that, as long as he got the same warm, sweet smile he was getting now.

"Kennedy, calm down," Mark said. "We're going to decorate Cassidy's house and bake cookies, and we're going to make sure he has a good Christmas. I don't think he needs an action figure to make that happen."

Kennedy's lower lip wobbled. "But he didn't have any toys when he was little! Uncle Mark, he needs *toys*!"

"Naw," Cassidy said cheerfully, touched that she would be so passionate on his behalf. "I don't need toys—I get to sleep with Gus-Gus the dog! When I was a kid, I wanted a dog more than anything, and now I get to borrow your uncle Mark's—it's great!"

Mark scooped his niece into his arms and kissed her on the cheek. "See? Now go down to the end of the hall and wash your hands so you can help Grandma and me make cookies."

She hugged him tight and kissed him back before burying her face against his neck. "But he didn't have any toys," she said softly.

"He's fine," Mark said. "Look at him—Grandma's going to teach him how to crochet, he got to play with you guys today, there's going to be cookies. If you guys keep coming to see him, it will be like he gets to be a kid all over again, okay?"

She nodded, but like she didn't agree with anything that had been said. Still, she trotted down the hallway to wash her hands without any more fuss.

Brandon stood up without prompting and showed Cassidy his picture. "It's a parade!" he said proudly.

Cassidy stared at the crude line drawing—but the man in the wheelchair was obvious, as was the stick man behind him pushing and the potato-shaped dog with the giant head who was attached. The balloons were purely Brandon's invention, though, as was the clown stalking, erm, following the entire parade.

"That's fantastic!" he said brightly, while behind Brandon's head, Mark was mouthing, *Run away! Run away!*

"Do you like it?" Oh, the kid was so sincere.

"I do." Cassidy nodded with emphasis. "Why don't you go put it on my refrigerator before you go wash your hands, okay? That way I can see it every day!"

"Yes! I'll show Grandma too!"

Brandon disappeared, and Mark sent Cassidy a droll look. "And you both will have nightmares for the rest of your lives."

"Is he the only kid in the world not afraid of clowns?" Cassidy asked, keeping his voice quiet. "That's terrifying!"

"I know!" Mark rolled his eyes and laughed and then scooped LizBet into his arms, where she giggled and shrieked before he hauled her to the bathroom too.

Yvonne came out of the kitchen as he left the living room. "Here," she said, handing Cassidy a spoon laden with cookie dough. "You finish that off while I set you at the table. We're going to take turns, you see? Mark and one kid are doing decorations while I ice cookies with the other kid, and we'll switch off in the middle.

"Isn't there a third kid?" Cassidy asked, not sure he could be counted on to chase LizBet down his hall, even though he was getting mildly more proficient at steering the chair.

"The third kid is going to sit in your lap and drink from her sippy cup and hopefully fall asleep," Yvonne said, nodding like she could make it so just by wishing. Then she sighed. "At least I hope so. If she gets too wound up, she's going to have to cry herself to sleep tonight, and she'll be a nightmare between now and then. Let's hope you're as good with her as you were with the other kids."

Cassidy snorted. "I wasn't great with them," he said. "All I did was talk."

"But you made them feel special," Yvonne told him, getting behind the chair and pushing. "Sometimes that's all kids really need. Do you think that boy draws a killer clown about to devour strangers in a parade for just anyone?"

"It really is scary?" Cassidy asked. "It's not just me, right?"

"Oh my God, no—that's nightmare fodder right there. Now eat the cookie dough, sweetheart, or you're going to hurt my feelings."

Suitably chastened, Cassidy began to lick the spoon, falling into an ecstasy of butter and sugar and vanilla.

"Good?" Yvonne prodded.

"Should be illegal," Cassidy said after swallowing. "I'm not even sure how it's not."

She laughed, delighted, and Mark came back in, herding children. Cassidy was suddenly the still center of a warm tumble of children and cookies and the Christmas decorations he'd bought on the cheap the year before but had yet to strew across his living room.

He held LizBet, who cuddled right into the crook of his arm, content as he'd never seen a child as she dozed. Yvonne and Brandon decorated cookies while Kennedy and Mark strung tinsel and lights around his window frames, the laughter and chatter quiet enough not to disturb LizBet, but *present*, all of it, through a fog of Christmas music that Mark had Cassidy pull up on his computer.

For a moment—a lovely moment—Cassidy wasn't just a party to the Christmas fantasy of his childhood, he was the *center* of it, an active participant, not an observer hiding in the shadows.

About a half hour in, Mark came and pulled a sleeping LizBet from his arms.

"Where are you—" Cassidy began, but Mark shushed him and moved the little girl to a blanket in a corner of the living room, where she curled into a ball. He covered her with another blanket—this one obviously one of his mother's creations—and she snuggled down, far enough away from all the hubbub to be able to sleep comfortably, but close enough that she could be seen and comforted when she awoke in a strange place. Mark and Kennedy had finished decorating his windows, and Kennedy had run to the kitchen to rewash her hands and help with the cookies.

Mark returned via a stop at the kitchen counter for a rack of cooled cookies. One more trip brought some mini bowls of frosting and some sprinkles, and a towel to cover the table.

"You think of everything," Cassidy said, grateful.

Mark shrugged. "You know we're going to eat half of them anyway." He gave a wicked grin and invited Cassidy into this fantasy world, where good boys really *did* get cookies and people sang Christmas carols while stringing tinsel.

"I hadn't planned on it," Cassidy said. "Don't we… I don't know… save them for Christmas?"

"But Christmas is in two and a half weeks!" Mark laughed, waving a butter knife with a dollop of pink frosting on it. "By then Mom will have made two more batches. We have to make room! Why aren't you decorating?"

"I've never done this before," Cassidy said helplessly.

Mark blinked. "Okay, that had not occurred to me, and I'm sorry. But never fear—I am the son of Yvonne and Harvey Taylor, and they taught me well! Here—you've got a butter knife over there. Choose a cookie and a frosting color."

Cassidy did so, picking a cookie that was shaped like a snowflake and a fluffy glob of white frosting. "Done."

"Now smear—but gently. A gentle smear. All over the front of the cookie."

"Smearing—oh!"

"Lucky you!" Mark all but sang. "You broke off a piece of cookie, and it's *already frosted*. That means you have to eat it for luck."

Cassidy laughed and popped the piece in his mouth. For a moment their game drifted away and he was consumed by the heady taste of sugar cookie and frosting.

"Good?" Mark asked, his smile absolutely irrepressible.

Cassidy nodded shyly. "Yes. Now what?"

"Well, your snowflake is crooked. It won't do. I think you should eat that one for symmetry—"

"Symmetry." He managed to say it with a straight face.

"Yes, symmetry. Because, you know. You ate the other piece."

"And it was delicious," Cassidy said. "Wouldn't that be... I don't know. Self-serving. To eat the rest of the cookie?"

Mark cackled, frosting his own reindeer-shaped cookie. The head broke off, and he held it up, *very* seriously. "Of course not. It's for art! Art, you understand. That is the *only* reason you're eating that cookie," he said, before popping the head in his mouth.

"Of course," Cassidy said, taking another bite. Then, with his mouth completely full, he said, "Who's Art?"

Mark laughed so hard he sprayed crumbs across the table, and Cassidy barely managed to swallow his own cookie before he did the same.

It took them a good long time before they managed to overcome their giggles and start frosting cookies again. This time, Cassidy kept his cookies intact so he could arrange them back on the cooling rack. The quiet after their giggle attack soothed him, and he relaxed into Mark's conversation as though he always had a good-looking man to play with on the weekends. Surprisingly enough, Cassidy found he had some questions of his own.

"Your father's name was Harvey?" he asked.

"Yeah," Mark said, sighing. Behind them, Yvonne and the twins were singing to Brenda Lee while they cut out cookies and put them on the cookie sheet, and he lowered his voice, probably so his mother didn't hear. "Late-diagnosed pancreatic cancer, which sucked. He was a good guy. The best."

"What made him so good?" He wanted to know what made a good parent. Yvonne and Rose seemed to be good parents—the best—but what made a man a good father?

"He only yelled a little," Mark said promptly. "And only when we got on his last nerve."

Cassidy frowned. "He yelled?"

"Only a little." Mark nodded. "And we were all pretty young when it hit us that he was mostly joking when he did it. He just had this great booming voice that made the yelling sound worse than it was. Mom would keep us all quiet and out of his way, and then he'd clean something—the garage, the kitchen, the living room—and then, when he was done, he'd make dinner or go get takeout and the world would be all okay again. I think he just needed to vent steam and have his family hear him, that's all."

Cassidy thought about that for a moment. "That made him a good dad?" He was having trouble understanding. Yelling scared him—it always had. He'd never been sure there was a good thing at the end of the yelling.

"He never yelled *at us*, you understand," Mark said. "He just... would walk into the kitchen and notice the cracked tile and yell at the house for falling apart. He'd see the dent in the molding of the foyer and yell at that. He never yelled at things that had feelings that could be hurt. He just yelled at inanimate objects because the real living people were giving him fits. I... I remember one day when a—" His eyes flicked behind him. "—a student died in a car accident. Dad was close to the kid, and he was devastated. He came home and yelled at the kitchen table for having dings in it, and at the counters for being old, and then he sat on the kitchen floor and cried. Mom came out of her room and sat down next to him, and they cried together, and then they took us out to eat. I was in grade school at the time, but I'll never forget the two of them sitting next to each other and leaning against the cabinets, and how I realized then that he really wasn't yelling at us when he did that. Like I said, he just needed the people he loved to hear what was in his heart, and that's all he had."

Cassidy nodded. "So a good dad isn't perfect," he said, getting—just a little, probably—what Mark was trying to say.

"Exactly," Mark said. He closed his eyes and smiled faintly. "And he liked to tell dumb dad jokes. He and Mom would swing by fast-food places on Friday sometimes, for a treat. One day before a holiday break, he had me in the back of the car and asked me what I wanted. I said a sundae, and he said, 'But it's Friday,' with a completely straight face, and I just couldn't stop laughing. It was such a dad thing, you know?"

Cassidy nodded. It wasn't that any one thing hit him, as Mark spoke. It was like there was an entire picture, and each story told one shade or one brushstroke—or one piece of wood—in who Mark's father had been.

"And he coached our soccer teams," Mark said. "I mean, he loved the sport way more than we did—even when me, Dani, and Keith were playing. But that didn't matter. Because when he was coaching us, we got to talk to him when we were helping him set up and take down, and he told dumb jokes and got excited about the plays and the team and how well he wanted us to do. And we'd get excited because he got excited, and it didn't matter how much we all sucked at soccer, we wanted to do well for *him*, and he wanted us to do well so we'd have fun. And it became fun because we got to be with our dad. It was sort of a big happy circle, instead of a vicious one, you know?"

Cassidy nodded again. He didn't know—not really. But it was one more color in the palette, and Cassidy's picture was getting clearer.

"And he believed in us—in whatever made us happy. Keith said, 'I'm going to be an accountant,' and Dad said, 'Sure!' And Dani said, 'I'm going to work in finance!' and Dad said, 'Sure!' And I said, 'I'm going to be a doctor!' and Dad said, 'Of course—but, you know, we wouldn't mind if you wanted to join a band either.'"

"Was he kidding?" Cassidy asked.

Mark shrugged. "Only a little. They knew med school wouldn't be easy, and, well, Mom was still hoping for that artist. But I really wanted to be a doctor, and what he really said was, 'We'll do whatever we can to help.' And then they did."

Cassidy *hmm*ed. "That's the most important thing, isn't it?"

"Yeah," Mark said, eyes growing red-rimmed. He'd answered enough of Cassidy's questions, Cassidy thought. "Did you have any good foster dads?"

Cassidy swallowed. His turn. "A couple," he said vaguely. "Ed and Cora were nice. I… I went to live with them when I was fourteen. I was so very obviously gay by then, and they were fine with that. Kind. I think… I think I might have stayed with them until I aged out, but when I was sixteen, Ed was in a car wreck. I…. Cora said she was going to the hospital to see how he was doing, and while she was there, the placement people came and took me and my foster sister away. Tilda was eight—I'd only known her a month, and she got placed somewhere else. I got put in a halfway house for teens. I… I asked about them, in the halfway house, and they told me Ed had died, and that was policy, to take the kids away when there was a sudden upheaval in the family. I… I don't even think Cora was given a chance to say goodbye."

"Damn," Mark said, looking horrified. "That's… that's terrible. Cassidy, I'm so sorry."

Cassidy shrugged. "Anyway, after that I aged out into college, got a scholarship for a degree in media, and, you know. Got a job with Rose and her magazine. I… I was just wondering if all good dads were like Ed, but I guess they're not."

"What was Ed like?" Mark prodded.

"Quiet. He liked to read aloud to me and Tilda, and that was better than TV. He really loved Terry Pratchett. And even though I spent less than a year there, I… I started reading sci-fi then, and then I just kept on reading, as much as I could. It was like a huge gift he never knew he gave me, you know?"

"That's really nice," Mark said softly. "Anything else you remember?"

"Old things—my watch," he said, showing Mark the old timepiece that Ed had given him when he'd been with them for a couple of months. "He liked old models and old clocks—he repaired this, but he had a lot of his own, so I kept it."

"I'd wondered," Mark said softly, glancing at the watch. "What about Cora?"

Cassidy smiled. "Cora liked to knit—like your mom crochets, I guess. I… I have one scarf she made me. Our only Christmas together. That's why I noticed your sweater. I just… just really like things that are handmade."

Mark smiled softly. "My mom's yarn stash is… well, impressive. It takes up an entire bedroom, and that doesn't count the boxes in the hallway and the living room."

Cassidy found his eyes bulging. "Her… yarn stash?"

Mark nodded, that soft smile not fading. "And Dad never complained. He'd ask her why she needed so much, and she'd say— still says—it's potential. Every skein, as pretty as it is, has *potential* to be something *fabulous*, and she feels like she's surrounded by all the things she could possibly make, and they're just waiting for her time and attention."

"That's amazing," Cassidy said. "And he understood that?"

"Yeah."

Yvonne came to the table in that moment and looked critically at their handiwork. "Well, they're decorated," she said bluntly. "I think they need sprinkles."

"We're getting there," Mark said. He held up a little bottle full of tiny colored candy. "See?"

"Sprinkle away!" she urged. "What had you both so involved, though? I was asking if you were ready to clean up so I could start dinner."

"Oh!" Mark looked around guiltily. "Sorry—having too much fun! Anyway, we were talking about your yarn stash. I was trying to explain your theory of potential."

"I think I get it." Cassidy smiled at her, well aware of their small conspiracy not to mention fathers in front of her for fear of spoiling the glow that seemed to envelop her after the day. "It's why I get buckets of wood chips for my woodworking pictures. I don't need all those scraps, but... you know. Potential!"

"Exactly!" Yvonne clapped her hands in excitement. "You know, since you can't really use any of your woodworking tools until you're back on your feet, I should bring by some yarn and teach you to crochet. You like to play with color, and you're good with your hands. You'll be a natural. Would you like that?"

Cassidy smiled up at her and tried really hard not to send Mark a glance as well. "Of course," he said, feeling only a little like a fraud. "I'd love that!" The idea of learning something to do with his hands while he was laid up—something that didn't need the total absorption of woodworking and could still engage some of the same skills—really did appeal to him.

But the excuse to spend more time with Mark and Yvonne and the kids and this family appealed to him more.

DINNER WAS—SURPRISE!—LASAGNA, and Cassidy was effusive in his praise. Yvonne laughed and told the kids that this was how it was done—she was tired of hearing complaints from her children that she was trying to make them fat.

Of course the grandchildren loved it, and Cassidy felt... spoiled.

By the end of the evening, he was exhausted from all the noise, from the kids, from the excitement, and as happy as he'd ever been in his life.

"I'll be back in a minute," Mark said as he stood up to follow his mom out. "I need to get my clothes for tomorrow. I'm sleeping on the guest bed again, if that's okay, but I need to leave you in the morning after I walk Gus-Gus. Work."

"Of course," Cassidy said. He hadn't told Mark this, but just knowing the other man was under his roof at night had led him to dream... things. Fantasies, spun sugar, about how he would wake up in the morning and this man would be there, smiling at him, and his life would be happy and warm.

He knew it would end. His leg would get better, and Yvonne and Mark would go back to their regularly scheduled lives. Perhaps a little warmer and friendlier—Cassidy would ask if he could walk Gus-Gus, and he'd definitely keep mowing the lawn. Mark, for all his devotion to his mother, would be working residents' hours after Christmas, and they'd both been so kind. Cassidy would find ways to repay their kindness, to stay in their lives, but he had no delusions.

Mark Taylor was every boy's dream—handsome, kind, so much fun—but he'd long ago reconciled himself to the fact that Cassidy Hancock did not get every boy's dream. He would content himself with the joy of having new friends and of knowing that if another tree fell from nowhere and hit him on the head this time, more people than just Rose would miss him.

But in the meantime, he was going to treat the whole situation like the Christmas he'd never had as a child, and he was going to accept his good fortune as some sort of karmic balance for swimming in the smoky depths of disappointment for so long. Good people were being kind to him.

He would be kind in return and enjoy their company.

DIFFERENT PLANS

MARK WASN'T sure when it happened.

Maybe when Cassidy was quizzing him about his father, so obviously interested in what it was like to have a dad.

Maybe it had been when they were laughing about eating cookies, like any two kids in the world.

Maybe it had been when Cassidy had sat at his kitchen table, a sleeping LizBet in his arms, looking bemused and happy and grateful.

And maybe it had been the rapturous way the man had eaten Mark's mother's lasagna.

But somewhere in all the ruckus, all the *Christmas* that had permeated Cassidy's lovely home—that he hadn't freaked out about *once*, in spite of all the people invading him—Mark had decided he absolutely, positively, without any teeny wiggle of a doubt, needed to kiss Cassidy Hancock.

It was imperative.

It wasn't just the wide hazel eyes or the knife-edge cheekbones or the way his mouth twisted into a smile a lot more than Mark ever would have thought—although it was partly that.

It wasn't just the way he drank in family, turning his face toward the conversation and the rhythm of it—even the chaos of it—like a sunflower to heat and light, although that was attractive too. Brad had claimed to love family, but every time he'd been around Mark's, he'd been more disdain than delight. It was more like he loved the *idea* of family, but the reality of it was messy and imperfect. Mark had heard Brad use his mother's yarn collection and his father's propensity to yell at furniture as punchlines at parties, and while he'd been inclined to laugh at first, because these were quirky characteristics of people he held dear, he'd come to realize that Brad had been full of contempt.

He found these imperfections the things he'd remembered most when he lived in the Bay Area, away from his family, and the things he'd been the happiest to see when he'd returned.

Cassidy seemed to embrace them as well.

Mark wanted to kiss him for that too.

But that wasn't the whole of it. There were so many kissable things about him—his humor, which took Mark by surprise, and his devotion to Mark's dog, which went a long way toward assuaging the bad taste left by Brad's seeming hatred of Mark's beloved tube-of-weird. His loneliness—and the way it hadn't left him bitter—seemed to call Mark's name, as did the absolute gentleness that emanated from every pore.

And the adorable little twist in his lips when he thought of something that made him happy.

Mark just really, really *liked* him—and while he was wondering when the other shoe would drop, he was also wondering if he could tease Cassidy into a first kiss before it did.

"Aw, man," Brandon muttered as they walked across the lawn to Mark's mom's house. "I thought we had until tomorrow morning."

"Me too," Yvonne said unhappily, shifting LizBet in her arms. "What's your father's car doing here?"

Keith sat at the battered oak kitchen table, drinking bourbon from a tumbler and looking exhausted. He greeted his kids with big hugs and admonitions to go upstairs and get into their pajamas, telling them he'd be up in a minute to tuck them in.

As they ran upstairs, their mother turned to him with an arched eyebrow, requesting—not demanding—an explanation.

"I, uh…." Keith let out a breath. "Mom, she left me."

Keith was a big man with Harv's receding hairline and grayish eyes. When his voice cracked and his lower lip wobbled, Yvonne moved in to hug her boy, even though he was in his thirties, and comfort him as best she could.

Mark made eye contact over Keith's back.

"Go!" she mouthed.

"He can sleep in my bed," Mark mouthed back, since the kids were in the two spare bedrooms, which was one of the reasons he'd converted the space over the garage into his own apartment when he'd moved in.

The other one was that she'd waited until all three kids moved out to use one of their bedrooms as a craft room, and he wasn't going to take that from her now.

She nodded and patted Keith on the back, and Mark made himself scarce, Gus-Gus at his heels. In just a few moments, he was heading back over the frosty grass, his breath smoking in the foothills chill, some of his ebullience faded.

"Hey," he said when he let himself into Cassidy's house with barely a knock. He and his mother had made themselves comfortable over the past week.

"What's wrong?" Cassidy called from his bedroom.

Mark followed the sound of his voice. He'd been getting more and more mobile, although he still needed help changing and using the bathroom. For Mark and Yvonne, that was such a part of their jobs that they'd had no problem helping him, but Mark recalled that Cassidy had blushingly asked the nurse who came by in the morning to check on him to help him take a shower that day. Now he surprised Mark by not being in his wheelchair at all, but leaned back against the pillows and props in his bed, wearing a tatty sweatshirt and the sleep pants Yvonne had modified by cutting off one leg with a pair of scissors.

Mark smiled at him, thinking he looked comfortable and sweet there, ready to watch television and relax, and Cassidy's cheeks pinkened a little.

"Come sit," he said. "We can watch sappy Christmas movies, if you're still in the mood."

"I am!" Mark was a little surprised to hear himself say it. "Here, let me change into my pajamas too and I can sit on the bed with you. I'm getting a crick in my neck from looking sideways."

Gus-Gus hopped up on the bed next to Cassidy—the big traitor—and Mark disappeared into the guest bedroom, hoping Cassidy didn't detect his bald-assed lie.

There was no crick in the neck from looking sideways. That was a line and a half. Mark hadn't been that shameless since high school.

No. Mark wanted to be next to Cassidy in his pajamas so he could be *next to Cassidy in his pajamas*, and that was pretty much the endgame right there.

Mark emerged from the guest room and made a stop at the bathroom to wash his face and brush his teeth.

When he got back to the bed, Cassidy had picked something schlocky and schmoopy and totally predictable.

Mark hopped onto the bed, completely on board with all of that. God, predictability was really damned underrated.

"What's wrong?" Cassidy asked again, in a sort of gentle reminder that Mark hadn't answered the question the first time.

"My brother was home when we got there," Mark said, unable to forget the sight of that lonely figure in his mother's dated kitchen with the green-flowered wallpaper and chipping tile. Keith had always been so full of big-brother bluster, so absolutely sure of his path, his place in the world, the things he wanted. It had been one of the reasons Mark, Yvonne, and Dani had difficulty talking to him about Tanya. Yeah, sure, she was rude to all of them, but Keith had *loved* her, and that certainty that all was right with the world was one of the things that made Keith *Keith*.

"Is everything all right?" Cassidy asked, which was kind, because he'd never met Keith.

"No. I guess Tanya finally left him—and the kids, I would imagine, since they're here. Anyway, Mom did her mom thing and hugged him, and I bailed. I was coming over anyway, but I was definitely not needed tonight."

"Oh no!" Cassidy stared at him in concern. "Are you okay? Will your family be okay?"

Mark smiled at him to see if he could get that wrinkle on his forehead to relax, and it did. "I think we'll be fine," he said softly. "But you—you are really sweet to ask."

Silence fell, and Mark allowed himself to fall into Cassidy's eyes for a moment, wide and infinite, clear as water. Gus-Gus made a happy little grunt with his head on Cassidy's lap, and Cassidy shifted his attention just long enough to break the spell.

"I just really like your family," Cassidy mumbled. "I, uhm, don't want… okay. I'm totally selfish and I want them to be happy so they can entertain me. Is that okay?"

He tried to put a spin on it at the end, but Mark heard the sincerity. He reached out and covered Cassidy's hand as he patted the dog. "It's not selfish to want people you like to be happy," he said softly. Hoping—ah, hoping—that Cassidy would take the hint and turn his hand palm up so they could lace fingers, he rubbed the back of Cassidy's knuckles with his thumb.

Cassidy's hand twitched underneath his, but Cassidy scrupulously avoided his eyes.

"It's just been such a nice fantasy," he whispered. "To have a family like this. I... don't want to... I don't know. Superimpose, I guess, my fantasy on your real life. That would be wrong, and not fair to you."

Mark blinked before taking a risk and threading his fingers between Cassidy's and making his intent very clear. "How do you know my family wasn't just waiting for a Cassidy Hancock to fill a void?" he asked. "I mean, I'm a pretty good 'fun uncle,' but it's a lot easier as a team."

Cassidy still wouldn't meet his eyes. "But that doesn't mean *you* wanted to fill a void," he whispered. "I'm—"

"If you say handy or convenient," Mark said sharply, feeling his exasperation rise, "I may have to make you watch detective shows instead of Christmas shows."

Cassidy met his eyes, finally, but he had a stubborn set to his jaw. "When I was in high school," he said, seemingly out of the blue, "after Ed died and I got moved to the halfway house, sex was easy and free and I thought it meant people loved me."

Mark felt his mouth fall open softly in surprise—but he didn't let go of Cassidy's hand.

"That's not what this is," he said softly.

"I... I threw myself at boy after boy," Cassidy continued. "And I let them do whatever they wanted. And I might have gotten hurt, or sick, or... or anything at all, but a teacher pulled me aside and showed me all the scholarships I could get and told me... told me I was worth more than the boys who kept using me. And I don't even hold it against them—"

"I do," Mark said darkly.

Cassidy gave him the ghost of a smile. "They were young, and I was willing," he said firmly. "It wasn't their fault I was looking for... I don't know. Mom, Dad, brothers, sisters, magical Christmases and birthdays, all of that in a blowjob or a quick fuck. I... just... I haven't done that since. I got out of high school and...."

"Reinvented yourself," Mark said. He let go of Cassidy's hand, but only so he could turn on his side and scoot closer. Close enough to rest his head on Cassidy's shoulder. Close enough to thread his hand under Cassidy's arm and rest it on his soft abdomen.

"Yeah." Cassidy blinked at him, acknowledging the move, noting their proximity. He seemed as mesmerized as Mark was to feel the heat and softness of another male body so very, very close.

"I… I could be talking out of turn here," Mark said, voice a low purr, "but I think you missed a spot in your reinvention."

Cassidy's dry roll of the eyes told Mark he was aware. "No, I have no personal life," he said with a sigh. "Derp."

Mark let out a surprised laugh. "Why not?" he asked.

"I told you. I… need to be on time. I need to be groomed, and my house needs to be straight, and I need to be—"

"Perfect." Mark got it now. He bent his elbow and raised their twined fingers to his mouth to kiss. "Was today perfect?"

Cassidy closed his eyes like he knew where this was going. "Yeah."

"But nothing was perfect," Mark murmured. "Not even the cookies. I know you know that in your head. What's it going to take for you to know it here?" He rested their twined fingers against Cassidy's chest.

"I have no idea." He sounded unhappy about that, and Mark thought now might be the time.

He tilted his face up and murmured, "Cassidy?"

And that undeniable connection sizzled between them as Cassidy locked eyes with him. "Yeah?"

"Kiss me and see if it's perfect."

Cassidy's lips were gentle against his at first, soft as a whisper, but firm too. Mark yielded, and when Cassidy pressed just the slightest bit, he opened and invited Cassidy in.

Cassidy's tongue was tentative, almost anxious, but Mark was patient. A flutter here, a sweep there, and Mark's other hand ventured under Cassidy's T-shirt, the better to glide his hand along bare skin.

Cassidy gasped and slid down so his head was on the pillow but the rest of his body lay flat. Mark propped himself up on one elbow and gestured sternly to Gus-Gus.

"Go on," he said.

Gus-Gus looked at him, surprised. Yes, he knew the command, but Mark hadn't used it in a while.

"You heard what I said—do you need a sock on the door?"

With a little whine, Gus-Gus hopped down off the bed and wriggled his way underneath, and when Mark looked back to Cassidy, he could sense the bemusement.

"He's not allowed on the bed when anyone's naked," Mark said, feeling his cheeks flush. "It's, uhm, the one command I really managed to get him to follow."

Cassidy's slow smile was so delicious, Mark had to taste it.

Delicious—and beautiful. Mark took over the kiss, grateful that Cassidy was using his hands to slide under Mark's T-shirt as well. He smelled like cookies—but also like man, and a little like sweat because it had been warm in the kitchen for a while.

Mark palmed his way up to a pointed nipple and then rubbed with a thumb, and Cassidy moaned and bucked, needing. Mark reluctantly pulled away from his mouth, but only so he could tongue the responsive nipple. It was adorable and pink, so he teased it first, and then plied it with his tongue and teeth until Cassidy moaned again.

"We should—oh! God! We should stop before I—oh man!"

Mark pulled off with a pop and checked Cassidy's face for clues. "Stop?"

"I'm going to come!" he panted. "And I'm wearing the cast, and there's not much I can do to recipro—"

Mark stuck his hand down the front of Cassidy's pajama bottoms and stroked.

"—cate?"

"So," Mark muttered, scooting down to Cassidy's midsection and wiggling his bottoms and boxers down enough to see what he was handling. Mm… nice. Proportional and hard. "Be clear. If I'm willing to suck you, are you willing to come in my mouth?" He punctuated his question with a hard stroke, and Cassidy tilted his head back and cried out.

Mark barely got his mouth to the head of his cock in time to catch it.

Cassidy came long and hard, his hands tightening in Mark's hair as his hips bucked, little cries issuing from his mouth as he finished off. Finally Mark swallowed—salty and bitter—and cleaned him off with his mouth, shaking with arousal as he shoved himself up so they could be face-to-face.

"Wow," he said, feeling smug and full of himself. "You did *good* for a guy who hasn't done that in a while."

"I think I did *exactly* what a guy who hasn't done that in a while would do," Cassidy said archly. He took a few more deep breaths and turned his head, watching in fascination as Mark moved one hand to his nipples to play and the other hand down under his waistband to stroke his own aching erection.

"That's not fair," Cassidy said, and reached out to still the wandering hand. "Don't I get to touch?"

Mark grinned at him, eyes half-mast. He felt sultry and a little slutty and on display. "Do you want to touch?" he baited.

"Yes," Cassidy breathed. "Please let me touch you."

"Okay," Mark told him. "As long as I get to beg. Can I strip for you?"

"Yes—yes, please."

Mark scooted out of his pajamas and left them in a pile near the top of the bed, then pulled the covers down so he was lying on the sheets. Sheets were easier to clean.

"Wow," Cassidy said, smiling and drifting his fingers down Mark's abdomen.

"Wow?" He wasn't above preening.

"You're... you're fun to look at."

Mark laughed throatily. "Are you going to touch? Please touch."

"Where?"

"Nipples first."

Cassidy did, rubbing first one, then the other with his thumb, then leaning over and taking one nipple in his mouth while he pinched the harder-to-reach one.

Mark *hmm*ed and splayed his knees, opening himself up to the air and enjoying the touch. Cassidy began to get into his work, bobbing his head rhythmically as he suckled. Ah! Everything tingled, and Mark wanted... *everything*. He usually thought of himself as a top, but as his lower body was happily exposed to the possibilities, he felt like any touch to his body would make him happy. A hand on his cock, or a mouth. A finger skating his rim—or a tongue. Cassidy was laid up now, but in another eight weeks, he'd be able to take off that cast, and oh! The things they could do!

Mark didn't even question that they'd still want to do those things. As he made sexy-sexy nom-nom noises just from having his nipples sucked, all he could see in their future was the endless potential between the two of them. The secrets they could learn, the promises they could make.

Cassidy lifted his mouth from Mark's nipple and turned slightly glassy eyes toward Mark's. "Can I touch your cock?" he asked breathlessly, his hips arching with what looked like more arousal.

Mark nodded and made an abrupt move to his knees, then shuffled a little until Cassidy could reach his bobbing cock with his hand and his mouth.

"Can you suck it?" he begged. "God, please, Cassidy. I need your touch and your mouth and your—ah! Yes!"

Oh, he felt so good. It wasn't that Cassidy knew what he was doing—although he did. It was that he wanted to do it, he was eager and warm and willing, and he seemed to be as much into touching Mark as Mark had been into touching him.

His mouth moved, and his hand, both of them in concert, and Mark shifted one hand to the back of Cassidy's head to tangle in his hair and the other hand to his own nipple, and then he gave himself over to it, allowed it to flood him with sensation, with pleasure, and when Cassidy gave a particularly deep thrust of his mouth, allowed himself to come.

He came until he shook with it, then pulled out gingerly and slid down next to Cassidy in naked, sweaty repletion.

Cassidy was staring at him, wide-eyed. Mark took him in—swollen, glazed mouth, hair tousled from Mark's fingers—and thought he looked beautiful and sexy and... perfect.

He lunged into the kiss with more passion than sense, but Cassidy met him, devoured his mouth greedily, gave Mark agency and want and need.

Mark took it and gave it back squared. Eventually they had to part, panting, because it was a little chilly in the room, and neither of them was quite ready to go again.

"You've got goose bumps," Cassidy said kindly. "You probably need pajamas and to cuddle under the covers."

"Can we?" Mark asked. Part of him was aware that he'd taken dreadful liberties. He'd planned for a kiss—had needed a kiss so desperately—but once he'd had a kiss, he'd had to take touches, and then tastes, and since Cassidy had wanted them too—had participated consensually and fully—he wasn't sorry, could never be sorry, but he was more than aware he'd trespassed.

Cassidy was a beyond private person, and Mark had snuck into his bed on a tourist's pass. If he wanted residential privileges, he was going to have to earn them.

"Yeah." That normally shy, reserved smile bloomed, wreathed his cheeks, crinkled his eyes. "I... I uh, really want to cuddle," he admitted, a little embarrassed, but not enough to hold back.

"Excellent! Gimme a second to get dressed, and then we can help you get into bed and—"

"I, uhm, may need to visit the bathroom first," Cassidy said, suddenly humble and obviously mortified. "I still, uhm, need help." As Mark watched, the blush intensified. "And I need to shower. I was going to tomorrow, when the nurse was here." He squeezed his eyes shut. "And isn't that incredibly pathetic and not romantic at all. Gah!"

Mark caught the hand he was trying to press over his eyes. "Hey," he murmured, kissing his knuckles again. "Don't stress needing things. I have had an *awesome* time on our first date—wait, is this our first date?"

Cassidy managed a shy little peep through slitted eyes. "I guess if meals count as dates, it's, like, our fourth."

That was his boy. Mark grinned, irrepressible. "I've had an awesome time on our *fourth* date, and our first sleepover that counts as a sleepover, because being in the guest room in case you fall out of bed doesn't count."

Cassidy's eyes opened fully, and his smile showed signs of returning. "No," he said. "It doesn't. I... I thought this—what we're doing. What we just did. I thought it was all a fantasy on my part. You're, uhm, going to have to bear with me, because I'm not sure how to deal with it when it's for real."

Mark nodded, suddenly completely sober. "I'll be here," he said. "As long as you let me. You'll let me, right? Help you deal?"

Cassidy nodded, but without much enthusiasm. "I... I wish I was... I don't know. A normal part of your life."

Mark frowned—and then shivered. "Look, we need pajamas and trips to the bathroom stat, and then you're going to explain to me exactly what 'normal part of your life' means. But first—" He shivered again, not exaggerating by much.

"Fine," Cassidy agreed. "You go first—I'm going to need help sitting up."

"Excellent! It's a deal."

Mark squirreled into his pajamas and then hustled over to the other side of the bed to help Cassidy into the chair for the short trip to the bathroom. Next week, his bulky cast would hopefully be replaced by a sleeker, more mobile model, but the injury had been done really close to the knee—no walking cast for a good six weeks.

He paused as he bent so Cassidy could slip his arms around Mark's neck to facilitate the lift to the wheelchair.

"What?" Cassidy whispered, and the act, which had been so very clinical for the past five days, was suddenly so very intimate.

"I...." Mark sighed and nuzzled Cassidy's temple. "I'm just so glad to be touching you," he said with a little gasp. This hadn't occurred to him, this switch from caregiver to lover. He felt odd, off-kilter, as though his chest had swelled and he had trouble catching his breath.

Cassidy made a hum, but no words. With a shake of his head, Mark got down to business, hefting him into the chair and then wheeling him into the hall bathroom, which had been outfitted with rails. Cassidy had his britches down around his bottom and the side of the chair dropped before Mark could even offer to help. The next part was tricky, though— he had to heft himself out of the chair and onto the commode, and over the past few days, he'd needed Mark or Yvonne to do it.

At first he'd been mortified. He hadn't said a word, but Mark was pretty sure he'd had digestive issues from sheer performance panic. Mark and his mom made a point of going into the kitchen and turning on music to let the poor man perform in peace.

But the more they'd done it, the more he'd been able to put his mortification aside for practical purposes, and Mark admired that about him. Mark had dealt with too many patients who'd been freaked out about cosmetic things—a scar from a bad break, for instance—and not focused on the important things, like how lucky they'd been to survive the accident that had put them in his care.

Cassidy was just as pragmatic now. When he was situated, Mark left and closed the door to give him time to finish, get back in the wheelchair, wash his hands, and brush his teeth.

When he came back, he knocked first and then opened the door, and found Cassidy squinting at himself in the mirror.

"What?" Mark asked, laughing a little. "What do you see?"

The look Cassidy gave him was troubled. "I don't know. But I'm not sure if it's what *you* see," he said.

Mark sighed. "I see only good things. Now let me get you back to bed so I can brush *my* teeth and use the facilities. Then we can cuddle and talk. Trust me, I haven't stopped wanting that. Have you?"

Cassidy gave him a wistful smile. "No."

"Good."

THE NATURE OF THINGS

MARK HAD to work the next day, early, and he insisted on Cassidy sleeping in until the nurse got there to help him bathe.

Cassidy conceded, but mostly because he wanted to stay in his bed and pretend the fairy-tale night before still surrounded them both.

After they'd returned to bed, he and Mark had talked, and in a way, it had been much like their other conversations—the meaningful mixed with the absurd, the lighthearted mixed with the real.

Snippets of what they'd said would haunt Cassidy in the best of ways, possibly for as long as he lived.

"I remember being surprised," Mark said, eyes dark and serious. "I thought my dad was invincible. You sort of make vows not to take your loved ones for granted after that. It's why I came home to be with my mom."

"You just keep hoping," Cassidy admitted, feeling embarrassed in the extreme. "Sometimes I'll go to sleep and dream about having a family when I was little, and I wake up and I'm surprised my childhood doesn't feel like the dream."

"I love being a doctor. I love being able to help people. I know some doctors are super ambitious and want to climb the ladder and be on the hospital board. I just want to treat people. I like the surgery part—I'm good at it—but I'm also good at setting broken bones and diagnosing muscle placement and strains. I... I want to work with people. I know its cliché, but I'm good with them."

"Putting out the magazine is a blast," Cassidy said, feeling himself grow animated. "Everybody has their jobs, and then we try to mesh everything like a big jigsaw puzzle, and then we work for aesthetics and trying to fit in as much as possible. I... I could be happy doing something like this for the rest of my life."

And then, right as they were falling asleep, he remembered Mark's hand on his cheek.

"You are so pretty," he'd slurred. "I don't know how I didn't notice before. How I thought you disapproved of me for this entire last year.

When really you were just taking us all in, my family, my dog, me. You were looking out your window and being a part of us, and we never knew it."

"I'm sorry," Cassidy had answered, embarrassed. "I... that's probably wrong or voyeuristic. I just never had a family before. You, your mom, even your nieces and nephew. Watching everyone play in the front yard this summer, hunt for eggs over Easter—I got to pretend. That's probably terrible. I don't know how to take it back or wish I hadn't done it."

"Then don't." Mark stroked his lower lip with a tender thumb. "Now you know us. Now you're ours. It's not voyeurism if you're ours. It's watching your family play."

Cassidy still couldn't believe he'd said it—God, Mark had probably been too tired to realize what he was so cavalierly offering. A family. *His* family. A chance for the day before to not be an isolated thing, an embroidered embellishment, but a repeated detail, a true part of the fabric of his life.

It couldn't possibly be real.

But the touches of Mark's hands on his skin had been real. Cassidy's searing orgasm into Mark's mouth had been real. The taste of Mark's spend, bitter and earthy and good—that had been immediate and true.

That disparity between what he knew to be real and what he'd always hoped for rode him all day. The nurse had to come shut the shower off because the water had run cold and his skin was pruney. The nurse—a stolid, taciturn man who seemed quite content to leave Cassidy to his thoughts during the shower and breakfast—had to ask Cassidy twice if he'd be okay as he made to leave.

When Yvonne showed up right after lunch—which he'd been able to fix for himself, thanks to her modifications—Cassidy finally snapped himself out of it.

"No kids?" he asked, mildly disappointed. Mark had left Gus-Gus there after briefly walking him that morning, and Gus-Gus too looked behind her in confusion.

"I'm afraid Keith has them at the moment," she said, sighing. "He's going to take them to lunch and explain to them that—" She frowned. "Mark told you, right? I mean, I *assume* he told you. It's not like we've spared you the family business so far."

Cassidy gave a faint smile and remembered Mark's pointed observations about perfect and imperfect. If anybody asked, he'd reply staunchly that Yvonne and Mark were perfect. But if anyone were to outline their faults, he could concede that spilling the family business on a dime was one of them. "No, he told me. I'm so sorry—for the kids especially."

Yvonne grimaced and swung the giant bag at her side onto the kitchen table. Brightly colored noodles of fiber trailed from the top, and Cassidy's smile bloomed. Apparently she took her promise to teach him to crochet seriously. He was grateful—he really did miss the detail work and craft immersion of woodworking.

"Well, I wish I could say I'm surprised, but I'm really not. Tanya and Keith were young when they got together, but I always got the feeling she had children because they were expected of her and not because she really wanted them. With any luck—and if she has any decency—she'll take the alimony and leave Keith with the kids. She can go off and do whatever she wants with her life, and the children can be with the parent who is more interested in their growing." She growled. "Gah! There is no way to talk about this without sounding like a shrill harpy! I don't mean she doesn't love them—I just mean she doesn't seem equipped with the tools to help them right now at this age." With a groan, she sank into the kitchen chair next to him and banged her head softly on the table.

Cassidy patted her back, surprised that he had that much instinct for comfort. "Keith is your son," he said. "I think there's probably a rule out there that says you get to be partial."

She paused in her banging and turned toward him, managing a watery smile. "That is a very good point," she said after a moment. "I'm going to take that to heart." She sniffed a little and took a napkin from the holder in the middle of the table, used it to wipe under her eyes, and then delicately blew her nose. "I think Keith and the kids are going to be living with me for a while, which, you know, makes for a full house. It's good, because the kids can go to the same school—I'm in district—but it's going to be crowded."

Cassidy nodded. "Well, you know—I've got a guest room." He could feel his face heat so hard and so fast that he was pretty sure sweat beaded on his hairline. "Mark, uhm, is welcome to stay. In the guest room. Until Keith and the kids have their own place."

Yvonne's lips quirked, and he felt the sudden weight of her regard. "The guest room," she repeated mildly.

"Yes," he said. "The, uhm, guest room."

"That's certainly handy, isn't it? That he can stay here. In the guest room."

Cassidy managed a smile, but he also knew a bead of sweat had gathered and actually dripped down to the back of his collar. "Very convenient," he said. "Uhm, you two have been so kind and done so much for me. It would be… uhm, natural, really, for me to return the favor." Wow, that was a whopper. It *should* have been the truth, but their activities—and that beautifully intimate conversation—were strobing behind his eyes, and he knew it for the biggest, most decadent lie he'd ever told.

"A favor?" she said archly, barely containing a smirk, and he broke and covered his face with his hands.

"I'm sorry," he whimpered. "I'm… I'm a bad person?" His voice rose at the end because he felt guilty—guilty and wicked for despoiling her baby boy, even though every recollection from the night before seemed to indicate that much of the despoiling had been Mark's idea.

"No!" she protested, finally laughing. "You're not a bad person at all! But you certainly do seem to fit in with our lack of discretion. Forget lying to save your life; you can't even let a secret hide behind your eyes."

"I don't even know how to deal with it," he confessed, welcoming her pat on his back much as he'd hoped she'd welcomed his. "I… I've never done a grown-up relationship. There are rules. Probably lots of rules. I don't understand any of them!"

To his horror, his own voice was breaking much as hers had been.

"Sh, sh, sh," she murmured, wrapping her arms around his shoulders and pulling him in. "Honey, it's fine. Mark *is* a grown-up, and he's had a couple of these. He's going to guide you, but you need to give him input, okay? Yes, there are rules, but they're unique between couples, and you both need to make them. Just remember that. You *both* need to make them. Okay?"

Cassidy nodded, feeling somewhat reassured. "I just… just really liked it when he stayed… in the guest room," he whispered. "I… I would like him to feel comfortable there."

Her snort of laughter rebuked the "guest room" ruse—but gently. "Well, you need to discuss that with him. But give him a moment if he seems to forget that you get input. I love my son, and his intentions are the best, but he can be incredibly self... involved, I guess, but even that's the wrong word. It's not so much that he's self-absorbed as it is that his plans and hopes for people and relationships seem to wrap everyone else inside. On the one hand, it makes him pretty attentive when he puts his mind to it, but on the other...." She sucked air through her teeth. "Well, it makes him oblivious."

She was obviously holding back, and he tried to remember all of his newsroom interactions, watching as Rose and the other reporters teased the guts of a story from a few cosmetic details.

"You're trying not to dish about his last boyfriend, aren't you?" Cassidy hazarded.

Her relief was palpable. "God, yes. I just—I would have liked Brad, I think, if he hadn't hated *us* so much. Not letting the kids visit, when Mark has loved them since before they were born. Threatening to euthanize poor Gus-Gus. Yes, Mark can be a little self-involved, but Brad wasn't listening to who he was in the first place. And I guess that's what you both need to learn from. *Listen* to each other. Try not to jump to conclusions." She sighed. "And don't put too much stock in what Mark's busybody mother has to say about things, because you've already seen me stick my nose into everybody's business to an embarrassing degree."

Cassidy nodded and allowed himself the comfort of leaning against her shoulder. "I can see why you do," he whispered. "You just want them all to be happy, and you can't... can't make their other people do what they should do."

Yvonne gave a bitter laugh. "Well, it's not my place, is it? If I could have accepted Tanya as easily as I accept you, maybe Keith would have had an easier time of it." She gave a sigh. "And maybe not." She pulled away enough to grin at him and ruffle his carefully water-combed hair. "Maybe I just like you," she said simply. "And that would be a first, because I haven't approved of any of Dani's beaus either."

Cassidy grinned back. "Well, I feel lucky, then," he said—and he meant it.

"Excellent." She took a deep breath, and they separated, which was a small relief because his wheelchair was not made for hugs like that. "So, how about we learn to crochet, and then we'll have an *excuse* to gossip, and you can learn what it's like to have a craft you can carry to all the rooms of your house and even to work with you."

As Yvonne dug into the big canvas tote bag, pulling out balls of wool in various colors and then hooks in an array of sizes, Cassidy thought of the pleasure he got from woodwork and how wonderful that would be to put in a bag and carry around.

He straightened and smiled, the possibilities flowing through him, and suddenly he understood what she'd been trying to tell Mark about yarn in the first place.

Potential. Every color and skein had *potential.*

TWO HOURS later, he was staring critically at the six inches of lumpy fabric in his hands. He hadn't changed his mind—he still thought the yarn and the hooks and the craft had potential—but he understood that he was in the middle of the fidgety, irritating phase where *unlocking* that potential got to be hard work.

"Ack!" he said, pointing to the sides of the fabric. "I'm doing it again!" The thing was going to be a scarf, because he understood that scarves were what beginners did. It was either scarves or hot pads, but Yvonne seemed to feel hot pads meant working too tightly with yarn that was hard on the hands. In this case, the sides of the work were "coming in"—instead of a potential rectangle that would just get longer and longer and longer, he had a trapezoid, where the width of the thing was narrowing and he was threatening to make a triangle, which as far as he knew had no use at all.

"Well," she said patiently, "count it, honey. How many stitches did we start with?"

"Thirty-six," he said automatically. It had taken them half an hour to get those perfectly sized, not-too-loose-and-not-too-tight stitches worked into his beginning chain.

"How many do we have now?"

He went back and counted. "Thirty," he sighed. "I'm forgetting to work the first stitch of the last row, aren't I?"

She nodded. "Yup. Beginners often do. It's because you chain three to get that stitch and it doesn't look like the others."

"What do I do now?" he asked, although he knew the answer.

"Sorry, honey. You've got two choices. One is to work an extra three stitches into each end of the work, which will make it as wide was it was at the beginning, but you'll have big lumps in the side—"

"Ugh."

"Yes. But the other option is to frog it."

"Frog it?" he asked.

"Rip-it! Rip-it!" She made the motion of pulling the live end of the yarn as she said it, and Cassidy gave an exasperated sigh.

"Of course." But he had to admit, making the noise did make him smile as he ripped out half the work. By the time he'd made up the lost inches, his body was a little sore from not shifting his weight and his fingers were cramped—and he was so proud. He looked up, holding six inches of scarf that were *not* trapezoidal, and felt triumphant indeed.

Then he realized Yvonne had been cooking dinner for the past half hour, and the thin winter light from outside had dissipated, allowing the complete dark of December to blanket the sky. The bushes outside his kitchen window moved frantically, scratching at the glass, followed by a patter of droplets.

It seemed to be raining.

"Oh no!" he said, looking around frantically. "It's dark! It's late! I'm late! I didn't realize—and where's Mark?"

"Calm down!" she laughed. "You can't be late for anything— except maybe using the bathroom, because you've been sitting for *hours*. And it is dark—you were really involved, but then, so was I. I thought I'd let you work because you seemed so happy." She gave a little shrug. "And as for Mark? Well, he's late, but he's late a lot. I'm sure you've heard of doctor's hours by now, right?"

Cassidy nodded and swallowed hard. Of course. Of course he'd heard of doctor's hours. *Everybody* had heard of doctor's hours, right? "Yes," he whispered, his heart hammering in his throat. "Yes. He wouldn't think to call."

"No," she said, frowning. "He wouldn't. Especially not because he was used to living with Brad through his internship and first year of residency—from what he told me, neither of them checked in, even if they had plans."

"No?" Cassidy hated the way his voice cracked. God, he had to calm down. This was what he'd been afraid of, the thing in himself he'd thought would destroy any relationship he attempted.

"No," she said, keeping her voice gentle. "And the past few months he's been living with me. He has the room above the garage so he doesn't feel trapped, you know, like he's living with his mother. So... so he's not going to be as thoughtful as he should be—not at first. You're going to have to speak up, remember? Negotiate rules."

Negotiate rules—she was right. He had to remember that. He had a plan. He wasn't late. He hadn't done anything wrong. This wasn't his fault. He just needed to.... He squirmed violently in the wheelchair and remembered he needed to use the facilities.

"I'll be back," he rasped, and wheeled himself back to the bathroom as quickly as possible.

It was a struggle—he'd needed Mark's help the night before and the nurse's help that morning, but God, after exchanging hugs and confidences with Yvonne and trying so hard to squelch his panicky anger toward Mark, he was sweaty and irritated and shaky with emotion and repressed anxiety when he finally cleared the bathroom.

Yvonne had put down place settings for them both by the time he came out, and he settled himself at the table and tried to pull himself together.

Every second ticked loudly in his brain, only partially tuned out by the roar of blood in his ears.

He worked hard at dinner conversation and tried to keep his panic at bay, but toward the end of the meal, she took a deep breath and put her hand over his, telling him he'd failed. "Would you like me to call him?" she asked softly. "I—"

He shook his head. "I'm being stupid. He's a grown man and I don't have any claim on him and—"

At that moment, the door burst open and Mark blew in, his face red from the cold and his hair tousled and windblown. "Wow, it's blustery out there!" he said. "Did you guys notice the storm coming in?"

And all of Cassidy's careful rationalizing broke loose from its moorings and he shouted, "*I can't do this!*" before backing the wheelchair out from the table and setting his own personal record for getting down the hall and into his bedroom.

He slammed the door on Mark's surprised face before he allowed the full-blown panic attack to take over. Mark knocked frantically on the door and called his name, but he was sobbing too hard to answer.

OLD GROWTH

"COME ON, honey," his mother said, tugging gently at his arm. "Come on. You need to give him some space."

"What just happened?" Mark asked, baffled and hurt.

She gave him a crooked smile. "You were late," she said simply, and he opened his mouth to say that happened all the time, but between the time he thought of the words and the time he could say them, everything Cassidy had ever said about being late came crashing through his thick head and stopped his tongue.

"Fuck."

"Mark!"

He shook his head, suddenly overwhelmed by the enormity of what he'd done. "Fuck fuck fuck fuck fuck!"

"Mark, he was tired and a little overwrought. I think—"

"I'm an insensitive prick? Because yes. Yes I am," he said bitterly. "God—Cassidy!" He raised his hand to bang on the door, but before it hit, they both heard what sounded to be muffled screaming.

"Oh, baby," he murmured, leaning his face against the door. "Mom! I've got to fix this!"

"Give him his space," she said softly. "Let him calm down a little. He's been trying not to work himself up into a state for the last two hours—I had no idea he was so upset."

Mark shook his head. "Mom," he said painfully. "I just... I just fed into every nightmare he's ever had about a relationship. Do you understand what I just did?"

She let out a breath. "You were late home from work," she said softly. "And you forgot to call. It was thoughtless, but it wasn't a crime."

"It was to *him*," he said, miserable to his bones. "So many people have let him down, Mom. So many people have not shown up in his life. And I know it's only been a week, but... but we're the most important thing to happen to him emotionally for a really long time."

"That I knew," she said, patting his cheek. "And I also know that you threw a monkey wrench into things, taking them up to another level so soon. But it's not necessarily a bad thing—just, you know. Needs extra care." She frowned. "But you need to decide right now that you're up to the extra care. This was once—and of course it will happen again. You both need training up. But are you up to the job? Because if you aren't, you need to pull out of this relationship right now."

"I a—"

She held up a hand. "Go. Just, I don't know. Take Gus-Gus for his walk. Do your laundry. Take a break. Let him get this out of his system and you both can cool down. But think about the question while you do. Mark, I'm really starting to care about this boy. You two don't have to be an item for me to pull another one into the fold, but it sure will make things hard if you're constantly at odds."

"I'll—"

"Think about it," she said implacably. Then she sighed. "And I'll try to get him to open the door."

Mark sighed and went, calling to a confused Gus-Gus as he walked out. The two of them ventured into the blustery night, and Mark thought she might have a point. He crossed their front lawns and made his way around to the back entrance to the garage apartment, the one behind the house. He was surprised to see the glowing tip of a cigarette as he neared, and the blocky silhouette of his brother.

"Mark?" Keith asked softly. "You're home late."

Mark grunted. "And you're *out* late. Where are the kids?"

"In bed," Keith said, blowing out smoke. "LizBet was asleep when I got them home, and the kids…. Well, it was a shitty day."

"Giving them space?" Mark asked, thinking of their mother's admonition to him.

"Yeah. Too many adults checking on them. I asked Brandon if he was okay in the middle of dinner, and he shouted, 'I'm eating pizza!' I, uh, told him to carry on."

Mark smiled a little, sad for them all. "Yeah, well, it wasn't going to be an easy time."

Keith grunted and leaned against the door. Gus-Gus waddled next to him to lean against his leg, probably because it was under the overhang and drier there. Mark took a hint from Gus-Gus and leaned against the house, shoulder to shoulder with his brother.

"You all saw this coming, didn't you?" Keith asked bitterly.

"Wasn't ours to see," Mark said diplomatically. "I'm pretty sure you all saw Brad coming too, but, you know...."

"Wasn't ours to see," Keith agreed after taking another drag. "Brad was a prick."

"Mm. Am I allowed to say bad things about Tanya now? Because I've got some saved. But if it's too early, I can hold on to them for next year."

Keith gave a humorless laugh. "Give it a month or two, then take me out and get me drunk and lay them all on me."

"Fair enough."

"Your new guy sounds promising."

"My new guy?" Mark hadn't even really spoken to his brother since Cassidy had come home from the hospital.

"Next door." Keith gestured with his chin. "Kids love him. Say he's nice. I mean, I don't think they even remembered who Brad was."

Mark thought about it, about all the family events Brad had been to where he'd paid the kids only cursory attention, and about all the family events Brad had missed because he just hadn't wanted to go.

"Small things," he said. "When you're a child. It takes so little to make kids happy." And the thought of all the moments Cassidy had missed—and had known he was missing too. "God. I'm such a fuckup."

Keith snorted. "My marriage broke up and I'm living with my mother, Mark. My wife is about to get the house in the divorce settlement just so I don't have to fight her for custody for the kids. I have to start from scratch. Don't tell me what kind of fuckup you are."

"I was late tonight," Mark said.

"So?"

Keith was really looking at him funny, so he tried to explain. And every time he talked about Cassidy's past, he felt the hugeness of his crime all over again. "So Brad was probably right about me," he said bitterly. "I'm an irresponsible child who can't be trusted with people or nice things."

Keith snorted. "I think we covered that Brad was a prick," he said. "He hated our family, he hated the dog, and I'll be honest, I think the only reason he was interested in *you* was that you're hot and you're a doctor. He just looked at the outside and didn't see that being a good person—which includes loving your family—is the thing that makes you tick."

"I can't believe my brother said I'm hot," Mark muttered. "Ew."

"Shut up," Keith retorted, sounding so much like the older brother he was that Mark couldn't help but think *Keith*, at least, was going to be okay. "What I'm trying to say is that you're right. Cassidy's been broken, and he's been broken in the place that's sort of your weak spot too, so you're going to have to work on that. But I think he's also got your priorities. Did you say Mom's teaching him how to... you know?" Keith flicked his cigarette to the concrete strip next to the house and made little motions with his hands. "The yarn thing she does."

"Crochet," Mark said dryly.

"Yeah—she tried to teach me, she tried to teach Dani, she tried to teach Tanya—"

"And me." Mark had been able to do it, but he hadn't really loved it.

"And she said this guy was excited to try. So this guy is, like, the anti-Brad. I mean, they may have the same pet peeve about time, but they definitely have different priorities about how you *spend* your time. And Cassidy sounds... I don't know. Maybe it's because I'm sort of raw, because I think my kids are *fucking awesome*, and Tanya doesn't seem interested in them, and that hurts. But he *also* seemed to think they were fucking awesome. Brandon said he put Brandon's drawing on the refrigerator—do you know Tanya wouldn't let them do that? She wouldn't let anything go on the walls that wasn't in a frame. I had to take all their artwork to my office and then show them pictures of it posted up there so they'd know it was up. So this guy's a little broken. I say you fix him, and learn how to write a goddamned text, and see if this can go somewhere, you think?"

"I was planning to try," Mark said, loving his brother in that moment. God, one of the most frustrating things about watching Tanya treat him like a cash machine was knowing that Keith was so much more than a provider. He was such a good father—and he'd make some woman a really good partner; Mark was absolutely convinced of that. "But... but I can't be the one that fixes the damage. Not all by myself." Mark sighed. "I mean, I can do my part, but... you know."

Keith's mouth twisted. "Am I about to become the world's greatest brother-in-law? I am. I'm about to become the world's *greatest* brother-in-law. I'll fly kites with this guy, I'll take him fly-fishing—"

"Do you even know how to fly-fish?" Mark asked, surprised.

"I am the fly-fishing *king*—as you are about to find out when I move all my equipment into the garage, along with my woodworking shit—"

"He's got woodworking shit," Mark said, thinking about all the machines in the garage that he and his mother had covered with tarps so the dust wouldn't damage them while Cassidy was laid up. "He's really talented."

Keith let out a chuckle. "You're killing me here. I love this guy. I'm going to be a *stellar* brother-in-law. You need to make this work."

Mark smiled, comforted by Keith just like he'd been as a little kid when he'd had monsters under the bed. He could hear Keith's voice in his head now. *I'll kill them for you, Marky—I swear I will. But first you need to pull that bastard out from under the bed so I know what I'm fighting.*

That was Mark's brother. He'd slay any dragon you needed him to, as long as he knew what it looked like.

In this case, it looked like Cassidy's fears and Mark's unreliability, and in the light of Keith's die-hard practical nature, that monster didn't seem so big.

"I'll fix it," Mark vowed. He remembered telling Cassidy that one late arrival shouldn't have changed the entire course of Cassidy's life. There *should* have been lots of chances besides that one.

He certainly hoped it was true.

"I know you will." Keith slung a protective arm over Mark's shoulders, and for a moment they just stood there, staring out into the rain. Then Keith shivered. "Are you cold? I'm cold. Did you need something from your room? Because I... I gotta tell you, Marky, I'm beat. Today was sucktastic, and it's great I can be your Jiminy Cricket and all, but I need some fun television and zero conversation, stat."

Mark leaned his head on Keith's shoulder for a moment before straightening. "I need some clothes for tomorrow," he said. "And another pair of pajamas. And my shower stuff. I'm sort of moving into his house if he'll let me, and I miss my own stuff."

"That's my boy," Keith said tiredly, giving him a squeeze before pulling away. "Always thinking ahead."

And with that, he led them both into the garage and up the wooden staircase to the apartment so Mark could pack a duffel bag and hope for the best.

HE STAYED for another half hour, having a beer with Keith as Keith settled down on Mark's denim couch with Mark's wool throw, recovering from their stay in the rain. The apartment itself was snug—the walls textured drywall, and Mark's mother had chosen a sweet shabby-chic blue wallpaper to decorate. Not particularly masculine, but Mark had thought ruefully that it was her house, and he was living in the little studio rent-free. There was a kitchenette with an oven, a mini fridge, a microwave, and a sink, as well as a bathroom with a shower cubicle just big enough for a grown man to possibly soap his pits. Mark had brought his couch, recliner, coffee table, a couple kitchen chairs, and the queen-sized bed he and Brad had kept in the guest room when they'd lived together, and with the bed stashed in one corner and the living room furniture ranged around a big-screen television, the space was big enough not to feel claustrophobic but small enough to keep *I've got to get my own apartment* singing through the back of a grown man's mind as he lived there.

Mark and Keith shot the shit as they sipped their brews, and Mark kept his cell phone on the table so he could see if his mother needed him, and he popped up like a jack-in-the-box when a message from her flashed.

You ready to come back?

"Good news?" Keith asked.

"Hope so," he said, texting *OMW* before sliding the phone in his pocket and grabbing his duffel bag. "See you tomorrow, maybe."

"Yeah. I may need you and Mom to help me with the kids at school. I know Dani gets back from her business trip next week, so she'll be in town to help too." He closed his eyes and shook his head. "That thing about taking a village is not bullshit."

"No it is not," Mark said, making his way to the door. "Thanks for the beer."

Keith grunted. "Thanks for not sucking as a brother, Marky. Talk to this guy—you're probably a decent boyfriend once you get past the being-late thing."

Mark chuckled to himself as he left, duffel bag slung over his shoulders, Gus-Gus once again at his heels. Keith deserved all the good things for Christmas this year—Mark would have to ask Cassidy what he thought they could do.

The idea made him square his shoulders and head purposefully back into the rain. Cassidy was waiting on the other side of the yard, feeling miserable and left behind and forgotten. Mark hoped that now they'd both had some time to think, Mark could make that better.

WHEN HE walked into Cassidy's house, his mother was in the front room, crocheting, and he saw what must have been Cassidy's work—done in a stormy blue worsted wool—sitting on top of a canvas bag at the other end of the couch.

"See what he did?" she said with pride.

"I saw that when I came in," he told her. He'd known immediately who it belonged to. "Why'd you put it there?"

"So he knows he can work on it when he's watching television." She gave him a smug smile. It was when she got most of her yarn-work done.

"Very clever." He grew sober. "How is he?"

"Awful," she said with a sad smile. "But he unlocked the door when I told him if anything happened we'd have to break it down. I haven't heard any sounds in a few minutes—he might have fallen asleep. Where'd you go?"

"Talked to Keith," he said briefly, and her eyebrows went up.

"It's been a day all around," she told him with a sigh. "How is *he*?"

"Ready to not talk about it," Mark said, grimacing. "And I think the kids are asleep, but you may want to check."

"Mm." With a little sigh, she packed her ubiquitous project tote, pausing to toss a couple of yarn cakes on top of Cassidy's bag. "So he can finish it in his own time," she said.

"Scarf?" he asked—but he knew her answer. As far as she was concerned, all "larval" crocheters were in the scarf stage. Eventually they would learn to cocoon themselves in their passion for the craft and emerge able to create blankets, sweaters, and accessories, but first they had to make a scarf.

"Yes," she said, and her lips quirked into a smile. "Don't tell him, but I think it's for you. He asked what your favorite color was."

Mark bent and fingered the yarn, recognizing the pricey hand-dyed small-mill brand. "It's the good stuff," he said, surprised. "You gave *us* the crap yarn to start with."

"*You* were all acting like I was forcing you to go to school," she said archly. "*He* was happy to learn, so he gets the good stuff." She sobered too. "Go make things right, sweetheart. I have hope for both of you. Oh! And there's dinner on the counter for you when you're ready."

Mark nodded and kissed her cheek before seeing her out, making sure she'd pulled her umbrella out of her crafting bag so she wouldn't get too chilled as she crossed the yards.

Then he looked down at Gus-Gus, who had curled up on the kitchen mat because he'd decided that was his sleep cushion, because he was Gus-Gus apparently.

"You think he'll talk to me?" he asked.

Gus-Gus thumped his tail experimentally, and Mark took some hope with him as he walked down the hall.

"Cassidy?" he called softly, knocking on the door. "Cassidy, baby, are you in there?"

"Go away," came the wretched reply, and Mark laughed softly.

"Uhm, no. Here, I'm going to let myself in, because talking through the door is stupid."

The room was completely dark, the only light coming from the bathroom. Cassidy was lying partially on his side, the cast keeping him from the full fetal curl, his back toward Mark. Mark thought about going to the other side of the bed so they could face each other, but maybe he should let Cassidy make a move of his own. Instead he drew up the chair he'd sat on previously and placed himself at Cassidy's back, hoping Cassidy would turn toward him when he felt safe.

Meeting each other halfway was going to be essential.

"Cassidy? I, uh, just wanted to tell you I'm sorry. I should have texted. It was stupid. I got caught up in what I was doing and forgot. It was so thoughtless of me."

"It wasn't your fault," Cassidy said, voice clogged. "I mean, yeah, you should have texted, but…." He let out a shuddering breath and said, "Ribbit. Ribbit."

Mark's eyes widened. "I'm sorry?"

Cassidy let out a miserable little laugh. "I… I wish I could rip back the entire last hour. Like with my project. Rip-it. Rip-it. And then when you walked in, all happy and excited to see me, I could have said, 'No, we didn't see the rain coming in! Gee, you're late.' And then you could have said… well, what you just said. That you were sorry and you should have texted. And it could be normal, and everyday, and not a problem. And I wouldn't have overreacted and had an anxiety attack and—" His voice started to tighten, his emotions ratcheting up again, and Mark rubbed a circle in the center of his back, his chest starting to loosen for the first time since he'd walked in.

"Hey," he murmured. "Hey, don't get upset. Baby, were you in here having an anxiety attack? Is that what happened?"

"I tried to make it go away," he whispered. "I... I haven't had one in years. Since Rose told me my probationary period was over and I was hired full-time. I... felt it coming, and you were late, and I couldn't stop it and—"

"Sh...." This time he leaned forward and kissed the crown of Cassidy's head. "It's okay. It's okay. Don't worry. Don't apologize. I know enough people who've had those to know you can't just wish them away. And...." He laughed a little, bitterly. "And this has been a roller coaster week for you, hasn't it? The leg and my family and... and us. So much, so soon. And then I was late and it just sent all of that spilling over. It's no wonder."

"But I like us!" Cassidy sniffled. "I like your family. I... well, I could do without the stupid cast and the ache and the wheelchair, but I'll get used to that, and then I'll get past it. I mean, I may need a cane for a while, but... but I'm *alive*, and the tree could have crushed my skull. I... I'm fine. It's just...."

Mark wrapped his arm around Cassidy's shoulder this time. "It's a lot," he said softly. "I... I'm sorry I rushed things. Do you want me to go? My mom can come over—"

"No," Cassidy whispered, and tried to look over his shoulder. Mark helped him out by standing up a little so they could make eye contact. "No. Maybe no... uhm, nakedness tonight—"

"Lovemaking," Mark clarified, and was relieved when Cassidy nodded.

"I just want you to be here, with me. I... I want the other stuff, but right now...."

Mark opened his mouth to say something the perfect boyfriend would say, and his stomach growled instead.

Cassidy chuckled weakly. "Go get food," he said. "I'll... you know, work to sit up. We can watch television and—"

Mark smiled. "Rip-it?"

"Yeah." Cassidy nodded. "Rip-it. And we can start again."

"Good."

GROWN ACCUSTOMED

"WIGGLE YOUR toes," Dr. Chu said, running a small tool along the ball of his foot as it pudged out from the cast.

Cassidy did as ordered, and Dr. Chu grunted approval.

"Good. Good—you have plenty of feeling there, and mobility. Your X-rays say it's healing well, but not quite ready for a smaller cast."

"No?" Cassidy asked, disappointed. In the two weeks since he'd returned home, he'd come to loathe the cumbersome thing—and the chair he was confined to.

"No," Dr. Chu said kindly. "It was a big injury, Mr. Hancock. I hope you know how lucky you are that Dr. Taylor was there when that tree fell on top of you. He routed you directly to me—we were able to operate much sooner than we would have been otherwise. He may even have saved your leg."

"No, no," Cassidy said hurriedly. "I'm not complaining. Mark's been—" How to complete that sentence? A godsend? A guardian angel? A friend?

The man in his bed who kissed him every night, whether or not they touched each other naked?

"—awesome," Cassidy finished weakly. "He's been so much help. I'm so lucky to have him and his family in my life."

Dr. Chu's mouth crinkled at the corners. "You're dating him, aren't you?" It wasn't really a question, and Cassidy's face went up into a quiet ball of flame. "It's fine—he's not your doctor, I am. But he's my friend, and he's been insufferably happy these past two weeks."

"Yeah," he rasped, surprised his sweater, the mutilated sweats that exposed his leg, the loathsome wheelchair, all of it, didn't just immolate right then and send him down to the core of the earth to be turned to ashes. "Yeah, we're, uhm, sort of a thing."

"Excellent!" Dr. Chu said happily. "Oh my God, you are such a nice guy. And don't tell Mark I said this, but Brad and I were in medical school together too, and he was *such a prick*. I'm so happy Mark's with someone I don't mind inviting to the office Christmas party. Do you want to come to the orthopedic ward Christmas party? It's in three days, in the evening, my house. Mark isn't working—I did that on purpose so he'd have no excuse not to come."

"He'd make up an excuse not to come?" Cassidy asked, surprised, because this didn't sound like Mark at all.

"I think he's afraid Brad has been trash-talking him," Dr. Chu confided. "Which he has. But I've known Mark since med school too, and he's such a nice guy. I want him to fit in here. He's a gifted surgeon and an excellent practitioner. It's my way of sweetening the pot."

Cassidy smiled, thinking he'd never heard so many confidences in his life as he had in the past two weeks. "Well, his family is here," he said. "I think that's his sweetened pot, right there."

"And yet another reason he is beloved," Dr. Chu said grandly. He patted Cassidy's cast with a sigh. "Try not to hold the cast against us, okay? We're going to take this one off, check your stitches—although I don't see any inflammation in the exposed areas and you have no pain, so I'm pretty sure that'll be shipshape. But we're going to have to put on the same model here—padded fiberglass. Next trip, maybe we can do one of the sleek 3-D printed ones. Don't lose hope."

Cassidy sighed, and he tried not to think about the things he wanted to do with and to Mark when he had mobility again. "I won't," he said.

"And definitely come to the ortho ward party," Dr. Chu insisted.

"I'll try," Cassidy told him, smiling warmly. "I don't have anything to wear."

"Who cares! People will be getting drunk and sleeping in the basement—I've got couches all over for company. Jeans and a sweater, it'll be fine—or in your case, one-legged sweats. It'll be fantastic. Just come."

"We'll see," Cassidy promised. "Thanks, Dr. Chu."

"Call me Harry!" They shook hands, and Harry pushed him out into the waiting room, where a pretty woman with Mark's brown eyes and Yvonne's pale blond hair awaited.

"How we looking?" Dani asked.

"Like you need to go down one floor to have the cast replaced," Dr. Chu said.

"Will we see Mark?" Cassidy hadn't meant to ask, because Mark told him he'd be in surgery all day and he hadn't wanted to sound needy, but it sort of slipped out.

"Probably not," Dr. Chu—Harry—said with a smile. "But you will see me. While you're getting checked in there, I'll see this next patient, and then I'll come down to supervise the whole thing with the saw and the new cast. And then we can all dish about Mark—how's that?"

"Mark's boring," Dani said flirtatiously. "Let's find something else to dish about."

"How about my Christmas party in three days," Harry told her, obviously charmed. "You're welcome too."

"I'll be there!" She giggled, and Cassidy shook his head as she turned his chair and started pushing him to the lab.

"You're terrible," he told her. He'd fallen a little in love with Dani Taylor the moment she'd breezed through his door last week, smelling of jasmine and—in her words—stale airport air. She'd been carefree and exciting, just like Mark, but unlike her brother, she didn't carry all the emotional weight of rapidly becoming the center of Cassidy's world.

"Yes, well, I had to do something," she said easily. "Because we both know you're going to politely back out and leave Mark to go all by himself."

Cassidy's cheeks heated in the cool of the hospital. "That obvious?"

She bent down and put her back into pushing the wheelchair, making him gasp in surprise—and, he could admit, excitement. She slowed for a corner, and they both laughed, and she answered his question.

"Not your thing, honey," she said softly. "Anyone can see it—well, except for Harry, but that's because he's a good guy and he desperately wants my brother to stay here and be his second chair in ortho. But it's okay if you don't like parties or crowds. Remember? You and Mark are working on your boundaries?"

That had been one of the things that had come about after that terrible night when Mark had arrived late. Mark would do his very best to give Cassidy a heads-up if his timeline was going to change—and in the past two weeks, it had changed a lot. What was supposed to be a light schedule as Mark made himself comfortable in the hospital and his new home had evolved into full-time very quickly, and Mark had cursed repeatedly as his pager had gone off just when he was starting to relax.

In return, Cassidy needed to let Mark—and his family—know when too much was too much. He'd gone back to work—online—in the past week, and he'd had to regretfully ask Yvonne and then Dani if they could only come over during his lunchtime or after work. He was surprised to realize his company was in demand. Yvonne likcd to sit and crochet with him, and she'd continued to teach him new things. Dani's job as a consultant for a financial firm involved traveling about once a month, and when she wasn't in the air or online, she confessed to enjoying the chance to sit in Cassidy's living room and comment on stupid television with him.

"I know it's dumb," she'd said the Saturday before, "but I love living in the same town with everybody. Meeting someone nice who knows all the same people is really a treat."

Keith had brought the kids over during the weekends—both when Mark was and wasn't at home. He'd been so respectful of Cassidy's woodworking gear—and so genuinely regretful that he was going to have to sell or store what he owned until he found another house—that Cassidy offered to let Keith use his.

It was such a simple, small thing, after all Mark's family had done for him, but the big man had gotten a little misty-eyed over it and asked for ground rules.

Cassidy had set them, and Keith had been so amenable. "This is great," he said, still looking like he could cry. "You don't understand— I've made little wooden toys for the kids since they were born, and I hadn't even started this year. I…. It's so dumb, but after everything else, I just really hated to break the tradition."

"I'm so happy to," Cassidy said, meaning it. "Your family— they've saved my life this last month. It's nice to be able to give back."

Keith chuckled and shook his head. "You are *so* much better than Brad," he said, and Cassidy didn't know how to reply.

It *was* nice to hear, right?

But the point was, as Dani had said, he was setting boundaries and standing up for himself, which was good, because it meant that ball of anger, of resentment, of panic, that had built up in him the night Mark had been late hadn't been allowed to form—and day by day, Cassidy had grown more comfortable with having these people in his life.

With *having* a life, actually. With having people who would watch out for him and care for him—but who would let him care for them back.

The day before, he'd tried to explain to Rose how the Taylor family had woven themselves into the fabric of his life.

"It's so strange," he said after logging back on after a lunch during which Mark had run in with sandwiches, then kissed his cheek and run back out to work in his mother's yard. "I... I have my work family, everybody I talk to and you, and I really love that. But... but this is different."

Rose grinned, the flatness of the screen not hiding a whit of her animated beauty. "Oh, honey, I'm so excited for you. I was so worried about you for so long. You'll be able to make the Christmas Eve party? Please tell me you will. I'll send a car for you myself—it's just everybody in the office has talked about how much they miss you."

Cassidy frowned. "But... but I'm so quiet."

She cocked her head. "Yes, honey, but it's what you did while you were quiet. It was the way you always made sure the break room had snacks, or that people got a plant or a card on their birthday. I know you're my assistant, but that was never part of your job. You're the one who requisitioned money for gifts when some of the girls went out on maternity break. You know how you got flowers yesterday?"

Cassidy smiled, warmed. "Yes—thank you. They're very pretty."

"You've been laid up for two weeks, darling. They're late. Those are some very pretty, very late flowers, because Lucy in the billing department asked why we hadn't sent them yet. She said you two had talked for an hour about who we needed to pay this month, and she realized she hadn't seen a single bouquet of flowers in your home—and then she threatened to quit. So whether you realize it or not, you have made an indelible and beautiful mark on my company and my office culture, and I think the people here would like to thank you. Please say you'll come."

"I'll have to ask Mark," he began, blushing.

"Bring him," she said. "I know you probably have one big social event a month inside you. I insist on making it mine."

And he blinked, realizing it was true.

"Is that bad?" he asked.

She shook her head. "No. You can be a perfectly wonderful person even if you don't thrive on big groups of people. It's just that in this case, it's Christmas. And your coworkers miss you, and we'd like to see you. Just for an hour or two. Is that too much to ask?"

And the last sentence wasn't flippant or manipulative. It was completely sincere. He realized she was worried, having seen him at Christmas parties in years gone by, because he'd never been more during those things than the person on the fringe of the crowd.

And he remembered that, while always maintaining her professionalism as his boss, she'd been a good one, warm in her way, and kind. She might not have remembered everybody's birthday, but she'd been more than complimentary when Cassidy had, and while she'd always expected perfection from him as he helped schedule her time and gave input to the magazine itself, she'd also been willing to talk things out with him, so if an idea didn't start out as perfect to begin with, it ended up as perfect between the two of them.

And of course, the fact that he'd just been hired to keep her schedule and get her coffee, but she'd promoted him so quickly up the ranks he'd been able to fulfill the dream he was living in right now.

"Of course it's not," he replied right then. "I'll see if Mark can come."

Mark couldn't.

Lying in bed that night, Mark's head on his shoulder because that was the easiest position with the cast keeping him mostly upright, Mark gave his regrets.

"I can't. I'm sorry—Harry's been scheduling me more and more this month, and I put my foot down for Christmas, but the only way I could do that was if I—"

"Worked Christmas Eve. I get it," Cassidy said, and the wonder of it was, he did get it. God, he'd been so worried. That terrible day—that terrible outburst—the storm of weeping later. What if he couldn't pull his emotions together? What if he was too broken to have the relationship he'd always dreamed of offered to him on a platter?

But Mark had been so patient—and it turned out he'd been right that night. Cassidy *had* been through a lot, and even the good things were hard on the emotions. Allowing himself some space—and imposing boundaries on Mark's family—had given him the strength he'd needed to be an equal partner in their relationship.

It had given him the space to become used to being a son, a brother, an uncle, and a lover, all in the span of less than a month.

And now it gave him the courage to suggest something he might not have done a month ago.

"So, uhm, Dani?"

"Yeah?" she said, slowing the wheelchair and then parking it by one of the chairs in the waiting room. "Wait—hold that thought. I'm gonna go give your paperwork to the nurse."

She returned in a moment and went through his wallet, which was stashed in a small bag hanging from the handle of his wheelchair, so she could return his medical card. He watched her with bemusement—boy, she was awfully familiar awfully fast, but she was just as irrepressible as her brother.

"There you go," she said, patting the bag. "Right next to the yarn. And I love that magenta color. Whatever you're making, it had better be for me."

Cassidy snorted. "Your mom can make you whatever you want, and better than I can."

She rolled her eyes in return, her little elfin face practically hidden by a thick, fluffy, *homemade* scarf in deep purple. "Yes, maybe, but *you* are a much better story. I have so much stuff from my mom, people are like, 'Yeah, yeah, your mom rocks,' but if I say, 'It's from my brother's boyfriend who had a tree fall on his head and learned to crochet,' I mean, *that's* an icebreaker for cocktail parties, right?"

He shrugged. She wasn't wrong. "Uhm, speaking of parties?"

Her breath caught. "What? You have one to go to and I get to be your beard?"

"Well, since you've offered to take my place with your brother, is there any way you can take his place with me?"

"In a way that's sick and wrong," she said, sounding judgy, "but since I know what you mean, then I have no problem with that."

He gasped in horror. "Oh God. Yeah. Gross. Forget I said anything."

"No, I will not. You were about to invite me to a party!"

Cassidy smiled—winningly, he hoped. "See, my office Christmas party used to be the only thing I ever got invited to, and I'm awkward and weird and shy and stupid. Anyway, it's Christmas Eve. I'm sure you've got something with your family—"

"No, no—we all gather on Christmas Day," she said. "I'm pretty sure Mom, Keith, and the kids are doing Christmas Eve small-style, and then we all converge on my mother's house and make her think that three was a much bigger number than she supposed when she was pushing us out."

"That's terrible," he said. "I don't even know if I'm invited Christmas Day—"

She laughed so hard she snorted, and then covered her mouth to hide the snort and continued to laugh. "My God, you're dense. Pretty—I can see why my brother's so in love with you—but stupid. Very, very stupid. It's a good combo. I'll try for pretty and stupid for my next boyfriend. It sure beats pretty and manipulative or pretty and unfaithful. No, no—Mark had the right idea."

"Stop it," he said, but he was laughing because no, she really did never quit. "Okay—so Christmas Day is all family, and Harry's thing is in three days, and Christmas Eve, I need a ride, I mean a date," he teased, liking the way her brown eyes lit up over her hand as he said it.

"I think I could be your ride," she returned soberly. Then—actually sober—she said, "It sounds pretty frantic. There are things you could be late for. Think you can manage it?"

"Only because I'm bailing on Harry's party," he said, feeling a little guilty.

She bent and kissed his cheek. "Honey, you are a dyed-in-the-wool introvert, and you are suddenly surrounded by people during the crazy time of the year. I think you're doing outstandingly, if that's a word, and I'd be happy to come with you to the Christmas party and meet all your work friends. And then dish to Mark about them later, and he'll be terribly jealous, and that will be fun too."

Cassidy's cheeks heated, which was what they did whenever Mark's name came up. "I, uhm, don't want to make him jealous," he said. "I mostly want to make him a hat to match the scarf I made him for Christmas."

"Why don't you?" she asked.

He shrugged, feeling sheepish. "Well, your mother was going to teach me in three days. She won't have the kids, and, uh, you just volunteered to go to that party."

She laughed. "Oh, you little schemer," she told him fondly. "Okay. We've got this beat." Then she paused. "But you *are* going to give me something for Christmas, right? Something homemade. In that color that's in your bag there."

Cassidy nodded at her, knowing he'd been caught. "Well, yes. If I wasn't stuck with the leg, I'd make you something in my shop, but right now, unless you want perfume, this is what I got." He blew out a breath. "I just wish I wasn't using all your mother's yarn. She says she has a lot, but I don't know if she has enough for the both of us if we're both obsessed."

She gave him a look of pity. "You poor, sad boy. You have no idea what you're letting yourself in for." Then her eyes widened. "And I have a dilemma on my hands. Let's see...." She pretended to consider. "I could let my mother clear out some of her craft room by feeding your addiction, which is only fair since she's the one who got you hooked in the first place, or...."

She pulled out her phone. "I could text you all the places Mom buys her yarn and let you go to town for yourself." Playfully, she tapped her lip. "Decisions, decisions...."

"You're terrible," he said again, but God, he couldn't remember laughing this much with anyone.

Except maybe Mark.

"I am," she agreed. "Now grab your phone, son, 'cause we're about to go online yarn shopping. And believe me, I've heard my mother say those words enough times for them to hold some weight."

And that's what they were doing when Cassidy got pulled into the cutting room to have his cast replaced. He was so intrigued by all the links she sent him he didn't have time to mourn that he was stuck in that tremendous bulky cast for another two weeks at the very least.

It was like all the good new things in his life really did outweigh this hundred-pound chunk of fiberglass on his leg.

HE TOLD Mark about his and Dani's plan that night as they lay in bed, watching television. Well, Mark might have been watching television, but Cassidy was watching Mark. He'd been assisting in surgery for a vehicular trauma most of the day, and he'd texted Cassidy he was going to be late about a minute before Cassidy truly got worried.

Then he'd slid into the house without his usual bluster and excitement, and Cassidy found he was worried about something completely different.

"What?" Mark asked, catching his gaze.

"I was going to ask you the same thing," Cassidy said. "You're sad."

"Today was hard," he said simply. "There's a reason surgery isn't my favorite. I mean, it's the job and I'm good at it, but Harry's got the heart of a surgeon."

"Will the patient be all right?" Cassidy always hesitated to ask. As much as he loathed the monstrosity on his leg, he was also acutely aware it could have been so much worse. He'd been given a second chance at life—and a group of people to assist him in taking it.

"No," Mark said softly. "At least, I don't think so. Harry's going in after he's stabilized, but he took one look at the X-rays and agreed that it was a fool's errand. We should have just amputated the leg and saved the risk of infection. But... but it's not just a leg, you know? It's this person's whole plan for his life, his self-concept. And they're doing wonderful things with prosthetics now, but it's just so unfair." He shrugged. "But there you go. Life's not fair. If life was fair, you and I would have met while fixing up my mom's yard and you wouldn't have needed a tree crashing on your poor body."

"But... but we *would* have met working on your mom's yard, right?"

Mark rolled onto his side, and Cassidy hit Pause on the remote. He loved it when Mark did this, looked at him seriously with those bright brown eyes, talked to him like every conversation was important.

"Yeah," he said, smiling slightly. "One day, Gus-Gus would have broken loose and run straight to you, because he's smart enough to know that someone who loves dogs like you isn't to be taken for granted. Or you would have shown up to clean my mom's gutters and I would have come out to talk to you, because you've got pretty eyes. Something— something. I don't think life would be that cruel to let us just sit there, day after day, as neighbors, when we could be so much more."

Cassidy laced their fingers together and raised Mark's knuckles to his lips. "I'm sorry your job was hard today," he said sincerely. "But I'm so glad you're the kind of person who will work to do the right thing. You're so smart—you're so good. I... I want to be someone in your life who makes that easier—who supports that."

"You are," Mark said. He scooted forward so he could cup Cassidy's chin and kiss him, his body warm and his lips soft. It was a tender moment, but as happened so often when Mark kissed him, it flared from tender to inferno in a matter of heartbeats.

For a few moments there was no sound in the room but their muffled *hmm*s of pleasure as Mark made free with his hands, rucking Cassidy's shirt up, grinding their groins together. Cassidy tried to keep up, but he moved slower, more methodically. He just hated to miss any part of Mark's body that might make him wriggle and moan.

But that usually meant he was the one wriggling and moaning and out of his mind first.

"Here," Mark whispered, pushing him onto his back. With deft movements, he stripped off Cassidy's wide-legged sleep shorts and boxers, and then his T-shirt.

Cassidy's eyes popped open as he realized he was well and truly naked, with the exception of the hated albatross on his leg. "Uhm.... Mark?"

Mark sat up on his knees and pulled off his shirt, grinning. "What?"

Cassidy swallowed and chinned toward his erection, which had not deflated one bit as the air—and Mark's eyes—stroked along its length. "Feeling awfully, uhm, naked?"

Mark cackled, mischief in his every move. "Really? That's great! I *like* you naked!"

"But the lights?" he whispered. That first night, they'd kept partially clothed, and after that, well, Cassidy was more comfortable in the dark.

So many secrets—and so alone—for so long. Was it any wonder? But being comfortable naked still didn't come easy.

"Leave them on," Mark said, shinnying out of his own pajamas in a quick movement.

Cassidy was torn between gaping at his fit, rangy body or protecting his own body, which was becoming a little softer than he'd have liked, in spite of the upper-body workout. "But...."

Mark rolled over and kissed him, their bare chests rubbing, their body heat mingling, and Cassidy lost the thread of everything but that kiss. Then Mark straddled him in one quick movement and bent over, nibbling down Cassidy's neck.

"Nungh!" Cassidy tried again to ask what he was doing, but that same sound came out, and he just abandoned himself to it.

Mark fumbled with something under his pillow, and Cassidy felt the cool slick of lubricant smoothed over his cock, and had a light bulb. "We're doing this?" he asked. "I thought.... You said you usually topped!"

"I do," Mark mumbled, positioning Cassidy's erection right at the place he *wouldn't* be, if Mark was going to top.

"But what are we—"

Mark paused. "I want this with you," he rasped. "Do I want to be inside you? Yes. Can I do it the way I want right now? Not without hurting you. This, we can do. Do you want me?" He inched his body down, just a little, enough to stretch his entrance, and Cassidy's eyes rolled back in his head.

"Yes...," he hissed, lost in it. Mark's slow, easy descent gave the lie to his gruff words, and in a moment they were lost in the thrust-and-recede pattern of lovemaking that made the world go softly around.

"Wow," Cassidy mumbled. "This is... wow!" Mark's body engulfed him, hot and satiny, and Mark supported his weight with hands on Cassidy's chest. It was like he was surrounded by all things Mark Taylor, and all things Mark Taylor were so, so good.

"Mm...." Mark closed his eyes and concentrated on his rhythm, and Cassidy took the opportunity to touch him some more. Pinching his nipples never got old—they were sensitive and pebbly, but now, as Mark shifted his hips back and forth, the motion seductive and undulating, Cassidy wanted them closer. He cupped Mark's neck, feeling Mark's pulse against his palm, and closed his eyes in awe.

"You feel so good," he said brokenly. "So beautiful. How is it you're here with me?"

"Mm...." Mark's sensual mouth twisted a little in response. "Destiny," he replied. "Meant to be here. Ah.... God, Cassidy, you're awesome. Stay here inside me. Stay."

Cassidy's hips had begun to pump of their own volition—albeit crookedly, one part of him mobile, the other not. But the grip around his cock stayed tight and velvety, and Mark arched his back and cried out. His own cock bounced up and down with his movements, and Cassidy moved one hand from his neck to that jutting piece of flesh.

Mark moaned again, head tilted back, and to Cassidy's surprise, he came, semen arching out from his tip, landing across Cassidy's abdomen, hitting his chest. The sight of him, abandoned in pleasure, in the two of them, sent Cassidy over the edge, and he grabbed Mark's hips and gave an awkward thrust, groaning in completion and seeing stars behind his eyes.

He was still spurting when Mark collapsed across his chest, and for a moment Cassidy's breaths carried the two of them, until Mark gave a little grunt of unhappiness.

"I should probably roll off you, but I don't wanna," he whined.

"I am not having a problem with this," Cassidy told him, eyes still closed. "I could be here forever."

"Okay," Mark mumbled, still sprawled. "Let me move my clothes in. I'll keep them in the guest room dresser. I'll be here forever."

Cassidy's breath caught, and he stopped breathing entirely, stunned by the suggestion.

Mark's body stiffened, and he slid off Cassidy's cock in a mess of come. "Unless, of course, it's too soon," he said, sounding chastened.

"No," Cassidy gasped, surprised at himself. "I mean, probably, but I don't care. You're practically living here anyway. Stay here until your brother's situated. Or, uhm, after, if we're still happy. I'm happy. Are you happy? The sex we just had was wonderful, by the way. Are we moving in?"

Mark rested his cheek against Cassidy's chest. "I'm really happy," he murmured. "But we should wait a while. Still, keep it in mind. I mean, I was freeloading off my mom before I came over here. We do what we just did much more often, I'll be freeloading off you for the rest of my life."

"Every night," Cassidy said dreamily. "We could do that every night."

Mark laughed throatily and licked a path across his nipple. "We could try," he said.

Sanity asserted itself. "Maybe," Cassidy mumbled, "we should, you know, wait until I get the cast off, at least. I'll have a sad little spider leg until I can work it back to health. You may want a chance to run away once you see it."

Mark laughed some more and licked again. "I doubt I will," he said, "but that's fine too. Maybe now that you've topped, you'll have to wait until I can top *you* to see if I'm the kind of lover you want living here full-time."

"I do," Cassidy sighed. "I don't see that changing."

The moment went still, and the face Mark turned toward him was completely serious. "I felt so shitty when I left work, and you made me so happy tonight. I know it's too soon—I do. But Cassidy?"

"Yeah?"

"I'm falling in love with you. I'm probably already there. I just want you to know that's where I'm headed. If you're not ready for happy-ever-afters and two toothbrushes and my nieces and nephew's pictures all over your fridge for ever and ever, you need to let me know now so I don't get my heart ripped out."

Cassidy caught his breath, his eyes burning. "You know you're talking about all I've ever wanted for my entire life, right? You and me, together, your family all in my business—even your dog, who is cowering under the bed—you know that's… that's my fantasy. That's like my reward for clean living. I'd be stupid to turn my back on that— and I'd really be stupid to turn my back on *you*."

"You don't strike me as a stupid man," Mark murmured. "I think this just might work."

Cassidy laughed again, not sure how much of what they just said was foolishness and how much of it was promises, but determined to show Mark that it was all possible. "Only stupid thing I've done so far is wait for a tree to hit me so we could meet," Cassidy said. "Once is enough. We've met. I'm going to count my blessings."

Mark gave a rumble of laughter and pushed up to take his mouth. "I care about you so much, Cassidy Hancock. You're *my* blessing, and I want to count on you every day."

Cassidy had no words for that—but then Mark was kissing him, and he was flying and words were unnecessary.

Even when they were true.

CHRISTMAS TUMBLED down upon them at warp speed. Cassidy regretfully dodged Harry's Christmas party, but he was able to finish the matching hat for Mark, which, as far as first Christmas presents went, he was pretty damned proud of.

He also managed a scarf for Dani, and a sweet quilted project bag for Yvonne, which he bought online from one of Dani's sources. He bought the kids small gifts, even LizBet, but after seeing the doll furniture, carved action figure, and very basic string puppet Keith produced from his woodshop, he promised himself he'd up his game next year. Crocheted toys were very en vogue right now, he thought. He would have to investigate.

And he'd also made a scarf and hat for Rose. He gave them to her on Christmas Eve, when Dani, true to her word, took him to the Christmas party. His coworkers seemed thrilled to see him, and for the first time, he realized that he'd never been invisible. That thing he'd said to Mark right after surgery, about having nobody—that hadn't been true.

He'd always had people who would have cared about him if he'd let them.

It just seemed that Mark and his amazing family had been the ones to show him that.

Dani brought him home that night, happy and breathless and still so very, very ready to have a break from people. Gus-Gus, who had been staying in his house for longer and longer intervals without incident, jumped about the wheelchair until Cassidy dropped his hand to fondle the oddly blocky head. He wondered for the millionth time how he could have lived his life so long without a dog.

"Now, remember," Dani told him as she pushed him down the hallway, "the kids will be up at ungodly a.m., but you're not expected to be, okay?"

"But I don't want your mom to have breakfast go cold." He grimaced. "Although I should probably not worry too much about breakfast. I need to count my calories if I'm ever going to be able to put weight on my leg again."

Dani blew a raspberry. "Only you," she said bluntly. "Only you, Cassidy Hancock, would be worried about your diet on Christmas Eve. Now I'm going to help you get into your jammies and take Gus-Gus out for a quick piddle." She paused. "After I take *you* in for a quick piddle, of course."

Cassidy winced. He recalled a time not too long ago when he would have held it, anxious and in pain, because he didn't want *one more person* to help him undress. But Dani had insinuated herself as easily into his life as everyone else in her family. He wasn't ecstatic about the situation, but he was grateful for the help.

"As long as you remember the rule," he said soberly.

"When you get the cast off your leg, nobody in the family shall ever speak again of how Mom and I got to see you wee. We get it, Cassidy. We've signed on the dotted line, in blood—it shall never leave our lips."

Cassidy snorted. What that possibly meant was everybody he ever met from this moment on was going to hear how Mark's entire family had to help him to the bathroom in the early days of their relationship. A month earlier, it would have been the end of the world.

Now he was merely hopeful he'd have other, better, happier, and funnier memories to contribute to the Taylors, so this one could quickly be forgotten.

But not all of it, he thought, after the embarrassing part was over. With Dani's help, he was changed and comfortable, sitting on the bed under the covers with Gus-Gus sprawled on the bed between him and Dani, both of them asleep in front of *A Christmas Story* when Mark arrived home.

"This is frickin' adorable," he said softly, walking into the room and kissing Cassidy on the cheek.

Dani yawned and blinked, and then grinned at her little brother. "And so is that," she said, indicating the kiss. "But now I'm pretty sure you want me to be gone."

"You can sleep in the guest room," Cassidy said. Dani apparently lived a couple of miles away in an apartment with a roommate who watched her cat when she was away for business.

She smiled softly but shook her head. "All my presents for people are at my apartment," she said on another yawn. "But thank you. Next time I keep you company while Mark's at work, I'll definitely do that." And with that she walked around the bed and gave Mark and Cassidy both kisses on the cheek before heading out.

Mark stripped quickly after that, dressed in his pajamas, and cozied up to Cassidy while the movie wound down. When it was done, he turned off the television and rested his head against Cassidy's shoulder.

"Good party?" he asked, sounding half-asleep.

"Yeah." Cassidy launched into a highlight reel, mostly designed to make Mark laugh, which was pretty much what Mark had given him about Harry's party.

When he was done and Mark was somnolent against him, he reached to turn off the light, and Mark slid down next to him.

"Cassidy?" Mark mumbled, burrowing closer.

"Yeah?"

"I have so many plans for us next Christmas. About how we'll make each other's parties. And what I want to give you. And how we'll spend the year between now and then. Tell me I'm not the only one."

"No," Cassidy whispered, his eyes burning. "No. I have so much hope for us. I want to tell you I love you, but it's probably too soon. I should probably wait until my cast comes off and you don't have to help me around my own house. But I'll save it for then, okay?"

"Yeah," Mark said. "I don't think that's how it works. I think if we love each other now, we get to say it now. Merry Christmas, Cassidy. I know it's quick, but I love you."

"I love you too."

A LATE START

MARK GOT up in the middle of the night to get a drink of water, and when he came back, instead of walking around to Cassidy's side of the bed, he had Cassidy scoot over to his side.

Cassidy did it without much complaining, which was nice of him, because he didn't realize Mark had plans.

Mark had been thinking logistics in terms of their lovemaking, and how much he wanted to take Cassidy's willing body. When he woke up the next morning spooned along Cassidy's back instead of his side, with Cassidy's cast on the *bottom* of his body, Mark thought his plan might work.

At around seven, which was probably when his brother's completely insane children were awake terrorizing their grandmother and father, he began his campaign.

"Cass?"

"Mmm?"

"I'm gonna get us naked."

"Sure."

He didn't sound like he believed Mark—or was particularly awake—but Mark figured he'd wake up enough to decide by the time Part A of the plan was finished. Being tender—and with playful kisses on bare skin—he slipped off Cassidy's pajamas and boxers under the covers, and then his own. He slid back into bed and pressed his naked body against his lover's, kissing between his shoulder blades and beginning a slow seduction as Cassidy tried to swim up from the depths of his sleep.

"Wha're we doing?" he slurred as Mark slowly stroked his burgeoning erection.

"We're going to have sex," Mark said, hoping he didn't sound too predatory. Damn, he wanted this. He wanted Cassidy to be all his. Forget waiting for the cast to come off—if they could do this and make it work, he was going to declare tentative victory, get the rest of his stuff tomorrow because he was moving in, and Merry Christmas to them both.

"Mm… that feels nice," Cassidy rumbled. "But don't we have to be there for breakfast?"

"Forget breakfast," Mark mumbled. "They'll start breakfast when we get there." He slid his hand under the pillow for lube and slicked up two fingers. Then he propped up Cassidy's good leg, foot on his cast, and opened Cassidy's body for pillage.

"Oh my!" Cassidy said, sounding very awake when Mark began to toy with his entrance. "That's a surprise!"

"A good one?" Mark hoped, stroking one finger in and out. "The kind with tinsel and bows?"

"Yeah, sure—that kind of surprise—oh! Oh wow!" Mark had added another finger. "And that's an even bigger surprise!"

Mark chuckled, wanting his hand back so he could stroke Cassidy's chest and play with his nipples and stroke his cock. "Want an even *bigger* surprise?" he asked, placing himself at Cassidy's entrance.

"*Yes!*"

Oh yes.

Mark's rhythm wasn't too fast—it couldn't be—but coupled with Cassidy's beautiful responses, the way he rocked back and forth just as Mark needed him to, the way he begged for touches, his nipples, his cock, and then used his own hands because Mark only had one that could reach—all of it made the experience exquisite and beautiful.

Mark wanted this. He drove himself into Cassidy's body like he'd driven himself into the man's life—without reservation or conscience.

And Cassidy gave back without inhibition or fear.

It was beautiful, perfect, and as Mark's climax snuck up on him, a surprise convulsion of need and seed, Cassidy gasped and clenched down, pulling Mark into the here and now with the force of his own orgasm.

They both gasped and cried out and then went limp into the mattress, and Mark kissed his way down Cassidy's spine as he waited for the moment they absolutely, positively must separate.

"Mm," Cassidy mumbled. "That was glorious. Why'd we do that?"

"Because I love you," Mark said. "And I don't want to wait until your leg is better. I want to tell you now. Merry Christmas, Cassidy. I love you. I want you in my bed all the nights we can manage. I'm moving in tomorrow—is that okay?"

"Yeah," Cassidy said. "I love you too. I won't argue. Move in. We'll make it work. Merry Christmas, Mark. Thank you for all my gifts."

Mark chuckled. "I haven't even given you your gifts yet."

"Yeah, you have," Cassidy mumbled, obviously falling back asleep. "My life. It's still my life, but it's got all the things I ever wanted in it. Those are your gifts, your family's gifts. I can't unwrap them, but I'm not giving them back."

Mark chuckled softly and nuzzled his cheek against Cassidy's spine. "I won't ask for them back," he promised, and then he fell back asleep too.

THEY BOTH woke up two hours later because Mark's phone was buzzing.

It was his mother, asking when they'd be there for Christmas.

What followed was a frantic, almost comical effort of the two of them to get dressed and ready to go one house down to celebrate Christmas. Brushing teeth, putting on pants, using the bathroom, all of it made more cumbersome and more irritating by Cassidy's cast and Gus-Gus's frantic need to pee. Finally Mark had to take Gus-Gus out and leave Cassidy to dress himself.

When he came back inside a few minutes later, Cassidy had struggled back into one of his pairs of "modified" pants, complete with boxer shorts, and into a dress shirt and sweater. He grinned proudly at Mark, showing off white teeth, and Mark laughed and promised he'd be out in a sec.

He dressed in record time, and when he came out, he helped Cassidy gather the pile of presents they'd put underneath the tinsel-decorated window and put them in a canvas grocery bag to bring to Mark's family.

Cassidy didn't have to tell Mark this was the first time he'd done this—*really* done this, not as an obligation from a lonely child, but as an opportunity for a happy adult.

Finally they were ready for Mark to push him down the walkway to the sidewalk, then down the sidewalk to Mark's mother's house, and Mark's chest ached as he saw Keith had installed a makeshift wheelchair ramp to get Cassidy up the two porch steps and into the foyer.

Mark bent and whispered in his ear as he saw that. "This is going to be a good day."

Cassidy sent a smile over his shoulder, and they entered the chaos, the happy children chattering, Keith and Dani and Yvonne discussing what needed to be done for breakfast, and even the stereo playing Christmas music loud enough to be heard over the noise.

Yvonne broke off from her business in the kitchen and gave Mark a big hug and a kiss, and then bent to do the same thing for Cassidy.

"Glad you could make it," she chided, and Mark saw Cassidy blush.

"Sorry," he mumbled. "Didn't mean to be late for Christmas."

"Oh no, my boys," she said happily. "Christmas is whenever you show up with the people you love. It's impossible to be late for Christmas. Now come inside and ruin your breakfast with cookies."

Mark pushed the chair through to the living room and bent down to whisper in his ear. "Hear that? It's impossible to be late for Christmas."

Cassidy laughed softly. "Since Christmas started in bed with you this morning, I think you might be right."

Mark kissed the top of his head before nuzzling his temple.

Yeah, he thought. Yeah. There was a lot for them to do as a couple, but he had all the hope in the world. After all, if he could get Cassidy Hancock not to worry about being late for Christmas, it was possible they'd be on time for many Christmases to come.

CHRISMYTHS

CHAPTER 1: NOBODY EVER MISSES THE BIG CITY

"ANDY—ANDY, IT'S time to get up. Your train leaves in an hour."

Andy Chambers rolled over in bed and pulled the pillow over his head. "You can't make me," he said. "I live here, I pay rent, you can't make me."

Eli Engel, boy of his dreams, cosigner of his lease, welcome pain in his ass, smacked him on the backside.

"Andy, you have to. It's *your* family. I'm just some schmuck that's stolen you away for the last three years."

Andy groaned and eyeballed the man he loved more than life. "I keep telling you they don't think like that."

Eli's mouth—full and smiling most of the time—went crooked. "And yet they don't visit either."

"They think New York City is evil," Andy muttered. "And Brooklyn's the moon." With ill-disguised reluctance, Andy swung his feet over the edge of the bed and straight into his moccasins while he reached for the sweatshirt he kept by the end table. Their apartment in trendy Williamsburg had great hardwood floors, but those floors got chilly in December. The whole apartment got chilly in December. Mostly, Andy and Eli fought the cold by wearing layers around the apartment and by fucking like monkeys. Even though he was launching straight into the shower from bed, Andy didn't want to make the trip without an extra layer.

"Well, family is important," Eli said. "You go visit your family for Christmas, and I'll be here when you get back. Now shower. I'll go make you breakfast."

Andy watched his retreating back miserably. "Family is important," he'd said. But Eli didn't *have* any family. He'd been kicked out of his parents' house for being gay and had spent months on the streets before being taken in by Rainbow House, a shelter down in Bedford/Stuyvesant. They'd helped him apply for college and get scholarships—he'd gone to NYU, gotten a degree in management, and turned right back around and started working at Rainbow House, doing everything from fundraising to organizing sports programs for the residents. Rainbow House was open to everybody, but it specialized in LGBTQ youth, and Eli was their biggest success story and most ardent advocate. He loved the employees there with all his heart, but when all was said and done, they all went home to their families for Christmas.

For the last three years, Andy had spent Christmas with Eli, celebrating with the residents of Rainbow House.

Having Eli tell him "Family is important, go visit yours," was painfully generous—and Andy hated it.

But his mother had been absolutely incessant.

"Two phone calls a day, Andy," Eli had told him at the beginning of December. "I mean, I get your family is super close, but two phone calls a day? Man, you've *got* to go visit them or they'll never leave us alone. We'll be answering their calls in the middle of sex into our sixties!"

Andy had snorted at that unlikely scenario, but he'd also softened. "Our sixties?" he'd asked winsomely. "You promise?"

Eli had looked away, biting his lip. Andy had done his best to help his lover believe in forever, but Eli had a lot of damage to overcome. That was okay—Andy was up for the job.

"Just go," he'd said, not looking Andy in the eyes. "Your job practically shuts down during those two weeks. Take the time off, go visit your parents, and come back to Brooklyn."

Andy had sighed and rubbed the back of his neck. It was true that his job in a local tech firm really *did* shut down over Christmas, but that's not what Eli was saying.

Andy knew because Eli had been saying it from the very beginning of their relationship.

Back Then

"OH! HEY! You dropped your umbrella!"

Andy was the kind of guy who bought trench coats with an umbrella pocket and then had an extra spot on his waterproof briefcase for a spare. But this guy, with curly dark hair falling into brown eyes and a bony jaw covered with stubble, looked like the kind of guy who went out in the rain frequently and then wondered why he caught cold. Andy had been watching the guy on the train for the last few weeks, feeling vaguely protective over him. Andy had been rooming in Park Slope then, with a group of new hires for his tech firm. They all commuted to Williamsburg, and Andy had seen this guy getting off in Bed/Stuy and had worried for him. He'd looked so earnest, so focused on being somewhere else. Andy, who had grown up in the country, had loved the city because it meant he had to be focused on the *now*.

"Oh," said the sloe-eyed stranger. "Thank you." He gave a shy smile. "Good luck, this." He shook the umbrella Andy had handed him. "It looks like rain."

"Well, stay dry," Andy had replied awkwardly. "Maybe I'll see you tomorrow?"

For a moment he saw hope in the stranger's eyes. Excitement.

"You'll have better things to do tomorrow," the stranger told him with a wink, and then his stop had come and he'd been gone. Andy had turned to Zinnia, one of his roommates, and sighed.

"What's wrong?" she asked. "I've seen him on the train before. I think he thinks you're cute."

"I thought so too, but he seems absolutely certain I'll have something else better to do."

Zinnia snorted. "Prove him wrong!"

The next day, Andy had tucked three kinds of protein bars in his pocket—one with chocolate, one with nuts, and one that was a veganese delight. As the dark-eyed stranger stood to get ready for his stop, Andy held out the breakfast bars and said, "Here, breakfast on me."

The stranger had gaped at him in surprise. "I, uhm—"

"I bet you skip it, right?" Andy said. "I mean, you look super focused on your job or whatever, but you should have breakfast."

The subway hissed in preparation to stop, and Andy felt a little desperate.

"Please?" he said. "I'll bring you one tomorrow too!"

"Tomorrow's Saturday," the stranger told him, his wide, full mouth quirking up in a smile.

"Then I'll bring you one Saturday," Andy said, pretty much past pride. This man's brown eyes were fathomless, like the night sky full of stars.

"Okay," the man said, taking the one with chocolate. "I'll bring coffee."

"Lots of cream and sugar," Andy said, trying not to be embarrassed. Since he'd come to the city, it seemed like all New Yorkers took their coffee black.

The next day, Andy dressed casually, wearing his wool peacoat from his Vermont winters instead of his slick lined trench coat. But he still carried an umbrella—and a selection of protein bars—and took the same train as usual to Williamsburg.

This time when the doors opened three stops before Bed/Stuy, he saw the dark-eyed stranger get in, carrying two paper cups of coffee.

With a shy smile, the man came and sat down next to him, handed him the coffee, and accepted the breakfast bar in return.

"My name's Eli," he said, and Andy noted he'd tried to shave in the last twenty-four hours, but there were still patches of stubble like he'd forgotten a lot.

"I'm Andy."

"So, Andy, where are we going today?"

Andy had grinned. "I just got a raise. I was hoping to find an apartment in Williamsburg. Want to come with me?"

Eli grinned. "Sure. I work for a nonprofit—it'll be nice to dream."

And Now

THEY'D EVENTUALLY found the perfect apartment, and by then, Andy wanted Eli to move into it with him. The only problem, he realized, was that to Eli, all of it—Andy, the job he loved, the safety of the home—all of it was a dream, and he still dreaded waking up to an awful reality of being alone every morning.

And now Andy was *leaving* him for Christmas.

Andy raced through his shower and getting dressed. His suitcase was already packed, including gifts that needed wrapping. He wanted as much time with Eli as possible before he took off for the train.

Eli was already dressed when Andy got out, and he'd scrambled eggs with some toast for breakfast. Andy looked at the plate waiting for him on the counter in the kitchen and wanted to cry.

He'd been the one who'd made Eli eat breakfast for three years. Eli *never* remembered to eat—had become too used to *not* eating when he'd lived on the street or been broke and going through school. Three years of Andy stuffing his pockets with breakfast bars or getting up early so breakfast was on the table, and now Andy was leaving him and Eli was the one sending him off with breakfast. It didn't seem fair.

He'd even sliced some green onion and tomato to put on top.

"What?" Eli asked anxiously as Andy stared at the plate. "It's not good?"

Andy forced himself to take a bite. "It's delicious, babe. You're getting better."

Eli rolled his eyes. "You left enough food for an army."

As if. "The refrigerator is too small for an army. And you'll run out in a week, so, you know, don't forget to eat."

Eli shrugged. "Most of me will still be here if—when you get back." He grimaced and clapped his hand over his mouth, but he'd said it, and Andy knew he'd meant it.

"*When.* Oh my God, *Eli.* We've lived here for three years. What do you think is going to happen? I'm going to go visit my parents and forget I'm in love?"

"It's Vermont over Christmas, Andy. You've seen the propaganda. You'll go home, your parents will convince you the city was a bad dream, and I'll be the first thing you forget."

Andy gaped at him, suddenly angry. Three years? Three years and Eli didn't trust him more than this? "You complete asshole," he said, voice choked. "You think I could forget you? I'll show you. I'll come back in two weeks, and you're gonna have to eat those words."

Eli regarded him with deep skepticism. "You gonna cook them up like pizza?"

Damn him. Andy's mouth quirked. "Yes, asshole. I'm going to cook up a giant pizza that says Eli, I Love You and make you eat the fucking pizza. Two weeks. Love to Mom, a few handshakes with Dad, some bonding with my siblings while I convince them to get the hell out of Vermont, and I'll be home before you know it." His whole demeanor softened. "And maybe then we can get a pet for the apartment?"

They'd put it off because Eli didn't think it was fair to bring something into a situation that could change. Andy wasn't sure how three years didn't make a solid enough foundation to bring a pet into but dammit, he wanted a cat!

Eli shifted. "Do you think we're ready for pet ownership?"

"Yes, Eli! I work from home three days a week. Why can't we get a cat?" He tried to remember his patience. "Baby, we live a good life. We live a *great* life. Don't you want to, I don't know, *expand* that life a little? A cat would be a good thing, don't you think?"

Eli took a deep breath and closed his eyes. "I'm sorry. I don't mean to be so insecure—"

Andy abandoned his eggs and moved to the other side of the table, breathing out, and rubbed Eli's arms briskly with his cupped palms. "Maybe when I get back from this trip, you'll see. Nothing's going to break us apart, okay?"

Eli leaned forward and rested his cheek on Andy's shoulder. He did that when he was feeling soft, and it always made Andy feel like king of the world. He wrapped his arms around the boy of his dreams and squeezed him tight.

"I've got to go," he whispered. "I'll call you every day. I promise."

"I love you," Eli offered, still taking comfort, and Andy took it as a win. Eli wasn't demonstrative by nature—too many years of having nobody had left him wary of being affectionate, even in private. But an unsolicited "I love you," from him was like gold.

Andy hugged him even tighter and then moved back enough to tilt his head up and take his mouth, softly at first, and then as he remembered this had to last through two weeks of his parents, his sisters, his damned hometown, he deepened the kiss, took more, pulled as much of Eli's sweetness into his soul as he could to sustain him for the coldness of winter in Vermont. In these moments he felt like the power of his six-foot-plus, two-hundred-pound frame wasn't wasted. His entire purpose was to keep Eli Engel—*his* angel—safe from all the harm the world had to offer.

Finally Eli pushed him away, reluctance written in every line of his body. "You need to leave," he said. "You're gonna miss your train, and then your mom's going to make you go next year!"

Triumph! "You said next year!" Andy replied, his face lighting up. "I'm bringing you crow pizza when I come back—you just watch!"

And with that he had to run. Eli was right. Between the slow elevators of their building and the struggle to get a cab to get him to the station, he really might miss the train!

And he had to go now so Eli would know he'd be back.

CHAPTER 2: HARD TO BE A SAINT IN THE CITY

AFTER ANOTHER frantic kiss, Andy dashed out the door, leaving the apartment a cold, vacant place, and Eli tried hard not to get too emotional. There were things to do, right? It was the Christmas season; the kids at the shelter needed a thousand things, and Eli was in charge of Christmas with them this year. It didn't even bother him that he was Jewish by birth. Christmas was all about the fantasy. The idea that there was a perfect day and a perfect love and that children would be cared for by magic or fate or a responsible adult were all equally unlikely in the minds and hearts of the kids at Rainbow House.

Andy had asked him to come to Vermont, but this was the one year Eli absolutely, positively could not leave. The fact that Andy understood this sort of made him the perfect boyfriend, but it could also mean Andy was totally okay with leaving Eli behind.

Argh!

Nobody kissed like that when they were totally okay with leaving someone behind, right?

In the end, that was the thought that got Eli going. He made quick work of the kitchen—but first he finished the eggs Andy hadn't eaten. Eli didn't waste food, ever. He'd known too many hard times when food was a luxury. Andy had known that when packing little homemade dinners for him, Eli noticed as he put the eggs in the fridge and took stock with a little lump in his throat.

Ten days' worth of dinners—along with a note that said there would be a food delivery on the twenty-ninth of December so Eli would have food until the third. Eli also knew Andy had stocked the freezer with frozen burritos, but Eli wouldn't let Andy's hard work go bad. Andy knew that.

Andy knew him so well.

That first day after they'd met on the subway, the one thing that had drawn Eli to him—besides his big blond good looks and country-boy smile, of course—had been his way of paying complete attention to

Eli, as though Eli was his favorite subject and Andy was studying him for the big test.

Back Then

"SO YOU know everything about me," Andy said, taking Eli by the hand and pulling him off the subway car at the Williamsburg stop. "You know I'm a tech coder, you know I grew up in a tiny town, mom, dad, two kid sisters—so boring, yawn now. But what about you?"

"Nothing to know," Eli mumbled. The streets of New York were always so busy. He liked being able to tuck his hands into his pockets and keep his head down and go. Walking hand in hand with someone was harder. He had to be aware of his space and Andy's space and—oh. Andy drew nearer to him, bumped shoulders, and kept up that grip on his hand.

This was nice. Andy's body heat radiated out from the protective wool of his peacoat, and Eli felt like a lizard basking in the sun.

"There can't be nothing!" Andy laughed. They came to the real-estate agent's office, which had a small blue-and-white striped valance to protect people from the weather. Still smiling, he drew Eli under the valance and looked into his face. "You have the prettiest eyes," he murmured before bending to place a quick kiss on Eli's lips. "There's got to be a story in there somewhere."

Then he lifted his head and turned to open the door and let them into the small office, greeting Elaine Stritch, his agent, with a hearty hello. Eli was left, heart pounding, to listen as Andy negotiated the three visits they were going to do that day and introduce Eli as his new friend who was helping him get a feel for Brooklyn.

It turned out to be bullshit, of course. Andy worked in Williamsburg and had for nearly a year. He walked down the street with that shoulder-swaggering confidence that made people part for him, and Eli began to cling to his hand just to ride his wake.

The agent was competent—which meant she showed them the apartment, talked for a moment about the features, and then left them alone to decide.

But as they looked around each place, Eli started to realize that
Andy was looking for more than just an apartment. He was looking for
a life, a future, and that… that blew Eli's mind.

"No," Andy murmured at the first one. "No windows. We need
windows to the outside. I don't care if they're in the front, in the kitchen,
or in the back—there's got to be a window so we can look outside and
see what kind of day it's going to be."

Eli had snorted. "So *you* can look outside and see what kind of day
it's going to be."

"So me and the person of my choice can look outside and see what
kind of day it's going to be," Andy corrected him. "I'm not going to live
here alone. I'm going to settle down."

"Just like that. You assume you're going to settle—"

Andy had kissed him then too, until Eli couldn't remember what
he'd been going to say.

"And we need a guest room," Andy said breathlessly when they
came up for air. "Because my family's going to visit. And yours too."

"I don't have any family," Eli confessed in a daze. This wasn't
first-date conversation. Hell, this wasn't even *date* conversation. Eli
didn't tell *anybody* this. The facts of his somewhat pathetic existence
were locked behind his eyes, because he hated pity.

"Well, you'll have mine," Andy offered blithely. "And if not
visiting family, visiting friends. And if not visiting friends, we'll adopt."

Eli sputtered. "Adopt? You're already planning for kids?"

Andy had paused then, gazing into Eli's eyes with absolute
determination. "You want kids, don't you? At least one? To open your
home to a small person, someone we can shower with affection and
spend time with, and love?"

Eli had been helpless then. Absolutely helpless. He'd been kicked
out of his house when his parents found out he was gay. Ever since, he'd
lived with the fantasy of having a child of his own, whom he swore he
wouldn't let down. Someone who would be treated like a child should
be—with love and care and attention and laughter. It was his pet plan,
held close to his heart even as he built up his credibility and trust at
Rainbow House. Someday he'd learn enough from the kids at Rainbow
House to feel like he could give a child a childhood, make his house a
home.

And here was this giant of a man who brought him breakfast and found his umbrella and grabbed his hand to dream impossible dreams... and they had the same dream?

He'd almost run away then, terrified by all the promise in Andy's sparkling blue eyes. But when he took a step back, he realized he was already in Andy's arms, clinging to his casual shirt underneath the peacoat, sheltered by the peacoat like a duckling under a parent's wing.

"Someday," he rasped.

"Me too," Andy murmured. "So yeah. We hold out for a guest room that can be a kid's room. And windows so it doesn't feel like a prison. And hardwood floors and arched doorways."

"Arched doorways?" Eli asked, looking around at the very pedestrian lines of the apartment they were in.

"Damned straight."

"Well, now you've gone too far."

And Andy had grinned then, blinding him with his vision, his dream for the future, the intoxicating fantasy that Eli would be in on that dream from the ground floor.

It took three more months and countless visits to the real-estate office for Andy to find the perfect apartment. By the time he did, he'd had Eli so wrapped around his heartbeat that subletting his own tiny hole in the wall to a recent graduate from Rainbow House and moving in with Andy had seemed inevitable.

But Eli had lived with him for two years before he gave up his lease and let the graduate have the apartment for real.

And Now

"HEY, ELI! Are we getting the tree today?"

Eli smiled at Lola as he walked through the door of the shelter. The outside of Rainbow House was pretty impressive. Taking up what used to be an old theater, before extensive remodeling, the scalloped overhang that took up nearly a quarter of a city block had been painted with a series of rainbows over the stucco. Yes, time and weather kept trying to dull their luster, but every two years or so, somebody wrangled some extra money for paint out of the budget and let the residents do the paint job. The rainbows had turned into murals, and this last one had turned into watercolor rainbows that bled into flags representing as many countries as the kids could possibly fit on the marquee. The result was slightly chaotic but very universal, and it made Eli smile every day he worked.

On this day, he'd walked through the grand entryway, between the tables set up to admit new shelter residents or simply pass out food to those who didn't want to stay but were hungry, and into the foyer of the house itself.

The foyer had been kept grand, and while the theater had been renovated to a two-story house—top story for dormitories, bottom story for schoolrooms, offices, and medical facilities—the foyer still gave a sense of greatness to the battered old girl that Eli loved as much as the rainbows.

Sometimes old things did need to change, but sometimes they just needed some paint and some elbow grease to not just *change* but *transform.*

"Yeah, honey. I promised. The delivery guys are supposed to get here to set up in an hour."

Lola nodded as though of course that would happen, but Eli caught her look of suspicion. Well, Lola had been thrown out of the house a year ago, at sixteen, when she'd come home with green stripes in her long hair and high heels. She'd been out on her first date as Lola instead of Chris, and she'd gotten caught, and that lovely champagney joy of first love—and first love with a boy who knew her for exactly who she was at that—had quickly become a fight for survival on the streets.

It had taken her a week to find Rainbow House, and Eli didn't want to know what she'd been through in that time, although much of it was plainly written in her distrustful eyes and the way her full lower lip trembled whenever something threatened happiness.

But Eli had made it a rule not to make promises to these kids he couldn't keep, and he had done the fundraising—and Andy's firm had pitched in a *lot*—as well as made the order, ensured the order, double-checked the order and delivery, to make sure *this* promise, of all the ones that had been broken to these kids, would be fulfilled.

"See here?" he said, pulling out his phone. "What's that say?"

She narrowed her eyes and studied the readout. "It says delivery in an hour. The car is coming in from upstate now."

"Truck," he said. "We're getting a ten-foot tree, delivered and set up, complete with pedestal."

"And decorations?" she asked suspiciously.

"No, not decorations! That's our job!"

She rolled her eyes. "Popcorn strings and paper chains?"

"Well, yes," he said. "But we also have glitter, felt, popsicle sticks, and a whole lot of patterns that Mrs. Wheeler printed out. Have you *been* to the craft room today? I promise you, there are some prime craft supplies in there. Go look."

She thawed a little. "Okay. But someday, I'm going to have all glass ornaments. No janky shit on my tree."

"Fine, but if a kid you love makes it, it's not 'janky shit.' It's 'sentimental decorating.' I swear. It's a thing."

That got a small smile. "It's janky shit, but you're a nice guy for trying," she said.

"Then go do some trying yourself," he said, laughing. "Shoo! I know the younger kids need someone to ooh and ah over their own janky shit."

And that got a laugh; Lola missed her own younger siblings, but she'd done a nice job of adopting some of the kids at the shelter as her own. And any kid who'd been thrown out of the house at ten, eleven, or twelve for things that they barely understood themselves was desperate for someone to tell them they were okay.

Eli suppressed a sigh at the thought and walked through the foyer to check on Mrs. Wheeler.

Mrs. Wheeler was a retired schoolteacher who devoted three afternoons a week to the shelter, usually helping with lessons and continuation school packets, but this close to Christmas she was all about the arts and crafts—and so were the kids. Thanks to Mrs. Wheeler they had glitter candles and glitter lights and glitter banners and sprays of hand-crocheted stars in every corner of the foyer, all of them awaiting the big tree.

"How's it going, Margie?" Eli asked as he poked his head into the craft room. As expected, her demesne was a combination of military organization and happy chaos that probably would have driven Eli absolutely bonkers but that the kids seemed to really thrive on.

"Go away, Eli," Margie said happily. "Your need for order stresses the kids out."

"Aye aye, chief," he said, ducking his head as he went to close the door. Before it clicked shut, she stopped him with a little wave before she pushed her ample body up and moved creakily toward the entrance.

"It's coming, right?" she said softly. "The kids are so excited."

He held out his phone and showed her the delivery truck, now ten minutes closer than it had been when he'd shown Lola. "So it says," he told her. "But they haven't called me yet—"

At that moment, his phone buzzed.

"Don't get excited," he muttered. "It's Andy."

"Isn't he on his trip?" she asked.

He nodded and stepped back into the hallway, hitting Call as he went. "Eli Engel," he said crisply, because he didn't *get* gooey when he was here. It was absolutely imperative that the kids believe the adults around them were drama free. Most of them had gotten enough drama from their homelives and were getting a continuous supplemental dose from draconian politics, uncertain futures, and their own hormones.

"Hello, Eli Engel," Andy said teasingly. "Your tree is on its way."

Eli blinked. "Wait, they called *you*?"

"Mm-hmm," Andy replied, keeping his voice deliberately vague. "No, I don't know why, but I know you and the kids are probably freaking out a little by now, so I thought I'd let you know you should have the tables cleared out in the next half hour."

Eli nodded, remembering the first three times they'd done this, when Andy had been the driving force behind it.

Nobody had thought they could get a Christmas tree that first Christmas.

Andy had been the one to suggest some fundraising, to hit up his bosses, to give Eli a list of other contributors—particularly those located in Bed/Stuy who wouldn't mind big gold foil stars with their names on them.

And Andy had been the one to spend a week of evening dinners on the phone proving to Eli that it could be done.

"We can do that," he said. "Thank you. How's the train ride?"

Andy grunted. "Not as quick as a plane ride but with much less risk of getting snowed in."

Eli laughed softly and found an alcove—once upon a time it had been a phone nook—and he backed into it, pretending it meant real privacy. "Thanks for the heads-up, babe. I appreciate it."

"Not a problem." Andy's voice was laced with fondness. "I know how you worry." He paused. "And there should be a couple of boxes of big glass ball ornaments in different colors to go on the tree. The guy said there was a special or something—I have no idea. Anyway, I know Lola thinks it can't be a real tree without super fancy ornaments, so be sure to put her in charge of making sure those get on the tree. Tell her you're taking pictures for me, so I expect a full report."

Eli nodded. "Yeah," he said. "I'll tell her. She'll be *so* excited."

"Good," Andy said, a satisfaction in his voice Eli couldn't identify. "Now tell me you love me and then go have your day. I know you've got a busy one planned."

"I love you," Eli said wistfully. "I'll take lots of pictures."

"I love you back. And you'd better. Now, bye."

And with that he ended the call.

He was right about Eli's day—from checking to make sure the kitchen was stocked to looking in on a couple of new residents to having a meeting about funding, his day was packed, and that didn't include the tree decorating and the trays of hot chocolate and the donated, kid-decorated sugar cookies.

All of it was a breathless flurry of activity and productivity that made Eli proud every day.

It wasn't until he was helping to clean up after the tree had been decorated—and wondering if he was going to get home before nine at night so he could eat one of Andy's premade dinners—that he saw a spare piece of paper on the ground by the tree.

It was from a box of ornaments, and it had the usual stuff—number of boxes (five), color of ornaments in box (one box of silver, one of gold, one each of blue, red, and green), number of ornaments per box (twelve), and person to be billed for the ornaments in the boxes.

Andrew Matthew Chambers.

Eli knew the address—it was his address too.

"Whatcha got there?" Margie asked, heaving by him with a trash bag and a broom.

Eli shook his head and wiped his eyes with the back of his hand, and she snatched the paper away.

It took her a moment, and she put the paper down and handed him a ripped-off portion of industrial paper towel.

"Aw, baby," she said softly. "That boy really loves you."

Eli nodded. "I know," he said through a constricted throat.

"He really did hate leaving you for the holidays."

"I know." His lower lip was wobbling.

"Maybe you should trust he's going to come back, you think?"

"M-m-m-m-ayyy—"

"Don't hurt yourself," she murmured, setting her cleaning supplies down on a table and holding her arms out.

Eli found himself engulfed in a big, squishy Margie hug—a thing he'd seen her offer countless kids before him but had never once been subjected to himself.

What was he going to do when Andy decided not to come back to Brooklyn?

CHAPTER 3: EX-BOYFRIENDS ARE ALWAYS HOTTER THAN YOU EXPECT

"OH DEAR God," Andy said as he got off the train. "No. No. No no no no no no."

Porter Burrell grinned at him, his famous eyebrows-o'-lust dancing in response to Andy's less than enthusiastic salutation.

"Aw, come on, Dandy. It's not my fault your family needed an extra hand to pick you up from the train station. St. Albans is a long way off!"

Andy scrubbed at his face with his hand and double-checked his backpack and his big suitcase. He looked around the train station unhappily, but he knew what he'd find. By the time the train had gotten this far north, there had been a small crowd coming from all the cars put together, and they'd all gotten off on the platform. Most of them were either moving into the small but hopefully warm station or being greeted by a friend or loved one in the cock-shriveling cold that came with Vermont this time of year.

If Andy couldn't see his family—or his father's rather beat-up Chevy Suburban—from the platform, it wasn't like they could be hiding behind in the parking lot.

And given that Foxglove was about thirty miles from the station, it wasn't likely his family had simply forgotten to mention they couldn't make it to the station to come get him. Nope—this had setup written all over it.

"Keep your hand off my ass or I swear to Christ I'll get right on the next train back to Brooklyn," Andy snarled. "Which one of my soon-to-be-disowned family members sent you anyway?"

Porter grimaced and went to hoist Andy's suitcase over his shoulder—he was unfairly tall and unfairly muscular, and when they'd been in high school, that had turned Andy's key.

Eighteen was not exactly an age known for its sound reasoning or penis-free decision making.

AMY LANE

"That would be your mother. But you don't need to sound so snotty. I think they were hoping we could catch up."

Andy gave him an unfriendly glare. "I can carry that," he said, and Porter shrugged.

"Throw me a bone, here, Andy. It's not like there's another gay man in a forty-mile radius of Foxglove. Coming out to the station is sort of a big deal for me."

Andy scrubbed at his face and tried not to be a dick. Porter hadn't been a bad guy—or even a bad boyfriend—and this really wasn't his fault.

"A bone but not a boner," he said on a sigh. "And thank you for getting my bag."

"That's the sweet guy I knew in school." Porter gave a happy grin. "So tell me why your mother wants us to hook up again. As I recall, she was not all that thrilled about the event when we were seniors in high school."

"Because it kept happening in her SUV," Andy said, wincing in embarrassment. Ah, to be young and horny and to not give a thought to the future boyfriend who might not think high school shenanigans were hilarious. "She saw the container of wet wipes and took it all the way to Pawlet to have it disinfected."

Porter winced. "Yikes. Okay, so maybe that wasn't real considerate of us. Teenagers are *dicks*, aren't they?"

Andy had to laugh. "Some of them, yes. Blue Tahoe?" Because the ginormous blue Ford was the only vehicle in the lot that made sense for someone like Porter, with his larger-than-life shoulders and larger-than-average cock.

"You know it," Porter said. "And I swear, no wet wipes—I get laid in my house like a human being."

Andy grimaced and glanced around, noting the one restaurant, the pharmacy, the post office, and the gas station, all of which were situated on opposite corners of a remote edge of St. Albans. Many of the towns in Vermont—including the one he and Porter had grown up in—looked just like this.

"That, uh, happen a lot these days?"

Their graduating class had consisted of thirty people, twenty of them destined to spend their lives in Foxglove and ten of them hell-bent on the holy grail of Get The Fuck Out. Porter, in fact, had been a charter member of the GTFO contingent, but then his mother had gotten sick in his first year of college. He'd written Andy an email saying he was going home for a semester to help out, but Andy had read it and he'd known. There was no way to financially recover from his mother's medical bills, whether or not she recovered.

She did, eventually, recover, but Porter had been stuck in their hometown, running his own computer service from their home and doing odd jobs for the local contractors so he could continue to assist with her health needs.

Andy wasn't asking his friend if he was *single*; he was asking him if he had any hope of *not* being single, and Porter knew it.

"There's enough closet cases to wax my knob," Porter said with a sheepish smile. "But you know. It's Foxglove. The only reason *we* hooked up was we kept catching each other checking out other guys."

Andy laughed, the last of his resentment drifting away like snow. It wasn't Porter's fault his parents had thrown them together, and he really was a nice guy who deserved a break.

"That's not true," Andy argued good-naturedly. "I was checking you out at least part of the time."

Porter guffawed like he was supposed to and piloted them out of the train station and toward the interstate.

"Look," he said, checking conditions carefully as he merged. "I've been looking forward to picking you up since your parents asked me, and not because I wanted to get in your pants."

"You were in love with my brain?" Andy shot back, and Porter laughed some more.

"*No*. Man, I'm *starving*. There's one decent restaurant in Foxglove, and I'm *dying* for some Thai. I kid you not—there's a little restaurant about five miles up the interstate. Let's go there, eat, catch up, I'll get you home, and you can chew out your parents there and I'll…." He let out a breath. "I'll have a chance to talk to someone who actually knows what it's like in the outside world. Is that okay?"

"Yeah. Sorry I snapped, Porter. I just, you know, left behind a boyfriend who's absolutely sure he's going to lose me to the wilds of Vermont, and I'm heading to parents who won't visit me in Brooklyn because they're afraid of cannibal soup kitchens or something equally weird. I *really* didn't want to leave Eli over Christmas. Having you show up instead of my mother…." He shook his head, remembering the sixty-dozen-and-fifteen phone calls that had precipitated this visit.

"Ah, Cindy," Porter said, nodding. "That woman has never met a tabloid headline she didn't fall in love with."

"If you knew how many hours we spent talking about Bat Baby, you'd send the nice people in the little white coats to my parents' house to take her away," he said bitterly and then tried to let go of his irritation.

"She's bored, Andy. Foxglove is a boring place. When her kids lived there it was one thing, but Charlie's finished junior college and has a grant to get a teaching degree out of state—"

"She never told me that!" Andy exclaimed. It would figure his mother hadn't clued him in for the good news during all of those discussions about Bat Baby—and about leaving Brooklyn.

"I don't think your mom's admitted it's happening," Porter said. "And Mary Beth's got a scholarship to NYU."

Andy felt an absolute thrill of excitement zip through him. "Really? *Really*? She's coming to New York?" He tried not to dance in his seat.

"Wow, Andy. She's your little sister. Try not get all gushy!"

Andy blew a raspberry. "Look, just because I don't visit as often as I should, doesn't mean I don't miss the girls! And I felt bad about deserting them when I went off to school as well. I would *love* it if my little sister went to NYU and I could meet her for lunch once a month and have her for small holidays and stuff. And I *really* want them to meet Eli." *That* was the best part right there. He'd gone home for a week during the summer for the last three years, although Eli had opted out, citing a complete allergy to things like mosquitos and rural lakes and chickens, but Andy really knew he hadn't wanted to get between Andy and his sisters and parents. But this—having his sister nearby—this was like the Christmas present he hadn't asked for but really wanted anyway.

Porter frowned. "They haven't met your boyfriend?"

Andy blew out a breath. "Well, they're allergic to Brooklyn, and Eli… he takes that shit personally. I mean, we got an apartment with a guest room pretty much so *my family* could visit, but Mary Beth didn't even come by on a college visit?" He let out a breath. "It's depressing."

"Aw, man," Porter said. "That *is* depressing. What do you think the problem is?"

Andy grunted. "The problem…? Is that Cindy Chambers doesn't want to admit that Foxglove, Vermont, isn't the center of the earth."

Porter blew out a breath. "Oh, come on, Andy, you can't blame her for missing you a little."

"I don't," Andy said, sighing. "I just...." He grimaced at Porter and tried to remember what he'd told Zinnia as it had become clear this situation wasn't going to be easily resolved. "I don't think it's occurred to them that I'm never moving home," he said at last. "And as much as I love them, I'm going to have to make it really clear that if it's a choice between my parents and Eli, I'm going to pick Eli every time."

"Mm. Oh! Thai food!" Porter knew better than to swerve, but Andy had to laugh when he went for the off-ramp to the little restaurant strip with his Thai place. "Okay," he murmured, continuing to steer. "I hear you. Family drama—not my favorite." He hemmed and hawed to himself for a couple of moments while he negotiated traffic and snow. "Okay, we're here. I can tell you what I was thinking now."

"That's great, Porter," Andy said dryly, not stating the obvious, which was that some people could very obviously figure out how to talk and drive at once.

"Hey, Peanut Gallery, no comments until you taste the Jasmine Blossom, okay? Their drunken noodles are to die for, and like I said, I'm starving."

Well, given it was the last chance to eat anything but Panda Express or Mom's home cooking, Andy couldn't argue.

"Fine," he said shortly. He disembarked from the Tahoe, pulling his hat closer over his ears and tucking his hands in his pockets for the trip through the parking lot.

"Okay," he said, after they'd gone inside and gotten a seat. He discreetly checked his phone messages too, not resting until he saw the text from Eli showing the Christmas tree being erected in the foyer.

Lola loves the decorations too. Please tell your sources at the delivery company thank you.

Andy laughed quietly to himself. Good. Eli didn't suspect a thing. He wasn't sure why it was important that the ornaments seem to come from a mysterious source, except that Eli didn't really believe in Christmas miracles or the kindness of strangers. If Andy could give Eli one thing, it was the hope that people would step up when he couldn't, because Eli was just one—admittedly awesome—man. Buying those big glass ball ornaments had filled Andy with a ridiculous amount of happiness over the past week, and knowing he'd done it anonymously only made that better.

Anything that made Eli happy made him happy, and he was pretty sure the Christmas tree would help do it. At least for now. Andy planned to make Eli happy for a lot of years to come.

"Okay what?" Porter asked.

"Okay, explain to me why I shouldn't get my panties in a wad about my parents trying to throw me at you like they're chucking a fish at a seal."

Porter chuckled. "Okay, so that should piss you off. I've got nothing. But...." He let out a big breath. "Look, man, I gave up a lot to go home and take care of my mom. And you know...." He sighed. "She's sort of a pistol." Tart-tongued and sharp-witted; Porter had his hands full....

"She loves you," Andy said, meaning it. Porter's mother knitted for him almost constantly. Perhaps because it was so damned cold in Vermont, or maybe because she didn't have words for how she felt about her baby boy, but she was always knitting sweaters with the most amazing colorwork and cables and such. Andy's mom knitted too, and Andy had to admit their work was breathtaking. Porter was wearing a hand-knitted sweater now, and it looked like something someone would buy in a boutique: cream-colored fisherman's wool transformed by two sticks and an irritable, bedridden woman.

"I know," Porter said. "And that's why I stay. But what I'm saying is, you have an actual life in Brooklyn. That doesn't mean break all ties—and I get that's why you came back for the holidays—but don't let them bully you home either."

"I can't," Andy said, meaning it. "Eli needs me."

Porter gave him a gentle smile. "That's awesome. But you know it means you've got to tell me all about your guy."

Andy's eyes burned. "That's like asking my mom if you want to see pictures of her dog."

Porter's laugh boomed through the little restaurant. "Oh my God. Start at his dreamy eyes, and don't stop until I'm half in love myself."

Andy nodded, for a moment so choked up he almost couldn't swallow. "You're a really good friend," he said, meaning it. "So, about Eli. The thing is, he left home when he was really young, so he forgets the finer points of taking care of himself. But at the same time, he wants to take care of *all* the kids without a home so they don't ever have to know what it's like. Let me tell you about the first time I saw him on the train...."

Back Then

"SO WHAT was wrong with that apartment?" Eli needled as they sat down to eat at Birds of a Feather. The place was a little pricier than their usual haunts, but Andy had noticed that Eli tended to love Chinese food the most, and he'd started to just casually invite him to places after their weekend apartment hunt. A part of him was dying to take Eli out to someplace special—to dress up, to wear ties and make a big-deal date of it, but he'd played his cards smart and close to his vest for the past few months. Weekend jaunts to go find his apartment had turned into texting during the week just to say hi. Texting during the week to say hi had progressed to Andy bringing Eli lunch once a week at work. Bringing lunch by at work had led to Andy devoting some of his weekend to volunteering at the shelter, and then casually suggesting he and Eli should go out to eat since it was Sunday and all.

And the whole time, Andy had kept up a subtle campaign of surprise kisses, twined fingers, cheerful good morning greetings, and free coffee to make Eli feel like his day wouldn't be complete without an Andy Chambers in it.

But his time was running out on his whole premise for seeing Eli on the weekends in the first place, and he knew it.

"Nothing," he said now, looking into Eli's eyes and trying to keep track of the question. God, those eyes, though, were fathomless. He had strong arched eyebrows and almost delicate features, but his eyes... dark and infinite, Andy would do almost anything to have Eli's full concentration on him.

Eli didn't do lies and didn't do bullshit. He'd almost put a kibosh on Andy's entire strategy when he'd discovered Andy didn't actually like protein bars or breakfast bars—he brought them on the train for Eli. Andy had been going to feed him a line of word salad about bringing the breakfast bars for Zinnia when he'd sensed that this moment here, this little white lie, could be the one that drove Eli away completely.

"I bring them for you," he'd confessed after a long moment of listening to the subway car clack down the tracks. "You don't ever look like someone's taking care of you. I want you to have breakfast and a good start to your day."

Eli's entire face had washed red, and he hadn't summoned a single thing to say for the rest of the ride. When his stop came, Andy had tucked Eli's favorite breakfast bar firmly in his pocket, and neither of them had mentioned it again.

Choosing a restaurant to go to after their weekend activities had been the same way. Andy had asked Eli his favorite takeout and then looked up places to go near where the real-estate agent had planned to take them during what had become their one Saturday a month of apartment hunting. Their other meals had been takeout in the front room with Andy's roommates, and while Eli was a welcome guest there, it was not exactly… intimate.

Andy was hoping—praying?—for an invite to Eli's apartment, which, according to him, consisted of a bed, a desk, a hot-plate, a minifridge, and a bathroom with a shower cubicle. It wasn't so much that Andy thought that would be the most romantic place in the world to make love—and he was *dying* to make love to Eli—it was that he knew once he got a glimpse of Eli's tiny apartment, Eli would trust him enough for the sex to actually mean something.

But that meant this question here—what was wrong with the last apartment?—was a potentially loaded gun. One wrong move, one wrong answer, and Andy might kill the relationship he'd worked so very hard to foster.

He went with honesty; it was the only thing that had worked so far.

"Nothing's wrong with it?"

"Not a thing," Andy confirmed.

"Then why did you tell her you'd get back to her?" Eli asked, barely looking at the dumplings that had just been set in front of them. "You're going to lose the apartment if you don't say something, like, yesterday."

"I'm not ready," Andy replied with dignity. He grabbed a potsticker, because *he* was starving.

"What do you mean you're not ready?" Eli asked, laughing. Finally he noticed the food and picked up a dumpling with his chopsticks. "You've been looking for an apartment for months!"

Andy sighed and bit into his dumpling, closing his eyes in appreciation because it was delicious, but also buying time. Yeah. No. He was out of time. He chewed and swallowed and managed to look Eli in the eyes.

"Okay, then. *You're* not ready."

"Not ready for what?" Eli asked, confused.

"You're not ready to move into the apartment with me." Andy watched as Eli froze, his mouth full of dumpling, his brown eyes enormous.

Eli swallowed with an effort and wiped his mouth carefully. "We... we haven't even...," he said in a very small voice.

"Made love?" Andy asked dryly. "I've noticed." So had his good right hand and his roommates. Nobody went through that much Kleenex if they were getting some on a regular basis. He was pretty sure they had a pool going as to when Andy and Eli decided to fish or cut bait.

Andy was rooting for fish, himself.

"Why...?" Eli swallowed hard, no dumpling needed. "Why haven't we?"

"Because it needs to be your apartment, Eli," Andy explained patiently. "And you need to trust me enough to invite me in."

Eli had regarded him for a moment in silent agony. His apartment was his sanctuary. He'd told Andy that often enough, and as Andy had heard the story of his childhood—being kicked out of the house at fifteen, living at the LGBTQ youth shelter until he'd gone to school—Andy had understood. In his *bones* he'd understood. Eli's tiny apartment was his, as very few things had been in his life. But Andy wanted to be Eli's too, and that sort of trust, that was something Andy needed in a partner. This wasn't Porter, who was good for a few—or many—blowjobs in the back of his mom's SUV. This was Eli, who only smiled in flutters, and who clung to Andy's hand like Andy could change the course of the sun.

Andy would do that for him—oh God, he would—if only Eli would let Andy see his heart.

Or his apartment. He'd settle for Eli's apartment and hope the heart would eventually follow.

"Why me?" Eli asked, looking wretched and afraid and as though he was about to bolt from the restaurant.

Andy smiled bitterly. "Because your eyes are beautiful," he said. "Because I love your taste. Because you work your fingers to the bone so a bunch of teenagers might never feel as sad as you did as a kid. Because even though you forget to feed yourself, you always remember to feed your kids. And because when I grab your hand and drag you through Williamsburg and Bed/Stuy looking for my future, you come with me, and you play the future game too, and I want your future in my life."

Eli's mouth parted, and for a moment, Andy thought, *This is it. I've lost him,* and his heart opened up in his chest and he'd mourned with all his soul.

Then Eli said, "It's not good enough," in a small voice. "My apartment... it's not good enough."

Andy's heart started to beat again, and he drew air into his lungs. "Why don't you invite me," he said, "and let me decide for myself."

And Now

HE ENDED the story there, because the rest of that night was personal, but Porter hadn't been asking for salacious details. Andy knew that.

Porter, for his part, took a thoughtful bite of drunken noodles and let out a wistful smile. "That's a good story," he said. Then with a wink, he added, "Did you get the apartment?"

Andy had to laugh. "We did!"

"Both names on the lease?"

Andy nodded, because this sounded like a lighthearted question, but the way Porter said it told Andy he knew it was serious too. "I insisted." It had almost been a fight.

"Then you'll be okay. I mean, the great Andy Chambers—student athlete, star quarterback, student activities wunderkind—the world doesn't let you down."

Andy shook his head. "Foxglove is a very small place," he said. "In Brooklyn I'm just a cog in a very big machine, even in my department." He grinned. "Which is pretty great, actually."

Porter grinned back. "Well, let me settle up here and you can tell me all about it. I'm getting to live vicariously through you. This is the best Christmas present ever!"

Chapter 4: Once You Leave the City People Don't Miss You

Eli MANAGED to get home by ten, and the sound of his footsteps echoing on the hardwood was one of the emptiest things he'd ever heard.

Hardwood is actually sort of warm looking, but we should get each other slippers for our first Christmas, I think.

He smiled as he remembered Andy saying that before they moved in. The day they'd officially unpacked, Eli had walked into their bedroom and found a box of moccasins on the new navy-and-cream-colored comforter, with his name sharpied on the top.

Andy wasn't great at waiting until Christmas. Eli'd felt his phone buzzing in his pocket as he'd walked from the subway station to the building, but he hadn't answered right away. For one thing, it was not particularly smart to lose situational awareness in Brooklyn at night, no matter how gentrified your neighborhood, but for another, he knew the texts were from Andy and he wanted to… savor.

He was going into an empty apartment; the texts would keep him company.

In a few minutes, he was curled up on the couch, covered with a throw and with the TV on for ambient noise—some sort of Christmas thing where a big city girl fell in love with a small town. Eli shuddered. There were *chickens* in the movie. It didn't matter how many times he and Andy took the kids on state-funded trips to a farm in the summer, *chickens* frightened him more than any of the big things. Horses, cows, alpacas, pigs—they were all big, and even when running full out, they still felt… well, *carlike*. Chickens were like rats, but without the intelligence and self-interest. And roosters attacked people. He'd *seen* roosters attack people!

He shuddered. So very many reasons he never wanted to move out of Brooklyn.

But he would for Andy. If Andy ever asked him, he'd go in a second. He hadn't told Andy that, though. He was really hoping it wouldn't come down to that.

On that thought, he pulled out his phone and looked at the series of pictures Andy had texted him.

One was of a Thai food place at a strip mall with a background of snowy woods behind it. In front of the place stood an unfairly handsome man with dark brown hair, a glossy brown beard, and thickly lashed brown eyes.

This is Porter—yes, THE Porter, the ex. My parents sent him to pick me up at the station. He says hi and really wants to meet you.

Eli swallowed and took a deep breath. So there it was: his biggest fear, out in the open, with the picture of the guy in the super-detailed blue-and-white Christmas sweater. Andy's ex-boyfriend from high school. But he was grinning and holding up his phone and... wait a minute. What did the phone say?

HI, ELI!

Oh wow. There he was, being all up-front and transparent about knowing other single men and making sure Eli had nothing to be jealous of or insecure about.

Tell him hi back, he texted, smiling a little.

I will, Andy replied. *Late night?*

Yes. Everybody loved the fancy ornaments, and the tree is lovely. He'd taken pictures all day and sent them to Andy.

I saw, but I had to wait until we got to Mom and Dad's place, because the Wi-Fi here isn't great. All the kids look really happy!

They were. Margie outdid herself with the glitter. Lola was thrilled. Her little sister was also excited.

He'd included a picture of the two girls. Josie was ten and had run away when her father had beaten her for confessing to a same-sex crush. Lola had taken the girl under her wing almost from the get-go, maybe because nobody had for her when she'd been that age. The two girls couldn't have been more different in appearance. Lola was tall and slender and blond, with a ponytail and mischievous green eyes, and Josie was small, soft, and round, Latina with darker skin and sloe eyes. It didn't matter. They clung to each other through thick and thin, two children displaced by the hurricane of the world.

They look really happy, Andy texted back. *Any news on Lola's college applications?*

Eli sighed. No, although they didn't expect to hear until after spring break. It was still sort of a monster in the closet for the girl. Going away to college meant leaving Rainbow House, and Rainbow House was not just the only home she'd ever felt safe in, it was also Josie.

Not until spring, you know that.

I do, but I want to run something by you about the two of them when I get back. I don't want her to feel like she's getting kicked to the curb because she ages out.

Eli's eyes burned again. *I'm open to all suggestions,* he typed, relieved. He could only do so much in his capacity at the home, and these girls—they were special to him.

I hope you like this one. Did you get my other pictures?

Eli had. He'd seen two young women, one Lola's age and one a little older, who could be recognized as Andy's sisters in the fog in the dark. They were both tall and lovely, with light brown hair and Andy's blue eyes.

Your sisters are getting grown up, he replied.

Charlie graduated from Junior College. She's going to Northwestern for her degree and her teaching credential. Mary Beth will be at NYU.

You'll finally get to use the guest room! Eli smiled, thinking Andy would be excited about that.

Maybe.

Huh. That was sort of noncommittal. But before Eli could reply to that, Andy texted again.

Baby, I'm beat. I will call you tomorrow morning because I want to hear your voice, but I'm crashing right now.

Okay. Enjoy your visit. Don't let the chickens get you.

In response, Andy texted a picture of a chicken in a hand-knitted jumper, made especially to accommodate wings and tail.

Oh my God! They're wearing clothes? When will they take our cell phones and take over the world? Eli was horrified—and only partially kidding.

If they do it will be in retaliation for things like this. I shit you not, my mom and Porter's mom went on a crusade to make sweaters for chickens this year. It's your nightmare, baby. Stay there and save yourself.

Eli laughed at that last one. *Come home and save both of us,* he typed.

I plan to. Love you.

Love you back.

And the conversation was over.

Eli grabbed a couch cushion and shoved it under his head, enjoying the warmth and the coziness of the couch since Andy wasn't in their bed.

When had he gotten so used to Andy's big body in his bed? Had it been those weeks after they'd first made love, when Andy was over almost every night? Had it been in that flurry of moving activity after Andy had agreed to take the apartment? They hadn't wanted to be apart, not *ever* during that time. Had it been after they'd moved in, when part of what made the place their home had been crawling in under the comforter and reaching out to stroke an arm or a shoulder, even when they were exhausted and lovemaking was completely off the table?

Or had it started at the very beginning, during that first night in each other's arms?

Back Then

"WHY DON'T you invite me?" Andy asked gently, "and let me decide for myself?"

Eli had stared at him in agony, his heart in his eyes. Oh God—these last three months had been delirious. Dreamlike. The Saturday morning meetings—sometimes to go look at apartments and sometimes to go work at Rainbow House together. *Together!* That had been so surprising that Andy would take on Eli's work, his vocation, and participate in it too. The Sunday morning breakfasts at Andy's apartment with all of his friends, all of them in various stages of flying the coop, including Zinnia, his best friend, who had gotten engaged while they'd been getting to know each other and whom it seemed Andy would miss enormously after she moved out.

Eli had loved all of that, but he'd been afraid, so afraid, of what Andy was asking now.

No, Eli wasn't a virgin. He'd been used and had used men from his teen years on up. But after he'd graduated from college, started working at Rainbow House, he'd been reluctant to do that anymore. Even he could recognize that it wasn't healthy, and he felt like he owed it to those kids to do healthy things with his life so he could give them advice for how to do the same.

But two years of celibacy had been lonely—damned lonely—and suddenly he had a man who wanted his time and his company and his opinion, and who liked making him smile.

And this same man—this beautiful, broad-shouldered, big-smiled mountain of a man—wanted to take things to the next level, and the way he was looking at Eli right now, across the dishes of Chinese food that had just sort of arrived at their table while they were staring at each other, hearts in their eyes—was looking at him in a way that oh, made Eli's pulse throb in his ears from intensity alone.

"It would…." He swallowed, hating this feeling of vulnerability but unable to stop himself. "It would kill me if you didn't like… my apartment."

Underneath the table, Andy bumped knees with him, and he sucked in a breath, the contact steadying him, helping his lungs work, giving him comfort.

"I'm sure I'll love it," Andy said, leaning over to squeeze his knee. "But you've got to let me see it first."

Eli's face was on fire, and still Andy's eyes were hypnotizing him, making him say things he normally wouldn't dare. "Okay," he whispered. "Tonight? After dinner?"

Andy gave one of those nods that people used when they were trying not to tell you that you were being dense.

"Yeah, Eli. Tonight, after dinner. But don't worry. We can eat first. Get some gelato on the way. It'll be nice. I promise." He gave a winsome smile, and Eli was completely lost. "You do trust me to make it nice, right?"

Eli had swallowed, unsure of how to answer, and the look Andy gave him was a little sad, but not surprised. Oh God, it was like he knew all of Eli's secrets and wanted him anyway.

"You will someday," Andy said softly. "Hopefully tonight too."

Eventually they left the restaurant, Andy taking the lead like he tended to do and holding the door open for Eli. Eli walked out first, and when they got to the sidewalk, he paused and deliberately held out his hand, palm up, waiting for Andy's larger, wide-palmed hand to cover it, to lace their fingers together, to walk him down the more sparsely populated street to the dessert shoppe down the way.

"You trust me to pick dessert, right?" Andy asked chidingly as they walked.

"Yeah."

Andy's brief kiss on his temple promised sweetness to come. "Good."

EVENTUALLY THEY ended up at Eli's fourth-floor walk-up, and their footsteps rang hollowly on the wooden stairs. Eli fumbled with the key in the lock, and only Andy's hand, covering his own, gave him the courage to go forward.

This was so stupid. He'd had sex before. Faceless, nameless hookups—lots of them.

But not in this place. His old apartment, maybe. That had been a rat hole. The door hadn't sealed right, and he'd had to share a bathroom with the meth addict next door. All of it had been awful.

But he'd gotten his job and had been able to afford, well, an improvement. Not a perfect place by any stretch of the imagination. Certainly not the place Andy had just looked at, his face shining with hope and promise.

But this place. The door had opened on his apartment: the neatly made bed that doubled as a couch, the small television perched up on his one dresser, the two cinder-block bookshelves that held paperbacks. He dusted and vacuumed periodically and kept his one window clean.

Like Andy, he felt like a window was an important feature in an apartment.

He gazed at the place for a moment, trying to see it through Andy's eyes, and then felt the door close behind him and turned.

And realized that Andy's eyes weren't really on the apartment.

Andy moved in on him, that magnificent chest crowding Eli until he was back against the door, gazing up into Andy's face in the darkness.

"I'm going to kiss you now," Andy whispered, cupping his cheek. "And I don't want to stop until we're done. I mean, I *will* stop if you get uncomfortable, but I'm telling you right now, I don't want to."

Eli grinned at him, calmed somehow by the humor, by the reassurance that Eli's enjoyment mattered, and by the desire, the implication that Andy wanted him that badly.

"Then don't," Eli whispered. "Stop, I mean. Don't stop."

Andy chuckled, and Eli wanted to clap his hand over his mouth, but then Andy lowered his mouth to Eli's and Eli had better things to do with it.

So easy—it was so easy to fall into Andy's kisses. To return them, to taste him and to open his mouth and let Andy possess him with that casual farm-boy ease.

The kiss was tender and thorough, and it went on and on and on, and somewhere between Andy lowering his head and pulling back to gulp in breaths, he'd managed to insinuate his big-palmed hands under Eli's shirt, under the waistband of his jeans, under his briefs.

Eli shoved at Andy's shirt, needing his skin, all of it, and Andy dropped his shoulders, letting his denim jacket fall to the floor. Another shove and enough buttons had come undone for Andy to grab his shirts by the back of the neck and pull them over his head, and there he was, smooth-skinned shoulders gleaming faintly in the ambient light.

Eli gasped and heard a needy sound that he was surprised to find he'd made himself, but he didn't care. He ran his lips along Andy's collarbone, the column of his throat, along his jaw.

Andy let him, pushing at his pants and his shirt as Eli peppered him with kisses, tasted all the grand romantic paths between knee-melting kisses and bare bodies searching each other out in the darkness.

One article of clothing after the other, one kiss at a time, they made their way to Eli's twin-sized bed against the wall. Andy paused, pulled the covers back, and then sank onto the sheets and rested his head on his palm, waiting for Eli to come to him, and suddenly it wasn't easy anymore.

Andy waited, though, smiling gently, and with a deep breath, Eli took the last two steps to the bed and slid under the sheets.

Andy's body, bare and strong, was his reward. Suddenly "easy" wasn't the word anymore. Necessary. Imperative. Life-giving. *These* were the words running through Eli's mind as they resumed their kisses, their caresses, and he was pulled forcibly into a world in which sex wasn't a hard, impersonal release anymore.

Sex was *this*. Sex was Andy's soft whispers in his ear. "Mm—good. I'm going to touch you now, okay?" Gentle laugh. "Your cock, Eli. I'm going to... ooh... nice. Can I taste? Please?"

Sex was the little grazes of Andy's lips against his skin in transit. He moved his lips gently from Eli's lips to his jaw, down his jawline, along his neck, from his neck to Eli's collarbone... and then to his nipple, where he suckled just hard enough to make Eli cry out, his body arching without his permission, his arousal in the stratosphere without him ever acknowledging a launch.

Sex was the guttural sound of Andy's enjoyment when he tasted the precome on the bell of Eli's cock. It was the playful feel of his chuckles when Eli was deep in his throat and pleading breathlessly for something, anything, to give him release.

Sex was the tender stretching of a lubricated finger along Eli's opening, ramping up his need, fueling his desire to pure conflagration.

Sex was the glee in Andy's eyes when Eli shyly admitted he was on PReP, because Andy was too and who didn't like no condoms?

And sex was, now and forever, the tenderness in Andy's eyes when he positioned himself carefully and merged their bodies together, mindful of all the nerve endings that had the potential to be injured in the breach but that he stroked to pleasure instead.

Sex was the glorious flood of climax as it crashed over them both, the way Andy's soft moan of release tickled Eli's ear, the way Eli's breathless cry was swallowed by Andy's urgent kiss.

Sex would be, for the rest of Eli's life, the gentle stroke of Andy's fingertips along Eli's jaw as he searched Eli's face for reassurance, his body still lodged inside Eli's, his spend dripping down Eli's thighs.

"Good?" he murmured.

"Yes," Eli whispered back, voice catching.

"You look...."

And then Eli had buried his face against Andy's neck and cried softly, not having the words to explain. Not merely the orgasm—although damn! And not just the sex—which was *wow*! But all of it: Andy's care, his patience, his gentleness, and in the end, his power, which he only released when Eli had begged.

In his life—his entire life—he hadn't known love could feel like this, this gentle descent into afterglow after a brilliant, soul-freeing moment in the sun.

How had he never known? And would he ever find his way again when Andy left him forever?

And Now

ELI REALIZED he'd been gazing into space in the quiet apartment for quite some time. Those moments in Andy's arms had been a beginning for them, a true one. Eli's faith had grown, a little bit at a time, until not the next apartment, or the one after that, but about a month later, they found themselves standing in *the* apartment.

This apartment.

"So," the exhausted real-estate agent had asked. *"Is this one it?"*

Andy had met Eli's eyes, his full mouth flirting with a nervous smile. "Is it?" he'd asked. "Can you live here?"

"Yes," Eli had responded without thought. *"Absolutely."*

He'd worry about it later, after that magical moment when worry wasn't a thing and hope was the only feeling in the world. Later he would let his doubts eat at him through three years of breakfasts, lunches, dinners, and outings. Later he would try to figure out why that voice, the one screaming that he could never do enough, learn enough, *be* enough, to have an Andy Chambers in his life, was so loud and so insistent.

But every day he woke up in Andy's arms, to Andy's kisses, to breakfast in the morning, and that insidious little voice got smaller and smaller and smaller.

Eli stroked the face of his phone for a moment, remembering the ridiculous picture of the chickens in sweaters. There was no reason to listen to that voice now, he told himself.

And on that note, he snuggled down into the couch and set his phone for morning. He didn't want to sleep alone in their bed, but finally, *finally*, he could sleep.

CHAPTER 5: ONCE YOU GET HOME, ALL THE OLD FEELINGS COME FLOODING BACK

THE FAMILY had been gone by the time Porter had dropped him off at six the night before. There'd been a covered dish in the fridge for him to microwave and a note on the table saying everybody was at choir practice and that he and Porter should make themselves at home.

Porter—who had lived up to his name and brought Andy's suitcase inside—looked at the note and whistled. "Wow," he said.

"It's not my imagination, is it," Andy stated flatly.

"No. Just...." Porter shook his head. "Dude, I'm so sorry. Have you sent them a picture of—oh." As he spoke, Andy had stalked to the mantle where the picture of him and Eli that he'd sent them the year before was tucked behind his graduation picture from ten years ago.

Muttering to himself, Andy took down the graduation picture, set Eli up front and center on the mantlepiece, and turned back around to the cold dish on the table.

"Porter, I'll give you two hundred dollars to take me back to Brooklyn right the hell now."

Porter rubbed the back of his neck. "No can do, bro. My mom needs her medication, and I need to get *her* fed. I can come back later tonight—"

"No." Andy shook his head, feeling bad. "No. You've got responsibilities, and dealing with my family crap should not be one of them. Tell your mom I'll be by tomorrow to chat, and I'll make do here." He yawned. "My room probably still has the little TV in there—I'll hit the hay early and be ready to tear the folks a new one when I wake up."

"Or, you know, you won't be tired and cranky and oversensitive and you can deal with this like an adult," Porter said, and Andy shot him a look that should have peeled paint.

Porter gave a goofy, lopsided grin under his beard, and Andy couldn't help it. He laughed.

"Well, maybe we can compromise. I'll wake up feeling like an adult who can have an adult conversation with his parents about the fact that I'm not leaving Brooklyn. How's that?"

Porter laughed. "Fair." He sobered. "Seriously, though, if you need me to get you the hell out, brother, I'm here. One of us should." His face fell wistfully, and Andy's heart twisted. Not romantically—not even a little—but out of sympathy.

He'd wanted so badly to get out of his little tiny town, but so had Porter. Porter was being the dutiful son, but he was paying for it.

Andy went in for the strictly-bro handclasp with the double-tap fist bump on the back, and Porter took him up on it. Andy half expected a pass, but that's not what happened. A sincere hug and then a respectful step back.

With a little salute and a wave, Porter was out of there, and Andy was left thinking his friend needed a way out for real.

He ate dinner and unpacked and then wrapped his gifts to put under the tree. He was just about to retire to text Eli when his family arrived.

The girls rushed in first, looking stressed but happy to see him.

"Andy!" Mary Beth first, coming in for a hug at his chest, and he engulfed her completely, like he had when she'd been a little girl. She didn't look so little now, wearing a tight glittery sweater and glossy pink boots.

"Biminy Beth!" he cried, using the nickname he'd made up for her when he'd been ten and his mother had brought her home. She'd been a happy baby, and he'd spent hours of middle school blowing bubbles on her stomach to make her laugh. She giggled a little bit now, just enough for Andy to smell the brandy on her breath.

He scowled down at her, his eyebrows raised, and she grimaced.

"Don't tell Mom," she mouthed, and he grunted unhappily. He and Mary Beth had always been close, but he really didn't like being the diplomat to the country known as Mom.

"Give me one reason not to," he murmured, and at that moment, Charlene walked into the kitchen.

"Charlie!" he exclaimed happily, and she gave him a more reserved—but definitely more sober—hug.

"You got in okay?" Charlie asked. "I wanted to go get you, but Mom...." She scowled and shook her head. "*Mom* said it was too far to drive, and then she said, 'Oh, why don't we ask Porter—he and Andy haven't caught up in a dog's age!' Then Dad looked panicked, but she called Porter anyway." Charlie blew out a breath. "God, you were so lucky to get the hell out of here."

Andy shrugged. Yes, his own resentment felt righteous and justified, but seeing it in his younger sister was sobering. Their mother didn't deserve all of that—she really didn't. But then, the three of them deserved to fly and be free.

He gave Mary Beth a censorious look, because drunk at choir practice was *not* acceptable, and as big brother, it put him in a sticky position. "Look, guys, let me take a picture of you to send to Eli, and we can chat in the morning." He yawned, not feigning in the least. "It was a long day, okay?" He shook his head. "For one thing, we had to stop on the street for at least fifteen minutes while Mrs. Jenkins's chickens crossed in front of Porter's truck."

"Oh God," Charlie said, clapping her hand over her eyes. "Were they wearing their little jumpers?"

Mary Beth giggled. "They're *adorable*, and I swear that's not just the brandy talking."

"They really are cute. Where's Mom and Dad, by the way?" He stood back to line up the shot, frowning for a moment.

"They were having a *discussion*," Charlie said dryly. "I think Dad really wanted to be the one to go pick you up."

Andy sighed. "That would have been nice," he admitted. "I gave Porter a hell of a time." He looked into his camera screen at his sisters— Mary Beth shorter, rounder, more bubbly than Charlene, and Charlie tall and willowy, but both of them with elegant oval faces and rich dark blond hair back in ponytails. Like him, they had ditched all their cold weather gear on the neat hooks in the mudroom entryway of the lodge-style house, and they were wearing happy seasonal sweaters and jeans underneath, as well as thick woolen socks knitted either by their mother or Porter's.

Andy took a couple of shots and told them thanks while Charlie went to the fridge and broke out a pie with some ice cream.

"We ate dinner early," she said, "and I'm still starving. Mary Beth, you in?"

Mary Beth nodded and flopped down at the table. "C'mon, Andy sit down and talk. How's Rainbow House? And Eli? Did he at least *want* to come meet us?"

Andy's heart twisted, knowing that's probably how it felt to them.

"Of course he wanted to meet you," he said, sitting down. "A tiny piece, Charlie. I'm still full from dinner."

"Course," she said, grinning. "Sour cream apple is always best eaten in tiny little bites."

He groaned. "Medium. Medium piece. Anyway, Rainbow House is doing good. Eli should be sending me more pictures tonight. They put the tree up in the foyer. It's always a big deal for the kids."

"How's Lola?" Mary Beth asked anxiously. "And Josie?" Perhaps because Mary Beth and Charlie were so close, Andy's description of the two girls at Rainbow House had pulled at their hearts.

"They're doing well," he said. He sought out his little sister's eyes. "I think Lola's worried about leaving Rainbow House for school. It's hard, when you don't think there will be a home waiting for you after you leave."

Mary Beth swallowed, looking suddenly vulnerable—and very sober. "No serious stuff," she said thickly. "Not right now. I keep asking Mom if I can come visit, you know? Like instead of you spending ten days here, how about if I go into the city with you for a few days and volunteer or something. Like, you know, Margie? You sent us pictures before? I want to help kids decorate!" She gave a suspicious sniffle. "All the kids here are spoiled. I asked a kindergartner if he was going to string popcorn for the tree, and he was like, 'My mother said that for as much as she's paying for decorations, I'd better not wreck it with art stuff.'"

Andy grimaced and pulled his phone from his pocket. "Well, decorating's all done, but I'm sure Margie would love your help on another day." His heart fluttered in his chest a little, mostly with hope. "You know, we *got* an apartment with a guest bedroom hoping you guys might swing by and visit." He peered at Mary Beth in hurt. "I mean, you visited NYU and didn't even tell me? I would have taken an afternoon off and had lunch with you at the very least."

Mary Beth folded her arms and rolled her eyes. "I *wanted* to," she growled. "But *Mom* insisted that it was on an entirely different island and you wouldn't be able to get there in time. We were at the hotel for two days!"

His eyes widened involuntarily, and Charlie put a comforting hand on his shoulder as she slid a plate in front of him. "Have some carbs,

Andy. They're antimatricidal. And let me see the pictures of the tree. Mom insisted we couldn't get ours or decorate it until you got here."

"I'm sorry, you guys. She didn't have to do that."

"It's not your fault, Prince Andrew," Charlie said, giving him a sly look with her blue eyes. "We know you can't help being the oldest and a boy and a football hero…."

"Oh God, please stop," Andy moaned. "Don't forget, I'm the one who also came out and moved to the city and ruined all her dreams about bringing my family back to Foxglove. *You* two had the perfect openings to be the perfect children—"

"And then we had to ruin it by getting scholarships to anywhere but here," Charlie said, plopping down at the table.

He regarded her with pride. "Congratulations, by the way. Porter was *all* about you and your scholarship to Northwestern to finish up your BA and credential. He really does love you guys."

"Well, he keeps us sane," Charlie admitted frankly. She took a giant bite of pie. "Oh my God, how that woman can drive us to eat a pie and then bake the best pie in Vermont is just the definition of irony. Anyway, Porter brings us over to his house to watch anime while his mother naps—he's *so* excited about *Jo Jo's Bizarre Adventure*, and, you know, that kind of thing is catching. It's all very big city and forbidden, and it's probably the only reason we both haven't gone searching out a meth rave in an abandoned warehouse or something and come back addicted and pregnant."

Andy stared at her in horror. "If I had ovaries, you would have made them shrivel. God, you're terrifying."

Charlie let out a sound of exasperation and looked over to where Mary Beth was yawning over her portion of the pie. "Look, I'm not saying I approve of spiking the church eggnog—"

"I didn't do it." Mary Beth yawned. "I just took advantage of a prime opportunity."

"I'm just saying," Charlie overrode firmly, "that when that's what we're doing for fun around here, you should just be glad someone's having some."

"Well, you're both poised on the precipice of something greater," Andy cautioned. "I mean, c'mon, Mary Beth, can't you wait a few months until you're at a dorm party or something? Also, don't do that. Girls get roofied at dorm parties. Stay away from alcohol altogether. And boys. And raves. And meth." He blamed that entire panicky attempt at parenting on Charlie, who chortled because she obviously knew it.

"I'm *dine*," Mary Beth hiccupped. "I mean, *fine*. Anyway I promise not to drink spiked eggnog again until next year if you promise to leave early and take me to Brooklyn for part of this year. Please, Andy? Pretty please? I've *got* to get out of here!"

He was about to say yes, unequivocally yes, please God come use our guest room yes, but at that moment the family juggernaut entered the kitchen from the mudroom, and his chance to hear a thing his sisters had to say was gone.

"*Andy*! Oh my baby, I'm so glad you're here!"

Andy shoved one more fortifying bite of pie into his mouth and swallowed it hastily before he stood up to greet the enemy.

"Mom! I thought you two were going to freeze out there—become 'rentcicles. Glad you came inside!"

Cindy Chambers was a midsized, slender woman in her mid-fifties, one of those balls of energy that everybody assumed was much younger. She volunteered with her church and with her women's group and knitted for charity and baked cookies for charity and was basically exhausting on every level. Her hair was tinted blond and artfully tousled, and her eyes were Andy's shade of sky blue—but her nose was tiny and pert, and bless her, she'd managed to pass it on to Mary Beth, although Charlie had a slightly more aquiline nose, inherited from her father.

It wasn't that his mother was a *bad* person, Andy thought grimly as he gave his mother a hug and a kiss on the cheek; it was that she was a *strong-willed* person, but she hadn't had a really good place to *wield* that will. She could have been a congresswoman or a world leader or run a nonprofit in a third-world country, but she'd been born and raised in a small town, and her children *were* her small country, and she was having trouble deciding whether or not to be a dictator or a diplomat.

She was, in fact, both, which was frustrating as hell.

"Your father and I were just mulling a few things over," Cindy said, laughing merrily. Andy caught his father's expression over Cindy's head and grimaced.

"Divorce?" he mouthed, and the way Matt Chambers shook his head, Andy was pretty sure that no, maybe not a divorce in their future, but it was probably a near thing.

"Well," Andy said firmly, wanting to get his two cents in about this, "while you're mulling, the next time you tell me I absolutely have to be home by a time, and then you send Porter out to get me, is going to be the next time I don't come home but turn around and catch the next train back to Brooklyn."

"Oh, honey," his mother said, looking indulgently dismayed. "That's no way to be about your old boyfriend—"

"He's my friend, Mom, and you threw me at him like I was a steak and he was a dog. It demeaned us both. I'm serious about this. Next time, it's you or Dad or one of the girls, but Porter is working two jobs and taking care of his mother, and it wasn't fair to do that to his time."

His mother swallowed and looked down, then smiled briefly again, a conciliatory smile. "I wasn't trying to—"

Andy's temper—which had cooled off a little when he was talking to Mary Beth and Charlie—tried to flare up again. "Sure you were," he said with a sigh. "Mom, I'm living with someone I love *very* much. Someone I've tried to convince will have my family as his family when we marry. You don't make a very good case for that when you're trying to set me up with my old boyfriend just to get me to move back to Foxglove."

She flushed. "That was never my intention," she said stiffly. "I was just trying to point out that you have friends here too."

"I have *a* friend, Mom. And he's like my brother, but I'm not moving back here for him." Andy didn't do temper well, and he found his burst of it fading. "But sit down. Talk to me. Tell me about choir practice. How's the Christmas pageant doing?"

The Christmas pageant was one of two town events that people poured their hearts into in Foxglove. The other was the Fourth of July pageant, which Andy had managed to be a part of every year even after he left home, but that paled in comparison to the fervor over the Christmas pageant.

Every mother tried to bake the most cookies, and every father tried to put up the most lights. Every young homemaker worked to create their first quilt or their first afghan to give to the city charity stores, and prizes were given for the best homemade item and the church that raised the most for the disadvantaged. It was an orgy of giving, and much of it was for a good cause. The choir crawl literally lasted all of Christmas Eve—each of the three churches had a fifteen-minute presentation a a different part of the hour for twelve hours straight. Practically every man, woman, and child was showcased in the town, talented or not, and Andy sort of missed the days when he got to solo. He'd loved choir so much more than football, truth be told, but choir wasn't going to get him the scholarship or the help through school, which he'd always thought of as a damned shame.

But what mattered for the Christmas pageant was the involvement. The entire town came together, quite literally, during the tree-lighting ceremony the week before Christmas. They all but held hands and sang the Whoville song from *The Grinch*, and the only reason they didn't was because they needed the rights to that song, and there wasn't room in it for a solo.

Part of Andy's mom's insistence that he come home for Christmas was wanting his participation and wanting the family together. Part of that he got. If the girls were leaving home, this could be one of the last times in a while all the kids *did* get together in one group.

But that didn't mean Andy welcomed his mother's meddling.

So the question about the Christmas pageant was something of a peace offering; it was a way to tell his mother he was happy to help while he was there.

What he got in return was a barrage of places, dates, times, and Christmas obligations that left his head swimming and had him yawning as he sat, chin resting on his palm, as he tried to stay upright at the table.

Like he had when Andy was a kid, his father came to his rescue.

"Cindy, give the boy a break. He's asleep where he's sitting. It's been a long day for him—the train, the car trip here. How were the roads, Andy?"

Andy struggled to sit up. "Rough," he mumbled. "Good thing Porter's truck is indestructible. I still feel bad that he had to drive all the way down to get me."

"Well, your mother promised him help with his mother over the holiday," his father said. "Here, son, let me guide you to your room."

"We should be helping with his mom anyway," Andy grumbled. "He gave up his entire future to come here. He should get days off to go to the city and get laid!"

His father chuckled sadly. "You're right there, son, but I'm not sure how to arrange that. Slim pickings up here for guys like you and Porter."

Andy wanted to grump, but his father's hand at the middle of his back, guiding him down the hallway, kept him from getting snippy. Nothing but love and acceptance from his parents from the moment he came out onward, and even for Porter, too, when they realized that what they'd thought of as two guys bonding was really, well, two guys *bonding*. So no, being gay had never been a problem for his family, and he was grateful. He'd seen what those prejudices had done to Eli as a teenager, and it had made him cherish his family even more.

But by the same token, all that love they had for him made them want him home, and it was such a pervasive heartbeat of a tune that it was starting to drive him away as much as urge him back to the nest on the odd holiday.

All of which he put out of his mind as he curled up in bed to text Eli. A part of him wished Eli was *here*, to help him laugh at his family a little, to assure him Mary Beth was not going to get pregnant at a meth rave, and to remind him that he was loved, he'd been provided for, and he had too many blessings to count.

But most of him—the adult part of him—wanted to be *there*, to celebrate another successful Christmas tree, to talk about Lola and Josie, and to look across the river to the Manhattan skyline from Marsha P. Johnson Park. His childhood bed was too small, and his family loved him, but they were the family from his childhood as well. He was a better adult with Eli, and in a way, he was almost afraid of Eli seeing him with his parents.

Eli might find out he wasn't a superhero after all.

Back Then

"HEY, ELI, come over here and sign this," Andy muttered, doing paperwork on the dinner table. They'd moved in together in August, and while they waited for a desk to put in the tiny "den" off the guest room, paperwork, office work, all of it was done at the little table off the counter.

"More lease stuff?" Eli complained from the other room. He was exhausted, Andy knew, because he'd fallen asleep while Andy had been loading the dishwasher. They'd gotten a sudden influx of residents in September. Eli told him that it happened after school started and the kid who'd been alone in his or her or their head all summer, questioning their sexuality and identity, suddenly came into contact with peers and the whole situation crystalized.

And then the parents got into the act and everything went to shit.

"No, just some health insurance stuff." Andy made sure everything had printed out, and the scanner—which currently sat on the kitchen counter—was ready to scan Eli's signed paper. He wasn't really paying attention to Eli's reaction until Eli was suddenly standing at the table, looking over his shoulder.

"I don't have insurance," he murmured. "I mean, the basic stuff, but you know. Don't bring me in even if I'm dying, and even then, don't call an ambulance because you'll be paying for my rotting corpse forever."

"Yes, Eli, I know that," Andy said with grim humor. "That's why we're doing this—so you don't have to give up a limb to save another one."

Eli had sprained his wrist when they'd been moving in. Andy had danced around him, freaking out about maybe it was a break and shouldn't they see the doctor, and Eli had snapped, "And pay the hundred-dollar copay, are you kidding me?" Then he'd wrapped a tube sock—a TUBE SOCK—around his wrist and tied it tight using his teeth and had proceeded to pick up the kitchen stool he'd been moving and finish the job.

The first thing Andy had done when he'd gone back to work that Monday had been to go to HR and ask for the paperwork to put his life partner on his health insurance, and God bless New York and his progressive company for not making that a pain in the ass.

"But what does it say?" Eli muttered. "Wait, I'm on your health insurance? How's that work?"

"You're a member of my household now," Andy replied patiently. "See. The box checked there for Partner? Yes. You. Eli. My partner. It's almost romantic, except when it's romantic I get to check Husband, which I would like to do someday."

Eli's eyes grew humongous. "But… Andy. This is permanent!"

"Well, yes. So's moving in."

"But I could always move out!" Eli protested, and if Andy hadn't known—at least a little—where this was coming from, that sentence alone would have broken his heart.

"Yes, but I could also drop dead tomorrow. Bad ticker." He clutched his chest and grinned. "But odds are good that I won't. And if I do—" He held up another sheaf of papers that he'd just finished signing. "—I've got insurance and a trust." He gave Eli a mock suspicious look. "You're not thinking of, you know, offing me for the apartment now, are you? I mean, we just moved here. Let me at least get my desk and chair and stuff."

Eli stared at him, his lower lip wobbling. "Don't even joke about that," he rasped.

Oh God. Could Andy ever do this right? "Then don't joke about moving out," Andy replied, letting his hurt show. "I just got you here. I like you." He turned his kitchen stool enough to pull Eli close, his hands on Eli's hips. "I like sex on tap." He offered a big, toothy grin to make Eli laugh—and it worked, thank God.

"I'm just worried. What if you, you know, regret putting me on your insurance. I mean, life and death decisions and stuff."

"So you're saying you'll pull the plug?" Andy asked, keeping his face straight.

"You're being obnoxious," Eli told him, eyes narrowed.

"Well, you're making this way too complicated. Is it too much to ask that the next time you sprain something, we can get a nurse to wrap it up in a bandage instead of rubbing some dirt on it and using a tube sock?"

Eli's lips twitched. "The tube sock really bothered you?"

"It offended me to my toes," Andy reassured him. "Now sign the paper, because you were falling asleep, and now that I mentioned sex on tap, I want some."

And that got an actual laugh out of him. Andy felt like it was a win. He especially felt like it was a win when Eli signed the damned papers and then kissed him, wide-awake and wanting.

It was funny how some of the least romantic moments of a relationship could mean so very much. Andy was pretty sure he'd be celebrating the signing of insurance papers for the rest of his life.

And Now

"ANDY! ANDY darling, are you up yet?"

Andy kicked futilely at the baseboard of the bed he'd slept in until he'd left for college. A full-sized pedestal bed that used to hold hi clothes but now seemed to hold as much yarn as Porter's mother's house, the bed was a little too short for full-grown Andy, and the blankets? Forgetaboutit. He'd needed to grab two more from the closet to cover him from toes to nose, which was absolutely imperative because his parents didn't believe in turning on the heater until the temperature dipped below fifty-five degrees in the house.

"Andy!" His mother poked her head into Andy's room and gave a chirpy little smile. "Oh good, you're awake."

"Sure I am."

"Don't be grumpy. Now, I called Porter's mother, and she said you were planning to go over and visit, which is great, because I need you and Porter to make cookies for the Christmas pageant today so we can provide them for our family's little moment in the sun. Then you need to get home tonight in time for dinner so we can practice our Christmas carols. Did I forget anything?"

"That this is my vacation?" he grumbled.

"There's no vacation over Christmas," she contradicted gaily. "Now the girls and I are going to Lewiston for pageant costumes—"

"Please God, no."

"Don't be snippy. They've got some of those adorable novelty Christmas sweaters on sale."

"Mom, why don't we just wear what you've made us? I mean, we get a new sweater every year. I brought a couple, and I wear them to the office all winter."

Suddenly his mother stopped, a look of such simple joy on her face that he cursed himself for being an insensitive boob.

"You do?" she asked, as eager as a child.

"Yeah. I do. Everyone at work is jealous, I swear." It was true. When he was a kid, Mom's hand-knit sweaters were a cross to be borne, but as an adult? Each one was an individualized creation that would have sold for an obscene amount of money at a local boutique but that Andy just threw on. He'd been dying—*dying*—for her to make Eli one, and he thought this might be the moment.

"Oh," she said, her voice small. "That's so sweet."

He opened his mouth to ask her about Eli's sweater, thinking that his moment of quiet might last, but no, not with Cindy Chambers. *His* mom fanned her face and said, "Well, as sweet as that is, I'm afraid

I didn't knit for the whole family to match, and we need costumes. It won't cost much, and we'll be home in time to bring takeout."

Andy grimaced. Compared to New York, takeout choices were *very* limited. "Panda Express?" he asked, remembering when the franchise had arrived in the neighboring town when he was in eighth grade and the entire family had celebrated small victories with takeout from Panda Express.

She bobbed her head excitedly.

"Your favorite!" she chirped. "Now hurry up and get dressed. Porter's mother is expecting you just after breakfast!"

He nodded and tried to pull on his big boy jammies. "Sure, but Mom, before you go, I need to talk to you about Eli."

The look on his mother's face was... what? Dismayed? A little frightened? Sad?

"Honey, he can miss you for ten days—"

"Yes, but it would be great if you guys could meet him!" Andy said, but the last part was called to her retreating back.

"Sorry, we'll talk about this at dinner," she promised, pretty much as she ran across the house and out the door.

Well, shit. Apparently he was baking cookies today and adulting when he could pin his mother by her tailfeathers some way she couldn't escape.

But thinking about Eli—and remembering moments from their past—had him pulling his phone up from the charger where he'd plugged it the night before.

Good morning, sunshine, he texted, after grabbing a hooded sweatshirt and a pair of moccasins to ward off the chill. *Sleep well?*

Oh I wish came the irritated answer. There was a pause while the little bubbles danced on the text screen, and then a picture came through.

Oh no! Andy stared at the picture in dismay, wondering how on earth he was going to help Eli through *this* when he was a more than four hundred miles away.

CHAPTER 6: CITY PEOPLE ARE SOFT

ELI GOT the panicked text from Leon, one of the supervisors who stayed over four nights a week, when he was still asleep on the couch. Leon's job wasn't easy. Part counselor, part troubleshooter, part repair man, Leon was the guy who fixed leaky roofs, repaired windows, and made emergency grocery orders when something went wrong with their stores, because he was the guy who was there when shit went wrong.

In this case, shit had gone very wrong.

"It froze last night," Leon said without preamble. "The pipes burst in the basement. Eli, the water's rising and all the Christmas stuff is getting soaked."

Oh God.

They had such a limited budget. They scrimped, they saved, they got stuff on sale, they hit up charities and overstocks; getting up to sixty kids, aged ten to eighteen, Christmas presents that were both practical and desirable was no easy feat. Scrupulous planning and a whole lot of forethought—not to mention money they didn't have—went into having the gifts ready to open on Christmas Day. And while some of the gifts were things like socks, underwear, and personalized sheets, some of them were favorite books, a coveted sweater or phone case, makeup for an emerging young woman, or shaving supplies for a vulnerable young man.

All of which had been wrapped and decorated the week before. It had been Andy and Eli's last weekend together, hunched in the basement of the aging duchess of a building, wrapping presents and pretending they weren't there. None of the kids even saw them, although plenty of Andy's coworkers saw the bump on his head from where he ran into one of the water pipes set in the too-low ceiling.

"Get it out of there," Eli said through a constricted throat. "Wake the others up and get the presents up and out of there. Save everything you can, and for God's sakes, fix the pipe. Get a move on. I'll call in reinforcements on my way."

He'd fallen asleep in the Henley tee he'd worn under his sweater the day before and a pair of Andy's old sweats that he had to double knot and haul up over his narrow hips, and that's what he walked out of the apartment wearing, the warm wool coat Andy had bought him for their first Christmas holding his phone, his keys, and his hat and gloves in the pockets. He'd barely managed to lace his boots he'd been so panicked, and he'd been doing everything one-handed while he called up employee after employee and had them descend upon Rainbow House in what would become known as the Great Christmas Rescue.

In the end, they only managed to save about half the gifts, and the basement was still flooded while Eli tried to find a serviceman at six in the morning three days before Christmas.

They'd managed to wrap duct tape around the pipe, so at least it wasn't spewing water all over the basement, and Leon had found the water main to shut off. Half the presents were in a room upstairs drying off, and the other half were submerged and unusable. They had someone who was supposed to arrive around lunch with a sump to at least empty the basement out.

Eli was sopping wet, filthy, and freezing right down to his toes when Andy texted, but that's not what he was most concerned about.

Despondently he sent the picture of the presents floating in the dirty, hip-height water as he stood at the top of the alley stairs and aimed the camera into the basement.

God. What was he going to do?

When the phone rang in his hand, he noted Andy's number dully, not sure what Andy could do, and was surprised when someone *not* Andy was on the other end of the line.

"Eli?" said the pleasant, rumbly older voice. "This is Andy's father, Matt. He's panicking over here about your basement. I don't know what to do about the presents, son, but I ran a string of hardware stores up here for forty years. I've got some contacts down there that will do you folks right. Give me half an hour and somebody—I swear to you—*somebody* will show up to fix your pipe, turn your water back on, and pump out your basement."

"We have a guy with a sump on the way," Eli replied weakly wanting to cry out of sheer blessed relief. "So you don't have to worry about—"

"Two will do twice as well," Matt Chambers said. "Now I know this is a setback. Andy's been trying to tell me what a big deal this is, and I had kids. Christmas for three was hard enough, and you're trying to pull off Christmas for sixty. And believe me, I get it. These kids need the best Christmas you can manage. So you do what you can on your end—maybe get an inventory together of what you lost and what you need—and I'll see what we can do on our end, okay? Don't worry, son. You've got some help, okay?"

"Yessir," Eli breathed, trying to ignore the burning eyes. "You can't know how much I appreciate this. We had a cold snap last night."

He heard a note of humor enter Matt Chambers's voice. "I can tell, kid. Your teeth are chattering."

Oh no. "I've been wet for an hour," he confessed.

"Dear Lord," Matt muttered. "Andy, talk your boyfriend into going to put on some warm clothes. I'll hit the horn and see what I can do from up here, okay?

"Yeah, Dad. Thanks. Seriously, *thank* you." Andy's voice grew clearer as he took back the phone. "Baby, you there?"

"Yeah," Eli mumbled. "Can he really help us?"

"Of course he can," Andy said, and his faith in his father took Eli's breath away. How did somebody simply *believe* like that? "But the gifts are another matter. You know, I could be back by tonight to help you—"

"No," Eli muttered. "No, Andy, you're with your family. Seriously, just stay. I'll deal with—" He had to stop to shiver, and Marge's voice penetrated his misery.

"Eli Engle, your boyfriend just texted me to get you out of the damned cold. Now come next door. They've got hot coffee and blankets for you and Leon, and you can let the next shift go to work."

"That's Margie, right?" Andy asked. "She's getting you warm, right?"

Eli nodded and then managed a "Y-y-y-y-esss...."

"Good. I'll text some backers, get ahold of the old roommates and some of the volunteers who moved out of state. Lots of people have good memories of Rainbow House. Let's see if we can spread some Christmas spirit, okay?"

"Andy—" He was trying to say "Don't worry." He was trying to say "Stay home." But his throat and his ears were tight with cold, even as Margie moved him to the coffee shop next door, which had apparently opened its doors to help the people in Rainbow House out of the goodness of their hearts.

"I love you, baby," Andy said. "Let me talk to someone and see if and when I can get a ride to St. Albans, and maybe I can get home early, okay?"

"I'm not taking you away from your family," Eli said, finally pulling himself together. It helped that Margie had led him away from the basement stairs and the heat from the restaurant across the alleyway was starting to permeate his wet clothes. "Your dad is finding me a plumber. Please, Andy. Just stay there and have fun and do Christmas, and next year I'll come with you—"

"Next year we're going to Martinique," Andy said darkly. "Merry Christmas to us! I want someplace I can feel sun on my toes."

Eli chuckled weakly. Andy was always the first person in the park to take his shoes off in the spring. "Next year you're going to Vermont," he said fondly. "Stay. Be with your family."

"Eli!" Leon came trotting up quickly in the alley. "Eli, you've got to move. Apparently we've got *two* guys with pumps coming, and I'm fielding calls from a company that wants to come fix our pipes. Man, this is above my paygrade. I need you!"

"I gotta go," Eli mumbled.

"I love you. I'll see what I can do from here," Andy replied, resigned.

"Love you too," Eli said, but Andy had already signed off.

Grimly, Eli turned to Leon. "Can they meet with me next door?" he all but pleaded. "Leon, I've got to get warm."

"Yeah, I'll go talk to them." Leon stood six foot six if he stood an inch. An enormous Black man with midnight skin and graying braids, he had a rumbly voice and shoulders as wide as a barn. Eli had known him as a teenager because Leon had been at Rainbow House for over ten years, and Eli would trust him with his life, but Leon tended to lose his temper with idiots and was not always the most reasonable voice of the organization.

"Tell them where I am," Eli said, shuddering again.

"Come on, Eli," Margie said. "Let's get you warm."

"Wh-wh-what about the kids?" Eli asked. "Is the heat out all over the building?"

"The furnace and radiators are out," Margie said, "but you know most of the rooms use space heaters in addition. It's not Florida, but they're all huddled in blankets while they do their schoolwork. They should be fine."

Eli let out a small breath. "Better if we get this fixed," he murmured. Then, only loud enough for Margie to hear: "The presents, Margie. Half the presents are toast."

She sighed. "Yeah. Yeah, I know. I've got the volunteers making piles to see which kids lost the most stuff. It's… it's going to be hard to make that loss up."

Eli swallowed and nodded, remembering Andy's pledge to see what he could do from all the way up in Vermont. Part of him wanted to scoff and simply assume he was on his own, like he'd been since he was seventeen.

But part of him remembered the first holiday disaster he and Andy had weathered with Rainbow House… and he hoped.

Back Then

HOLIDAYS WERE always high pressure for organizations like Rainbow House, particularly because kids were involved. Kids had such high hopes for holidays, especially if they'd celebrated with their families before they'd been displaced or disowned and left to fend for themselves on the streets. They equated that happy holiday with being secure and cared for and loved, and they wondered if they'd ever feel that way again.

Rainbow House couldn't heal all the wounds—they couldn't even come close—but they could try to let kids know that they were secure and cared for on *this* day, whatever day it was, with the people they were with.

So getting the kids costumes so they could go trick-or-treating at a local shopping center was a big deal. The merchants did it for the entire neighborhood, giving candy and coupons for merchandise and decorating their storefronts, even the ones inside the building. The kids weren't required to go, but the older kids got points toward chores for helping to supervise younger kids, and Eli had noticed that the older kids enjoyed dressing up too.

this was your night off." He gave a winsome smile. "You, me, Chinese food… remember?"

Eli had stared at him for an absolutely fraught moment, not sure if he should grab his phone back and run out the door, never to return again, or simply beg off as having a work emergency and go back to the shelter to pace the floor and try to come up with something… anything… to help fix the situation.

He opened his mouth and closed it, brain still caught between the two extremes. Until this moment he'd done his best to keep any work problems he might have had to himself. Andy had helped on the weekends when they'd been dating—and even now after they'd moved in, to tell the truth—but Eli had sworn to himself, up and down and back and forth, that he was not going to make Andy's life all about Eli's job. It wasn't fair. Eli was more than that, wasn't he? He saw the occasional movie, right? Read a book once in a while? Held a political opinion? He didn't have to begin and end with Rainbow House, right? Shouldn't Andy get more than that in his life?

So he opened his mouth to say, "I've got to go take care of something. I'm sorry." What happened instead was half an hour of emotional word vomit involving padding and wings and fairy boys and twenty-five yards of missing rainbow gauze.

Andy stood through the whole thing, hands on Eli's shoulders, before he said, "Here. This sounds involved. How about let's go eat some Chinese food, get some gelato, and we'll think of a solution while we talk."

Eli gaped at him. "But isn't that date night?"

Andy grinned. "Yes. Because I can think much better over Chinese food and gelato than I can standing here in the kitchen wondering when we're going to eat. Let's go!"

Andy had asked questions on the way there, and Eli had pulled up some photos on his phone of sketches the kids had drawn for their costumes. Andy looked at the sketches and hemmed and hawed and then had asked if he could take the four boys to the local craft store the next day after school.

"We have a budget," Eli had told him, hopefully and also proudly Andy didn't have to give up all his disposable income to Eli's job.

"That's fine," Andy said. "Let me know how much we have to spend. I think we have some options."

They had the best time.

Dorms would plan themes—often from anime or popular cartoons—and the shopping center had costume contests that judged individual and group costumes.

In general it was a fun way to celebrate the holiday—but the possibility for disappointment was always there, hanging just out of sight, like a beam just above eye level ready to take out an unwary walker.

In this case, the beam took the form of a bolt of rainbow-colored gauze that was rerouted in shipping, leaving a dorm of four boys who'd been planning to dress as fairies (Get it? 'Cause they were gay!) without material for wings or robes or tunics or whatever they'd been planning to sew with it when it should have arrived two weeks before Halloween.

The week before Halloween, the boys were despondent.

Now that he was no longer an adolescent, Eli recognized the distress that kids could put on themselves over something like this. He liked to think of the emotional support kids got from mostly functional families as "padding." People with "padding" could bounce back better from setbacks. They could think through a problem because the pain from falling on their asses wasn't as acute. They could cope with hard emotional dilemmas, secure in the knowledge that they could recover because their "padding" gave them resilience and strength.

His kids didn't have any of that.

He spent a day running around trying to drum up a bolt of cloth to get into that boys' dorm or to find a seamstress willing to donate some time since the boys didn't have enough time left or… or… or….

Eli's brain shorted out at this point because this had been his first year in charge of holidays of any sort and the same year he and Andy had moved in together. He spent a lot of time trying to get his mental and emotional feet underneath him and combating the terrible, gut-wrenching fear that somehow, something was going to rip this entire life of cobwebs and daydreams down around his ears.

So the kids were panicking, the staff was panicking, he was panicking, and Andy came home from work to find him chewing out some poor fabric-store owner for not having rainbow gauze by the bolt.

"Hey, hey, hey…." Andy laughed as he pulled the phone from his hand before Eli chucked it across the kitchen. "What's up? I thought

In the end, they had gone with T-shirts in neon colors, opalescent ribbon, florist wire, and brightly colored cellophane wrapping paper—and black hair dye. They'd called themselves "punk fairies," and their costumes cost half what the bolt of wayward cloth had been going to cost.

And they'd won the group costume contest.

Andy had stayed up for two nights running on his weekend helping the boys with their costumes, telling them about how he'd come out to his hometown by wearing his sister's fairy wings with his football uniform and making them laugh about the story of his ex-boyfriend who had come out to his own mother by borrowing the wings himself. Eli had wandered into the dorm between his other duties and listened as Andy spoke, warmly and with patience, to the excited adolescent boys.

God, he was such a good man. The kind of man with "padding" who enjoyed sharing that emotional stability, that kindness.

And it hit Eli suddenly—this man was *his*. His man. His boyfriend. His partner. Andy had patiently and tenderly pulled Eli into his arms, into his home, into his life, until they were so completely intertwined Eli wasn't sure where he stopped and Andy started.

His heart beating in his ears was the first sign of panic.

Margie had found him hyperventilating under the staircase to the dorms, and she had needed to give him coffee and cookies and calm him down in order to ferret out the reason why.

"He's perfect!" Eli managed to gasp out. "Just… perfect!"

"His eyes are a little crossed," Margie said practically. "And, you know, he broke his nose, I think, playing football. And I don't think he'll ever be president of the company. I see him as a happy cog in that machine for the rest of his life."

Eli squinted at her. "I have no idea what you're talking about."

"A perfectly ordinary, perfectly decent man with a really wonderful heart. Why does this scare you?"

Eli scrubbed at his face, understanding what she was saying but not sure she could ever get what he was saying. "My whole life," he rasped. "My whole life I wanted somebody in my life that good. And I thought I had it, and then my parents found my copy of *Magic Mike* in my room and figured out what it meant."

Margie gave him a sympathetic look. "Joe Manganiello?" she asked.

"Channing Tatum!" he retorted, and she chuckled.

"Who bears a striking resemblance to the man making fairy costumes upstairs, because he's terribly in love with you."

Eli blinked and then found a reluctant smile teasing his mouth. "They do sort of have the same mouth," he admitted. "But you see what I mean."

She nodded. "Padding," she said softly. "Your parents kicked you out, and all of that protection you had in your heart against the bad stuff that could happen in the world, all of that disappeared. So now you have something—someone—really wonderful in your life, and you're barely holding it together because you're afraid it's going to get ripped out of your arms again."

Eli swallowed, ready to panic over again. "Yeah," he said.

"Honey, all I can tell—besides the fact that even a blind woman could see how much that kid loves you and thinks what you've got going is forever—is to let the relationship strengthen you while you have it. You're right. No one relationship can be counted on forever. Even if his heart is forever—and I think it is—fate and general cockup could screw you both over. But he's willing to pour all this love into you, so take it. Take it and return it and let it make you stronger. Believe in it, even if it's only for today or tomorrow or this month or this year. If things go wrong and somehow you lose him, be strong enough to tell yourself, 'I was loved once for who I am, and I will be again.' And value the time you spent with a really lovely human being. And maybe someday you'll believe that it will last forever." She gave a small smile. "Like I do. But I'm just a silly old woman and a hopeless romantic. Who cares what I think?"

He took a shuddery breath, feeling like maybe he could go back to his job and pull his shit together. "I do," he said, standing up to kiss her on the cheek.

And he did. He did care. He didn't start to believe he'd have Andy forever that night, but he started to treasure every moment they did have together.

When Andy's mother started calling after Thanksgiving, begging her son to come home for Christmas, he'd started to repeat Margie's mantra over and over again.

"I was loved once for who I am, and I will be again."

Because he figured his time was up with Andy. Nothing as good as Andy Chambers was meant to last forever.

And Now

ELI STARTLED up from the chair in his office, where he'd nodded off after the sumps had cleared out the basement and the heat had been restored. The plumber had gotten started and planned to finish up in the morning, and he'd hit up the city to make sure they at least had potable water being delivered over the next few days. And he had a neatly inventoried list of how many gifts each kid had left in the piles—with a rating for what the gift might be. Socks and underwear were a one-star gift. A small stuffed animal was a two-star gift. A necessary smartphone for a kid going back to public school or starting a job search was a five-star gift, and so on.

Eli still had the original lists of what the kids had been going to get—he didn't throw that away until February!—and the number of three-star and higher gifts that were littering the floor of the basement in a sodden heap was truly staggering.

He'd been formulating strategies and calling in favors to try to replace what they were missing for Christmas when his body had remembered that he'd gotten about four hours of sleep the night before and spent the morning freezing his ass off as he worked to unload the basement.

When he tried to place what had interrupted his sleep, he reached into his pocket, pulled out his phone, and saw texts from Andy.

I've got lots of gifts wrapped and ready to deliver tomorrow. Send me your finalized lists so we can see what else you need.

Eli blinked hard, and for the first time since he'd gotten jolted awake at 5:00 a.m., a little warmth started to creep into his chest.

You shouldn't have to do this, he texted back. *YOU'RE ON VACATION.*

Whatever. Margie says you need to wake up, eat something warm and go home and sleep. She told me you'd only listen to me, but I think she just didn't want to hear your backtalk.

Eli chuckled, the humor surprising him. *You lie—I'm an angel.*

You are. You're MY angel. Take good care of my angel, okay? Margie will tell me if you haven't eaten and left in an hour. We're a conspiracy, Margie and me. Listen to her.

"Eli!" Margie called as she walked down the hallway. "I've got a hot sandwich and coffee for you to get you home. Now move it!"

When he turned to Margie, he had a tired smile on his face, but it was a real one, and that was something. "You and Andy are tag-teaming me."

"We are," she agreed. "Is it working? Are you ready to—aw, baby." She bustled in, a bag of takeout dangling from her hand. "You fell asleep at your desk, didn't you?"

He nodded and yawned and looked at the clock. Oh Lord, 8:00 p.m. already? His phone buzzed again.

Eli? Are you eating?

Damn. *Yes, I'm eating now. I'll text you when I get home.*

Okay. Promise?

I do. He paused because he wanted so much to say more, to tell Andy how much his support had meant during this miserable day. *I love you,* he texted instead. *You've been so much help already. Your father's a lifesaver.*

You say that and I haven't even told you about the plasterer that's going to arrive the day after tomorrow. I'm sorry I couldn't make it sooner.

Eli's eyes burned. *Are you kidding? The earliest we had for a plumber was December 28th. Your dad's the BEST.*

Yeah. But then, so are you. Love you back. EAT!!!!

Eli did, Margie briefing him on the kids and their day with the cold and the knowledge—running like wildfire gossip through the school—that Santa might be a little short on gifts this year.

"Oh no," he groaned, mouth full of pastrami on rye. "I was hoping they wouldn't find out!"

Margie grimaced, and she must have been really tired too, because her eyes grew bright and shiny. "You know what Lola said to me today?"

Eli girded himself. "What?"

"That if it was a choice between presents for her or presents for Josie, we needed to make sure Josie had her presents first. She said she knew that Santa didn't always show up, but Josie still believed."

Eli suddenly found it hard to swallow. "Wow," he said after the bite finally went down.

"I'm saying," Margie murmured softly.

"We've got to get those kids some presents," he said with renewed fervor. He was wondering how many Andy could actually have. He'd promised a delivery the next day. How would he do that?

"Yeah." She gave a bedraggled smile. "But first, you and me have to go catch our train and get home so we can come back tomorrow and fight some more."

Eli nodded. The night before, Margie's son had come to get her—he had a car and had known the night was going to be late. Most nights, Eli and Margie walked to the subway together, because they both lived in Williamsburg. Margie got off the stop after Eli, where her husband would be waiting to walk her home.

"Which we can do," he said. "Thanks to my boyfriend."

"He's a keeper," she said with emphasis.

"He is indeed."

Together they finished up and left the night watch in charge of the house so they could go back to their homes and drop, exhausted, into their beds.

The next morning, Eli was awakened at 6:00 a.m. with a text telling him that the water had seeped through the walls in the kitchen and shorted out the freezer. Everything from Christmas cookies to the five turkeys they'd had stored in the giant freezer was inedible, and it's not like the kids stopped eating.

Chapter 7: Baking Cookies Solves Everything

Earlier on the day the pipe broke…

"I CAN'T believe I'm doing this," Andy grumbled, throwing flour into Porter's mother's giant mixer. That's why they were making the cookies at Porter's mother's house—she used to run a bakery and had kept some of the industrial-sized appliances. And her kitchen was top notch.

"Baking cookies or making a mess?" Porter asked, grinning.

Andy gave him a remorseful look. "I'm sorry," he said, taking a moment to wipe down the counter so he could continue to bake cookies. "I'm just distracted. I should be in Brooklyn right now, you know?"

"Yeah." Porter blew out a breath. "Man, that sucks, what Eli's going through. I wish I could be there. I'm getting damned good at fixing plumbing. You sure your dad's got a guy?"

Andy nodded. "He does. And as worried as I am about that, it's the presents that are killing me. You don't understand. We've been budgeting since *August* to get those kids the stuff they need. There were laptops in that room for the kids graduating and going to college. There was high-end makeup for our trans girls—their identity is so tied up in their appearance at this age, and feeling pretty and made up is so important for their self-esteem. Binders for our enby or trans boys so they can feel like themselves. Or, hell! Just clothes that don't have holes or haven't been worn by anyone else, phones to help them get jobs—"

"Or surf porn," Porter said with a wink.

"Well, yeah, teenagers." Andy chuckled because he and Porter had been that age together. He sobered, grateful for the lighter moment. "But you know, important things for kids growing up without the support system they thought they'd have."

"I get it," Porter said. Then he paused and sort of shifted on his feet. "Uhm… so, how picky are these kids? I mean, does it have to be Aeropostale and Abercrombie & Fitch?"

Andy squinted at him, not sure of what he meant. "I know *you* were the clotheshorse in school, Porter, but these kids were out on the street. They'd be pretty happy with Old Navy."

Porter looked abashed and all but dug his toe in the tile of his mother's kitchen floor. "But, you know, could it be handmade?"

Andy thought about it. "I know a number of the kids are nuts about my mom's sweaters, if that's what you're asking. Why? What do you have in mind?"

"Hold on a sec," Porter said. "I've got to go clear it with my mom and Pastor Dan first."

Andy stared at him. "Pastor Dan?" he asked, at a loss. "What happened to Pastor Martin?"

"Pastor Martin retired to the old Unitarian's home or whatever last year. Pastor Dan took his place. He's, uhm"—Porter blushed—"sort of young."

"Is he cute?" Andy teased, not sure how else to explain that intense pink between Porter's beard and his eyes.

And then it got darker.

"He, uhm, comes a few nights a week for dinner," Porter said. "You know. My, uhm, mom asked him the first time, and then, well, it became a thing."

Andy tilted his head suspiciously, remembering what Porter had said—that if he had company, he had it in his own room like an adult.

"Doesn't your mom fall asleep at, like, seven?" Andy asked, more and more fascinated with where this was going.

Porter was practically doing the pee-pee dance. "Look, do you want me to see if I can get some presents or not?"

"Sure. I mean, as long as they're nice. I mean, I'm assuming it's clothing, right?"

"Yeah, they're… well, I think they're awesome. But, you know. I've been stuck here for the last six years. What do I know? Look, let me go make some calls and talk to my mom and… give me a sec, okay?"

And with that, Porter practically ran out of the room. Andy stared after him and then turned his attention back to making Christmas cookies—and getting some of the flour off the kitchen counter.

He had the second pan from his first batch in the oven and was whipping up the second batch when there was a knock at the back door

Andy checked the timer on the oven and went to answer it, inviting in a handsome, fresh-faced man his and Porter's age with water-combed hair under his stocking cap and an earnest expression in his brown eyes.

"Are you Andy?" he asked, extending his hand. "I'm Dan Green. You know, from Porter's church."

"You're Pastor Dan?" Andy asked, holding up his own flour-covered hands apologetically. "Sorry, I'm a mess. But come in! I—"

"I'll be right back," Dan told him. "I've got a couple of boxes in the SUV outside. Porter said it was something of an emergency?"

"Yes, but he didn't tell me what you're—"

But Dan was out and back and Andy was left to pull the browned pan of cookies out of the oven and put the next pan in before returning to the mixer bowl for the next batch, this one snickerdoodles.

Andy watched in surprise as Dan—and then Porter—went out to the SUV and returned a number of times, each arriving with a big plastic box embedded with cedar chips. The tops of the crates were opaque, but he'd seen his mom keep yarn in them and started to get a hint as to what was inside.

But as he started to push dollops of dough onto the next clean pan, Dan and Porter—talking quietly and animatedly together in the way that intimate companions tended to do—began to remove the lids.

"Oh my God," he said. "Where did they all come from?"

Each box held sweaters. Hand-knitted or hand-crocheted sweaters, each one unique in color, size, shape, and technique. There were delicate women's cardigans with embroidered flowers on the pockets and chunky men's ski sweaters with a miracle of colorwork at the yoke. Jackets, pullovers, cables, lace, intarsia, and fair isle in sizes infant to adult XXXL, it was like a magic garden of beautiful, unique handcrafted clothes, and Andy was in awe.

"You *guys*," he said, when he could manage words. "Where did all of this come from?"

"The knitting circle," Dan said, obviously preening. "I mean, I kind of inherited all of these. The women are fabulous, you know? They knit every day, and they wrap and store the finished products, so no moths or predators. But the old pastor told me he didn't know what to do with them! Everybody in town has someone who will make handcrafts *for* them. There's a hat-and-mitten club for kids in disadvantaged households, but even that gets overstocked sometimes. I've been meaning to find another charity to give these to, but I only took over a few months ago—"

"He took over in July," Porter said, and they both nodded.

"And, well—" Dan grinned and shrugged. "—Porter asked his mother if she thought it would be appropriate, and I honestly can't believe he had to ask!"

"Well, Mom's a big contributor," Porter said, and Andy could see the flush again, and then Dan gave Porter a worshipful look that almost took Andy's breath away.

"That's not fair," Dan said, his heart practically in his eyes. "Your knitting is amazing, Porter. I know you don't like to brag, but your colorwork is some of the most intricate I've ever seen!"

Porter grimaced and looked anywhere but at Andy, who was staring at him with his mouth open.

"You knit?" he asked, trying not to let his voice squeak.

"You cook?" Porter shot back as the timer went off for the next pan of cookies.

"My mom taught me so that I might not starve when I got to be an adult," Andy retorted, lunging across the kitchen to get to the oven before the delicate cream-colored disks turned too brown. "You used to give your mother a *terrible* time about knitting, remember? Teased her unmercifully about not having anything better to do?"

"Oh God," Porter mumbled, burying his face in his hands. "I remember. I do. Teenagers are terrible people. But winters are *long* here, Andy. And the nights last forever, and I get bored in front of the television and... you know." He smiled sheepishly. "I always did think better when I was moving."

Andy pulled out the tray of cookies and used the spatula to scoop them to the cinnamon-sugar station. "You do," he conceded and then sent his friend—and his friend's lover, if he was any judge of nuance—a fond look. "And if you made some of these sweaters, so much the better. Because I think these are *great*. I mean, it's not the end of the problem, but oh my God, if the kids at Rainbow House got one of these—and maybe even a little note, saying how it was handmade by someone with love—you guys. You have no idea. I mean, there's a program that gives knit scarves to kids who are aging out of foster care—our kids get one too—and those scarves are treasured. This is like *gold*."

"How many do you need?" Dan asked. "How should we do this?"

Andy put the next pan of cookies in to bake and then scooped two snickerdoodles—still hot—onto a plate to give to Dan and Porter.

"Well, if Porter can take over in the assembly line, I'm going to go call Eli's people—"

"Not Eli?" Porter asked.

Andy shook his head, remembering how exhausted—and cold— Eli had sounded during their phone call that morning.

"He's up to his eyeballs in water mains and restoring power and heat right now," he said. "Let's get this done without him and he'll have one less thing to worry about."

"God, you're a nice guy," Porter muttered. "I don't even know how you do that!"

Andy gave him a flat look. "You design and knit sweaters for charity to keep your mom company, Porter. And your boyfriend is a pastor. I think you have me beat."

Both Dan and Porter looked at him in shock, and he rolled his eyes.

"Don't even bother to deny it," he said. "But don't worry, I won't tell a soul." He was so totally telling his sisters. "Now if you'll excuse me...." He gestured to the kitchen, the sweaters, and the phone he was pulling out of his pocket all at the same time. "You two carry on, and I'll go do my thing."

Margie was so relieved she almost burst into tears. "Oh my God, really?" she asked. "You could do that? Because Andy—it's heartbreaking. All that work, and it's all in a trash heap on the floor, and the kids were getting so excited, and Eli's *exhausted*. I'm so worried he's going to catch cold or something because this morning was a mess! His lips were blue!"

Andy whined in his throat. "I'll see if I can find a way home tomorrow," he said, thinking about shipping the sweaters down to Brooklyn before Christmas and maybe renting a truck to get that done anyway.

"Not yet," she said, obviously trying to rein in her panic. "Stay there, honey. Your mom seems to need you, and Eli doesn't want to be a bother."

"But it's not a bother," Andy said. "It's *Eli*—"

"Yes, but these things happen. I think he can handle this, Andy. Let's give him a chance to try, okay?"

"Sure, but I'll still try to wrangle some donations up here. Do you have a list of what you're missing?"

"Yeah," she said, blowing out a breath. "We're working on one. I think Eli had a master list in his office."

"Okay, well, send me what you need as soon as you know. I'm calling my bosses to ask for business donations and for other businesses who might give. I mean, I can't magically wish this all away, but I'll do what I can." He'd already left several messages with businesses in Brooklyn and was hoping they'd get back to him as he worked.

He'd have a lot more luck, he thought darkly, with his laptop in front of him instead of big vats of cookie dough. *Eli* would have more luck with him at home, helping him through this mess.

"I'll let you know if anything changes," she said, blowing out a breath. "And I'll get you that list as soon as we get it. How's that?"

"Brilliant," he said, clutching the phone tightly in his hand. "Thanks, Margie."

"Thank *you*, Andy. You're doing a great thing here!"

"I didn't knit the sweaters!" he said, and then he signed off.

He didn't go immediately back in to talk to Porter and Dan, though. God, he wanted to go back home and help—so much. It wasn't that he didn't think Eli could do it. Andy had all the faith in the world. It was just that he knew Eli wasn't great at asking for help, even when he really needed it.

Andy knew that all too well.

Back Then

THEY ALMOST broke up that first Christmas...

Eli—who had blossomed around Halloween—seemed to withdraw into himself after Thanksgiving. Andy had been engaged in a silent war with his mother—all of it done over his cell phone, because she hadn't acknowledged the landline in the apartment yet—and in the middle of a push for a promotion, the better to be able to afford their new apartment.

The two of them had fallen into the classic trap of retreating further and further into their shells, each one preoccupied with their own worries, neither one asking the other for input.

They might have become completely isolated, lonely while being forced to interact like roommates, if not for two things.

The first was that they kept date night—Chinese food and gelato—almost religiously. Andy may have been new to living with someone, but he'd learned from his parents that holding that time sacred was one of the keys to making the relationship work.

The second was that nobody had told Eli about that.

The week after Thanksgiving, Eli had been moody and withdrawn, working late hours and getting up to leave before breakfast. Andy was irritated, but he tried to stay calm. He told himself he'd talk to Eli about it on date night.

But date night came and Eli didn't show.

Nothing. Nada. Not a phone call, not anything.

Andy's temper went through the roof. He and Eli played the "would you find my phone" game all the time, so it was no problem at all to track Eli's phone and find out that he was still at Rainbow House. By the time Andy had taken the train to Bed/Stuy and walked the three blocks to the house, he'd worked up a real head of steam, telling himself—and an imaginary Eli—in no uncertain terms that this was unacceptable, and if Eli couldn't remember how to tell someone at home where he was or to even check in, then Eli was obviously not ready for this kind of commitment.

Everything hurt. He would remember that forever. His joints, his head, his eyes, his throat—it was all swollen and too tight and angry and hurt. Especially his chest. His chest hurt.

His heart hurt.

Finally he stalked through the doors, barely remembering to be civil to Leon as he checked in.

"Where is he?" Andy asked, swallowing his temper.

Leon sighed. "Probably filling out more paperwork. You know, the police won't let him alone about it."

Andy's rage vaporized, his anger forgotten. "About what?" he asked, genuinely puzzled.

"You know... Ambrose?"

"The student?" Andy had gotten to know a lot of the kids there, had gotten to like them and enjoy being in their lives. And the kids had been so grateful—mentors, volunteers, examples of happy-ever-afters—all these things were precious commodities on the island of misfit toys.

After that, Andy took the plates to the kitchen before returning to take Eli by the hand and dress him in his hat and coat before leading him docilely past Leon and into the quiet city to the train.

When they were finally in bed, and Eli had cried again, all without saying more than five words, Andy had held him as he'd drifted into what had probably been his first sleep in days and had made a silent vow to himself. Eli took care of all the kids—that was his job. It was the thing he did with most of his heart. The thing that drove him and fulfilled him and made him light up in the morning and feel satisfied when he went to bed.

Eli was that thing for Andy.

So it was Andy's job to keep Eli going so Eli could keep Rainbow House going. Yeah, Andy enjoyed his job, did it to the best of his ability, and took on extra projects when he could, but he was in no danger of becoming a workaholic.

Eli had claimed top place in his hierarchy, and the thing that drove Eli would be Andy's passion as well.

The next morning over breakfast, when Eli was more animated—and more awake—Andy served him eggs with tomato and chives and some sour cream on top and said, "Eli?"

"Yeah?" It was hard to say with a mouth full of eggs, but he was eating so Andy didn't mind.

"You need to promise me something."

"Okay," Eli said. He looked away. "If I can."

Andy let out a patient breath. "You need to promise to tell me. Bad shit's going to happen, baby, but you need to tell me when it does. You can't do it all alone. I mean, yeah, running the shelter is your job, and you have a grant and get paid for it and everything, but I can help you with the hard stuff." He set the pan down on the stove and rubbed his chest. "The heart stuff," he clarified. "And even the hard stuff like kids and fundraising and grant writing and all the other stuff. But mostly the heart stuff. I can't be there for you if you don't tell me where you are."

Eli gave him a shy smile. "I'll try," he said. "I'll… I've never had that person before. And just when I realized I had you, we were moving in together. I still don't know what I can tell you that won't make you run away screaming."

And leaned against the counter and crossed his arms. "You can tell me when you get your heart broken," he said soberly. "Because I think

"Yeah." Leon frowned. "Eli didn't tell you?"

"No. What happened?"

"Well, first his parents came and fought Eli for custody. And won. And the day they brought that kid home, swearing they would beat the gay right out of him...." Leon swallowed. "Ambrose tried another way out."

"Oh God." Andy didn't want to say the word. He'd known—on one level he'd known. Kids who'd been rejected, for whatever reason, were so damned fragile. And sometimes being in a position where the people they loved sought to actively harm them—and the person they were destined to become—made the most extreme option of escape seem like the best one.

"Is he okay?" Andy asked, barely daring to hope.

"Yeah." Leon nodded. "He's in the hospital right now, and when he's released, he'll be sent to a foster home. But in the meantime, Eli has to fill out all the paperwork again and again because he was the one who said this would happen, and you know in this world, they really only punish the people who tell the truth."

"Amen," Andy whispered. "I'll go check on him. Has he eaten?"

Leon shrugged. "Probably not."

Andy stopped in the kitchen and cadged a couple of leftover plates from the night cook, who was prepping for the morning's breakfast, before heading down the hallway to Eli's office. He entered quietly, nudging the open door with his hip, and found Eli resting his chin on his arms, staring into space as he sat at his desk.

His face was streaked with tears.

Andy set the plates down hurriedly on a filing cabinet and came around the desk, kneeling down and swiveling the chair until Eli turned to face him.

"Baby," he whispered, "I'm so sorry."

Eli came undone, silent sobs that Andy might never have heard if he hadn't taken a breath to talk to Leon. Andy did nothing but hold him, rocking him back and forth and murmuring softly. When Eli was done, Andy made him eat, and he did, without comment, shoving the food in like he hadn't eaten in days. He might not have, given how stressed he'd been.

it's going to happen sometimes, and it's my job to put it back together when it does."

Eli's lips flickered in a smile. "Do you want to hear about it?" he asked tentatively.

"I really, really do," Andy said, sighing in relief. "Let me pour myself some OJ and sit down to my eggs."

They didn't always make date night after that—Eli really did work long hours. But Eli never forgot to text again. And they always started out their mornings talking about their doubts and fears over breakfast. Yeah, sometimes breakfast consisted of protein bars and five minutes before they dashed for their separate trains, but more often, breakfast consisted of the two of them conferring quietly over orange juice, oatmeal, and eggs.

And Now

ANDY FINALLY pulled himself together enough to go inside and continue with the cookies. While he was there, Pastor Dan suggested they wrap the sweaters but tape a brief description tag on the top—so, *Adult Woman, L, Red cardigan, embroidered flowers on pockets,* or any of the myriad other styles they had. That way, the presents were good to go, and Andy could switch the tags out for a name tag once he had a list of Eli's needs.

That didn't stop Andy from snagging the red cardigan for Lola and a smaller white one in almost the same pattern for Josie. He thought the two girls loved flowers and color, and the cardigans would be adorable in the spring, when it was too warm for a heavier sweater.

And basically he wanted to see his girls smile, whether or not they'd lost Christmas presents in the basement debacle. He figured that even if they hadn't, these would be special presents, from him and Eli.

Andy was deep in the middle of another batch of cookies, wishing he could go help with the wrapping, when Charlie and Mary Beth showed up, comfortable enough with Porter's house not to knock. "Porter texted that you'd need help," Charlie said. "What can we do?"

"I thought you guys were in the next town?" Andy said, so grateful he wanted to cry. He was covered in flour and baking his ass off, but the sheer numbers of cookies his mom wanted him to bake had him exhausted already, and it was only afternoon!

"We just got back," Mary Beth said, wandering over to try an iced sugar cookie. She closed her eyes and exhaled blissfully. "You still have the touch, Andy. I don't know what you do—"

"Lemon extract in the icing," Andy said, grinning.

"Well, Mom refuses to do it like you do, and yours are always better. Anyway, what do you need?"

Andy explained the situation to them, from the flood to the ruined presents to the mad bout of wrapping going on in the next room. Charlene and Mary Beth both exclaimed over the loss; they were young enough to remember when not getting a Christmas gift really would have been the end of the world—and then they both started talking at once.

"Wait, I've got an idea!"

"Oh my God, I know something that can help!"

He calmed them down and pointed to Charlene first. "The junior college got a *huge* donation of new prepaid smart phones for the students to buy at a discount. They've been sitting in the bookstore, drawing dust, because most of the kids have the newest iPhone and they're not needed." She grinned. "I knew that job would pay off!"

"Oh wow," Andy said, taking a deep, delirious breath. "We don't need too many of them, Charlie. They were meant for about twenty of the students, and I don't know how many of them survived the flood."

"Let me go call my boss," Charlie said, looking excited. "I can go pick them up today if she can do it. She's super generous. She always keeps a bowl of granola bars for kids she thinks haven't eaten yet, mothers the bookworms, that sort of thing." Charlie gasped. "Hey! Do you have any bookworms?"

Andy grinned. "We have a couple—and a lending library, why?"

"Same reason. We have to send the covers back of the books we decide not to restock. Let me see if she can donate some of those too!"

"Charlie, you're a genius!" Andy gave her a big, floury hug. "Go do magic! You're amazing!"

"But I haven't even talked yet!" Mary Beth protested. "Let me talk!"

"Of course!" Andy said. "Apologies, Bimini Beth. Your turn!"

She grinned, all excitement. "My anime club was going to sell these book/collectible sets to raise money. One of the girls got them donated by the artist because she wrote fangirl letters and stuff. But it turns out the only people who *wanted* this set already had five of them from the series already. My friend Avery was really depressed because she was going to have to write the author and say we couldn't sell any, but this would be so much cooler. The books are very sweet, YA level, with all sorts of queer representation in them. We've got twelve sets. Would that help?"

Andy's eyes actually burned. "You, too, are a genius! Oh my God, you guys, go make your calls! I'm going to stay here in cookie hell, but if you can get some extra wrapping paper, go get the other stuff and come in and join the party, okay?"

It didn't end there. Andy kept on with the baking, and Porter's kitchen became a portal to Santa's little sweatshop. Young men and women Mary Beth and Charlie's age began to stream in, bearing mint in-the-box laptops that had been hanging around since a birthday or brand-new snow boots that hadn't fit quite right and had never been returned. Mary Beth's friends brought in stuffed animals, fresh in the wrappers, explaining that they'd gotten three of them for their birthday and they were *very special* anime animals and he wouldn't understand, and the entire school football team came in with brand-new sports equipment—footballs, volleyballs, baseball mitts—all of them still with the tags on.

The true scope of what his sisters had done didn't start to dawn on him until Porter and Pastor Dan started trooping presents outside to Dan's SUV.

"Where are all of these going?" he asked, a little dazed—and a little sugar crazed too. He'd been eating nothing but cookies since breakfast.

"Dan's got a cargo plane," Porter said, like didn't everybody? "It's out at the hangar by Mr. Portenby's airstrip, so the presents should be safe. I talked to a buddy of mine—"

"Ex-boyfriend," Dan said, giving a sly little glance.

"Ex-hookup," Porter corrected, looking *very* embarrassed. "Not boyfriend. There's a difference." He gave his own sideways glance. "As you very well know." He cleared his throat. "Anyway, his cousin always goes back to New York with an empty truck. He leaves tomorrow night, and we figured that if he hauled some of the presents down, and Dan flew down at about the same time, they could deliver all the presents, and then Dan could fly him back to Foxglove, because his wife was afraid she wouldn't get to see him Christmas Eve."

Andy paused for a moment, putting all this together to see what it really meant. "You offered him a flight home," he said softly. "So he'd get to see his wife, and the presents would get to Brooklyn."

Dan shrugged. "Porter likes to fly," he mumbled, his face bright red.

Andy tried to wipe his face with his palms and realized he couldn't without leaving flour paste all over. "You guys. I'm a mess. All I'm doing is making a diabetic nightmare, and you—"

"And your sisters!" Porter laughed.

"You've literally become the elves who saved Christmas."

Pastor Dan shrugged. "We were going to leave tomorrow night after the pageant." He and Porter looked at each other, and Porter nodded. "I, uh, know you really want to be back there with him. Do you want a ride?"

Andy thought about it, the memory of Eli, chin propped on his fists, crying alone in his office, still fresh and raw in his heart.

"Yeah," he said. "I don't know what I'll do with my luggage...." He shook his head. "Don't care. I'll have a go bag ready for after the family choral presentation. How's that?"

"Perfect," Porter said, grinning. "Your guy's gonna be super happy to see you."

"He's going to be super happy to see all of *this*," Andy said excitedly. "Wait until Margie sends me the list and we can compare what we've lost to what we've got—I think this is going to be his best Christmas surprise *ever*!"

'OH MY word, Andy. You're late! We need to practice for the choral presentation tomorrow. Please tell me you got all the cookies done?"

Andy looked at his mother dully, his eyes gritty with fatigue. He'd finished the cookies by four o'clock, but they'd needed to work for another three hours to get the rest of the presents wrapped. On the one hand, he'd gotten to talk to Porter's mom, which had been nice. She had a tart tongue, it was true, but she was often very funny.

"Did you see our chicken jumpers?" she'd asked, cackling.

"Yes. They're terrifying." He remembered Eli's horror at the idea of wee chicken sweaters and smiled.

"Right? I mean, chickens aren't smarter than people, but the people don't know that!"

He'd laughed and grabbed some wrapping paper and a package, and she knitted while he started to help. When she asked where Dan and Porter had gone, he'd told her they were taking presents out to the airstrip, and she'd snorted.

"I think that's code for getting busy, what about you?"

He'd snickered but then shushed her. "If they wanted the world to know, they'd tell the world," he whispered, looking around at the animated teenagers all having their own discussions.

"Well, if they didn't want *me* to know, they need to keep it quiet! It may look like I fall asleep in my chair at seven, but it's a nap, I tell you. By the time I wake up from my nap...." She shook her head and *tsk*ed. "Not pretty. I'm saying."

He'd snorted another laugh, and the scissors slipped in his hand, making a hash out of the wrapping paper.

"Are you seeing what you're making me do?" he told her, part in outrage but mostly in affection. Porter's mother was what his grandparents might have called "a pistol"—not all butterflies and candy corn, but not boring either.

"That stuff's terrible for the environment anyway," she sniffed. "Recycle some brown paper with some pretty ribbon."

Charlie heard her and said back, "Yeah, but this was going to get thrown out by the book store anyway as surplus after a fundraiser. So, you know, we're just letting it be used before the landfill."

Porter's mother looked at Charlie in admiration. "You kids are gonna save the world, you mark my words."

Charlie came by and kissed her on the cheek. "Maybe, Mrs. Burrell, but *you're* going to save all the chickens. Andy, let me have that piece you just cut off. I've got something smaller I can use it on."

So catching up with Porter's mother had been fun, but between the cookies and the wrapping, he'd needed to send Charlie out for pizza because after cleaning up after the cookies, he couldn't even *look* a the kitchen again, and his blood sugar was on such a roller coaster he'c contemplated getting sick.

He was in no mood for his mother's demands at the moment.

"Yeah, Mom. They're in the boxes in the mud room, on top of the washer." The mud room wasn't heated, so it was the next best thing to keeping them in a refrigerator.

"Well, Andy, don't just sit there. Charlie told me you ate pizza for dinner. Come get ready to go use the piano at church!"

Andy took a breath and stood, every bone in his body cracking. "Did Charlie tell you what else I was doing all day?"

"Something about getting last-minute gifts for the kids at the shelter. Honestly, if your boyfriend's going to wait this long, he's going to have to take what he gets—"

"He didn't wait this long!" Andy interrupted, needing her to understand this point at least. "The basement sprang a leak, and they were destroyed. He's been planning Christmas since August! He almost couldn't find someone to help with the plumbing. Dad had to call in a favor."

His mother's expression softened. "Well, that's too bad, honey. I'm glad you could help him a little with that. But you promised you'd be here for the holidays, and it would be really nice if you were, you know, *here*. So I need you to come practice with us. Please, don't fight me on this."

He stared at her. "You're not hearing me," he stated flatly. "This was huge. A huge undertaking. The entire town donated stuff to help him out. Pastor Dan and Porter are transporting everything out tomorrow night so it can get there in time for Christmas Eve. This was enormous. Mary Beth and Charlie and Porter and Dan and Porter's mom—they all pulled off a miracle here—"

"While Andy worked three jobs at once," Charlie chimed in, standing up to their mother for the first time in Andy's memory. "Mom, he's exhausted. He was baking cookies, making calls, wrapping presents—he was killing himself to help out his boyfriend and his boyfriend's kids. Do you think you could give him a break tonight? There's nothing in the child handbook that says you have to kill yourself to come home, okay?"

"Don't be melodramatic," Cindy snapped. "He baked some cookies. I do it every year. It's not going to kill him to come sing with us."

Andy's temple gave a throb. He reminded himself that he was leaving immediately after the presentation the next night, and he hadn't told his mom.

Charlie opened her mouth to protest, but Andy shook his head. "No, no," he said. "Don't worry about it, Charlie. The pageant is the last thing I'm doing here anyway, so let's go practice and make it super-duper great." His voice cracked with sarcasm, and Charlie's eyes got really big, as did Mary Beth's. Both of them gave him wary looks but said nothing as he stomped to the mudroom to grab his coat, hat, and boots.

Their mother glared at them as they got ready, but Andy's father actually came to talk.

"Son?" he said, looking worried. "What did you mean by that?"

"I'm going with Porter and Dan to take the presents down to Brooklyn, Dad," he said softly. "I'd appreciate it if you didn't tell Mom about it. I'll just go, and she can fuss all she wants, but I'm tired of it. Eli is literally the most important thing in my life. He is *my* family, and I wanted him to have you guys too, but she won't even acknowledge he's alive." His voice broke bitterly as he remembered those piles of sweaters, some of which had his mother's unmistakable color choices or needlework. "She won't even knit him a sweater. Dad, I can't be here with you guys if you're not going to be part of his family. I just...." His voice fractured again—and this time not with sarcasm. "I'm exhausted," he confessed. "Let's just go. I'll learn the choir part, and we can practice. I'm actually looking forward to it. But if she wants to see me ever again after tomorrow night, she's going to have to get off her high horse and get her ass to Brooklyn."

His father nodded. "How are you getting down there?" he asked.

"Porter's driving with the trucker, who's taking the bulk of the presents, but I'm going in the cargo plane with Pastor Dan."

"Ask Dan if he's got room for one more," his dad said. "You're right, son. *I'd* like to meet Eli. I realized this morning that I was talking to him for the first time in two and a half years, and he sounded like a really great ki—erm, young man. And I really liked the sound of the two of you together. You guys have a guest room, right?"

Andy nodded, his eyes burning. "Yeah."

"Well, if you're taking Christmas down to Brooklyn, I can join you if you can put me up."

Andy found himself engulfed in his father's best hug, and then the girls whispered, "Guys, Mom's coming. Get a move on. Let's go practice so we can come home and sleep!"

As his father guided him, once again, with a hand in his back so he might not fall apart in exhaustion, Andy thought that finally, *finally*, he could bring the family to Eli that Eli so desperately deserved.

Chapter 8: Our Romantic Hero Realizes You Can Go Home Again

Eli stared at the mess in the kitchen and tried not to hyperventilate.

"Oh dear God," he whispered. "The hell. What in the actual hell?"

"The pipes were leaking in the walls," Leon said, sounding as stunned as Eli felt. "We didn't notice it yesterday because, well...."

"The basement was floating," Eli said. "Leon, what are we going to feed these kids! Not just today but, you know, *Christmas*. All of the flour, the cookies, the turkey—the only thing salvageable is the potatoes."

Leon sucked air through his teeth. "Mmm...."

"Yeah," Eli said, looking at the sludge on the floor. "I don't know if I'd want a potato that had been floating around in that. Okay. So we've got a plumber coming today, and we've got a cleanup crew." He looked at Leon for confirmation. "We do, right? We have a cleanup crew?"

Leon grimaced. "Buddy, I'm sorry. I think between the staff and the maintenance crew, *we're* the only cleanup detail available in the five boroughs. And since you're the one who's going to be on to feed us all, I use the term 'we' loosely."

Eli sighed and rubbed his temples. Okay. Okay. He could do this. He'd managed to survive on the streets by begging, borrowing, and stealing—and by offering to sweep or clean up for some of the local merchants in exchange for a meal. It had been a bodega owner, in fact, who had walked him to Rainbow House after he'd gotten sick one night sleeping in the rain. In spite of the fact that they were deep in the heart of the "big city," as Andy's mom labeled it, like any matter, a big city was made up of molecules, and Eli knew that they had some first-rate molecules in their orbit.

He'd start with the vendors who sold them the food in the first place. A lot of the truck guys were really nice about giving Rainbow House their surplus—fresh fruit that would be left off the turnpike so drivers didn't have to pay for the extra when they weighed in, or produce that a merchant couldn't afford but was about to expire. When Eli had taken over, his predecessor had fed the kids almost exclusively off those offerings, but Eli had applied for grants so the shelter was a little more food-secure.

He was going to have to go back to the old days, he thought with resolution, and just as he'd shored himself up to hit the phones, his phone rang.

Don't worry about presents, Andy sent. *Margie sent me your list, and we've got a truck coming in.*

He sent an inventory sheet, with the lost presents ticked off, and the addition of "handmade gift" next to each name.

Holy crap.

You're welcome. Truck should be there tomorrow morning.

Eli's shoulders sagged, and his knees wobbled. In his entire life he could not remember actually experiencing the term "weak with relief," but here he was.

How did you do this?

Magic! There was a pause, and then a picture came through. It was taken from the doorway of a smallish living room, lamplit and filled to the gills with teenagers and young adults wrapping presents—new presents, Eli saw in relief, not hand-me-downs, which his kids knew far too well. An older woman sat in the corner, her lap covered with a colorful afghan. She was knitting, but her face lit up with tender animation as she apparently talked to a girl Eli identified as Mary Beth, Andy's sister. In the background stood Porter and another man, this one freshly scrubbed and as earnest as a Muppet, taking inventory and obviously giving directions.

Magic and elves, Andy added after the picture came through.

Oh God, Andy. How did you even accomplish this?

I did nothing. I was baking cookies all day for my mother's shindig. Porter, Pastor Dan (Porter's secret boyfriend—hoo boy, do I have gossip), and Mary Beth and Charlie all pitched in. They called their friends, who called their friends, and Margie sent me the inventory sheets as soon as you were done with them.

Big ticket items too?

Prepaid cell phones and year-old computers—but mint in the box.

Oh wow. OH WOW. He giggled a little. *Andy, you're the greatest! You're a superhero!*

So's my boyfriend, Andy replied cheekily. Then, *How's everything else?*

Eli thought about not telling him—he did. Because this was Andy's vacation and he'd already done so much. But he remembered that night after Ambrose… well, after Ambrose had left Rainbow House, and how devastated Eli had been in the aftermath. And how, in the end, it hadn't been about what Andy could do for Eli, but how Andy had *cared* about what Eli cared about.

It had given him the strength to keep going. And right now he felt so very weak, so very inadequate to the task ahead.

All thoughts of Andy leaving him for Vermont fled. All fears of losing Andy because Eli wasn't good enough, or because he was too needy, or because his job was too all-consuming, fled. The only thing that remained was his conviction that he was in love with a good man, a man who would love him and partner with him and who wouldn't leave him hanging for a picture-perfect life with his adorable blond family, but who would stick with him through the thick and the thin.

A man who made everything in Eli's life better.

Abruptly the phone in his hand rang.

"Eli? You're scaring me. You didn't answer right away. What happened?"

Eli let out a sad little chuckle. It was a good thing he'd decided to tell the truth. Andy wasn't taking any risks.

"The pipes leaked into the walls," he said baldly. "We've got no food, and I'm about to go recruit the older kids to come help with the mess before someone calls the board of health and shuts us down."

"Oh for fuck's sake," Andy said, sounding stunned. "Okay, baby. Hang on. I'm coming."

"Andy…," he started to protest, but the Andy he knew and loved was on the other end of the line.

"Eli, do you *want* me to be there?" he asked.

Eli's eyes burned. "You have no idea how much."

"Then I'll make it so. Probably tonight. Now you obviously have a thousand things to do, but remember, baby. I'm coming. You are the only place I want to be right now. You believe that, right?"

Eli nodded and then cleared his throat and spoke. "I do," he said gruffly. "I do believe that." He remembered that time he'd spent on the street so clearly, the sense that he was standing on a precipice, looking into a vast abyss, flailing, nearly falling *every minute of every day*. He'd believed then that nobody was coming to his rescue. Nobody would grab him by the back of the shirt and pull him to safety. But here Andy was, and even if he couldn't yank Eli back, he was fully prepared to jump into the abyss with him.

The only way to reward that was with faith.

"Good," Andy said softly. "I love you. Let's get busy."

"Love you back," Eli said. "Can do."

They hung up then, and Eli threw himself back into the fight.

By midafternoon, he'd managed to drum up some soup-kitchen donations for the next couple of meals, and had some feelers out to some grocery stores and bodegas for Christmas dinner. He'd spent the hours *not* on his phone working with the older kids and maintenance crew, sweeping out the water and bagging the trash—and checking with the plasterer Andy's dad had hooked him up with, who immediately put his other projects on hold and showed up that day to work with the plumber. Together, they were making a massive effort to fix the whole works before the building crumbled around their ears.

By late afternoon, he thought he could see daylight.

The kids had enough food to last them until Christmas Day itself. The sources he'd called were asking *their* sources, since this close to the day most people were tapped out. The floor was clean, and there were power heating fans that painters used to speed the drying process in the kitchen, aimed at the walls and floor. The plumber—and Andy's dad must have been as awesome as Andy because this guy was the *best* and insisted it was an honor to return a big favor—had repaired the leaks and insulated the exposed pipes, declaring the whole works safe against more burst plumbing.

And Andy was coming sometime that night with presents.

Eli stood at the top of the basement stairs, his knees wobbling, his vision a little dark as he realized he'd skipped breakfast *and* lunch for the second day running, and got ready to go down for the final check to see if maybe the storage space was usable again.

He took a deep breath, promising himself a sandwich when this was over, and started down the stairs. He was so exhausted, by the time he realized his foot had slipped and he was falling, he'd already cracked his head, and after that, blissful, blissful darkness.

So," ANDY'S father said as they stood in the church foyer. "I'm coming with you, son, but you've got to tell your mother."

Andy nodded, checking his phone and scowling. "Are the go bags in the car?" he asked anxiously. "I gave Charlie and Mary Beth the presents to put under the tree the day after tomorrow, but I'm going to need some clothes when I get home."

"Yeah," Matt Chambers reassured him. "I took care of it, but about your mother—"

"Andy!" Pastor Dan said excitedly, hustling over to Andy and giving him and his father a droll look. They were dressed in bright novelty sweaters, lime green and pink, featuring kittens in little stockings hung on a Christmas tree. "Wow." He blinked hard. "As good as your mom is at knitting, you'd think…."

Andy shook his head. "Don't ask. What's up?"

"Okay, so I told the other three churches about Eli's dilemma, and besides the cookies left over here tonight—and there should be plenty, because God, what you made alone should feed the whole town—each church is each giving up a turkey for the big feast and a few boxes of stuffing, as well as about twenty pounds of potatoes. There's also a couple of grocery bags with green beans, cranberry sauce, and some apple and pumpkin pies. It's not the whole feast for sixty kids plus employees but—"

Andy hugged Porter's secret boyfriend spontaneously. "Oh my God, Pastor Dan. You and Porter—you're, like, the best. It's a huge start. Eli's asking grocery stores for donations right now, and…." He looked at his phone again. "And I don't know. He was giving me updates once an hour, but I haven't heard from him in a few. God, they don't need one more disaster, you know?"

Dan and his father both nodded, and Porter rushed up. "Guys I've got the knitting circle set to come over and help my mom with her medicine and stuff for the next three or four days. Dan may have to come back to Foxglove, but I can stay and do some work on the building, just in case." He gave Dan a sheepishly sad look. "Christmas will sort o suck," he muttered.

Dan grimaced. "I, uhm, have a gift. I'll… uhm…." He took in Andy's and his father's avidly curious looks. "If you'll excuse us?" he asked painedly.

Matt Chambers cocked his head at Andy. "Is that what I think i is?"

"Porter having an affair with the pastor?" Andy said. "Yes. Yes. Absolutely. And no, my mind is still blown, so I've got no words. I mean…." He and his father both flailed at each other. "How's that even work?"

His dad grinned. "Well, son, I think that works the same way it does for couples around the world. I just think, uhm, maybe they should make it legal sooner than they would normally, because… like… God and stuff."

Andy snorted, letting the humor of the situation ease his out-of-control worry.

"Andy? Matt?" Andy's mother came bustling out of a crowd of her friends, looking excited and happy and in her element. "Are you ready?

"Yeah," Andy said distractedly. A text flashed across his phone, but it was from Margie, not Eli. "Mom," he said, glancing up from the phone and remembering he needed to be an adult now. "Dad and I are going to clear out after we sing, okay? Dan and Porter are taking a bunch of presents and food down to Brooklyn so Eli's kids can have Christmas, and I'm going down to help."

His mom scowled at him. "Andy, you promised me you'd come home this year—"

"And I did," Andy said, holding on to his reason with all his will. "But my boyfriend, whom I love very much, is having a super shit time of it, and if I'm going to be the kind of guy he deserves, I have to sacrifice things like Christmas in Vermont." His phone buzzed again, and he frowned as he saw an entire text string from Margie erupt on the screen.

"Andy," his mother snapped, "we're about to go up and sing. We've put our all into this pageant so we can work together as a family—"

Andy tuned her out, his focus on the words in front of him.

Andy, Eli took a fall down the basement stairs at around four this afternoon. We just found him an hour ago—he was unconscious and hypothermic and perhaps suffering from broken bones. We got him checked into Bed/Stuy general, and they're looking him over now, but we thought you'd want to know.

"Andy!" his mother's voice cut through his rising panic. "Andy, are you even listening to me?"

"No," he said, his voice far away. "I'm not."

"Andy!"

He could suddenly focus on her, and the glow of home and glamour of "Christmas" fell away. "I'm not listening to you anymore. Because it's all bullshit, Mom. You, wanting us all to gather together to be this fictional family in this picture-perfect Christmas card moment. Mom, I've seen Christmas spirit. People in this town have been helping me for *two days* trying to get Christmas to a bunch of kids they've never met. The entire goddamned town has opened their hearts and their pockets and has come through in amazing ways to help my boyfriend be a superhero to kids he works his fingers to the bone for. And all I've wanted is to be *there*, working with him, because this means everything to him. And Mom, you can't even say his name. You knit five sweaters for charity this year—I know because they got donated to his kids through the church. But you haven't knit *one fucking sweater* for the man I love. And I'm done. Christmas isn't picture-perfect. Our *family* isn't picture-perfect. But I thought we could at least be Eli's family too. Charlie, Mary Beth, Dad—they all jumped in to help. But you? You're so wrapped up in what you think Christmas *ought* to be, that you haven't seen what it is. It's *hard*. It's hard to make dreams come true for children who've had all their dreams stripped away. The world is a hard place to make generosity and charity matter. But damned near every person in this town has worked their asses off to make it happen, just this once, for these kids. Every person in town but *you*"—his voice cracked—"who should have loved Eli best. He needs a mom, and I was so excited because I thought I'd be giving him a family. But the family I'm giving him is going to have to be absent one parent because you're not up for the job."

He sucked in a breath and realized he was crying. The entire church was deadly silent, all eyes on the painful tableau of him and his mother, staring at each other in anger.

"*Andy!*" she burst out, eyes filling. "Andrew Michael Chambers you take that back."

"No," he said, voice calm. "And I'm not standing up and singing with the family either. Eli's in the hospital, Mom. He fell down the stairs as he was cleaning up, and he's unconscious, and I *promised* him I'd get there today. I was going to do this one last thing for you, but you know what? I don't care if I have to wait in the car before we take off. I don't care if I *freeze to death* waiting in the car before we load it up and get to the airstrip. I'll be damned if I do one more thing for a woman who won't even say my boyfriend's name."

And with that he turned on his heel and strode toward the coatroom, not able to stand there one more minute.

FIFTEEN MINUTES later he was sitting in Dan's SUV, wrapped in one of the many lap robes Dan kept there since he was—in his words—often a granny taxi. He had Margie on the phone so they could trade stats about Eli, arrival times, and the food and gift situation.

"I was planning to get in around one in the morning," he said. "That hasn't changed. I need to wait to talk to my sources to see what needs to be—"

He was interrupted as Dan, Porter, his dad, *and* Charlie and Mary Beth all trooped out to fill the back with the bags Dan had gathered from the other churches. Included, he noticed, was the box of cookie tins filled with the cookies he'd baked the day before.

"Talk to you later, Margie. I should be in Brooklyn around ten."

"We weren't even going to get to these," Dan said by way of explanation as he put the box in the back.

"But the pageant...," Andy mumbled, confused.

"Your mother is in charge," his father said dryly. "Pastor Dan put her in charge before telling the congregation that our family was needed elsewhere."

Charlie gave an evil laugh. "That was some great shade, Pastor Dan," she said. "I mean, she won't need sunscreen in July after that!"

It took Andy a moment to process that. Shade. As in.... "You said she wasn't part of our family," he mumbled.

"You all mean everything to her," Dan said frankly as he got into the driver's seat and shut the door. "I think she needed to hear that she was losing you by trying to keep you all on a leash."

"And whether she learns or not," Matt Chambers said, "you and Eli need us right now, and the girls and I weren't going to ignore that." Behind them, Porter had started up his truck. He gave a little beep to signal he was leaving, and they headed out.

The supply truck usually hauled dry goods for an East Coast centered bakery, so it had a refrigerator compartment perfect for the perishable food. Between the truck and the cargo plane, they had two full loads ready to go, but Andy's dad insisted on riding in the truck with the girls since the cargo plane only sat three. That was fine. Andy wasn't sure how much conversation they'd get in anyway.

As it turned out, quite a bit, but not with his father, and not with Porter, who had worked his actual job that morning after being everybody's workhorse for the past two days. Porter sprawled on a tarp on the floor in front of the cargo netting and slept, and Andy sat in the front of the plane, peering over the breathless snowscape of Vermont.

"God, it's beautiful," he said, talking over the headset so he could be heard over the propellers. The dark silhouettes of conifers could be seen over moonlit snow, as could the occasional house standing in a clearing, split-rail fences lining the properties like black lace.

"And so peaceful." Pastor Dan flashed him a smile. "Feel closer to God this way. It's why I like to fly."

Andy grinned and then sobered, glancing back at Porter, who had turned out to be the best of friends. "What are you two going to do about each other?" he asked, a little afraid. He'd been so sure Porter had been meant to GTFO—it had always been his driving ambition, but after seeing him with Dan over the last two days, Andy was pretty sure getting out of Vermont was the *worst* thing Porter could do.

Dan winked at him. "Oh, that man is going to marry me. Don't worry. See, it's all part of my plan."

"Your plan?"

"Yeah. First I had to get him to see me as a hot guy and not a saint."

Andy had to laugh. "How'd that go over?"

Dan gave a very self-satisfied, very *masculine* smirk. "Oh, I think he bought it."

Oh my! "So, erm, step one achieved. What was step two?"

"Mm." Dan let out a breath and adjusted his course a little. "Step two was making sure he'd be happy in a small town." And wow—Pastor Dan, proving he wasn't just a pretty face. He really did know Porter.

"I think he is," Andy said thoughtfully. "Which is funny, because he was the one who wanted out the most. But look at him. He's… he's the town rock. He's like my dad. Making sure everybody's houses are ready for the winter, checking on the food bank, knows the snowplow guy. He's the backbone of the town."

Andy wasn't sure, but he thought Dan's eyes grew a little shiny.

"You get it," he said softly. "See, I really *had* been planning to stay celibate until marriage, sort of like you're supposed to. But... but I felt like I had to make him see, you know? What a good guy he was? I figured God and I could do a little reckoning if Porter could start to understand that he doesn't have to be a saint to be a great guy."

"Is he starting to?" Andy asked. Suddenly he wanted nothing more than to go back to Foxglove to attend Porter and Pastor Dan's wedding.

"I think helping you out is doing a lot with that," Dan said. "Something about helping people outside your own little world and extending charity to both strangers and your friends and family—I think it's starting to sink in."

"So after that, what's step three?"

"Marriage and babies," Dan said impishly.

Andy laughed. "Porter *and* his mother would love that, I think."

"Yeah, me too." Dan looked at him with serious eyes. "Fostering children would be good too. I think Porter and I could make a really good forever home for kids who have no place else to go."

Andy swallowed hard, thinking about kids like Lola and Josie, boys who wanted to dress as fairies for Halloween, and kids who would rather take a closet full of pills than go back to a home full of cruelty.

"I think the world needs you guys like you would not believe," he said through a rough throat. "I want to see the two of you achieve step three. You can do amazing things in a small town." He glanced back over his shoulder, thinking about all the help they'd given so far. "You already have."

He saw Porter looking back at him, eyes gleaming faintly in the running lights of the plane. When Andy met his gaze for a moment, Porter winked and held up three fingers, nodding like he'd won something.

"Step three," he mouthed, obviously excited.

Andy chuckled and nodded back.

Step three. It couldn't happen to a nicer bro.

CHAPTER 9: CHRISTMAS DAY IS SAVED BY TRUE LOVE

ELI GRUNTED and tried to move, but his head exploded in pain, and he abandoned that plan. "Ouch. Fuck. Andy, am I sick?"

Andy's soft-skinned palm cupped his forehead, smoothing back his hair before dropping to hold Eli's hand. "No, but you are concussed, baby. Don't move for a bit. The nurse is coming back with something for pain."

Eli grunted, and the hospital smell and coarseness of the sheets permeated his consciousness, as well as an all-encompassing dull ache in his arm. "I almost wish I was sick," he said.

"Yeah, either way, buddy, you're not going anywhere." Andy sounded exhausted, and Eli squinted against the pain in his head to open his eyes.

Andy smiled tiredly from the side of his bed. He'd dropped the side rail and was resting his head on his arm so he could watch Eli sleep. His hair was a finger-combed clumping mess, he had huge bags under his eyes, and he was wearing some hideous acrylic novelty sweater that Eli could not imagine he picked out himself.

"Wow, you look worse than I feel," he said, and Andy gave a brief laugh.

"Well you look wonderful. God, we were afraid you weren't going to wake up."

Eli groaned. "How long have I been out? What day is it?" He tried to sit up. "What's going on with Christmas at Rainbow House? Ow! Ow! Ow!"

Andy sat up and pressed him gently back into the bed with the palm of his hand and gave him a stern look. "To answer your questions: You've been out about twenty hours. It's Christmas Eve. We got in around ten last night, and I've been here since one in the morning…. My dad, the girls, Porter, and his pastor boyfriend are currently saving Christmas at Rainbow House—if the boyfriend isn't flying back the truck driver who helped with transport. They brought presents, a crapton of food, and are working with Margie and Leon to scare up the rest. Dad's been sending me pictures. He and Porter are going around making repairs and fixing the place up so you don't have anything like this happening again." Andy scowled. "They had a new stairway built by ten this morning. I mean, it took them *four hours*. It's terrifying. Give those two men a hammer and a crescent wrench and they'll fix the planet. I'm not kidding."

Eli wanted to laugh, but gah! He was so tired. "Did you say the girls are here too?"

Andy nodded. "They're giving cooking lessons since so much food got destroyed. They've got the older kids peeling potatoes and baking pie crusts and chopping vegetables. It's funny—my mom has insisted she's the only one allowed to make Christmas dinner for so long, I hadn't realized how much Charlie and Mary Beth had absorbed over the years. Anyway, they'll have Christmas Eve dinner ready by six, and they'll be back to cook Christmas breakfast, and then I think your staff at Rainbow House will be on for the turkey and stuffing, which was all prepped today."

"I was going to be there," Eli whispered, feeling awful.

"Nope," Andy said. "You're coming home with me, pal. And you'll be lucky if they'll let you out tomorrow night. We may end up all having Christmas here, but if that happens my dad promised he'll bring us some turkey and pie." Andy nodded his head toward a brightly decorated tin on a portable table near the door. "And Christmas cookies. When Porter's trucker friend dropped me off, Porter insisted I bring a tin of Christmas cookies in for the nursing staff. Because he's a good guy. They've been super grateful, by the way."

"That's your family," Eli said softly. "Spreading sunshine and miracles."

Andy's expression grew sad, and he looked away. Eli realized that here was one person he *hadn't* talked about in the last five minutes.

"Andy, what's your mother doing?"

Andy sighed. "Living in the past. Running the Christmas pageant. Wondering what to do with a Christmas meal and no family to eat it with. I really don't care."

But the way his voice broke at the end made that last one a lie.

"I'm sorry. Do you need to—"

"To stay right here?" Andy said softly. "Yeah. That's what I need to do." His hand came up again to stroke Eli's cheek. "Yeah. That's exactly what I need to do."

Eli wanted to talk some more, ask more questions, but at that moment, the nurse came in with his painkiller, and he was asleep before she left.

ANDY WOKE up when his father shook his shoulder gently. "Andy? Son? C'mon now—they say you haven't eaten."

Andy sat up, his body creaking as he yawned and stretched. "Dad?" He closed his eyes and reached above his head. "Ouch. Ouch. Crick in the neck!"

"This is why you should sleep *on* a bed, not next to it," his dad said.

"No. Didn't want him to be alone."

"Yeah, son—we got that."

The last twenty-four hours came flooding into his consciousness, and he groaned, much like Eli had. "Oh Lord. What time is it?"

"It's around six," his father said. "Here, I brought a plate for you. One for Eli too, if he wakes up. And pie. Rainbow House was sitting down to dinner as I left. I have to tell you, everybody wanted to know how Eli was doing. Those kids really love him—and you." His father held up his cell phone, grinning. "I sent your sisters a picture of you two asleep a minute ago. I think it might be the real Christmas present for everybody. What a bunch of great kids."

Andy squeezed his eyes shut, and he might have burst into tears on the spot, but his stomach rumbled. He father laughed and set the plate in his hands.

"Did you and the girls get any sleep?" he asked, taking the foil off and digging in. Mom's lasagna recipe, since turkey and stuffing were for tomorrow, but still, what wasn't to love?

"Yeah," his father said, yawning. "We got a bit last night, and we've all caught some naps during the day. I think we're going to make good use of your apartment again tonight, though. Thanks for the keys."

Andy kept eating, feeling more sustained with every bite. He looked at Eli, who was still sleeping, and smiled weakly. "He's going to miss most of Christmas," he said.

"Yeah, but so will you," his father reminded him.

Andy shrugged. "Christmas for me is being here for him." He realized how corny that sounded and rolled his eyes. "Sappy but true."

His father nodded, eyes a little bright. "Me too," he confessed. "With your mother. I-I hate the thought of her alone tonight, but... I think she needed this. She's been holding on so tightly to all of you. Not letting Charlie go to college unless she finished junior college, going on all those college visits with Mary Beth to try to get her to stay close to home. And what she did with you and Eli was... well, it was unkind, which is so weird. I would have said she didn't have an unkind bone in her body. But I think admitting you had a partner and a life in Brooklyn would have just made it real. She was losing you—she was losing all of you." He let out a sigh. "And it's like it never occurred to her that the only way to keep you was to make going back a good thing and not that... that bucket of stress she inflicted on you over the last few days."

Andy laughed, his mind blank. "I'm sorry, Dad. I wish I could think of something to say."

His father shook his head. "You look worse than I do," he said. He nodded toward Andy's go bag that he'd apparently brought when he'd come to the hospital. "They have a shower you can use. I asked. It's down the hall. Go. Wash up. I'll be here. Don't worry, son, we won't leave your boy alone."

ELI HEARD unfamiliar voices in his room and opened his eyes warily. He peered upward into the faces of two breathtakingly pretty young women and smiled.

"Charlie? Mary Beth?" he asked, recognizing them from the pictures and videos Andy had shown him. "Wow. It's great to meet you."

"Dad, he's up!" Mary Beth chimed. "It's good to meet you too! Are you hungry? Dad brought a plate for both of you, but only Andy ate his. Dad, is he hungry? Should we feed him?" She looked back at Eli. "Should we feed you? Your arm is broken. Andy said you'll have to wait until the swelling goes down before they put on a cast. That sucks. My best friend did that to her *femur* on a snow-skiing trip, and she said it hurt like *balls*. I think you only fractured your arm bones, but they popped through the skin, which is *gnarly*. Are you sure you don't want food?"

Eli found himself laughing in spite of the pain in his head. And, now that she'd mentioned it, his arm. "I'm not sure," he murmured. "It smells delicious, though. Where's Andy?"

"Taking a shower," said the other girl, Charlie. "Dad apparently sent him off because he didn't know we were coming. But we had to come. We ate with the kids at Rainbow House, who are great, by the way. They worked so hard today to make Christmas Eve nice for the little kids and prepare dinner for tomorrow. You had to see 'em. Anyway, they were sort of worried about presents for the little kids, and Mary Beth and I told them that we'd managed to gather presents for *everybody*, and you should have seen them light up. I asked if I could take pictures of them opening their gifts just to show the people at Foxglove how much they were appreciated. Pastor Dan said that should be okay, but we had to clear it with you first. Anyway—" She yawned. "—we were going to go to your guys' apartment and sleep so we could be there Christmas morning and send you pictures, but we had to see you first."

"See me?" Eli asked, bemused. "Why would you want to see me?" He was used to adolescents. He was. But these two girls, pouring their effusive chatter and goodwill over him—it was a balm of good cheer. And knowing that this family—or part of it anyway—had taken over the job when he couldn't? Oh, it soothed something to know that there were good people out there who would take care of his kids.

And that Andy was there to take care of him.

"Well, because you're Andy's boyfriend!" Mary Beth exclaimed. "Duh! I mean, my brother has talked about nobody *but* you for the last three years. Charlie and I have been mad to see you, but...." She bit her lip and shrugged, looking suddenly vulnerable when she'd been fearless the moment before. "It doesn't matter why, but we very much wanted to meet you. I mean—" She shrugged. "—he's *Andy*. He's not going to fall in love with somebody stupid, right?"

"I hope not." Eli chuckled. "But, you know, I *did* fall down a flight of stairs."

"Yeah," Charlie conceded, "but you were saving the world."

"He was," Andy said from the doorway, looking tired but clean and refreshed. Eli glanced up at him, feeling gratitude in every part of his body that didn't hurt. "And now we get to save him. It's a good cycle. It's the same thing that sustains Batman. I really think it is."

"No," Eli murmured. "Batman was a Gothic hero—his whole schtick is that he doesn't love."

Andy snorted. "Not according to the fanfic Charlie keeps sending *me*," he said. "Move, Mary Beth. You're in my spot."

She gave him a *look*. "No, you can sleep here when we leave. We get fifteen minutes of Eli time, and we're not spending it across the room. Go." She waved her hand. "Eat pie. Eli, would you care for some dinner? The nurse said you could eat if you didn't feel queasy."

Eli smiled again, but this time up at Andy, who was flopping good-naturedly onto the couch back against the wall. And for the next ten minutes he was cheerfully subjected to the girls and their questions. What had Andy told him about *them*, for instance, and when were they going to get a kitten. Andy had told them the apartment allowed pets for a reason. Didn't he understand that obligated him to a kitten? Could Mary Beth really stay in the guest room some weekends while she attended NYU? Could she drop in unannounced? Could she bring friends? Would they go visit Charlie after she got settled at Northwestern? He did his best to answer their questions, but when Mary Beth's, "And what is my brother's most *annoying* trait? Inquiring minds want to know!" made him pop his eyes open from what had almost been sleep, he knew the battle had been lost.

"His most annoying trait is he's not here next to me right now," Eli said through a yawn. "But I forgive him. I've been dying to meet you both."

"But you're exhausted, and it's time for us to leave." She yawned back. "Very smart."

And then the family did just that. They left. But first they stopped and kissed Eli on the cheek and then Andy—even Andy's father—and gave them hugs and told them they'd be back tomorrow after the Christmas package massacre at Rainbow House.

"We'll send Andy video," Mary Beth promised. "Swear to God, we're doing nothing but charging our phones while we sleep."

THAT NIGHT, the nurses set up a cot for Andy, although that didn't stop him from scooting in next to Eli on the bed so they could watch Christmas specials on television.

They were quiet, Eli resting his head on Andy's shoulder, when he hit Mute on the remote and spoke.

"We used to have a Christmas tree when I was a kid."

Andy's breath caught. Eli never spoke about his childhood. *Never.* It had been the one subject he'd dodged neatly during their courtship, the one thing he'd never discussed. Andy had gone on and on, ad nauseum, about Christmas in Vermont and how it really did look like a postcard, and the only sound Eli made on the other side of that was....

Crickets.

Andy let out a slow breath now and figured out what to say. "You said you were Jewish."

"I am. Bar Mitzvah and everything. But Dad never figured Christmas was a Christian holiday—not really. He said there was something sweet about celebrating the birth of a child, the birth of hope." He let out a sigh. "And I grew up with all of that and then got kicked out on Christmas Eve."

Andy squeezed his eyes shut. This, he'd heard about. His brother had found a copy of something stupid—something a growing gay boy would want for excruciatingly private reasons involving fantasies and hormones, and the resultant teasing had, in the end, spurred Eli to an awkward, earnest confession.

And then he'd gotten struck for the first and only time by his father.

He'd grabbed a backpack full of clothes and hit the streets, hopping on the subway with his school subway pass and going all the way from the Bronx to Brooklyn, ending up in Bed/Stuy.

"I didn't know it was Christmas Eve," Andy said through a dry throat, the thought of his boy—*his* boy—all alone and sad and confused wandering the streets of Brooklyn in the dark of a holiday night.

"I found an alleyway," Eli told him. "Next to a restaurant. They were open, you know. And when they saw me, hugging the wall because it was still warm, they gave me a plate full of food and let me sleep in their back room. I stayed there for a while, sweeping up, taking out trash. A social worker saw me and tried to pin me down, so I ran." He shrugged. "Lather, rinse, repeat."

"Baby...."

"But I never forgot those people at the restaurant. That they didn' want anybody to be alone and cold and hungry on Christmas Eve. I was a family-owned restaurant, and they treated me like I was human.

mean, I thought they were wonderful, and perfect, but...." He let out a sigh. "That's probably why I ran, you know? I'd thought *my* family was wonderful and perfect, and look what happened."

Andy kissed the crown of his head, wishing he could wrap his arms around Eli's shoulders and ward off everything: memories of cold, of hunger, of rejection. Oh God. His boy. *His* boy had been out there in the snow, cold and hungry, and Andy hadn't been there to keep him safe.

"I know you're mad at your mom," Eli said softly into the quiet. "Just remember—she didn't reject you. She didn't kick you out in the cold. She didn't even reject *me*. She just wanted her family around her so bad it sounds like it got in her way. Just... your dad and your sisters and friends, coming out here like you did? Being here for Rainbow House, for *me*? It's the kind of family I didn't think existed anymore. It's the kind of kindness, of *Christmas* for all its consumerism and corniness, that I didn't think was real. But it is. And you're part of it. And your mother, for all she's not perfect, she's part of it too. I... you know. If she ever speaks to you again, you should forgive her."

Andy laughed a little. "Only if she speaks to you too," he said. "And seriously, she has to come to Brooklyn first."

"Who wouldn't want to come to Brooklyn for Christmas?" Eli asked drowsily.

"I know I did," Andy murmured.

"Did I tell you what your Christmas gift is?" Eli said, just when Andy thought he was asleep.

"No. I thought we'd open gifts when we got to the apartment tomorrow."

"Well, yeah," Eli said. "But this one is something that will make you happy all day, just knowing it."

"I could use some happy," Andy told him with a smile. "Shoot."

"I have an appointment to visit the animal shelter in January, first in line on adoption day."

Andy laughed, his eyes burning. That thing he'd begged Eli for, the thing that would make their place a permanent home in Eli's eyes.

"A kitten?" he asked, his throat tight.

"I want an absolutely wicked one," Eli said decidedly. "One that sleeps on your computer when you're working from home and who steals all your socks. Extra points if he's got three legs and one eye and a rip in his ear."

"God, I love you," Andy said, and he couldn't keep the tears out of his voice.

"I know. Forever. You promised."

And the kitten was Eli's promise. Andy knew that. "Forever. Like I promised. Merry Christmas, Eli."

"Merry Christmas, Andy. I love you too."

CHRISTMAS IN the hospital sucked. Everybody knew that, including the doctors and nurses. Once Eli's vitals had been taken—and his head CT scans had been looked at—he'd been allowed home, on the condition that he stayed on the couch or in bed for at least another week. No alcohol, no pushing a broom, no work. His noggin had been banged around a bit, and he was to do nothing but sleep and let it heal.

That said, they were on their way to the apartment by early afternoon, and when Andy's father called to ask if they wanted him to bring Christmas dinner, Andy told him to bring some to put in the fridge (to replace all the little meals they'd apparently wiped out) but that he'd be providing a special dinner that Eli would appreciate.

He'd put in the order to the pizza parlor while Eli had been getting his head CTs, and Andy felt an evil little chuckle start whenever he thought of it.

With some help from the cabbie—and some more from his father and the girls after Andy had hit the buzzer to get in—he got Eli ensconced on the couch, pillows behind his head, happily watching the *many* videos the girls had taken of Christmas at Rainbow House.

Porter and Dan walked in quietly while he was watching the one of Lola and Josie, and he looked up from the phone, wiping tears from his eyes. The girls in the video were wearing the cardigans Andy had picked out and hugging each other because they matched and laughing like, well, children at Christmas, and Eli didn't see two averagely handsome men in his living room when he saw the two men who'd helped make that happen.

He saw superheroes.

"You two," he said hoarsely. "Look what you did. I... I have no words for you. Thank you."

Both of them blushed like schoolboys, and Porter stepped forward, hand extended. "So good to meet you, Eli. Andy here can't say enough good things about you."

Dan stepped forward too, and Eli had them come sit next to him, Andy dangling over the couch with his arms around Eli's shoulders, while they watched more of the videos.

"Look at all the sweaters," Eli whispered. "And look at them—the kids. Not one of them is like, 'Ew, sweaters!'"

"They loved them," Porter said frankly. "I hope you don't mind, but I took some videos myself, for my mom and her knitting circle. I mean, all the love that goes into their work, and I don't think anybody could appreciate it more, you know?"

"Some of the kids cried," Dan said, sounding a little choked up. Then he grinned. "And Porter, your sweaters were a *favorite*. Those two boys were so impressed when I told them you'd made them. I think you're going to have to come back just so you can give knitting lessons."

"Well, if you do," Eli said, "you're welcome to stay here."

"Finally," Andy joked, "the guest room gets some use."

There was general laughter, and then everybody agreed to let Eli rest—they needed some sleep themselves. Andy had gotten a text from the pizza place, telling him dinner was a go, and his news that there would be takeout for dinner at six was met with a tired cheer of approval. Christmas had been secured for Rainbow House; everybody was *done* with cooking. Andy gave Porter and Dan his room, since they were resting up for the flight back that night, the girls slept in the guest room, and his dad took the recliner.

Andy took the opposite side of the couch from Eli, and for a couple of hours, Andy got his first real sleep since he'd awakened to go to Vermont. He was home. Eli was happy. And his family was there under his roof. He looked at the tiny tree he'd made Eli put up in the corner before he left, lights twinkling through the halo of sleep in his eyes, and thought that this was what Christmas *should* be. This moment of peace between crises. This moment of gentleness to cushion their hearts from the harshness of the world.

He'd work to make sure all their Christmases were like this. Eli would never be cold and sad and alone, staring into the warmth of family on Christmas from the darkness outside, not ever again.

ELI COULD hear people up and about a little before six, but he was cushioned by pain relievers and pillows and the lovely floating feeling

Finally the door closed, and Cindy stepped back and wiped under her eyes. She hadn't been wearing makeup, Eli noted, as Andy led her into the living room in front of the couch. She looked vulnerable, a woman whose entire life was changing, and for a few steps, she had failed to keep up.

But the woman who had just sobbed in her son's arms wasn't cruel—not deliberately. She wasn't trying to reject her son, or even Eli. It's just that all her electrons were moving out of her nucleus, and it was scary. Eli had a sudden flash of insight that he felt the same way about Brooklyn. He knew every train and every corner, every street, every back alley. Andy was getting to be a native too, and maybe that's what this moment had been. Nuclear fission, a nucleus being split into two parts, releasing all its energy in a gigantic blast of Christmas cheer and reunited family fallout.

And leaving two separate molecules, with Andy as the covalent bond.

"Eli?"

Eli looked up into Cindy Chambers' anxious face.

"Mrs. Chambers," he said quietly. "I'm so happy to meet you."

She caught her trembling lower lip between her teeth and held out three wrapped packages in her arms. "Welcome to the family," she whispered. "I'm so sorry these are late."

He bit his own lip, and he fought against an image he'd kept at bay for years. The night he'd been kicked out, his own mother had closed the door behind him, her lower lip caught between her teeth just like Cindy's, before she whispered, "I'm sorry. I'm sorry. We just can't."

This woman can, he thought with a rush of emotion. *This woman can love me. And she's going to try.*

"Would you like to sit down next to me," he asked, "while I open them?" He winked at Andy, who was watching the two of them so hopefully it almost stopped his breath. "I, uhm, know handcrafters like to talk about their craft."

She gave him a shining, gorgeous smile from behind her tears and did as he asked, cozying up to him like he was her own child.

"Open this one first," she said earnestly. "It's the first one I made for you. I, uhm, didn't know much about you, so I made it to match Andy's from that year. Do you remember?"

that for this period of time, someone else was getting it. There was a knock at the door, and Andy said, "I'll get it. It's takeout," and Eli went back to sleep.

He was startled awake by a cold draft from the doorway and a gasp from the girls and Andy's dad, who were all sitting in the living room with him, watching Christmassy things on TV.

And by Andy's voice, cracking a little as he said the word, "Mom?"

Eli struggled to wake up, sitting upright as slowly as he could on the couch and peering toward the door.

"Hi, uhm…." Andy stepped back, and Eli got a glimpse of the trim blonde woman hovering on the doorstep, her face a study of contrition and uncertainty. "Can I come in?"

"Yeah," Andy said. "Sure. What are you doing here?"

"You left your luggage," she said. "I-I, uhm, got somebody else to buzz me in." Even Eli could see the tentative smile. "I, uhm, wasn't sure of my welcome."

"You came all the way here to return my luggage?"

Eli hated that sound in Andy's voice. That note of suspicion and hurt. Eli wondered how often *he'd* sounded like that when they first met.

"I…." Cindy Chambers took a breath. "It was the damnedest thing. I woke up on Christmas morning, and it seems my whole family was in Brooklyn without me. I"—her voice trembled—"I miss my family, Andy. I—"

"Say his name, Mom." Eli's heart quailed. No. No. Not all this over *him*. He'd never forgive himself if Andy fractured his family over Eli.

"I brought him a gift!" she said hurriedly, her voice breaking more. "I… you're wrong. I *have* made him sweaters. I made three. One for each Christmas. I just… I just kept telling myself, you know, that when you moved up home, I'd give them to him then. He could be part of our community, and I'd have my son back. But my son is gone, and my girls are gone, and my husband's gone, and home isn't home without you all. I'm sorry. I'm sorry. I didn't mean to make Eli feel bad or unwelcome. I just wanted him close, with the family, and I didn't know how to do that, and I guess I can't, and—"

And Andy stepped forward to hug his mother, and she sobbed into his chest while the family moved around them, dragging Andy's luggage inside, as well as another large suitcase filled with gifts.

He smiled and went to work on the paper as he always did, working the tape off carefully so they could use it later, but it was harder than usual because one of his arms was in a sling. To his amusement, she took the sheet of wrapping paper from him and folded it neatly as he worked on the box.

When they were done, they had three neatly folded boxes, three sheets of beautiful foil wrapping paper to reuse, and three sweaters that he'd treasure always. He let her descriptions wash over his head. Fair isle, cables, gansey—he figured he could study it all later. What mattered was that after the first, which really did match Andy's, only in blue instead of forest green, she took something Andy had told her about him and incorporated it into the next sweater. He told her that he was worried about Eli coming home at night, so she'd made the next two cream colored so he could be more easily seen. Andy told her how cold it got in Eli's office, so she used cables and other techniques to make the sweaters extra cozy. And he'd told her that Eli needed family, so the last one had a series of Xs and Os cabled across the front, for hugs and kisses—and love.

When he was done, Andy's father folded the sweaters up and tucked them in a corner of the living room, and Eli wrapped his free arm around Cindy's shoulder.

"Thank you," he said, from the bottom of his heart.

"I'm sorry," she replied softly. "I was stupid and misguided and—"

"And you love your son," Eli said. He gave her a quiet smile. "As it happens, so do I."

She nodded. "Good. He deserves someone who loves him." Her voice broke again. "Like I do." Eli rocked her back and forth until Andy's father returned from tidying up, sat on her other side, and held her. Because that's what couples do.

Not long after, there was another knock at the door, and Andy jumped up to get it.

"Pizza!" he cried. "Thank God. I'm starving." As he paid the delivery guy, Eli heard him talking quietly about "the special pie," and suddenly he remembered their conversation before Andy had left for Vermont earlier that week.

After some setup in the kitchen—there were apparently *three* pizzas to worry about—Andy came in bearing a large pizza box. And an insufferable grin.

"You ready?" he asked, and Eli found himself laughing.

"You didn't," he replied, knowing that Andy totally had.

"I did," Andy said. "You remember."

"I remember," Eli told him. "You told me you'd come back to me, and I said I'd believe it when it happened—"

"And *I* said you'd be forced to eat crow." Andy's laugh was all mischief as he opened the box. Eli groaned.

There, spelled across the sausage pizza in black olives, was the word CROW.

"Are you ready to eat crow?" he asked. He gave his mom a sly look. "There's enough for everybody."

Cindy Chambers did not disappoint.

"I'll take two slices," she said firmly, and then gave Eli a shy smile. "It's only right."

They all ate a little crow that night—and some pepperoni and sausage, peppers, onions, cheese, and mushrooms as well.

It was the best Christmas dinner Eli could ever remember.

THAT NIGHT they lay in bed, listening to the unfamiliar sound of other people in their apartment. Porter and Dan had flown home that night, but the rest of Andy's family was staying for another couple of days to help at Rainbow House while Eli was laid up. Mary Beth was staying a few days beyond that, just because, in her words, she really needed to get out of Vermont before finishing high school.

When it sounded like everybody was settled, Andy found himself looking at Eli in the darkness, raising his hand to smooth back the hair from his brow.

"Getting long," Eli murmured.

"You're always a bit shaggy," Andy told him. "I sort of love it."

Eli smiled and opened his eyes. "You're thinking too loud. Talk to me."

Andy smiled back and stroked his hair again. "I'm thinking," he said, "that we should have Lola here a couple of times before she goes off to college. And we should tell her that she needs to spend all of her vacations here, because we'd miss her. And we should have Josie here too, maybe as a permanent foster after Lola goes away to school. Josie can keep attending school where she's at now, and she can go to

Rainbow House afterward, while you're at work, but the two of them would be ours. Lola would always have somewhere to go. Mary Beth won't mind sharing guest room privileges—she and Lola get along really well. And...."

He didn't know how to put this, but Eli did.

"And Lola and Josie will never have to spend another holiday alone," Eli filled in softly.

"And neither will you."

Eli squeezed his eyes shut. "Did I mention how much I liked your Christmas present?" he asked, and Andy grimaced.

"New boots?"

"The boots are nice," Eli admitted. "But no. The family. Andy, you did it. You've given me all the family I never thought I'd have again. I didn't even tell you I wanted it. You're like my own personal Santa."

Andy felt that in his heart. "And you're my best gift."

They were both a little shiny eyed and wobbly, and Eli's eyes drifted closed. Andy kept watching him, breathing softly in the dark, until he fell asleep too.

He dreamed of happy children and kittens, of showing Brooklyn off to his parents, and of never, ever, leaving the man at his side.

ANDREW GREY is the author of more than two hundred works of Contemporary Gay Romantic fiction. After twenty-seven years in corporate America, he has now settled down in Central Pennsylvania with his husband of more than twenty-five years, Dominic, and his laptop. An interesting ménage. Andrew grew up in western Michigan with a father who loved to tell stories and a mother who loved to read them. Since then he has lived throughout the country and traveled throughout the world. He is a recipient of the RWA Centennial Award, has a master's degree from the University of Wisconsin–Milwaukee, and now writes full-time. Andrew's hobbies include collecting antiques, gardening, and leaving his dirty dishes anywhere but in the sink (particularly when writing). He considers himself blessed with an accepting family, fantastic friends, and the world's most supportive and loving partner. Andrew currently lives in beautiful, historic Carlisle, Pennsylvania.

Email: andrewgrey@comcast.net
Website:www.andrewgreybooks.com

Follow me on BookBub

By ANDREW GREY

Accompanied by a Waltz
All for You
Between Loathing and Love
Borrowed Heart
Buck Me
Buried Passions
Catch of a Lifetime
Chasing the Dream
Crossing Divides
Dedicated to You
Dominant Chord
Dutch Treat
Eastern Cowboy
Hard Road Back
Half a Cowboy
Heartward
In Search of a Story
Lost and Found
New Tricks
Noble Intentions
North to the Future
One Good Deed
On Shaky Ground
Only the Brightest Stars
Paint By Number
Past His Defenses
The Playmaker
Pulling Strings
Rebound
Reunited
Running to You
Saving Faithless Creek
Second Go-Round
Shared Revelations
Survive and Conquer

Three Fates
To Have, Hold, and Let Go
Turning the Page
Twice Baked
Unfamiliar Waters
Whipped Cream

ART
Legal Artistry • Artistic Appeal
Artistic Pursuits • Legal Tender

BAD TO BE GOOD
Bad to Be Good • Bad to Be Merry
Bad to Be Noble • Bad to Be Worthy

BOTTLED UP
The Best Revenge • Bottled Up
Uncorked • An Unexpected Vintage

BRONCO'S BOYS
Inside Out • Upside Down
Backward • Round and Round
Over and Back • Above and Beyond

THE BULLRIDERS
A Wild Ride • A Daring Ride
A Courageous Ride

BY FIRE
Redemption by Fire
Strengthened by Fire
Burnished by Fire
Heat Under Fire

Published by DREAMSPINNER PRESS
www.dreamspinnerpress.com

Published by DREAMSPINNER PRESS
www.dreamspinnerpress.com

Published by DREAMSPINNER PRESS
www.dreamspinnerpress.com

Writer, knitter, mother, wife, award-winning author AMY LANE shows her love in knitwear, is frequently seen in the company of tiny homicidal dogs, and can't believe all the kids haven't left the house yet. She lives in a crumbling crapmansion in the least romantic area of California, has a long-winded explanation for everything, and writes to silence the voices in her head. There are a lot of voices—she's written over 120 books.

Website: www.greenshill.com
Blog: www.writerslane.blogspot.com
Email: amylane@greenshill.com
Facebook: www.facebook.com/amy.lane.167
Twitter: @amymaclane
Patreon: https://www.patreon.com/AmyHEALane

Follow me on BookBub

Published by DREAMSPINNER PRESS
www.dreamspinnerpress.com

By Amy Lane (cont)

DREAMSPUN DESIRES
THE MANNIES
The Virgin Manny
Manny Get Your Guy
Stand by Your Manny
A Fool and His Manny
SEARCH AND RESCUE
Warm Heart
Silent Heart
Safe Heart
Hidden Heart

FAMILIAR LOVE
Familiar Angel • Familiar Demon

FISH OUT OF WATER
Fish Out of Water
Red Fish, Dead Fish
A Few Good Fish • Hiding the Moon
Fish on a Bicycle • School of Fish
Fish in a Barrel • Only Fish

FLOPHOUSE
Shades of Henry • Constantly Cotton
Sean's Sunshine

GRANBY KNITTING
The Winter Courtship Rituals of
Fur-Bearing Critters
How to Raise an Honest Rabbit
Knitter in His Natural Habitat
Blackbird Knitting in a Bunny's Lair
Weddings, Christmas, and Such
The Granby Knitting Menagerie
Anthology

JOHNNIES
Chase in Shadow • Dex in Blue
Ethan in Gold • Black John
Bobby Green • Super Sock Man

KEEPING PROMISE ROCK
Keeping Promise Rock
Making Promises
Living Promises • Forever Promised

LONG CON ADVENTURES
The Mastermind • The Muscle
The Driver • The Suit
The Tech • The Face Man

LUCK MECHANICS
The Rising Tide • A Salt Bitter Sea

TALKER
Talker • Talker's Redemption
Talker's Graduation
The Talker Collection Anthology

WINTER BALL
Winter Ball • Summer Lessons
Fall Through Spring

Published by DREAMSPINNER PRESS
www.dreamspinnerpress.com

By AMY LANE (CONT)

Published by DSP Publications

ALL THAT HEAVEN WILL
ALLOW
All the Rules of Heaven

GREEN'S HILL
The Green's Hill Novellas

LITTLE GODDESS
Vulnerable
Wounded, Vol. 1 • Wounded, Vol. 2
Bound, Vol. 1 • Bound, Vol. 2
Rampant, Vol. 1 • Rampant, Vol. 2
Quickening, Vol. 1
Quickening, Vol. 2
Green's Hill Werewolves, Vol. 1
Green's Hill Werewolves, Vol. 2

Published by Harmony Ink Press

BITTER MOON SAGA
Triane's Son Rising
Triane's Son Learning
Triane's Son Fighting
Triane's Son Reigning

Published by DREAMSPINNER PRESS
www.dreamspinnerpress.com

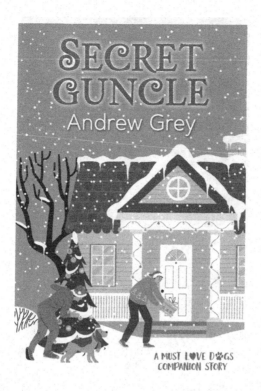

A MUST LOVE D🐾GS
COMPANION STORY

Veterinary student Dutton Glenroth isn't on speaking terms with his sister, Mary, but he isn't about to let his niece and nephew suffer because of it. He knows they have very little, so for the holidays, he makes up a basket of gifts for them and leaves it outside their door.

But the kids are getting older, and this year Dutton finds it difficult to pick out their gifts. When he asks for help at Foster's Toys, he runs into Randy Grant, his high school crush, who even volunteers to wrap and deliver the gifts with Dutton. Suddenly Dutton's normally lonely holiday has a spark of Christmas cheer. Will this be the year he gets the holiday he's always longed for?

Scan the QR Code
Below to Order!

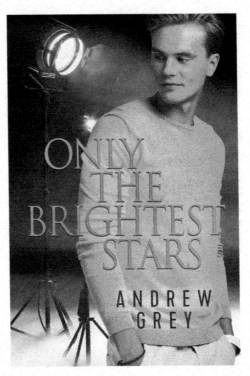

The problem with being an actor on top of the world is that you have a long way to fall.

Logan Steele is miserable. Hollywood life is dragging him down. Drugs, men, and booze are all too easy. Pulling himself out of his self-destructive spiral, not so much.

Brit Stimple does whatever he can to pay the bills. Right now that means editing porn. But Brit knows he has the talent to make it big, and he gets his break one night when Logan sees him perform on stage.

When Logan arranges for an opportunity for Brit to prove his talent, Brit's whole life turns around. Brit's talent shines brightly for all to see, and he brings joy and love to Logan's life and stability to his out-of-control lifestyle. Unfortunately, not everyone is happy for Logan, and as Brit's star rises, Logan's demons marshal forces to try to tear the new lovers apart.

Scan the QR Code
Below to Order!

An Amy Lane Christmas

Christmas with Danny Fit
Puppy, Car, and Snow
Turkey in the Snow
Going Up
If I Must

Celebrate the season with Amy Lane's own brand of holiday cheer. Enjoy five classic Amy Lane Christmas stories, imbued with her signature blend of humor, romance, and heart-warming satisfaction as businessmen, lawyers, accountants, and teachers all find love this December. Includes the stories:

Christmas with Danny Fit

Killian's life. How can Killian find time to fall in love with Lewis and ask him to stay if they're inundated with destructive furry poop-machines who all seem to need a home before Christmas?

Scan the QR Code
Below to Order!

Killian Thornton likes his downtown life, tending bar, and enjoying time with his friends and community. He'd given up on passion long ago. Then one night Killian offers his couch to help a friend's little brother find his feet in a new city, and everything Killian thought he knew about himself and his little life gets turned upside down.

Lewis Bernard can't believe his luck. After being forced to flee his parents' house, he was afraid of what came next, but Sacramento seems to be treating him just fine. The stunningly handsome bartender who lives downstairs from his brother offers Lewis his couch and doesn't even balk when Lewis discovers two abandoned kittens in a vacant lot as they walk home.

Vet bills, cat food bills, litter boxes—none of it was on Killian's Christmas agenda. How can Killian find time to fall in love with Lewis and ask him to stay if they're inundated with destructive furry poop machines who all seem to need a home before Christmas?

Scan the QR Code
Below to Order!